c.2

Hampel
   Wherever you go, there you are.

DATE DUE

Browsing Library

WHEREVER YOU GO, THERE YOU ARE

JOHN HAMPEL

BZFF *Books*

MILWAUKEE

C.2

BZFF Books
P.O. Box 27529
Milwaukee, WI 53227

First Edition

Library of Congress Catalog Card Number:
90–085289

ISBN   0-9627992-0-3

First Printing, December 1991

10   9   8   7   6   5   4   3   2   1

Printed in the United States of America

Printed and bound by The Haddon Craftsmen, Inc., Scranton, Pennsylvania

For my mother

There was an old woman lived under a hill,
And if she's not gone, she lives there still.
— Nursery Rhyme

In the sixties, the young expected revolution, but the revolution did not come. So the young went back to law school and the Yippies retooled themselves to become Yuppies. In the seventies, the New Age movement expected a millenarian revelation. Looking back on the seventies, it seems as if humanity had voted overwhelmingly for a postponement of the revelation. The alternative and ecological movements were resoundingly defeated everywhere. The New Age movement ended with Reagan and not Zen Governor Brown as the Californian President, and the spirit of the age made itself felt at every level of the culture ...
— William Irwin Thompson

The adventure of the Grail—the quest within for those creative values by which the Waste Land is redeemed—has become today for each the unavoidable task; for as there is no more any fixed horizon, there is no more any fixed center, any Mecca, Rome, or Jerusalem. Our circle today is that ... whose circumference is nowhere and whose center is everywhere; the circle of infinite radius, which also a straight line.
— Joseph Campbell

WHEREVER YOU GO, THERE YOU ARE

Welcome To Wasson's Bay

The disappearance of the leader of
an "electronic" cult draws a private
investigator to a sacred Indian mound
in rural Wisconsin where a pair of
unusual women, a haunted house, and a
mysterious teleporting device sent
him careening across time and space.

Other than Mystery Rock Hill, Wasson's Bay is not much different than any other touristy little burg on Lake Michigan, bustling in the summer and dreaming the winter away under blankets of deep, drifting snow. The village is located on the northern stretch of a peninsula that juts like a bony thumb some ninety miles into the big lake from the fist of mainland Wisconsin. To the east is the lake itself, to the west, Green Bay, a long body of water (a sort of negative thumb) at the vertex of which nestles the football-famous city of the same name. (Ironically, this city, proudly known as "Title-town" during the halcyon 60's glory days of Vince Lombardi's Packers, is also now the location of the Midwest chapter of the "James Dean Inner Space Institute"—the seventh in the country, the man himself actually having participated in the official opening, in 1971—this a fact that, when recalled, gives Basil and Synandra and Tiffany solemn and humble pause at the awesome power with which they are dealing. But never, it seems, pause quite enough.)

Essentially, the peninsula is the best of the Midwest contained in an almost-island. Dairy farms sprawl lazily over the gentle hills and valleys of the southern portion: lush fields of corn, oats, and alfalfa bordered by verdant copses, weedy creeks, and crumbling stone walls

3

that might protectively surround an ancient elm, while apple and cherry orchards romp northwards up the peninsula, the soil thinning considerably all the way, near the apex approaching the thickness of an old rug, worn so badly in places that the bare dolomite floor shows through.

This rocky superstructure, however, imparts a beautifully sculpted shoreline, crenated with harbors and coves, sandy beaches and bluffs, making this thumb tickling the second largest of the Great Lakes a resort area sometimes called "the Cape Cod of the Midwest." During the summer the population swells with vista-hungry visitors, who in an annual pilgrimage stream northwards into the coastal villages, engorging them with cars, campmobiles, and kids.

Wasson's Bay is one such village, hugging a blue gibbous moon of water rimmed with a bright corona of sand, and of course also containing the Mystery Rocks, which are the pride and joy and main tourist attraction of the small town. The rocks are situated on the top of a large hill that breaks through the trees a couple of hundred yards from the road that runs along the shoreline. From a distance and even closer-up the mound looks like an almost-bald head. Vegetation is sparse on the rocky slopes, but the baby moon of the summit is barren, save for lichens and small struggles of shepherd's purse and campion. The hill is an oddity in the area, a pimple on the back of the otherwise smoothly rolling and tastefully forested landscape. It is some sort of glacial goof, a kame perhaps, deposited during the Pleistocene as the last great ice sheet receded over the cruesta. But besides providing a fine view of the bay, the hill itself is merely a vehicle for the mystery—what matters are the rocks themselves, geologic strangers to the area, of deep black basalt, ancient igneous, inconclusively dated, but speculated by some investigating geologists to be more than three billion years old, dating back perhaps to the earth's fiery formation. The half-buried Volkswagen-sized boulders of mystery are thus strikingly different from the local telluria, generally sedimentary Niagara dolomite, often bearing the scratches of glacial horseplay. But besides their anomalous composition, it is, of course, the *pattern* of the rocks that for the past century has both baffled and charmed area natives and researchers from afar. They are arranged in the shape of a slightly lopsided heart.

In the past the singular mound had been variously called Heart Hill, Valentine Hill, and also, Love Hill—names still used at times by older residents. But due perhaps to a practical proclivity of the rugged northlanders to deny the romantic aspect of a geographic entity, or perhaps because of the rocks' solemn mysterious darkness upon the buff surface of the hill, or perhaps because the boulders do not actually form a perfect heartshape, the term Mystery Rocks has not only endured, it has prevailed.

It was also by this appellation that the rocks were first referenced in an early monograph by Sir Reginald Battlesea, a visiting British geographer with no penchant for romance: "A Description and Speculation Regarding the Phenomenon of the Mystery Rock Hill in the State of Wisconsin"; it being also the first published description of the hill, in 1861. His conclusion: "the indigenous redman" constructed the mound and placed the rocks, "quarried from a southerly location," and ultimately used for "pagan worship rituals and animal and perhaps human sacrifice."

Since then the Mystery Rock Hill site has been the source of continuing speculation by hordes of the curious, from university specialists to inquisitive tourists. However, through some workings of mystery or magic or simply local respect, the hill and its rocks seem to have been protected throughout time, remaining virtually undisturbed since, perhaps, its mysterious creation. Owing to the fact that both the town and the newly erected Wasson house (in 1870), a scant two hundred yards from the hill, miraculously avoided destruction in the terrible fire of 1872 that swept through the northern peninsula (following on the heels of the Great Chicago fire of 1871 and an even greater conflagration, though garnering much less press, the Peshtigo fire on the western side of Green Bay in the same year), the Wasson clan and, in fact, the townspeople regarded the mound as somehow sacred, exerting a protective influence on the village (and the venerable Wasson house, which it overlooks). Thus, none of the residents would dream of despoiling the great hill in any way, and it is perhaps this parochial protectionism that has spared the hill the ravages of ever-encroaching civilization. Indeed, neither the mound nor its immediate surroundings have ever been excavated, or even deeply probed, although, over the years, quite a few serious overtures have been made, all of which the Wassons have managed to ward off through various legal maneuvers, but with increasing difficulty in later years, as the Sacred has become science, and Magic, a modern-times misfit.

5

Probably the most current geological life-and-times description is provided in a brochure published by the Wasson's Bay Chamber of Commerce. Excerpted, it reads:

> ... The Mystery Rocks are indeed a mystery. Experts from colleges and universities throughout the world who have journeyed here to study them have arrived at mixed conclusions. The consensus is that the boulders are glacial erratics, left behind as the Labrador ice sheet retreated 10,000 years ago. But curiously, their large sizes and uniform balsaltic content are unparalleled in the rest of the peninsula; in fact, no similar examples have ever been discovered in the area. The prevailing theory is that the rocks may be a type of Indian "medicine wheel," like those found in Montana and Wyoming. These wheels were the North American Indians' version of the British Stonehenge and were thought to enable the tribal shamans, or medicine men, to accurately forecast the coming of the seasons by indicating the times of the summer and winter solstices. They were, in effect, giant calendars.
>
> But speculation that Mystery Rock Hill is a type of calendar is quite tenuous, and would be of singular importance because the dominant Indian tribes of the area, the Menominee, Potawotomi, and Winnebago, have never been known to build any similar structures, and also, because the rocks are arranged in the unusual, strikingly heart-shaped pattern, they bear no resemblance to any other known medicine wheel. Although several of the rocks, being slightly larger than others in the pattern, can be aligned with the cardinal points of the compass, scientists have proven that they bear no relation to the sun or moon or any of the prominent stars or constellations rising above the horizon to be of any use as a calendar.
>
> An interesting theory has been proposed by amateur historian Bernard Wasson, a direct descendant of the founder of Wasson's Bay and owner of the acre-

age upon which the rocks are located. He suggests that the rocks and hill may have been an ancient ceremonial site used for Indian tribal rituals, although it is unclear what those rites may have been. Mr. Wasson bases his theory on the prehistoric works discovered at Aztalan in southern Wisconsin and other works in Ohio and southern Illinois.

But even under the intense scrutiny of scientists the Mystery Rocks have remained a mystery. Perhaps one day the mystery will be solved. Meanwhile enjoy the splendid view of Lake Michigan from Mystery Rock Hill and enjoy your stay in Wasson's Bay. Welcome to the beautiful and mysterious Midwest. Welcome.

1

The clouds are madness today, scudding across the sky like tattered blankets lost to an east wind, the unkindest wind of all. The morning sun flashes only momentarily upon the head and shoulders of a windblown figure standing by the side of the road, Basil Lexington, a study in disabled-vehicle geometry, a point on the line of Illinois Interstate 55, *nee* the celebrated macadam queen, Route 66, the Way West ... and long before that an ancient American trade route conveying copper, salt, pipestone, obsidian, peyote ... what ghosts of neolithic businessmen do the salesmen in Buicks and the screaming semi-trailer trucks pass?

The year is 197-, the era, post-sixties, the climate, late spring, early June, summer beginning to prime her vital juices, and Basil (rhymes with razzle-dazzle!), blindly eastbound, is beginning to shiver slightly, not from cold, although the skies indeed are irregular, mottled, fickle, and the wind grabs at the lapels of his sport coat during fitful gusts. No, it is more the situation in which he finds himself, as cloud-shadows race past him and his broken vehicle, a dusty Chevrolet Vega smelling strongly of the heated oil that pools beneath it and marks, in arcing ragged patches on the road behind, the distance from which a piston rod managed to lose its bearings. ... Each time he becomes conscious of it, the acrid smell, Basil's heart sinks; he knows it is the mark of death for vehicles. Plus, he stands to lose his man, whom he has trailed for 2,000 miles ... and he is actually going to be paid two hundred dollars a day plus expenses for this job, just like the big guys. But it now looks like he's blown it for sure with "Captain" Jimmy long-gone northward in his sleek Ferrari and Basil stuck in this god-forsaken tortilla-flat cornland with a dead Vega, hood open, no garage in sight—must be able to see for hundreds of miles in each direction, too. Basil lights a cigarette, a Camel, with Pop's precious Zippo, the only object he has that might conceivably be termed an heirloom, and sighs, hates waiting, especially out here in this enormous oppressive emptiness. He has never been in the midwest before and all this *space* is getting to him, a southern California boy (L.A.-born), a confirmed bottom-dweller in the vast topaz basin of smog, accustomed to its harsh topography: cars, buildings, bodies at every turn, flowing freeways like ancient rivers of Coronado: San Diego, Santa Monica, Pasadena, Ventura ... not at all like here: an awesome clarity of angry sky and uncountable acres of wide open land, infinite untrammeled space with not even token hills in the distance, not a one, farm-clusters appearing like isolate islands in wet black seas stretching horizonward, the topsoil rich and dangerous, so deep here he can sink to his thighs in it ... yes, and all he wants right now is to get out of here, to get to a garage, to *get going*, the crummy old Vega never more than a piece of junk anyway, transmission was going too, he thinks. Vaguely, more out of desperation than anything else, feeling a little foolish, Basil extends arm and thumb and almost immediately—a ride! Hot Dog! Brake lights burning red, gravel grinding, an enormous Winnebago motorhome lumbers to the berm like a wounded buffalo with an arrow in its flank, slowing, lurching, and not quite rolling over on its side as it stops in a cloud of dust.

The man at the garage tells Basil that his car is beyond repair and that he will take it off his hands for the cost of the towing. Respectfully, Basil is left alone to think this over, sitting on the Vega's cold orange hood in the windy back corner of the station's lot among the fading shells of other wrecks whose lives have also ended here, an eternity of rusting oblivion in the infinite flatlands, what a way to go.... Basil feels another chill, wonders what he is going to do now. He has a moderate amount of cash, and the waning end of a Master Charge limit to toy with ... but certainly not enough for another car, and has no idea how much farther or longer this job will take him. Being a private investigator isn't quite as easy as it looked; he realizes that he isn't even sure how he should go about the billing on this case, lengthy as it has become ... Doesn't seem quite appropriate to wire back to L.A. for money now, before he has gotten his man—whatever, exactly, even that means—another of the creeping uncertainties that have come with this case, with the profession.

There is really nothing else to do. From the Vega, Basil retrieves his possessions, a battered leather suitcase and a smaller traveling bag, also of leather, which contains important detective-type equipment: a small cassette tape recorder, a Nikon F1 with an 80x200 zoom lens, a collapsible miniature tripod, a treasured pair of Zeiss 7x35 binoculars he considers absolutely essential, and, of course, his case journal.

"... An often overlooked, but extremely valuable portion of an investigator's equipment is his journal of investigation. Here he will record facts pertinent to his cases, personal observations, happenings in the field, and the like. Often a clue that was missed in fieldwork will be noticed during careful review of the journal ..." from *An Investigator's Handbook - A Guide for the Novice*, by Franklin "Hawkeye" O'Hara, Schrader Press, Los Angeles, California, 1963.

Impressed by such advice, Basil has diligently plugged away at the thing, which, besides having grown beyond meticulous case scribblings into something more inspired, has also begun to possess a certain hard-bitten style that Basil, aside from anything else, considers efficient. Yesterday, for example:

Kowalske lamming it on to Wisconsin, now, like a scared rabbit who has nowhere else to go but far away from his home hole, or like a weasel with a purpose, on his way to some sort of strange secret rendezvous with destiny, a destiny that lurks somewhere out here in these endless flatlands. Or whatever. I still can't figure the guy, leaving a set-up like he had going for him. My first instinct is that there's a broad involved.

*   *   *

Basil's next stop, upper Illinois territory, north of Waukegan and south of Kenosha, an essentially neo-primitive sector of Midwestern civilization, where, like a sort of central eye in the swirling confabulation of American destiny, the shining dream has lapsed into something more fundamental and urgent: bawdy roadhouses and billboards, gas stations and trailer parks.

From where he stands on the roadside, where he had been dropped-off by his last ride—a lonely traveling salesman by the name of Bill with a story all his own—he can just see the top of a green and white Sinclair sign about a half-mile or so up the road, and he determines to go there and rustle more smokes and some food, some chips and a Coke, maybe, *barbecue* chips, if he's lucky. He's starving; he hasn't eaten anything today yet and it is already midafternoon.

As Basil scuffles along in the gravel he becomes aware of what must be decades-worth of ankle-deep trash strewn in the narrow corridor of vegetation that fends between the highway and a choking growth of sumac and alder. Lots of it: wadded Kleenex, cigarette butts, styrofoam coffee cups, sodden newspapers, beer cans of Schlitz, Budweiser, Old Style, cracked glass bottles once filled with Rosie O'Grady and Ripple, a child-sized Cubs baseball cap, an old rusted ironing board (how does this stuff get here anyway?), a splintered fishing rod, cracked moldy shoes, condoms, candy wrappers, and, Jeeze, Basil feels a pang as he spots a woman's black slip floating mutely on top of the weeds, not yet compressed into the inorganic layers, not even yet dampened by rain. The lacy bodice appears to be ripped, split down the middle by some sort of violence and now discarded, ejected from some passing vehicle at terrific speed. Basil quickens his pace, doesn't look back, the slip is a weird omen, a vestige from his first and actually his only case before this one, just three—or was it now four? lean months ago when the Jack of Hearts Detective Agency had hung out its shingle. When he decided he had to do *something*, although what is left of the trusts set up for him and then nearly depleted by his parents is still intact, God and the financial managers at Bankamerica willing . . . hasn't seen them, his parents, for almost a year now, pictures them simmering in Palm Springs in comfortable retirement while their son, their only child, has decided to become a–a *private eye!* (". . . Say what, Harold? Did you say he— Let me see that letter. . . .") Idle roadside ramblings here as thunder-vehicles roar by. . . . But his first job, yes, was a divorce case, or about to be, a wealthy father who suspected his daughter's husband of philandering, and guess what? it was *her* instead, and, ha-ha, did she *ever*, wow, secret meetings all over town with all sorts of scuzzballs—Basil dutifully recorded it all in his case journal from which he then extracted the typed report and presented it and about a dozen 8x10 glossies along with the slip (a black one she had discarded during a late-night tryst on the beach a la *From Here to Eternity* and then never collected), seemed like a piece of evidence, something concrete to present to Daddy Warbucks who ("What?! Bringing me my daughter's *underwear*?!") was pretty upset, made Basil feel really like the rookie he was, but shelled out $1,350 for nine days work, not bad, but no bonus, should have told mom and dad that, about the money . . . not bad at all for the old Peeper, hey?

The highway and the stream of trash lead him to the Sinclair station which has looming grandly before it an amazingly large concrete dinosaur—maybe twenty feet tall—an entire brontosaurus, its green-painted skin cracked and faded from many seasons of pushing *Dino Supreme*. Its upward spiralling neck is inclined northward where in a frozen grimace its blank eyes stare out over Wisconsin and Canada, watchful perhaps for the coming of another ice age. Basil briefly pauses to admire the old beast, remembers having miniature plastic dinosaurs as a kid, it was a fad then dating back to perhaps when this baby was created, in the nineteen-fifties, this thunder-lizard the archetype of them all . . . but he never had much time to play with them, denied kidhood, a terrible thing when he thinks about it, wonders, as he hustles up past the pumps if those dinos will ever come back. . . .

"Oh, boy," intones a cultured voice behind him, "would you

please be sure to check the oil, too. After you wash the windshield?"

Basil whirls around, finds himself looking into the deep blue eyes of an extremely attractive young woman. Ooh. A real knock-out, the neurons in his brain detonating like Chinese firecrackers. She is sitting demurely in the white leather interior of a gorgeous maroon Mercedes Benz sports car and although, of course, Basil immediately falls in love with her, he throws in the car too, as if part of a package deal, maybe of the type often transacted here in this once saurian-inhabited wasteland, where men's values were simpler, or at least more honest: women and cars forming the essential substance of bargains for several thousand years. . . .

"Hey, I'm not the—"

"Oh, I'm sorry, from behind I thought you were—"

Lifting a bag in each hand, he manages to flap the lapels of his sport coat. "Does this look like a gas jockey, hey?" He is somewhat hurt, these days most young men his age are wearing surplus army jackets, and—it has been a long day.

"Well, I'm *sorry*." The voice more petulant than hurt, petulance not an unknown here, for this is none other than rich, young, pseudo-spoiled Tiffany L'Oreal, woman about town (Chicago), and heiress to the L'Oreal Food Company fortune. Yes, the very same, of the cakes and doughnuts and breakfast cereals, yes, and the famous—or infamous, depending upon your nutritional inclination, *Morning Candy Crunch*, the company known as LoFoCo, as displayed in the familiar logo on its brightly colored supermarkety packages. But she has nothing presently to do with the firm. She's an actress—by profession, if something must fill the space marked: occupation—but doesn't pursue it too hard, which goes along with her affectation of being spoiled; it simply seems like it should be a part of her character, rich and beautiful as she is, and so she plays it that way. Like now, on her way to vacation for the summer in northern Wisconsin where she accepts parts in a small summer stock company up there (she's got a *very* big in with the producer), and is in somewhat of a hurry, certainly never bothering with riff-raff along the way. . . . But something piques her interest here; she has been inching up the volume on the Mercedes' tape player on the drive up from Winnetka, Beethovan's *Ninth*, until it has become many hundreds of decibels loud, still ringing in her ears, having made its always amazing meta-morphosis from music to pure feeling, and she is currently infused

13

with its power, the *Ninth*, awesome—it always hits her like this, makes her feel, umm, really powerful and playful, even more than she usually does, operating out in the excessive regions while attached always to the massive anchor of her family's money.

"Say, listen—" she continues, becoming aware of the fact that he is perhaps in need of a ride, but by now Basil has pulled out his P.I. badge and is displaying the gilt ornament to the lovely blonde woman.

"I'm a private investigator, you see, and at this very moment I'm on an important case. But I've been hampered by some unfortunate circumstances."

The girl nearly breaks up. This is going to be fun. With considerable restraint she allows only a broad smile to surface and inquires if he needs a lift.

Basil tells her about the Vega: dead, his immediate direction: north, and, after he quickly rustles up a couple of packs of Camels and brunch: barbecue chips and a Coke, they're off.

2

In the hilly wooded Indian country of northern Wisconsin, Synandra Wasson sits quietly in the dappled shade of a great elm, intently watching the tall Indian doctor standing out in the sunny meadow. The sky is deep blue and a faint scent of wild mint carries on the breeze. Summer is beginning its dance; already the trilliums are thinning out, the pastel hepaticas and golden trout lilies have long gone. Now the hawthorne is florescent with snowy white petals and the green foliage of may apple, solomon's seal, spikenard, and bloodroot carpets the forest floor; ginseng is appearing on the cooler slopes.

Synandra picks at a loose thread on her bluejeans and sighs, hears the trill of redwings and the gawk of crows as she looks over again at the medicine man handling his bow and arrow. And again, as he arches the great wooden longbow to string it, she is impressed by the strength of the old man, whose name is Bo. He is an Indian, and he is a doctor—of ancient medicine—in the omnipotent eyes of shamans everywhere, and in the somewhat more myopic eyes of the AMA, "old medicine," Harvard Medical School, Class of 1929. His real name is longer than the exuberant amphibianic utterance "Bo," of course, but as it is a "real" name, conferred upon him in the course of one or more shamanic journeys he cares not to discuss with laymen, it has "real" power and is not to be carelessly revealed. Just more of the mystery surrounding the enigmatic doctor who over the years has acquired knowledge about a great many things, one of which is a practice that, to the uninitiated, appears a deadly sport.

Synandra catches her breath as the doctor nocks an arrow into the taut bowstring and slowly draws it back. The projectile is tipped with a razor-sharp broadhead that glints in the sunlight as the doctor makes minor adjustments in its anticipated flight path: straight up. It is aimed at the sky, possibly at a tiny puff of cumulus that seems to float directly above Dr. Bo's head. Synandra knows what the medicine man is waiting for: the right moment (she has seen this many times before) and what the arrow is really aimed at—in an antithetical way—Dr. Bo. Suddenly the arrow is released and Synandra watches it soar high, straight toward the little cloud . . . and it is probably a quirk of the eyes from staring into the bright sky after the arrow, now reduced to pure geometric point, but it appears to her that the cloud has suddenly darkened. Just then the arrow reappears, and Synandra glances quickly at the doctor who has placed the bow on the ground and is standing erect in the meadow, his eyes closed, lips softly chanting, arms angled slightly outward as in a gesture of supplication. . . . She looks away, she can't watch this part, never could . . . and the arrow flashes down, embedding itself in the ground about ten feet off to his right. The medicine man opens his eyes, glances at the arrow and then looks skyward. Synandra follows his gaze and sees that the little cloud is almost gone, its white form dissipating in the high morning breezes, the same fine winds that have influenced the arrow in its flight toward Dr. Bo.

Synandra shudders; she hates this type of divination, even though she must admit a certain fascination with the procedure. She remembers what the doctor has told her about the amount of effort required in the magical process: that you get out of it precisely what you put into it; this particular form of divination geographical in nature, its purpose to provide an inquirer with the particular direction, north, south, east, west, or variation thereof, of which some event, person, or expected object, will manifest itself. Dr. Bo has explained to her that it is imperative that you actually *expect* some sort of an occurence, too, particularly on very calm days, for it is when there is the least wind that this process is the most powerful; if there is no immediate force about to influence your being, nothing at all happening with you, so to speak, your time may be up, the arrow may find the top of your skull, and, on a calm day you may go forever.

"A lovely day," Dr. Bo says, eyes twinkling like the morning star itself.

"It sure is," says Synandra, sitting cross-legged now in front of the doctor's digs, a modest two-room shack that faces south, backed by a dense stand of firs. She looks out over miles of gently rolling forestland, patched here and there with the lighter green clearings of what once tried to be farms in the rocky northern soil, eventually abandoned to the might of the north wind, the harsh winters, the unforgiving persistence of the forest . . . all enclosed by the immense blue dome of the sky. She lies back and shuts her eyes against the sun's brilliance, watches rosy hearts meander behind her glowing eyelids, listens to squirrels chatter in the nearby pines.

"Do you see those clouds?" Dr. Bo asks softly.

"Where?" Synandra sits up, blinking, looks out where the doctor points with an oaken arm. Overhead, the sky is cloudless, azure, but to the south, above the horizon lies a cloudbank and out of it two fluffy cumuli drift northward, seemingly towards them.

"It is quite windy down there. Watch and see if they meet."

It is an omen; now she understands; the arrow indicated the direction perfectly. But these *two* clouds? Well, aeromancy being certainly not the least of his accomplishments, she knows better than to second-guess him; also, she just can't seem to calm the way her heart has foolishly begun flub-a-dubbing away. Why? She doesn't know, it's silly, probably nothing—she's so sensitive anyway. But listening to the doctor is always like putting together a jigsaw puzzle, and now she has a piece of the sky and a couple of clouds. . . .

"Watch," he commands.

She focuses southward. The two clouds are very close together now, and it appears that they are about to merge. Synandra squints. The two clouds become one and drift along toward them.

*   *   *

"Jimmy Kowalske, himself," Tiffany says, downshifting to about one ten-millionths the speed of light to pass a slow-moving semi-trailer as the small maroon Mercedes makes its way into the busy prairies of Wisconsin. "Imagine, him coming up here, to-to MacArthur, you say. Gosh, I don't think there's hardly anything there now, just a house or two where the roads cross. . . ."

"That's what my investigation has uncovered," Basil replies smartly, though he's lying. He doesn't have any idea what's there, couldn't even find it on the map, but reaches coolly for a cigarette and looks out the window, eastward, where the industrial essence has settled along the shoreline of Lake Michigan into the smoking factory towns of Kenosha and Racine; to the west rolling farmland spreads outward toward the shimmering lakes where the young F. Scott Fitzgerald spent impassioned summers. . . . Right now, however, it is Basil who is sporting impassioned thoughts, seated comfortably alongside one of the most classically beautiful girls he has ever seen—riding in style! As his journal will later recall:

It was one of the damndest pieces of luck I've ever had hit me. Like a ton of bricks, easy. This chick looks like a million bucks, which doesn't surprise me either, because she's in line to inherit plenty from the LoFoCo food business. She looks rich, dresses rich, she even smells rich.

I guess the jury's still out on whether big bucks mold a person or not, but it seems they sure must be able knock off some of life's rough edges here and there, because this chick is very smooth, smooth as the silk blouse that's trying its best to cover her gorgeous gazoombas. I'm not sure if she's got an angle or not. But the way she looks at me with those big baby blues, so innocent-like, makes me think that maybe she's one of the few in this world who don't. The thing that floors me, though, like a steamshovel uppercut from Kenny Norton himself, is that not only does she know where MacArthur is, but that she's headed that way. And I couldn't even find it on a map. Now what kind of luck is that?

18

"Say," she says, "what's he, Kowalske, going up there for any-way?"

"I'm really not sure, my informant wasn't clear about that. I tell ya, I was awfully lucky to be able to pin it down at all."

"You must have been very clever, too."

"Oh, of course, of course . . ." Basil wants to tell her exactly how clever he really was in tracking down this hot lead, but Tiffany starts gushing again over the fact that he—or they, now—are actually on the trail of "Captain" Jimmy Kowalske.

It is evident that she knows a moderate amount about him, says she read an article or two in the Chicago *Tribune*, and one in *Time* or *Newsweek* . . . and that's really almost as much as Basil knows too, even though he has visited their "church" factory outside of Barstow as a working private investigator. The Church of the Electronic Trinity has stonewalled him every step of the way, even though one of their own had hired him . . . and none of the church fanatics, the Trinnies, would consider talking. . . . But she presses him for more, Basil here being the local authority on the boy-wonder from Bakersfield.

"What are the three future things, exactly, that he's so ga-ga about, a telemarineophone or something? And a, a—"

"A teleporter, is one," Basil smiles. "Something that will supposedly take objects, anything, from place to place, through thin air. And then there's the telechronos, a time machine; and an anti-grav, an anti-gravity device, something that, I guess, should let you float around, fly with maybe. . . ."

"Ooooh," says Tiffany, "wouldn't it be wonderful to fly? I have flying dreams all the time. Maybe he found it and flew away with it. I would. . . ."

"Um, maybe, but then that would mean the beginning of a 'New Age,' remember? He says that the 'Coming of the THREE,' those three machines, will signal the beginning of world peace, prosperity, and, uh, I can't remember. . . ."

"Yes, well there's sure no 'New Age' around here that I can see. Maybe just the opposite. . . ."

"You're not kidding."

But according to Jimmy Kowalske, the leader of what has been termed "a company cult" by UCLA's Fad Religion Observatory, the New Age is on its way. The coming of the THREE will herald it, and those who wanted to reap all its wonderful (and vague) benefits would best be members of the Church of the Electronic Trinity—and therefore employees of Craxton Electronics, the manufacturer of the now-ubiquitous Craxton Sound-Pac. Formerly a small electronics components assembler that had fallen on hard times, Craxton made a terrific turn-around as the manufacturer of the 1970's integrated-circuit update of the transistor radio, the small AM/FM radio and cassette player with lightweight miniature earphones that is standard gear for joggers and music lovers on-the-go everywhere. The Sound-Pac, and the Church of the Electronic Trinity (providing the cheap labor to manufacture it), were the product of the inventiveness and intensely charismatic leadership of "Captain" Jimmy, a former honor student, M.I.T. graduate, and Captain of Infantry in Vietnam (where, as the church line goes, in a night-time firestorm near Long Binh during the Tet Offensive he suffered a vision of the THREE). It was a real setup, a businessman's dream, actually. The Trinnies donated all their possessions to the church, and then worked day and night assembling the Sound-Pacs, the church providing them with shelter in the church dormitories, food in the church cafeterias, and most importantly, *meaning*, in the church doctrine. How laboring long hours in the church workshops for wages that were eventually donated entirely back to the church would foster the pre–apocalyptic Coming of the THREE was never made exactly clear, but for the dejected and rejected souls that appeared at their door—or, factory gate—it was more hope in the future than they ever had before.

And then of course there was Captain Jimmy, who appeared in their busy midst from time to time like a gracious Immortal, joking and laughing with them, apparently *caring* for them, spinning tales of a future with the THREE, and (inadvertently perhaps) urging them onward to ever higher production goals.... Although articles antagonistic to the Church appeared occasionally on slow days, with charges ranging from tax-evasion to slave-labor, they got away with it, surviving investigations by both the press and the authorities, claiming first to be a religion, and secondly, to be caring for the homeless, providing them with jobs, education, and sustenance, and so why wouldn't everyone just leave them alone? Not a one of the Trinnies ever complained, and anyone was free to leave at any time, anyway. Weren't they?

Basil wasn't exactly sure, although he, like everyone else who toured the main facility outside Barstow, was impressed by their cleanliness, the abundance of food, and the absolute dedication to their cause the faithful seemed to possess. But there was one strange thing: everyone, at least all but the very young, wore Sound-Pacs. All the time. And these particular Sound-Pacs were company issue. Unlike the ones you bought in the store, they had no dial nor volume control. They were set at a common low volume and radio-frequency, that of the church. Which played mostly classical music, along with periodic church/company bulletins, shift change announcements, and the like. Basil had listened-in when he was there, hearing the busy Brandenburg Concertos at the time (although he didn't know what they were). Of course that in itself didn't explain the half-glazed look that everyone there seemed to possess. No one would look at him. They just stared straight ahead as if engrossed in the music—and their work. It gave him the creeps.

"Well, that's because they're all being brainwashed, silly," Tiffany looks over at Basil incredulously. "The latest rumor is that everything the Trinnies hear through their Sound-Pacs is underlaid with subliminal messages that are unconsciously embedded in their unsuspecting brains."

"I never heard of that," sniffs Basil. "It just sounded like music to me."

"Oh no. Department stores are notorious for it. You know that background music that plays all the time? Well underneath it are creepy little whispered messages saying: 'Don't ... steal ... from us,' or 'Spend ... spend ... spend.' Stuff like that. It's a constant barrage of propaganda. Yet we don't even know it's there."

Basil hmphs, "Well ... no wonder those Trinnies are so loyal—if what you say is true, of course. Then they're being brainwashed whenever they listen to those Sound-Pacs, which is all the time."

"You know," says Tiffany, "I also read that Kowalske wasn't really in charge anymore, that the church hierarchy, the businessmen Craxton had imported to help him with the day-to-day had pretty much taken over everything. They shoved Captain Jimmy aside, letting him remain there as only a figurehead."

Basil nods, has to agree that this was possible. He had that feeling when he was out there. He was given a short tour by one of the top church chieftains, someone named Murenger. He really wasn't allowed to look around anywhere that regular visitors weren't welcome, wasn't allowed to talk to any church officials, nor even any of the Trinnies. Especially none of the Trinnies. In fact, he got the feeling that all they wanted to do was get rid of him. And they had hired him to find their missing leader! He decides not to relate any of this to Tiffany, it's somewhat embarrassing, a more experienced P.I. might have found out more information, through some devious means, like they do on TV. . . .

"The paper said there was a power struggle going on, now that Kowalske has disappeared," adds Tiffany.

"That's the impression I get," Basil sighs. "It seemed pretty mixed-up back there. They weren't very cooperative, that's for sure. At least I was able to find out about MacArthur. On my own, of course. I can't believe you know where that is."

"Yes, it is strange, isn't it, but, you know sometimes I find myself part of funny coincidences like this. I have this friend who is positively mystical and it's usually when I'm with her . . . but, funny thing, I'm on my way up to see her now. She lives in Wasson's Bay. And that's where we're headed."

3

The last thing Synandra sees at night are hearts. After she emerges from her bath, delicately fragrant of neroli and musk, after she slips into her nightie (perhaps the one of watered pink silk bordered with tiny red hearts), and after she has blown out the flame on her massive brass and nickel hurricane lamp, they appear. Valentine hearts, white and pink and red and gold, dazzle and whirl across the dark palpebral curtains like the heavenly fire in van Gogh's "Starry Night." She doesn't remember exactly when the hearts first appeared; it seems they have always been there, in the same way that she can't remember exactly when it was her parents were no longer there; they just *weren't*; leaving her before her second birthday, although she swears that she deeply remembers being held, cuddled, comforted by her mother and father—before the freak accident that took them both out in one fell swoop. . . . And then there were the hearts, as though—she believes this, holds tightly on to this—when her young parents left her to be cared forever after by her grandfather, they left also a legacy of multitudinous glowing hearts, comforting tiny friends which would flash and cavort in the bedtime hours of little girldom until she drifted into sleep.

Later on, she began seeing hearts in the daytime. Usually they would appear only in the periphery of her vision, but now and then one would find its way free and flutter like a dainty butterfly into the cinerama of her sight. Occasionally the hearts seemed to have some significance, like an exclamation point in a phrase of her life, at other times not. It took her a while to learn that apparently only she was able to conjure hearts, and then, of course, that she was the only one who could see the little rascals when they popped into her outer vision—that is, the only one besides Dr. Bo.

This was something she discovered one day while sitting on the living room floor watching an after-school rerun of a popular television show of the sixties, *Leave it to Beaver*. Dr. Bo, who was visiting, was also absently watching the program while her grandfather was out of the room. In the show, one of the characters, Eddie Haskell, was being especially snotty to the Beaver, a boy who bore a slight resemblance to his namesake, when suddenly a beautiful little red heart, glowing soft pink around its border, flew from Synandra's eyes directly onto Eddie Haskell's forehead. It remained there for a second or two, then faded away. While Synandra stared, enthralled, Dr. Bo, standing behind her, suddenly let out a long low kai-eeeee. Synandra turned around, looked up and met the good doctor's piercing eyes. Afterwards he took her aside and asked her some questions. The next day was her twelfth birthday.

Henceforth, the symbol, the leitmotif of her adolescence, became hearts. While other girls sadly conjured up poltergeists, she inspired hearts. While other girls took a fancy to horses, rock and roll or movie stars, she took to the perfect abstract symmetry of the ♥ . She began to collect all sorts of heart-styled baubles and bangles, knicknacks and folderol. She baked tarts—in the shape of hearts.

So it was not mere whimsy that led Synandra to believe that the hill topped with a slightly imperfect heart, Mystery Rock Hill, was somehow hers. She believed that it had stood throughout time, waiting only for that great karmic carnival wheel to complete its whirl and drop-off, as it were, in the midst of the Eisenhower era, a girl with a penchant for hearts, a girl who might ultimately know the secrets of the heart-rocks and the hill and herself.

If there was ever a sound argument for a person to claim a portion of the planet as their own (at least for the duration), Synandra had a convincingly good case. Legally, she also had a good case. The hill, the Wasson house, and the ten acres that contained them were now hers, now that her grandfather, Bernard Wasson, had gone on, earlier this spring, to join her parents.

* * *

As the crow flies, the doctor's digs, though deep in the eastern forest of mainland Wisconsin, are not terribly far from Wasson's Bay. But by earthbound automobile, due to the intrusive tongue of Green Bay, the homeward-bound traveler has to jog around the green waters through miles of shadowy pinewoods, through the namesake city housing humming paper mills and impassioned Packer backers, and up the long peninsula.

Synandra, making the drive now and mulling over the medicine man's earlier disconcerting divination, idly recalls her own attempts at aeromancy, of watching the clouds for something significant, something of import ... but all she was ever able to see were fuzzy bears and bunnies and hearts, with the odd hippopotamus and dragon chugging by.... Except for the time, of course, less than a month ago, when she had seen *that*, an extraordinary perception—what appeared to be a gigantic cigar box in the sky, a colossal cosmorama of an intricate 17th century Dutch master's oil by Vermeer, perhaps, or Rembrandt. Strange enough, but the truly fantastic thing about it was that her *grampa* was in the scene, seated in a chair at the forefront of a circle of high-hatted Dutch burghers and merchants ... and he was animated, puffing tiny clouds from his favorite pipe.

Cruel perception. It was the day, the exact hour, she later learned, that he had died far away from her, drowned, along with his fishing buddy, a lawyer from the town of Sturgeon Bay. Their canoe had overturned in the frigid Canada-Minnesota boundary waters during a vicious spring storm. But of course she knew, at the moment of the vision ... she *knew* ... even now, she remembers the awful sense of grief that had taken her over....

And now, all she is left with is her love for him, and the wonderful memories, of garden-planting with him in balmy early June, apple-picking on autumn afternoons, after-school tobogganing in velvety winter twilights ... thoughts crowding her mind as she drives, causing several hearts, blood-red, salmon-pink, and ghost-white to burst before her misty eyes ... these being the same kinds of hearts, bouquets of hearts, that she had showered at the funeral along with a steady blurry stream of tears.

But only loneliness can crowd a void. Harsh memories well up with the others, all come together and must be given their due at times like this.... It had taken her quite a while to coax the story from her grandpa, but finally she learned the cause of her parents' death years ago—a reaper's grimmest joke: One August day they had attended the Wisconsin State Fair down in West Allis while grandpa cared for their baby girl, and buoyant as Chagall's gaudy lovers, the young couple decided to match the feeling by taking a spin on a small roller-coaster erected for the fair. It was a hot day, the first day of the fair, and also the first run of the ride. The cart, the coaster, to which they were directed unfortunately had been in rustic storage out in the Southwest somewhere, Arizona or New Mexico, and had borne a family of rattlesnakes beneath the seat. They had apparently remained dormant until roused by the heat of the day and the motion of the ride ... her parents' screams were not understood at the time for what they were.... At least she had been too young to sense that particular tragedy—or had she? Her grandfather reported that the normally quiet girl had wailed all that afternoon.

And now, not quite two decades later, Synandra lays dubious claim to being the last of the area's Wassons'—a once-hardy clan that had dug its roots into Wisconsin over a century before, dating back to a windy August afternoon in 1848 when a cargo steamer sailing from Buffalo to Milwaukee was suddenly caught in a northeaster and forced to seek shelter in the as-yet unnamed bay. While the gale blew itself out, the ship's captain, Milford Wasson, decided to explore this verdant woodland where Providence had so beneficently steered him.

History has recorded the bare facts: names, places, dates ... but there is no record, not even family legend that can relate what the Captain had thought when he first stood in the shadow of that oddly-appointed hill, nor what he felt after he had climbed to the valentine of rocks on its summit and surveyed the forest below. The heavens may have parted and the souls of vanished Indians ghost-danced before him ... or he may simply have sensed that this geologic malformation was somehow *special*. (Rumors abound that the Indians had considered the site sacred, but the Potowatomis and Winnebagos had been kayoed more than a decade before by the white man's classic one-two punch—firewater and broken treaties—and sent west, leaving the land virtually uninhabited and without historical record.) At any rate, Milford was impressed enough with the fine harbor and the area's abundance of timber that he gathered his savings and purchased a section of the virgin land, bringing his family and a few hired men to start a business shipping cordwood, railroad ties, and cedar poles to Milwaukee. Within a few years land was cleared, a sawmill constructed, a pier built out into the bay, and the tiny settlement, a dozen or so log cabins fronting a narrow road hacked from the forest, formally took the name of Wasson's Bay.

Over the next two decades the business prospered, more people moved in, and the frontier hamlet became a bustling lakeshore village. Schooners sailed in and out almost daily, dropping off supplies and loading their holds with lumber, and great lakes steamers began to make regular stops in Wasson's Bay. Stores and saloons sprang up, a new hotel and church were built, and small farms began appearing on cleared land to the west and northwest. Milford Wasson became a wealthy and locally powerful man. He was the first, in 1869, to represent the area in the State legislature. In 1870, the year before the great Chicago and Peshtigo fires, he constructed a large twelve-room house about two hundred yards northeast of the great hill which stood behind the village like a worn displaced pyramid, as though safeguarding it, providing an abundant flow of good fortune to Wasson's Bay.

But yin follows yang as inexorably as winter follows fall. The good fortune did not last. By the turn of the century coal and coke had become the predominant fuel in America's swelling cities and the cordwood business, declining steadily all along, finally fizzled out. The boom was over. Unemployed families and failing businesses began moving out in a wagon-load exodus for booms elsewhere, farther west. And in a few unforgiving years Wasson's Bay once again became a quiet little village of scrabbling farmers, fishermen, and the occasional vacationer. Milford Wasson had long since made his way to woodchopper's heaven, and his descendants, once so prominent in the region, scattered over the years like seed-fluff before the gusting winds of war, depressions, and the long, hard

Wisconsin winters, ultimately becoming anonymous names in telephone books across America, their sole forgotten nexus, a hill in
Wisconsin, a heart of stone.

Not every Wasson left, however. There was always someone who
remained to manage the family real estate, occupy the big house,
and ponder the mystery of the hill. After World War II, the area
began to resurrect from its big sleep, and then it was Bernard Wasson, great-grandson of Milford, who was there to help with the re-
vival. The town was becoming a popular summer resort and homes
and cottages and small stores grew along the town's main street as
vacationers, campers, sightseers, and sport fishermen began crowding
into the peninsula each summer. The hill, of course, became a great
tourist attraction, its rocks forever after bearing the monicker of
mystery rather than that of love, commerce triumphing over romance
every time in mid-twentieth century America. And in the early sixties, after some protracted negotiations instigated by Bernard Wasson, the hill, and the house, with its sturdy Victorian architecture,
were declared a scenic site to be preserved in their respective natural
states, forever. . . . And all might have been well for the orphaned
girl and her grandfather, had not Fate yet another unbeatable hand
to play, another prize to take during a violent day in May. . . .

Now the house seems so empty without her grampa's robust
aura permeating its century-old space. As she wanders through its
rooms she hears echoes that she had never noticed before. Especially, she recalls now with sadness and deep purple hearts, a time
after the interment when during a forgetful moment she had called
out to her grandfather about something and heard only her voice,
a ringing echo, and silence. No, it was not the house that was her
real legacy. She knew, and her grandfather would have agreed, that
it was the monolith of the Wasson clan that loomed through the
trees behind the house, Mystery Rock Hill, and the odd powers
she derived from it.

4

It is all in black and white, or, many scalars of gray, washed-out and distant as the planet Uranus in all the science books of the time. They exist here, dauntless little crew, where it is surely real, but—removed, all color squeezed-out somehow, nothing but this peculiar atmosphere left, gray as winter breath itself, the air he is breathing, and Pop Dawson and all of them, a supremely finer gray, perhaps less grainy than everything else here, but still essential for life in this peculiar realm.... And he knows by now there is no way out, the subtly fine monochromatic texture defining everything: sky, skin, sweat, tears, all into a world that exists nowhere ... and yet, there is something comforting about being here ... where the values, at least, the only true unperishables, are not so different from those outside: love, truth, honor, patriotism (lots of that stuff here), if anything, more pure, more, ha-ha, *black and white* ... maybe beauty the only one that doesn't really make it here, the one that it takes a firm connection with the celestial to apprehend and here there is precious little of that ... but ... then again, all is not totally removed ... he knows the sun is shining up there, can even see it when he chooses to look up, an infinitely bright gray, but never truly bright enough....

29

Anyway, there is no way out of this, and Pop again is getting himself into a jam, one that we all know the Peeper is going to help him get out of ... but each jam is more confusing than the last, it seems. ... Pop this time has invested the family savings in a business of some sort, a–a detective agency, oh Lord, yes, Pop Dawson has gone shamus on them, and good wife Martha worried sick about it with Mr. Preston from the bank expecting the mortgage payment this faded afternoon ... but the Peeper is going to figure out something, something stupidly simple in its naive child-logic-like way, he knows it, the family knows it, *all of America knows it,* but it is all so tiring for the poor Peeper, who is going to have to save the whole idiot clan again, he's just too young for this, should be outside somewhere, away from all of this, where sky is honest-to-God blue, grass is green, and—someone is calling him again—

He is being jostled, and none too kindly, "Basil, Basil, look, here comes the sign."

"Sign—?"

"The sign for Syndy's hill. Look, here it comes."

Up ahead, on the right side of the road is a small billboard.

See the World Famous
MYSTERY ROCK HILL
Ancient Indian Sacrifice Grounds
SCENIC PANORAMA   FREE ADMISSION
Ahead 2 miles in Wasson's Bay

"What is that all about?" Basil yawns.

"That's Syndy's hill. My best friend, you'll meet her."

"I will?"

"Uh-huh. If you want to get to MacArthur. She can take you there."

"And you can't?"

"Well, Syndy really knows where it is ... better than I ..."

"Oh."

"She hates that sign."

"How come?"

"The Chamber of Commerce put it up. There really wasn't any human sacrifice there ... we don't think."

"That's a relief."

They drive through a wooded stretch, snatches of cottages flashing at them through the trees, and then past older homes spaced on lawns edged with bridal wreath and forsythia. The shoreline opens up to the right and the bay appears, dark as sapphire in the afternoon light. Tiffany points left, landward, where the trees have abruptly closed in again, and sure enough, through them glows the bald dome of a hill.

"That's it?"

"That's it."

"Big deal."

"You'll see." She smiles.

Tiffany is staying at her parents summer home south of the village proper in woods that surround the lakeshore. Gravel driveways disappear into the trees, before many of them small vanity signs: Cottage-By-The-Bay, Whispering Pines, Harker's Hideaway. Tiffany pulls into a drive bearing the legend: Kingston's Kabin. And after winding through a canopy of hemlock and pine, stops before a three-car garage attached to a sprawling redwood beach house.

"This is a 'kabin'?"

"Well, daddy has a strange sense of humor."

Inside and later, after a spartan meal of brown rice and veggies that Tiffany has whipped up—turns out she's a hardcore health food nut—they chit-chat in the kitchen sharing one of her hand-rolled ganja cigarettes (*Gotterdammerung* grade) and a bottle of wine. It is preparatory to lovemaking, more or less. Tiffany is aroused by this cute private eye from Los Angeles, and he by her: golden daughter of the great Midwest grain barons—or, uh, some such thing.

She produces another bottle of wine which boy scout Basil decides he will open with the corkscrew on his red Swiss Army knife . . . but several shit-losing moments later it is apparent that the cork is not going to budge.

Basil motions to Tiffany, giggling uncontrollably now, to get up and grab the bottle, "yeah, like that, and I'll just—unnnghhhhh!" Basil gives a mighty heave, but *nada*. "Okay let's try it again— unnnnnGGGGHHHHHHH!" dragging her halfway across the kitchen. "Jesus," through clenched teeth, "is this some kind of trick bottle or something? The cork's glued in here, I'll bet, and you just bring this out when—UNNNNNNAAAAARRRRRGGGHHHHHHHH—" the cork floops out, sending Basil sliding ass-backwards across the floor into the refrigerator. Tiffany howls with laughter, nearly falling to the floor herself. Basil looks sheepish, but has to laugh too, "Boy, that's hard-won wine."

Tiffany shrieks. "Hard won wine! Basil, you-you hit your head and now you're speaking in *Chinese!*"

"Ah so . . ." says Basil from the floor, squinting his eyes like one of those pseudo-sino Charlie Chan's, "velly tough cork to pop, huh, Pop?"

Still giggling, she shoos Basil into the bedroom, a dusky expanse illuminated by candles and dominated by a large waterbed, "the waterbedroom," Basil thinks, and then immediately forgets as the theme of lovemaking tonight begins to materialize: "Africa, Land of Mystery," due to the effects of marijuana and this golden girl's stunning athletic imaginativeness, beginning with him being playfully flumped onto the waterbed apparently in order to watch her, uh, dance, amazingly erotic, to the sound, at first, of distant drums (far below brilliant white clouds in the high blue African sky and the sacred peak itself, Kilimanjaro) . . . the drums continuing, enlarging (as he presses rapidly, miraculously, across the open veld, velocity an unknown at this point, enormous geography racing below him, traversing easily entire *regions* as the insistent syncopation carries though the ether . . . onward now into greenery, vine and frond— steaming jungle and dusk, the light fading all along . . .) the drums much louder now, welling up into an incredible throbbing polyrhythm, voices chanting antiphonally, birds screeching in the background (. . . a convocation of natives revealed in the clearing before him, and the maiden unchained at last from the central totem, free to move, free to *dance!*) . . . with Basil a trifle uneasy here in the uncertain candlelight, albeit with terrific erection, watching her gyrate with voodoo-trance abandon, glistening with perspiration, hair fallen in straggles, eyes looking so far out into the bush, into nowhere, troubling nowhere . . . until after interminable minutes she collapses, calls for him. . . .

"Ahhhhhh!" Tiffany shrieks. "You were the *Peeper!* I can't believe it! The Peeper, here, you—I can't believe it."

It is usually some variation of recognition and disbelief when

Basil tells them who he is—or was. He knows he doesn't much resemble his childhood self, but once he tells them they always remember, can always see the likeness, this being a somewhat typical, perhaps even subdued, response. But what should he expect after she has experienced his terrific lovemaking? He yawns, figures she's lucky to have any energy at all ... especially after that crazy voodoo dance thing, gives him shivers just to think of it.... But it is now Basil's turn to relate his oft-told tale of how, yes, he really was the Peeper: impish, devilishly cute, and somehow young-wise with a sort of world-weary aspect that was so appealing in an eight-thru-eleven year old—probably one of the things that allowed the silly program to run so long, from 1959 to 1963, to begin with, before being unceremoniously cancelled, interestingly enough, several days after Kennedy was killed, and several months before the Beatles appeared on the *Ed Sullivan Show,* and the 1960's of legend and verse really began.

The show was *Those Doggone Dawsons,* and was one of many "family" shows of the era, actually a lesser clone of more memorable programs ... another adaptation of the nuclear-family mythos, which curiously, was decaying rapidly even as it was promulgated, perhaps desperately, in the nuclear age ... sending values, mores, role-models of happy, happy early-atomic America out into the ether, simple gentle propaganda *through space, at the speed of light,* into America's living quarters and the innocent eyes of those dwelling therein, forever transmuted by the constant darkgraylight roomblink jitter of the TV screen....

"You know," sighs Tiffany, leaning back into bed pillows, still a bit giggly from the pot, "I used to envy you, you know, how you were always so—clever, and able to get your Pop out of all those predicaments."

"Yeah, that was the way the writers slanted it, a clever little kid instead of, well—like the Beaver."

Tiffany laughs. "Did you hate him?"

"Well, there was a certain rivalry, I guess, after all we were on different networks, with different sponsors, different studios...."

Basil closes his eyes and yawns, doesn't much feel like talking about old times right now; it seems that he has developed another hardon lying next to this gorgeous girl and is contemplating nibbling on her fair soft shoulder or some such thing, despite the fact that he

33

is pretty tired after all this razzmatazz, as remembrances drift in, of the studio and the lights and the microphones, the directors that came and went, the silly scripts, and the crazy cast of that particular make-believe world: good old Stinky Harrison, his best friend both on and off the set, and then of course Jack Dougherty, who played the bumbling and insipid, yet very warm Pop Dawson, who possessed in real-life a depth and clarity you would never expect . . . and dear Nell, who played his fainthearted screen mother, Martha, and other transient cast members, including old Dud Lausser, who played Mr. Whithers, the supposedly-stern-but-with-a-heart-of–gold school principal on the show, the old fart, had once approached young Basil in the dressing room with his warty, veiny hands, tried to get uncommonly friendly, the old geeze, but Basil had kicked him perfectly below his distended fly, has to smile at that now, losing his present erection as he does, never told anyone, was near the end of the run anyway, funny how that even now the scene is replayed in shades of endless gray. . . .

There's a swath of sunlight reflected across the ceiling, and Tiffany is already out of bed. Showering-up with some terrific sandalwood-scented soap, Basil decides that he is never going to leave this town, this house, this amazing girl—although there is something sitting uneasy in the back of his mind . . . that he can't quite recall . . . but it's something, nagging . . . last night—that dance!

He mentions it during breakfast, trying not to make a big deal about the whole thing . . . but she says she's a dancer—also an actress, both semi-professionally, apparently taking roles when the mood strikes her—it doesn't matter, she blithely tells him, she's pretty good at both and anyway she's rich—

"How rich?" Basil feels impertinent enough to ask, also kind of excited in the presence of so much wealth and beauty . . . besides, there's a way actors can talk to each other, a subtle bond they understand, that they're always playing one part or another, if perhaps only on a subconscious level, and always know what they can get away with . . .

"Oh, fabulously. Daddy's company makes tons. I can't believe how people will buy that shit . . ."

"You're pretty lucky. To be born into it like that."

"Well, not that lucky," eyes flickering somewhat dangerously. "It's not easy being the daughter of a children's food pornographer."

"I never thought of it that way."

"Well, think of it . . ."

"Uh, about the dancing? I-I've never seen anything quite like that. What's it all about?"

"Did you like it?"

"Oh yeah, sure."

"Well, I suppose that's good, but in the end it really doesn't matter one way or the other. . . . You see, there's really not that much to explain. Maybe because there's really nothing that *can* be explained. The music came from some museum tapes I got ahold of, an early expedition into bongo-congo somewheres; I wanted—or needed—something absolutely primitive, something where I could feel the earth itself was really speaking to them and then of course to me. . . . But the dance, I don't know . . . it was the best I could do. You see, it's something I'm reaching for, something inside, I think. Something maybe I'll never really have . . . I don't know . . . maybe it's something I can only approach, never achieve. . . .

"But what?" Basil exasperated by her rambling, and also by a compelling sadness that seems to have taken her over. . . .

"I don't *know!* I told you I couldn't explain it." But then she brightens and says, "Say, you know my friend Synandra? *She* has it."

"Er, that Synandra Wasson?"

"Yes, in fact, she *is* it."

"But what's *it*?"

"I don't *know,*" she moans, petulantly again, "but maybe you'll catch a glimpse. . . ."

5

Tiffany's parents are due up this morning—this *morning?!*—and she has cleaning to do (since they are roughing-it up here in the wilderness, their housekeeper comes in only twice a week), and even though her mother wouldn't be *too* upset about his being here, Daddy is awfully conservative, and has a terrible temper, is prone to rages, actually . . . it is best that Basil leave, and probably the sooner the better. . . .

Well, she's certainly got *that* right, Basil furtively checking out escape routes, the back door, the kitchen window, the chimney, while he gathers up his bags with all possible speed, stuffs yesterday's Jockey shorts into his coat pocket . . . Tiffany's sorry, it's too late to even offer him a ride, but it doesn't matter, he's already halfway down the driveway turning to receive a blown kiss goodbye, a yelled good luck! and perhaps something else he doesn't quite catch. . . .

So, bags in hand, Basil trudges onward into the village, under lisping birches and pines along the quiet roadside, following Tiffany's hurried directions—it's on the main street, he can't miss it— toward her friend's little shop. He sighs greatly at this devolution of events but understands that he does have Jimmy Kowalske to catch up with, and it is this Synandra who can direct him to MacArthur. Out beyond his right shoulder a great melange of cumulus clouds, fading omens of fair weather, float above the lake, and overhead a ragged formation of fat herring gulls swoop and dither beneath a zinc-white sheet of clouds that have spread before the sun. He is sweating; the air has turned thick and humid and his baggage is heavy. Off to his left the bald dome of the hill glows through the trees and he passes a sign before an opening into the woods: Entrance/ Mystery Rock Hill. He thinks about climbing to its summit, but he is weighted down at the moment and considers himself on the job, so he stumps on until, near the center of town, he comes upon Synandra's shop, has to be, a cozy little place with a wooden sign hanging above the entrance, proclaiming, in serif-laden Olde English: *Ars Aromatica*. The door is open, allowing an assemblage of scents—sweet, spicy, flowery—to escape from the shop's darkened interior into the outside world, enticing the curious, the innocent, the faithless and as-yet uninitiated . . . and Basil steps inside.

The fragrance is stronger inside, but not overpowering, reminds him vaguely of his grandmother's home where sweet honeysuckle grew outside the kitchen window. Looking around, he sees floor-to-ceiling tiers of shelves upon which are arranged rows of glass jars—must be hundreds of them, containing, according to hand-lettered labels, decidedly unfamiliar substances: mugwort, vetiver, oakmoss, sandalwood, snakeroot, uva-ursi, periwinkle, deerstongue, skullcap, damiana, lobelia, and on and on. Other shelves hold scores of amber bottles, containing, a small placard indicates, perfumes and essential oils. Several antique tables hold baskets of fragrant dried herbs, herbal ointments and tinctures, salves and soaps, unguents and undecipherables. Hanging all around the ceiling and in almost every corner, nook and cranny are huge sprays of dried flowers and herbs available for uses he dares not attempt to imagine.

Strange how Tiffany has described Synandra Wasson as *young*; Basil hesitates to meet the old witch who must attend to this medieval curiosity shop. He even considers leaving, but the place is actually kind of interesting, and—he does have a job to do. On a wooden counter near the back of the store alongside a case of olde bookes of magickal spells and bottles of bat tongues and newt eyelashes stand two large jars containing glassy brownish pebbles; one labled frankincense, the other myrrh. And behind them, curled-up in an antique rocking chair, Basil spies—must be the witch's granddaughter—an attractive young woman. She has long brown hair, is wearing a long skirt and a peasant blouse embroidered with tiny hearts. On the wall behind her is a modest hand-lettered haiku: Dowsing/Reasonable Rates. The girl does not notice him immediately; she is engrossed in a paperback book, *Tertium Organum*, by P.D. Ouspensky. She looks up suddenly at Basil, her eyes large and brown, flecked with gold.

"Hi. Can I help you?"

"Er, yes, my name is Basil Lexington. I'm a friend of Tiffany's."

"Oh."

"And you're Synandra Wasson?" asks Basil, taking in, hmmm, her delicate nose, bright pale-rose cheeks, soft full lips. . . .

"Yes. Is Tiffany up here then?" the girl asks, suddenly, surprisingly, blushing.

"Up here?"

"Yes, here in Wasson's Bay."

"Oh, oh yes. Since yesterday—let me just put these down . . ."

Basil explains. He flashes his badge. He is a private investigator, presently without transportation, and that is how he ran into Tiffany—and he is still hot, or at least, warm, on the trail of "Captain Jimmy" Kowalske, whom this Synandra has not at all heard about, and certainly doesn't seem all that impressed that he (this very guy here, right in front of her) has been hired to track him, even as he tries to briefly explain the import and perhaps greater significance of his mission . . . and this apparent lack of interest bothers Basil more than he would care to admit, although he cannot quite figure out why. . . .

Thoughts echo off etheric cliffsides. Synandra has been expecting someone, via the doctor's prediction—he has never been wrong—but exactly *who* had remained a mystery until this moment, and a *private eye!* she wants to giggle at his earnestness, and, he is kind of cute. . . .

"Well, I have a car you could use if you need one—for your work," volunteers Synandra kindly. "For a short time . . ."

"Gee, thanks, but—you mean you just loan out your car to anyone that . . . like me, a stranger?"

She sighs. "Well, it's not much of a car, and you are a friend of Tiffany's—aren't you?"

"Oh sure, sure," says Basil, and then explains to her that what he really needs at the moment is a guide to MacArthur, wherever and whatever it might be.

Synandra's car is a black 1966 Chevrolet Bel-Air nightmare with balding tires, 98,000 miles on the odometer—Basil thinks it's more like *1*98,000 miles—and a bedevilling clinka-clinka-clinka somewhere in the engine compartment that incites vague worriment in the left hemisphere of his brain as they drive north, in the direction of MacArthur. "I'm not really very good with mechanical things," Synandra confides.

"Oh, me neither," Basil presently lost in thought, lights up a Camel with his Zippo without bothering to ask, wondering what it will be like to really meet Captain Jimmy, when and if he actually does. The guy, after all, is fairly famous, and to his followers, godlike. And here Basil is, hot on his poor hide. Suddenly he doesn't feel exceptionally pleased with himself, with his chosen profession. So glad was he to get the work, and so proud at being able to decipher Jimmy's cryptic last words into a location, an almost unknown town in Wisconsin, did he bother to give his mission much thought, in terms of a moral decision. But, just possibly, there is one to be made. After all, from what his investigation has uncovered, Kowalske is traveling on his own, no foul play involved. This he has reported back to them. So, *they want him,* that is it, it is unescapable. He is their leader, of course. But why do they want him?

"So why do they want him?" asks Synandra, frowning in the direction of his Camel.

"That's what I'd like to know," he sighs, exhaling smoke through his nostrils. If anything, Basil thinks that they probably *wouldn't* want him around, except, perhaps, on their own terms, which might be, hmm, rather stringent . . . but he doesn't tell her this, only, "I really think he's just trying to get away for a little while—"

"Or a long while."

"Yeah, could be."

"And when we—you, find him, you're going to turn him in."

"Well, I—of course I will. I mean I've got a job to do," he says. But the hesitation in his voice surprises him. Her question surprises him. Before now he had never considered not turning Kowalske in. And suddenly this "turning him in," sounds kind of weird too, turning him in to who? Kowalske hadn't done anything wrong; he wasn't wanted by the law, only by the church hierarchy, which seems to have by now, like most hierarchies run by higher arch-whomevers, gotten out of hand. But Basil is slightly angered by such considerations; he ought to be really happy right now, so near to closing in on his long-sought prey . . . but it is as if simply being in the presence of this girl is enough to cause a lot of vague doubts.

Weird.

Synandra is still curious, and Basil feels like talking, so as they drive, he explains how, after the Jack of Hearts Detective Agency had been essentially jobless for a while and the dunning notices had begun to pile up (he refused to dip any deeper into his trusts, feeling he really had to make this work, to prove he could actually *do* something in life, on his own, crazy as this might be . . . (but this he doesn't tell her either)), a man from the Church of the Electronic Trinity had walked in, a well-dressed lawyer by the name of Yates, a very slick guy whom Basil hadn't cared much for, but who had offered him work, an actual case to solve. Which turned out to be locating, very discretely, one of their members. Who turned out to be none other than Kowalske himself.

Basil sheepishly had to admit to this sharpie that he had heard only vaguely of the Church of the Electronic Trinity, and nothing of its popular leader, Jimmy Kowalske. But this hadn't seemed to annoy Yates in the least. Not at all. And he didn't even blink at Basil's fee (derived in large part from the cut of Yate's tailor-made suit): two hundred dollars per day, plus expenses. But he hadn't given him a lot to go on either, little more than Basil could have learned for himself in the newspapers: a brief history of Kowalske, his education, military service, the foundations of the church, and some sparse personal information (Kowalske had revealed surprisingly little to his comrades in the church). He had never married, both his parents were deceased; he had no known close friends, and his only apparent vice, a reported fondness for reading science-fiction—and, of course, an intense interest in technology, electronics, primarily, and the vision of the THREE. Sort of a super-mystic-nerd, Basil gathered. But there was one more thing Yates could tell him, Kowalske's cryptic last words, or word, heard uttered absent-mindedly as he moved about the Church's laboratories in one of his intensely creative states just before his abrupt disappearance, one word, Yates's voice had lowered almost to a whisper, as if in fear that the Jack of Hearts' tiny office might be bugged, one name: MacArthur.

MacArthur. It might as well have been Rosebud. Basil had had a tough time of it as it was, couldn't get near the church or any of its members, and was finally warned to stay away from them anyway by Yates. And he couldn't get anywhere up at Fort Irwin where Kowalske had been based, no military records, names, nothing—they had even laughed at him when he told them he was a private investigator. And then there was this word, MacArthur, which seemed to have nothing to do with anything. It looked bad, bad, Failure City just around the bend ... and then one night during a booming spring thunderstorm when Basil was sitting up late in his office tired and troubled and pondering what to do, suddenly someone came a-rapping, barely tapping, at his office door. It was a wet nervous young man, a Trinnie wearing the requisite Sound-Pac, who had somehow learned that Basil had been retained to find Captain Jimmy. And he had come to help. He told Basil he knew where he could find Kowalske's father. Basil had begun to protest that both Kowalske's parents were dead, but the man stopped him, told him that although that was the official line, he had been told by Captain Jimmy himself that his father was still alive in Bakersfield. However, his name was *Wolski*, which had been Kowalske's real name, which he had changed before entering the service, for unknown reasons. At any rate, the Trinnie told Basil that he hoped it might help him find Captain Jimmy. Well ... Basil had been overjoyed at this apparent break in the case, but as a suspicious shamus of the Hawkeye O'Hara school, he had to ask this Trinnie the obvious: why exactly was he helping him find Kowalske and—why he didn't do it himself?

The man replied that he feared that the Captain might be in danger and it was best that he was found. But he couldn't look for him on his own—he was taking a great risk even in being absent from the church complex for a while, let alone searching for their lost leader. Basil wanted to ask more about the goings-on in this wacky church, but the man responded fearfully that it was all that he had, in life. This church. And the wait for the Coming of the THREE. Then he'd run out. He'd struck Basil as being a kind of church trusty, higher-up than your run-of-the-mill Trinnie, yet still possessed of a brain as washed, rinsed, and hung up to dry as Basil could ever imagine.

The man had left an address with Basil and the next day the

41

dauntless detective had followed this lead to what turned out to be Jimmy *Wolski's* boyhood home, a small sad house on the industrial outskirts of Bakersfield. An unshaved suspicious man with a can of Schlitz in hand answered the door, but wouldn't talk to Basil, and was about to slam the door in his face when shazam! Basil had flashed his P.I. badge and the man, apparently impressed by the golden flash of ersatz authority, had let him in!

Mr. Wolski had Basil sit next to him on the couch, allowed him to talk over the crowd-roar grunt-and-boister of a professional wrestling match on a huge console color television. The Malevolent Masher vs. Aristotle the Apocalyptic at the moment, an exciting virtuoso display of strength and skill. Clearly the man did not understand his son's position in life as the head of the Church of the Electronic Trinity, nor did he understand the implications of his disappearance until it dawned on him that he might stop receiving the checks, "ever' two months," that son Jimmy apparently dutifully sent. Then he tried to become helpful, but no, he had no idea where his boy might have run off to, he certainly hadn't come *here* (a single tear had appeared in his bloodshot eye), and was wholly unresponsive to the name MacArthur. Uff, this was beginning to look like a dead end. Was he absolutely sure? He goddamn sure *was*, puffing up threateningly, perhaps absorbing some of the energy the Masher spewed via cathode-ray magic into the house ... but then allowed Basil to look inside Jimmy's old room, just for a minute—and twenty dollars offered in true TV-P.I. style. The room had been preserved more or less the way Jimmy had left it before going to Vietnam, although serving also as a storage area now, with a clutter of boxes and stacks of professional wrestling magazines covering the floor and dresser. Not much hope at first glance, but then ... there, inside, partly covered by the dresser, Basil spotted a weathered white sign painted in Department of Transportation black:

MacARTHUR
Unincorporated

His heart pounding, Basil rushed over to it, picked it up and read a small sticker in its lower right-hand corner: Wisconsin Highway Department. Basil breathlessly asked Mr. Wolski if his son had ever been to Wisconsin. Well, maybe, but it was so hard for an old man to remember things sometimes . . . but for another twenty dollars . . . come to think of it, he believed they might have sent him to camp there one summer, when the mill here was still going strong. And then, as if this had actually jarred loose some Schlitzified brain cells, he added that it was after that camp that their boy had changed— or something, "got real interested in science and other strange things, couldn't get him to go to the wrestling matches after that, we just didn't understand him no more, me and his mother, God rest her soul, it was like he was a different person. . . ."

Well, whatever . . . Basil thanked the maudlin Mashophile for his help, and the next morning, after checking some maps in a nearby Los Angeles library and finding absolutely nothing about the tiny town—Wisconsin no more familiar than the moon to this California kid—he was off to the great Midwest.

"Why do you suppose they picked you to find him?" asks Synandra. "I mean," she adds quickly, "there must be huge agencies out there with loads of resources, and you're only one person."

"Yeah," says Basil, "I've thought about that, and I think that they figured that I would be less confined by the bureaucracy that must go with those bigger agencies, like Pinkerton, all the administrative crap, you know, they probably thought that I would be more, ah, more fluid, or something . . ."

"Or possibly more controllable?" Synandra suggests.

"What?"

"Well, if he's running from *them*, maybe they don't want it to get out that they're after him. A big agency has more ties to law enforcement and, perhaps, a code of ethics that must be—"

"What? What are you saying that I'm not ethical or something? Look, that lawyer told me that he was a friend of the guy I had done my first case for, that I had been highly recommended by him—although," Basil thinks here, "I had sort of thought that he hadn't been too pleased with me . . ." Basil feels suddenly uneasy with the turn the conversation has taken, sticks another Camel in his lips, reaches into the wrong coat pocket for his lighter, finds his underwear, a bad sign, he's more shook-up than he thought, doesn't want to talk to her about this anymore, but he doesn't have to as at this moment they pull up before an old, obviously long-abandoned farmhouse perched upon a small much-overgrown rise.

"This," says Synandra with a certain smile, "is MacArthur. Or what's left of it."

"Huh," says Basil, detective-warily, getting out of the car, "this is all there is?" He stands under the lowering stuffy skies, looking around, for some reason feeling a shiver ripple up his spine. They are simply at an old crossroads of staggered wooded copses and open fields fallow with scrub brush and waist-high grass, orange hawkweed and yellow rocket in full bloom. A breeze is shifting around west-northwest, rustling the field grass, the greensoft leaves of wild apple and cherry and hawthorne that have grown up around the house.

"Not much to it, is there? There used to be a little store, like a general store, over across the road." She points to a ragged growth of trees and shrubs concealing the gray remains of an old structure. "There must be thousands of these little unincorporated towns in the state. All it takes is a couple of settlers and a name."

"How did you know about this place, with Kowalske swiping the sign so long ago and all?"

"My grandfather knew about it. He was something of a local historian, he went out and recorded what he could find out about places like this. He used to bring me out here when he'd poke around."

"No kidding. He studied this place?"

"To some extent. Come on." She starts to walk up to the house.

"Just a minute," says detective Lexington. He kneels down excitedly in the roadside gravel. He has spotted tire tracks; another car had been here sometime before them, and pulled out again. His instinct tells him that they are the Michelin's of Kowalske's Ferrari, this could be it! suddenly feverishly wishing that he had some plaster of paris and water to make casts so that the boys at the crime lab could make a positive I.D. But, heh-heh, let's not get carried away. . . . "When's the last time it's rained here?"

"Oh, about a week and a half ago, my gardens have been awfully dry . . . do you see something?"

"Might be Kowalske's car, but I can't be sure."

Basil tries to make some sense of the pattern of the tracks, but they aren't very clear, joins her to trudge up a path that obviously has been recently stomped into the weeds surrounding the house.

"Someone's been here," says Synandra.

"Yeah, yeah, I can see that . . ."

The house is smaller than it first appeared to Basil, and much older, thick log walls fronted with paintless gray clapboards, at one time a modernization, now ancient themselves. The door is boarded-up, and apparently has been for a long time. Some of the window boards have rotted away and they are able to peer in at bare wooden floors, an old chair, a broken table, cobwebs, and little else. Basil can't help feeling a vague sense of loss, of human transience, at the sight of this enclosed emptiness, the once-sacred space of a family's struggles with nature, the earth, the sky, the effort in time abandoned and leaving so surprisingly little to mark its stance.

"He's been here," says Synandra suddenly, firmly.

"Who has?"

"Your man, Kowalske."

"How do you know that?"

"I can feel it."

"Yeah, sure. . . ."

There isn't much more they can do in MacArthur, and on the way back Synandra asks Basil what his plans are, surprised at the sudden spark of joy that pings within her when he says that he has to stay, to stake out the old house, to find Kowalske. And then he asks if he can visit her tonight, to look through her grandpa's records on MacArthur. The question catches her by surprise, and she immediately says, "Yes, yes, of course . . ." before she can bite her lip, begin to worry that this might have sounded a bit too, eager, but he's rambling on, tells her that right now he needs a place to stay and asks her if she, uh, knows of any place, giving her his best Lexington smile, wonders if she too has a waterbed like Tiffany . . . but it turns out that she does know where he might stay, a small group of cottages fronting the lake, one of which just happens to be vacant, she knows the landlady.

"Oh, great, thanks. . . ." Basil sighing fairly audibly, Synandra pretending that she doesn't hear it, but the feeling emitted much harder for her to ignore, one that she feels she might even share, surprising, almost thinks that maybe . . . but by now they're in front of the cottages, there's a vacancy sign, and he's grabbed his bags and is out of the car, and then, and then . . . this crazy, lusty guy . . . calls her out to look at a supposedly low rear tire on her car, and as she bends down . . . boing! he pinches her soundly on the ass, leaving her standing astonished, angry, and what else? tears coming to her eyes, a nearly unsuppressible smile to her lips, as she holds her tingling bottom—God, he pinched hard!—watching him trot up to the cottages and turn and holler, "See ya tonight, babe!"

"You jerk," she mutters, "you're *not* gonna get away with that!" This she means with all her pounding heart, trying desperately to look angry, but can't stop smiling hugely as soon as she gets out of eyeshot, somewhat surprised at herself for not yelling back to him to forget about tonight, but—she knew that she was getting back, in a weird, perhaps somewhat imperfect way, just what she had asked for.

Had practically *conjured*, in fact, only a couple of weeks earlier, on the traditional witches' May Eve in what was, she believed, a first truly practical application of her powers. She hadn't mentioned it to anyone either, not Tiffany, not even Dr. Bo—but then he knew everything about everything anyway.

It was a hugely blue and bright May afternoon of soft, sun-warmed loam, burbling springs and creamy hepaticas, a light breeze, white sails dancing far out upon the blue lake waters . . . a day absolutely contrary to her brooding self, a day not long after her grandpa's death and the full negative force of loneliness had begun to weigh upon her. She felt she was approaching a peak—or a precipice, perhaps—of life, of youth, of blooming womanhood . . . and such a day, a time, filled the emptiness of her heart-center with magic. Magic, yes . . . useful, and perhaps even comforting to some degree, to those who needed its impersonal power, but it was not warm, smiling, sensuous . . . all it could do was, hopefully, bring one who could be. . . . So on that fine day she started up the trail to the great hill, not the established path that her grandfather had grudgingly widened to accommodate tourists—that was some distance from the house—but an older one, narrow and vague as a deer run that led directly from her back yard, a path that she had followed since she had begun walking.

She was still panting slightly from the climb as she looked out over the patchwork rooftops of the town below and the sprawling, sparkling bay beyond. She walked over to the center of the heart formed by the dark half-buried boulders and noticed that, even this early in the season, the offal of tourists had begun gathering: several

beer and soda cans, a candy bar wrapper, trampled cigarette butts. . . .
She sighed, it was always such a chore cleaning up the litter, but
she hated to think of putting a trash can up here. What would be
next? A steel railing around the top and a couple of those metered
telescopes you put a dime into to see Ann Arbor?

Well . . . she carefully centered herself in the rocky valentine
and faced the east, relaxed her slender body and took a long, fine
breath, which she held momentarily, then slowly released. She made
a quarter-turn to the south and repeated the process, then to the west
and then north, coming full-circle to face the east again. It was a
simple ritual Dr. Bo had taught her shortly after her twelfth birthday,
one to help open herself to, and ultimately make use of, the subtle
energies contained within the great hill.

Standing motionless, eyes closed, she began to feel a familiar
tingle in the soles of her feet, barely perceptible at first, but growing, the sensation gradually creeping up her ankles, knees, thighs
. . . until, after several minutes her entire body gently resonated with
the wonderful flow of earthly vibrations, a tiny tap of those incredible telluric currents from far, far below, where the constant rumble
is too gigantic to comprehend, the flow massive and dense, yet
constant, of soupy tons of primordial planet, eclogite and peridotite,
swirling slowly around the tense molten iron core of it all . . . the
energies winding inexorably upward, through gabbro and basalt,
mantle and plate, tendrils in the millions, crackling through quartz
veins, penetrating the fragile life-skin crust, one humble intersection
centering in the Wisconsin dolomite here, atop the hill, and she,
the present proud focus, a flesh and blood menhir receiving the
excruciatingly wonderful flow through the *yung ch'uan*, or "bubbling
well" acupuncture points, on the soles of her feet, channeling the
force upwards through her marvelous nervous system, all the way
to *ni wan*, at the top of her head, and onward, completing the ancient
incredible link with heaven above.

Ah, this wonderful hill. Multi-colored hearts whirled brightly
behind her eyelids, synchronized with her heartbeat, her quickened
breathing . . . and then she suddenly opened her eyes, leapt forward,
and in a few bounding steps stood outside the enclosure of the
heart. She stretched, she smiled, she felt gooood. Her body, excruciatingly lithesome and electrical now, made her feel—she couldn't
help it—like she was the amazing Amazon, Wonder Woman, trip-

47

ping lightly, fantastically, down the gravelly north side of the hill, into the woods below, humming softly, through a stand of ash and maple, onward to a loose cluster of feathery arbor vitae. Inside the trees was a shallow bowl-shaped depression in the earth centered with a large limestone boulder. The rock's surface was gently pitted and pocked with erosion and sprinkled with patches of soft green moss which, from a certain angle, gave the impression of a face, a kind of crazed—if you wanted to read that much into it—laughing man's face, of the type one might find in a bawdy 17th century European woodcut, a sort of earthly lusty laugh surfacing here where the alkaline bedrock broke lowly through. Next to it were a few broadleaved catnip plants and maple seedlings struggling in the cool blue shade of the cedars. But Synandra, radiant with energy, noticed neither chill nor damp as she brushed a few dead leaves from the stone face and sat down, directly over the gaping laugh, the only really comfortable spot, as it turned out, on its ragged surface. . . . She pulled her legs into a tight lotus and relaxed, looking upwards through a wide gap in the trees at the azure sky, dappled with billowy cumuli. Now she was ready to make her magic. . . .

Her magic, yes, well . . . her magic was not really of the type associated with the ancient art: fixed formula of rite and object, star and wand, cup and sword . . . no, next to the point-by-point rituals of legend and yore, her magic was virtual free-form . . . what blank verse is to iambic pentameter, shamanic diddling to priestly dogma, child's prayer to the high mass . . . mutable as the moment, like this very one, when she attempted to discern the face of her future lover.

A trifle old fashioned? Perhaps, but what was so modern about loneliness, and love? So be it. The medium of the moment was clouds; the force, the usual one: wandering daydreams . . . and as she gazed lazily up at the cottony billows that floated above the hill, they began to gently fold and flow, contract and congeal—directed by her magnificent energies? or had she simply become so-so sensitized, that she only perceived, perhaps only more perfectly, what was taking place anyway? even she didn't know—at first into a puffy ovoid shape, and then, expanding here, contracting there, into a reasonable facsimile of a person, and though the image was, well, cloudy, it appeared to be definitely male, fairly muscular, perhaps . . . and the face, the most important part really . . . the face pure cloud-blank at first, gradually swirling into features . . . but much *too* gradually for impatient her, she had to make it work, realizing, after many long moments the force of her intent, sweatbeads appearing on her upper lip, eyes crossing uncontrollably, straining to visualize the stupid face ... c'mon! watching for eyes to appear, yes, first eyes, then a nose, a mouth ... but where were they? It just didn't seem to be working and then, suddenly—something unexpected—the face just popped up like the image from a slide projector—only in the silvery gray of, say, black and white television, a face younger-looking than she had expected, a boyish face ... in fact, the face of a boy! smiling idiotically up there, down at her it seemed.... Of course it was like television, the face was one she thought she knew, reminding her of *Leave it to Beaver* on TV but it wasn't the Beaver, no, it was someone else, vaguely familiar, but she just couldn't place who it was ... and then the perception faded rapidly, the clouds began to fluff away, the crucial magic dissipating with them, her energy ebbing too, the magic couldn't last forever ... this she understood, feeling exhausted, sleepy, as she always did after something as taxing as this....

Afterwards she was confused, everything seemed to be working so well, and then that TV-kid face, the most important part ... and then it didn't make any sense at all.

6

"He pinched you—where?" Tiffany's voice, a compound of disbelief and glee, rings in Synandra's ear, which is presently blushing tulip-red. "And I don't suppose you're going to let him get away with that, huh?"

Synandra smiles. She knows Tiff well, and in the half-joking rote manner Tiffany made that last statement, it's obvious that she knows Synandra just as well. "Of course not. Who does he think he is anyway? Where did you find him?"

"Well, like he told you, I picked him up at a gas station down in Illinois ... his car blew up or something. Never could resist a guy in bluejeans and a sportcoat. Isn't he cute? What do you think?"

Synandra isn't sure, but has to admit there's something kind of interesting about him, and something warm and funny too. She tries to stifle a happy sigh here, one that well bespeaks how she is feeling now, about herself and Tiffany, how her crazy friend just, sort of—delivered this guy. And wasn't that just like Tiff? Her best friend, her only real friend actually, and though she only spent the summers up here, with an occasional winter visit to cross-country ski, they were as close as sisters, and in some ways, much closer than that.

They were both age eleven when they had met on the Wasson's Bay beach, Tiffany's parents having purchased the lakeside "kabin," designating the little village as their annual vacation site. At that time Tiffany was the quintessential poor little rich girl—and worse, actually a real little brat—spoiled, much overweight, and recently pronounced diabetic. A hazard of the trade, as it turned out, her family's, that of junk-food purveyor to the world (Tiffany's later disparaging description of her plutocratic clan's niche in the convoluted food chain of the twentieth century), she having grown up in a house perpetually laden with L'Oreal-brand treats: snack cakes, cookies, miniature doughnuts, and of course the notorious breakfast cereals. . . . The girls hadn't hit it off at first, either, in that feisty manner characterizing some of the most lasting friendships, and might never have come to be friends at all, were it not for that sublime gift Synandra had of intuiting what simply *had* to be done to remedy certain situations. And for this poor girl with diabetes, the prognosis was—a bold move. She kidnapped the fat little stinker.

Yes indeed, she knew that this unhappy girl needed medical help of a caliber that neither she nor her snobby parents would ever approve—administered by an Indian medicine man!—and so she lured her by a ruse: boasting to Tiffany about her skill at driving automobiles and then taking the obese brat up on the inevitable dare she made for a most illicit joyride in her grandpa's 1965 Rambler American. Not something your average eleven-year-old girl does for kicks. But then, Synandra was never average; she had meticulously prepared the vehicle with blocks taped to the brake and gas pedals, a book from her grandfather's study to sit upon, *Black's Law Dictionary*, a thermos of water, a couple of tuna-fish sandwiches, a coffee can to pee in. . . . And once she had gotten Tiffany inside she had roared off on their desperate emprise, planning not to stop, neither for gas nor toilet (and her victim's possible escape) until they had reached the great Wisconsin northwoods. Although beyond a certain point Tiffany's escape had ceased to be a pressing concern, thankfully before entering the town of Green Bay where the determined decadarian was prepared to run every stoplight if need be. . . . By then a spark of the essential Tiffany (evident to Synandra all along) had surfaced through the baby fat, through the torrent of terrific tantrum-tears (the very same that had always worked so effectively with her parents), and forced the little shit to realize that

51

she was truly engaged in an adventure—"Wow, so yer really gonna do this!"—the only semblance of one she had ever been a part of, and she settled down and waited to find out where this joyride with this amazingly crazy girl would end up.

And that, of course, was the woodland home of Dr. Bo, the venerable Indian doctor and Wasson family friend. The only one, Synandra knew, who could help her pathetic friend-to-be. The good doctor took the whole thing in stride, seemingly unsurprised by her outrageous arrival, the dusty Rambler bouncing up before his hut in the late afternoon light—though Synandra always remembered a hint of a grin cut across his stern face. He set straight to work providing for his new patient a regimen of herbal purgatives, sweat baths, and fasting, along with a lot of sound advice on what was good to eat, do, and think, and what was not, Tiffany's past repertoire consisting almost exclusively of the latter . . . until four days later when they pulled-up, totally unnoticed (the doctor's medicine was strong) in the midst of the largest missing-children-hunt in peninsula history, in the driveway of the Wasson home. Safe and sound. Their story was that they had gone for a drive and had "gotten lost," which both Synandra and a much-changed Tiffany, happier, healthier, and about ten pounds lighter, stuck to for many years—at least until they could be certain there would be no real repercussions for all concerned. . . .

What had they learned from such an adventure? Well, Tiffany, oodles: she singlehandedly changed her diet to much healthier, plebeian fare, and would in no way touch any of the L'Oreal sugared delicacies again, and Synandra, this: that if you're going to pull-off something, have a good purpose, and do it big. All the punishment she ever received was a wink from her grandpa, but it was enough. And about six months down the road there was even more good news: Tiffany had been pronounced cured of diabetes. The doctors, along with Tiffany's parents, were astounded. But the two now fast friends were not. In fact, it didn't seem that it could ever have come out any other way, so much like everything else when the wise Indian doctor had a hand in it; even now the memory of the experience flickers briefly as Synandra recalls Dr. Bo's sky-divination of the day before—and the subject of her and Tiffany's current telephone conversation. Her answer is somewhat evasive. "I think he could use some manners . . . and I hate his smoking."

"But other than that?"

"Well, he is kinda cute."

"Listen, Syndy, did he tell you who he is, who he really is?"

"Other than being a private detective?"

"Yeah, oh, you won't believe this, he's-he's the *Peeper!*"

"The—who?"

"The *Peeper!* From TV, remember? On the *Doggone Dawsons?* Remember now? He, this guy, Basil Lexington, was the little kid, the Peeper."

"My God. . . ." Synandra's heart skips a beat as, like finding a missing piece of a cryptic puzzle, the familiar boy's face she had seen in the clouds suddenly gains a place in her conjurations, an identity. The Peeper. Yes, that was him. Magic, strange stuff, certainly acts-up in mysterious ways. . . . "Well, I'll be, how'd he ever get to be a private detective?"

"He said it sounded exciting. Said he'd always see these guys on TV having so much fun. Plus he said he had to have some kind of job. I guess his parents spent a lot of the money he'd made on the show."

"Oh. Well, I took him out to the MacArthur place. He's looking for that guy, Jimmy Kowalske, of the weird church out in California. I gather he told you about it?"

"Yeah, I knew you'd want to take him there. Do you really think he's going to find him?"

"Think so. Someone—I have a feeling that it is this Kowalske— has definitely been there. Recently. Isn't it strange that it's the MacArthur place, I mean it being a center, like the hill, although of course, not as—"

"It's another one of your omens. Go for it, Syndy. I, ah, already got him warmed up. I mean I guess maybe I shouldn't have, but I just couldn't stop myself—"

"Tiffy, what did you—"

"Danced."

Synandra is surprised at the stab of jealousy she suddenly feels, along with a glimpse of a speeding tiny pale-green heart, a very rare one for her. . . . She knows that Tiffany collects lovers like she herself collects heart-things, it having evolved into a sort of hobby for the brazen girl, a series of men and memories, stories that Synandra has heard the best of, but never felt any envy over—until this time. "That, uh, jungle tape?"

"Uh-huh."

"Oh." That was a good tape. They themselves had tried dancing to it last summer—after getting a trifle loaded on some *Dom Perignon* Tiffany had splurged for. Synandra was a little surprised Tiff hadn't come up with a new tape by now.

"You're not mad are you?"

"No, no, of course not." And this is quite true. Ever since the very first, Synandra had always felt sorry for her. This was Tiff's way. Rebellious to the end. And why not? Knowing Tiffany has taught Synandra that wealth certainly brought as many problems as it could possibly eliminate, and perhaps Tiffany bears up as well as could be expected. She is, after all, the daughter, the product, really, of the tenuous marriage between *the* Harriet Hill of Chicago, flighty former-model-turned-socialite and Kingston Elliot L'Oreal, midwestern manufacturer of the earliest (and most enduring) of the great breakfast atrocities appearing in the 1950's: *Morning Candy Crunch*, *ChocoCrunchies*, and *Marshmallow Mush*. Because of their frightful perversion of the breakfasts' of innocent children (considered sacred by Tiffany) she hates these confections most of all, hates to be associated with them, and in direct retaliation has become an inveterate health-food addict and, for added spite, a notorious girl-about-town. It is only a deep, practically unaddressable true fondness for her parents, and the feeling that she must, in a way, care for their quirky psychological needs, that keeps her around them at all; from this she derives a sense of stability. Otherwise, she fears she would fly off somewhere and never return. Oddly, it is the distinctly opposite lifestyles of the two young women that seem to provide the bond for their lasting friendship. At times like this Synandra can't negate the sense it conjures in her, of Tiffany as *movement*, out there in the big outside world, buzzing around on myriad missions, bouncing from one episode in life, one lover, career, lifestyle, to another ... while she, Synandra, remains here, always here, with her land and hill and big house and gardens as a sort of safe haven for her active friend. But now she senses this arrangement is about to change, and if magic, the divine catalyst, is what it takes, well then, so be it.

"Maybe ... you're just a little too picky, Syndy,"

"Maybe ... yes, maybe I am ..." and this is the truth, both of them know, but neither speaking more of it, perhaps because of the inherently transitory nature of Tiffany's relationships. If they do, more than either of them really wants will come out here, on the phone. . . . It really wasn't the kindest thing to say. Though she is perhaps not as externally radiant as her golden friend, she is pretty and has attracted the attention of not a few young men of the peninsula, but is discriminating to such high degree that she remains yet a virgin, even in the midst of these times of sexual revolt. . . . Which, whenever she thinks about it, is odder still when it was actually she, on a long-ago bright spring day who more or less initiated Tiffany into her varied and spectacular sport of choice. . . .

"Oh, say," says Synandra, as much to change the subject as anything, "you know I got another letter from Mortell—"

"Professor Clyde! That unmitigated creep."

"He's really going to try to do it this time. He says he's gotten a fifty thousand dollar grant from the National Science Foundation, I think it is, to make a dig. And, of course everything would be so much nicer if I would agree."

"Of course. God, what a mess that would be. What are your legal rights?"

"At this point, practically none. Not if he returns everything to its 'natural state' after the excavation. We went all through it with my grampa's lawyers the last time. If he really wants to, we can't stop him now. There's going to be a hearing in Milwaukee in a couple of weeks, but I'm afraid it's going to be purely perfunctory."

Synandra is referring to Dr. Clyde Mortell, Professor of Archaeology at the University of Wisconsin. For the past five years he has made repeated requests to study the hill, actually, to excavate it. Which would, for all practical purposes—*her* practical purposes—ruin it forever.

"He *act*ually thinks that it's just a big Potawatomi or Menominee burial mound. How did he ever get to be a professor?"

"How did he ever get to be a person?" sniffs Tiffany.

Synandra chuckles, but truly wonders how one so thoroughly educated could be so completely dense, seeing the hill as a mute mound of earth, scraped-up over a pile of dead Indians. To her, to *everyone*, she thinks, it should appear as such a *living* entity, dynamic as a beehive, if not simply for itself, then because it is a part of our earth, and like the planet, humming with activity from within.

"Well, who knows?" sighs Tiffany. "I guess that's all the hill

55

looks like to him. Oh, Syndy, before I forget, one of the things I called to tell you is that mother has gotten daddy to go on a trip up north, up to Mackinac Island for a week or so and she absolutely insists that I go along. So, look, when I get back we'll try to figure out a way to stop Mortell. Maybe our Mr. Detective will be able to help us, hey?"

*   *   *

Basil's journal:

Hot dog! Caught up with Kowalske at last! I hope. Now begins the big stake-out. But first a little celebration. This Synandra chick has invited me over to her house tonight to go over her grandfather's records on the buildings at MacArthur. If she's anything like Tiffany, we'll be going over more than records, ha-ha.

This last entry quickly penned at a small oaken table in the small kitchen in the small cottage on the Wasson's Bay beachfront, where Synandra had dropped him off. Basil has rented it, one in a semi-crescent fronting the lake, for a couple of weeks, long enough, he figures, to complete his mission here. It's a very nice setup, too. Right out his back door, beyond the grove of airy pines the cottage nestles within is an expanse of sandy-white beach he fantasizes lolling upon, maybe a bit of well-deserved vacation in the warm days rolling up, after he files his report.

His landlady, Mrs. Frost, a sprightly, elderly woman with tightly curled silver hair and spectacled gray eyes that seemed to miss nothing when they first alighted upon him, alert for—head lice? malignant moles? insanity in the family? knew Synandra well and was immediately suspicious that he was "an acquaintance of Synandra's," but had not heard of the recent death of the girl's grandfather. Basil explained that he was actually a very, uh, recent acquaintance, flashed the old Lexington smile and managed to get her to relate the tragic incident as they walked along a sandy path back to the vacant cottage, a ring of brass keys tinkling softly in her hand.

"That girl's come into a lot of sorrow lately," she had said, unlocking the cottage door. Just before opening it she had turned and looked sharply at Basil, but spoke gently, "See that you don't cause her any more trouble, son."

"Yes, ma'am. I mean, no ma'am," Basil had replied, and then, "Is it, um, true, that she might sort of be a witch?"

Which had promptly broken Mrs. Frost up. When she had finally stopped snickering and snorting and had caught her breath again, she puffed, "Where did you hear that, son?"

"Oh, around . . ."

"Well, if she is, I sure wouldn't be hangin' around this town, witch indeed," Mrs. Frost harummphed. "Listen son, just because a girl learns a bit about herbs and medicinals and such and tries to do some helpin' out for ailin' people in the world doesn't mean she's a *witch*. That kind of talk only stirs up trouble. Is that what you're aimin' to do, son?"

"Oh no, I just—"

"Well, don't then," she continued. "That girl gives me some of those herbs for my arthritis, drink 'em in a tea, every day and it's darn near cleared up. Now if that's witchcraft, then I say this world could use a lot more of it!"

"Yes, ma'am."

"Now I've known that family ever since I come up here to the peninsula to retire, after Mr. Frost passed away, prit-near twenty years now. They're good folk, and even if some around here might think of her as strange, I think she's the best one of the lot. What a pair they make, what a pair . . ."

"A pair?"

"Her and the hill. That Valentine Hill yonder. *That's* one damn pair, the likes of which we may never see around here again, now mind. To me, that hill is something truly good upon this earth— don't ask me why, I couldn't tell you, it's a feeling I have, a deep feeling. . . . Why that's one of the reasons that I settled here, it's a just a feeling, a good, good feeling. . . ."

"So you rented one of Mrs. Frost's cottages?" Synandra's dark eyes gleam over the rim of her teacup.

"Yep," mumbles Basil, intently leafing through a small sheaf of papers within a bent-up manila folder bearing the fountain-penned inscription "MacArthur." Basil has already finished his tea, and has quickly lit-up a cigarette, the ashes of which he is absently flicking into the cup—which contains, smattered around its concave porcelain whiteness, an impasto of greenish brown tea leaf shards. Synandra, eager at first for a sly chance to gaze into and perhaps gain an impression of this boy's immediate interaction with the universe, has taken pause (evident enough in that she allows him to smoke in the house) and watches the graywhite ashes accumulate with the darker dregs, all random tailings together here, creating a scene which to some is as eloquent and decipherable as runes ... but the strongest, most immediate impression she receives here is of death and decay, softly, silently falling like radioactive waste upon otherwise vital lands—she averts her eyes from the cup. Never was much for reading tea leaves anyway. "You know," she says, "you really must stop smoking."

"Yeah, I know," Basil mutters, leafing through scrawled notes, in apparently the hand of Bernard Wasson, jottings like:

Present structure erected circa 1881 by Amos MacArthur, b. 1856, married to Mabel Guisewhite, b. 1863, in 1880.

Raised three children, Thomas, b. 1881, and Louellen, b. 1883, and Darlene, b. 1885. Mabel died in childbirth, December, 1887. Infant did not survive.

Farming proved unsuccessful, forcing MacArthur into bankruptcy. General store constructed in 1891 on NE corner of intersection with presumed inheritance. Only moderately successful, MacArthur evicted from both properties in 1895.

Evidence of previous structure with present one constructed over existing foundation. Unusual. Also signs of a root cellar previous to existing one.

... and various notations pertaining to plat maps, partial genealogies of the MacArthurs, successions of owners, and the like, Basil's eyes coming to rest upon what are two interesting entries on the last page of the notes.

Syndy lost for 2 days, found sleeping on the porch of MacArthur house. Age 4 yrs. June, 19—. (The year is coffee-stained, illegible.)

Rumors that the house is haunted begin again in 1963. Reports of noises, lights, at night. Infrequent. Unsubstantiated.

"Holy Cow," says Basil, "you were lost for two days, and found there, and-and the place is *haunted?*"

"What?" Synandra walks over to the desk he is sitting at, stands close beside him. "Oh!" she exclaims, briefly scanning the old papers, and grinning. "I almost forgot about that. I was always wandering off, as a little girl."

"But the haunting?"

"Well, rumor has it . . ." her grin broadens.

"Rumor has what? Is it haunted or isn't it?" He really wants to know, as his plans are to maintain surveillance of the place, perhaps after dark, and the very thought of spooks gives him the willies.

"Oh Mr. Detective," Synandra teases, "you're not scared of a few little ghosts, are you?"

"Of course not, I just . . . I mean for my investigation of course I should maybe know . . ."

"Well then, no, of course it's not haunted."

"Good."

"It's just—"

"Aha, what?"

"Well, it's just . . . let's say it's an area of the earth that is, um, a little more *lively* than other areas."

"What?"

She sighs. "Well, it's a center. Like the hill."

"What?" The only centers Basil has heard of are shopping centers.

Basil doesn't notice it, leafing again through the MacArthur folder, but she is looking at him now with an aspect of utmost anticipation, as though a crucial question has been posed.

"Huh?" Basil absent, more than anything else confounded by her warm closeness, by the delicious scent of citrus and musk that seems to follow her around, than what this particular moment demands. "What the heck are you talking about?"

59

"Oh nothing."

"Now wait a minute here!" Basil feels as though something has passed him by, as though the interview—it suddenly seems like an interview—is over. "Now look, uh, these—centers, what are they?"

"Oh, they're just—" she hates to tell him any of this, it is just *none of his business*, really, except that he is kind of cute, and perhaps the object of prophecy—"power centers," baby browns intent on the back of her outstretched right hand. "And you needn't raise your voice."

"Power centers, power centers? I don't quite follow . . ."

"Well, I didn't think you would."

"Hey now, *look*," Basil abruptly standing, first the place is haunted or *lively* or something and now this, "at least you could tell me what in hell you're talking about! I mean *pow*er centers?"

"Have you seen the hill yet?"

Up atop Mystery Rock Hill it is cooler, although still quite humid, the texture of the air complementing the dismal cloud cover. The lake below them to the east is gray as slate, barely stirring. They are alone on the hilltop; no one seems to be in the woods below.

"Jeeze, they are in the shape of a heart," observes Basil, not being able to resist nervously striding from rock to rock while Synandra attempts to tell him something about the hill.

". . . there are power places in all parts of the earth. Those people who—"

"But what are they?"

"They—?"

"The, heh-heh, power places—all over the earth. What are they? What are they good for? What do they do?" Basil smirks, perched finally atop a nearby heart-rock.

"I'm trying to explain that . . ." Synandra sighs. "Native peoples who live close to the earth, like our American Indians, or, say, the aborigines of Australia, have known about their existence and understood their benefits to man—or women—for ages."

"What benefits are those?"

"Why to provide power, of course."

"Power for what?"

"Power to do things, or for—"

"Like what?"

"Well, to gain knowledge about things, influence events, solve problems, you know."

"Oh sure."

"Also, there are healing vibrations that emanate from these places, as well as, ah, other kinds of vibrations—you don't look very convinced."

"I guess I'm not really into—vibrations, you know."

"Not many people are, yet. But I suppose that what I personally think about centers is that they are such a positive manifestation of the earth's energies. They're places that one can actually *feel*, if one is so attuned, the earth as a being, a huge, huge, wonderful nurturing entity. A sort of, great mother, is the impression I have, one that we ought to respect, and show our love for and . . . you look even less convinced than before," she smiles, wiping away a tiny tear that has appeared in her eye for some reason.

"Well—" Basil sighs grandly, smiles indulgently, sort of like, he fancies, Jack Nicholson. He feels as though he has had enough. Besides he's starved. "Look, why don't we just forget this crap about *pow*er centers and stuff," explosively emphasizing the pow!, "and we'll go out and catch some burgers and fries and a couple of beers. I owe you that for showing me that old house—" suddenly remembering the haunting thing, deciding to forget about that for now as he fumbles for his Camel pack, lights up a smoke . . . there does seem to be something strange about this place though, the quiet and the terrific humidity, he's sweating like a pig, and then the girl, mother nature's daughter here, makes him feel really edgy, jumpy as all hell. . . .

"Please don't smoke up here."

"Why the hell not?" Basil snaps at her.

"For one thing it's not good for you—"

Basil groans.

"—and I think it injures the spirit of the hill."

Basil laughs loudly, meanly. "Spirit of the hill my ass!" emphatically kicking a heart-rock. "We're talking rocks here, and—*dirt*, honey—"

"And don't call me honey!"

"Sure, honey," he continues blithely, for some reason the P.I. personna feeling appropriate here, always was quick to fall into

61

character ever since the old TV days, although even in the back of his mind the role models are, always, maddeningly, in the gray of black and white television, Jack Webb of *Dragnet* or Lee Marvin in *M Squad*, cool characters, all action and none of this chit-chat, so strange how he feels with her, angry at her scolding, yet somehow understanding on a much deeper level that she is very right here . . . and he resenting the hell out of it, feeling oddly desperate, as though his whole lousy *life* has been somehow wrong. . . .

"What kind of power could a woman have, anyway?" he blurts, blindly grasping for a point which has been eluding him here . . . then he catches it, "unless she's some kind of witch!"

"Then—shazam!" yells Synandra, suddenly grabbing Basil's old Zippo lighter which he has positioned carefully upright on the rock next to her and takes off down the south side of the hill. Just like that. It takes a second or two for it to sink in.

"Hey!" He leaps up after her . . . damn it, Basil had filched that lighter from Jack Dougherty himself after the feckless thesp had taught him to smoke, more or less by example, at the age of eleven; it's an extremely prized possession. . . .

She has stopped some distance out from the the hill in a small clearing that is almost completely surrounded by wild rosebushes, panting slightly, facing Basil with a wry smile mysterious as the Mona Lisa's, looking him right in the eyes as she places the lighter within the bodice of her blouse with one hand, calmly pushing long hair away from her face with the other. Well, well. Basil glances down at the soft mattress of grass growing within these prickly roses, and meets her gaze. It is going on twilight now, terribly humid, and he suddenly finds himself tremendously excited.

"If you don't think a woman has any power," she whispers, "then why do you have that silly hardon?" And she glides over to him, standing very close, the effect in Basil's muddled mind stunning and vivid: simple yet fetching peasant girl changed into wanton trollop in one fell swoop, her breath hot on his throat, oh God, is he ever excited, wants to just grab her but is finding it difficult to organize his thoughts . . . something, static electricity, weird mind-jamming interference, is bouncing between them . . . and then she grabs him. Right there.

Waves of anxiety fly instantly away, like crows from a shotgun blast, and a liniment of warmth floods from the locus of her touch, a strong tingling sensation—extremely pleasant—coursing through his entire body. He feels goood. And then she is at work, skillfully unzipping his Levi's, unbuttoning his shirt, while he cops feels, starts to pull off her blouse ... but she stops him here, cheeks glowing brightly, smiling demurely, softly biting her lower lip, whispers, "Let me undress for you."

"Oh *yeah!*" Basil somewhat paralyzed by lust here allows her to finish the job on him, even helps, kicking off his loafers, begins chuckling softly, fancies an erotic strip-tease, wow, just like Tiffany, but out here in the *woods*, it's sooo crazy-kinky. . . .

"Now don't you look," she begs primly, turning him around.

"Oh, sure," Basil compliant, sighs, didn't even think he was getting along with her, must be that old Lexington charm coming through at last, always did seem to be able to turn a fair lass's head . . . well, when it counted anyway, never really has let him down now, has it? Anyway, she sure was right about the "silly hardon." God, he is tremendously excited here, it's as though his entire being is just—*pulsing* with amazing lust, fantastic, these Wisconsin women sure know how to take care of a man, really bring out the old voyeur too, can't wait to watch her now . . .

Uh, *watch?*

The sound has been distant all along, the rush of wind through the treetops to the north, then nearer as it gusts against the uppermost branches of aspen, birch, and pine. Basil turns as if in a dream and feels the wind penetrate ground level, coming full-force and frigid through violets and buttercups and the now-swaying rosebushes and he feels the shocking first drop of cold rain on his bare chest, breaking at last the spell he has been under, then comes another drop, then another . . . and she is gone. Basil lurches forward, frantically looking for his clothes, which are, of course, also gone.

7

B asil stands in the roseate circle like a less than heroic version of Michelangelo's "David," scowling, too pissed-off at the moment to even move. Oh boy, did she get him good . . . and they had been getting along so well together, hadn't they? *Damn!* Just moments ago prepared to ascend the heights of human bliss, and now cruelly reduced to the ape, unmercifully exposed to cold pelting raindrops, Basil erectus-schmectus keenly senses that it's fight or flight time here, and since there's no one around at the moment to have her neck ungracefully wrung, and those thunderclouds up there aren't kidding around . . . it's got to be the latter, to get outta here, run!

Run! Lightning crackles overhead and thunder explodes as Basil bursts from the roses, instantly tattooing a fine filigree of scratches on his legs . . . dashing through the trees, skirting the great hill, which sits silently in the storm, patiently, being the rock-massive presence it must, observing this, another tiny incident in the snail-years of its geologic life . . . while Basil races onward through the torrent, trying to avoid protruding rocks, roots, snakes, hideously vicious toe-chomping shrews he has heard about . . . until he reaches the back yard of Synandra Wasson, but only in time to hear an engine gunning, tires spinning, and watch her black Chevy back into the street and speed away. Oh hell. He rattles the door knob: locked, natch, the front will be too, and the rain sweeps relentlessly across the back porch, so it's back into the woods. At least he'll have some protection there—or might have, had not the rain been blowing in, nearly horizontal now, in such driving torrents. Brrrrr-ruh! He is really cold now, gooseflesh risen on his skin like the Appalachians as he runs desperately, trying to make a decision here about an appropriate direction—"Owwooch!" He jams his big toe on an exposed rock, but the sudden pain and all other thoughts are instantly forgotten as another bolt of lightning slashes down nearby brightening everything to high noon, thunder roaring right behind. It is shockingly close, enough to start him running again through the dim woods in the general direction of Tiffany's place, doesn't really know where else to go, and she is less than a half-mile away, he thinks . . . the other choice, much less appealing, streaking through the village to his cottage, but the key is gone along with his clothes, and if he showed up at Mrs. Frost's door *naked*, she'd probably kick him out on his ass . . . which at this point might not be such a bad thing. . . .

So Basil crashes through the underbrush, scraping against hemlock bark, tripping over tree roots, avoiding the road till the last minute, it'd be easier going there, but—KRRAAAAAAAAAAAAAAK!! Lightning, sudden whiteness everywhere, a brilliance of sun, a deafening roar, bursts upon everything. And then everything slowly, softly, fades to black.

It is to the dull thudding of drums, very near, as in Tiffany's mad jungle tape, and to masculine voices speaking in jocular cadences, that Basil wakes to, although he can't quite make out what they're saying, what's going on . . . but that smell, oh God, it's got to be hamburgers—burgers and fries, the delicious fragrance overwhelming, he's starving, but-but he's warm too, and reasonably dry, wrapped in blankets fragrant of woodsmoke, and, uh, buffalo, antelope, mastodon . . . lying here on the floor of what seems to be a dimly-lit hut. A lantern is burning low on the floor.

"He's awake. And hungry, I'll bet," says a voice very near. Basil sees a man in the doorway, an Indian, dark of skin with a regal aquiline nose, wearing a dented fedora with a feather sticking from its broad band. He walks in and is followed by another Indian, much older, with a dark leather headband holding back his long gray hair. The older man holds the lantern near, silently scrutinizing Basil with eyes that appear in the lamplight to be quite blue. The whites of the younger man's eyes are wide and glow like pearls in the dim light; he is smiling broadly and is holding a white paper bag emblazoned with red and yellow arches containing, apparently, MacDonald's hamburgers. At that moment Basil's stomach growls loudly. Both of the men laugh. "See, what did I tell you," chuckles the younger one. "We'd better feed him soon. Huh kid? You want some grub?"

"Uh, sure. Wh-where am I?"

Both Indians chuckle again. "Safe from the storm," says the older one. "I am Doctor Bo. This is Keno."

Keno tips his fedora toward Basil and hands Basil a couple of paper-wrapped burgers from the bag and then a cardboard container of hot french fries. He also pulls out a paper cup of Coca Cola capped with plastic, inserts a plastic straw into its top and hands it over. "You like this stuff, don't you?"

"Yeah, sure."

"Sure, everybody does . . ."

Basil senses that the man is somehow mocking him, though he looks sincere . . . but anyway, he's got warm burgers and fries in hand now, feels a little better, pauses a moment to take inventory here, ascertains that his limbs are still all there and more or less functioning, feels dull pain from various bruises, his big toe throbbing like it had been hit with a hammer, but all in all he seems to be in a recognizable whole. . . . Then he starts in on those burgers, fries too, sucking down the Coke, too grateful at the moment to ask questions, just pigging out here in this somewhat smoky, er, shack. "Say," says Basil, pausing briefly to belch, "say, thanks a lot guys, I'm glad you came along, or—" A chill runs up Basil's naked spine as he suddenly recalls the terrific whitelight blast that preceded his awakening here, the fear coming on fast and hard that, oh no, maybe he actually *bought it* back there, and-and could this be the anteroom of death itself? And then has to chuckle, could there actually be *MacDonald's* over here? Last stop on the banks of the river Styx, man they *were* everywhere! Still choking down the second burger,

Basil feels he must demand, "Hey, guys, now where am I? Really. The last thing I remember was running in the goddamn rain—"

But both men have turned toward the entrance of the hut as the drums outside, plodding rhythmically all along, have suddenly stopped. Then, wordlessly, they each turn around and pick up a side of the boughs-and-branches pallet Basil is lying upon and spirit him across the room, through the entrance, and swiftly deposit him outside where a bonfire is blazing in the night. Basil holds frantically to his Coke and remaining french fries. "Hey, hey guys. Hey, now. What the heck . . ."

"Watch," commands the one called Dr. Bo, pointing toward a solitary Indian brave wearing a breechcloth, moccasins and head-band, who begins circling slowly before the fire as the drums start-up again.

Basil pushes himself up, realizes that he is quite naked under-neath the blanket, but dry, only his hair is still damp—absolutely surreal. He watches the brave perform an intricate dance, circling round, cutting back, then circling round again in the opposite direc-tion, stepping lightly to the drumbeats in 3/4 time, an earthy sort of waltz. . . .

"What do you think?" Keno whispers to Basil after several minutes of cadence.

"Well, it's hypnotizing. I get the feeling of broad movement."

"Good, good," Keno smiles at Dr. Bo, then circling the great eggshell-whites of his eyes back to Basil, "Movement where?"

"To the happy hunting ground?"

Both Keno and Dr. Bo laugh softly.

"Well, yes, ultimately, the dance always ends there. But move-ment where? Through what?"

Basil doesn't understand, doesn't really care, and, hell, doesn't even know where he is, sitting here in these smelly blankets, on the ground which is, hmmm, very dry, dust-dry, as though it never rained at all here, wherever *here* is . . . and he is presently dying for a cigarette.

"Through *what*, Basil?" Keno irritatingly insistent, but also, sur-prisingly, holding now a freshly opened pack of Camels' toward Basil, one perfectly extended as in an advertisement.

"Gee, thanks." Basil takes the cigarette, lights it on the match Keno also holds to him, and remembers the question. "Through the forest?" he ventures, exhaling a cloud of smoke.

Dr. Bo snorts. Keno snickers, though somewhat testily, and says, "No, man, he's been moving through *time!* Time. He danced the origin of the universe, the earth, and the time of animals, and then man. The people. He's moving into the present. Watch."

Basil drags thoughtfully on the Camel, wondering now how he's going to escape from these maniac redskins. The darkness beyond the fire is absolute, impenetrable, looks like he's gonna have to play this one out, somehow make the best of it, watch his options. . . . He sniffs. To think he missed the beginning of the universe . . . well, the twentieth century sure must be a bitch, because the dancer has really slowed down and the drum is booming much more slowly, the dancer looking like he's climbing up and down or around something out there on the firelit turf in a sort of elaborate pantomime, but these guys are really crazy, there is no way you could ever know what the dance really was all about—

"Hey!"

Dr. Bo's movement is precise and swift, shoving Basil forward by the shoulder as Keno raps him sharply on the back of the head. He exhales rapidly, cigarette smoke, and then inhales air cooler, but more acrid than even the smoke, an atmosphere tinged with chemicals, and the idea strikes him—decay. He blinks, and amazingly, the scene before him has transformed into daylight, smoggy daylight, the consistency of the dense atmosphere surrounding . . . say, Los Angeles . . . and here he now sees a vast junkyard of trashed-out appliances, washing machines, refrigerators, stoves, TV's, and just plain refuse: cans, bottles, furniture, bales of newspapers, disposable diapers, lots of fifty-five gallon drums . . . millions of anonymous, pudgy plastic garbage bags . . . acres and acres of it all, and out there in the midst of it is the lone Indian dancer, out *upon* this gigantic mountain of trash, doing the same movements Basil had seen in the firelight, as he attempted to move through the morbid mounds, climbing up and down or crawling around the junk. Amazing! Basil can actually *see* what the dancer is dancing, just amazing, the desolate scene appears to extend for miles, hills and valleys of nothing but endless garbage. It occurs to Basil that the dancer might have a destination and he is mildly curious about where that might be. But at the moment he craves more nicotine, having stubbed out his previous cigarette in the ground before him, one never seems to be enough anymore . . . and he is starting to feel pretty agitated, captivating as the scene before him is. He looks over at Dr. Bo and Keno, sitting on either side of him, and notices, oddly, the flicker of light from the fire on their faces, darkness behind, even though this daylit scene is before him. He looks back, and the spectacle is gone, only the brave out before the fire again doing his climbing, crawling dance . . .

"Aw, Basil," Keno shakes his head regretfully, the feathered fedora nodding in the firelight. "Didn't you care where he was going?"

"Well, actually, yes I did wonder that—" and suddenly all the strange craziness of what is going on here hits him. "But . . . hey, I just don't understand what this is all about, where this *is*, even," he whines.

Keno pauses for a moment, then speaks. "Yes, I can see where this might be a bit disconcerting, but we're trying to show you something important, can't you—?"

"Wait a minute," Basil interrupts. "I just want to get back to where I was, pal, this is too, too weird. Just too strange. And I don't understand any of it anyway!"

Keno tries again. "Listen, Basil, you'll have to prepare yourself. The kind of power that you're going to be dealing with requires that you have more understanding of the world around you, of the direction it's heading; you'll have to assume much more responsibility than, uh, you're capable of now."

"Hey, now just a minute here—"

"Try to understand, man, it's not just you, it's the whole planet we're concerned about," Keno continues. "We're talking power here, among other things, and it's something you don't really understand. Look what Synandra did to you. She's a powerful chick, more so than even she realizes. Check it out, man. You could be headed for trouble. You've got to prepare—"

"I have to prepare?" Basil sputters with righteous anger, feeling trapped and uncomfortable here, wanting his clothes, wanting just to get away. "All I *have* to do is what I want to do, which is what I've been doing all my life and it suits me just fine and I don't give a damn about any kind of understanding or about Synandra or about you guys or about anything! I just want a cigarette and I want to get back! Now! Get it?"

"Oh sure," drawls Keno, passing him another Camel, calmly

holding out a match while Basil puffs imperiously, furiously. And at the same time Keno looks over at Dr. Bo, who nods slightly, almost imperceptibly.

But Basil catches the nod too ... uh-oh, now what?

Keno sighs, places his hand upon Basil's head as if to pat it and says, "Pearls before swine, man. Bye-bye."

And instantly, the breath is sucked from Basil's lungs, darkness swirls around him, and he becomes acutely aware of wetness and numbing cold as he slowly turns over on the wet earth, an odd pale fish strangely beached here in the now-dark forest. The violence of the storm seems to have passed, leaving behind a steady murmur of rain to cleanse his wretched hide. He feels something slimy and wet between his lips, reaches up and wipes away the disintegrating remains of a cigarette, wonders where *that* came from and is suddenly agonized, has the unsettling feeling of having *been* somewhere, just now, somewhere far away, but he can't remember anything, just a remote feeling he has ... maybe the way it is when you've been knocked-out by a near ground-zero lightning bolt, hey, but-but, no matter what happened, he's gotta pull himself together here, the name of the game now is survival! He must get going, somewhere, to shelter, to-to Tiffany's, he figures, standing up now on battered feet, shivering terribly, swiveling back and forth to feel if anything is broken—apparently not, the only new pain a dull throbbing on his right buttock, must've landed on a stone or something.... And after several tortuous false starts Basil stumbles out of the devil-woods to the road, begins a fitful limping jog to Tiffany's. To warm sanctuary, to, hmmm, perhaps a warm bed, something he could use about now.... Then the sickening glare of headlights suddenly throws his shadow before him and—what to do?—he sprints back into the trees and crouches, watching, panting like a wounded animal, cursing under his breath—one of the distinctions between man and beast, how you can tell them apart on a strange planet—while a stopped carload of teenagers whoop and laugh from rolled-down windows at the hapless streaker, then honk the horn insanely for interminable minutes before driving away.

Finally, after running and hiding from several more dreadful duos of headlights, he reaches the driveway of Kingston's Kabin, lights glowing warmly inside, and notices, as he staggers to the door, a huge white car in the drive, Kingston's Kadillac. Oh jeeze, her parents are here. He had forgotten they were coming up. He is nearly too exhausted to care, but ... he slithers through the shrubbery and peeks in the window. Hot dog! Tiffany is at this moment walking through the living room, parents nowhere in sight. It is now or never. Basil ratataptaps on the windowpane, watches Tiffany start at the sound and cautiously walk over.... Basil waves, shrugs, tries a feeble smile ... and seconds later the door opens quietly, she whispering intensely, "Basil! What on earth?"

He doesn't tell Tiffany much, but he doesn't have to. "Aw, c'mon ... I know it had to be Synandra ..." Tiffany keeps giggling over the patter of rain on the Mercedes' windshield and the flop-flop-flop of the wipers.

"I d-d-don't w-w-w-want t-t-to t-talk about it," Basil's teeth chattering, shivering mightily beside her in the not-yet-heated car, unceremoniously wrapped in a clammy tan vinyl raincoat Tiffany has sneaked out for him.

Turns out the cottage is unlocked after all—careful detective Lexington—and Basil slips sheepishly inside, says goodbye to Tiffany.

"You sure you'll be okay, now?" Her big smile is infuriating.

"Yeah, yeah ... thanks." Basil feeling stupid and angry and sick (funny how he doesn't feel all that hungry—must be the cold), and is actually glad that the golden girl has to get back home. Next stop is a long soak in a hot tub, and then bed sweet bed. His second night in Wasson's Bay. What a bitch.

The next day dawns clear, bright, and cool, sun sparkling on the water and a stiff breeze in the pines. Basil sleeps late, gets up around noon, grumpy as a bear. He's hungry and there's nothing to eat in the place, but he feels it important to pause for a moment, light a cigarette (there is a full pack in his bag, thank Nicotinia, patron-goddess of tobacconeers everywhere) and record in his journal his somewhat-scrambled thoughts:

Tough night. One of the toughest since I've been a dick. Let's face it, that broad made a 14 carat sap out of me and I feel it all over. A real sucker. That's me. I feel like I've been on a binge so long and so deep that what happened seems only a weird, jangled dream. But if that's all it was then where did these ugly bruises

71

come from? Like the one dead center on my right butt? Looks like
a squashed grape. Hurts like hell, too. Not to mention my toe. No,
it happened. Just as sure as I sit here. In some pain.

There's something else too, the girl did something to me last
night. What it was I don't know, but it was something awfully
strange, something that turned me from a normally rock-solid sha-
mus into a plate of warm hamburger. No matter what Mrs. Frost
says, I'd have to say it was some kind of witchcraft. How else
could that bimbo have gotten the drop on me like that?

Right now my brain feels like a tossed marshmallow salad, hold
the hot fudge, please. But that reminds me, I've got a lot to do
today, the first of which is to get some food in me and then rustle
up some transportation. I've still got a job to do.

Transportation actually turns out to be first, quickly obtained
and cheap: an old red Honda 90 motorbike he picks up for ninety
bucks from the man who runs the nearest gas station, the guy asking
a hundred, but wheeler-dealer Basil getting him down after a test
drive revealed the machine to be smoky and loud—and a half-hour
or so of intense bargaining. But no big deal, he'll get better wheels
to blow this town—hopes it's soon too—when he wires the attorney
Yates with a progress report, and a bill, but not until he gets a
positive make on Kowalske. Which, he figures, should be soon.
Meanwhile he finds a bar in town, Maxwell's, that serves up what
they call "Paul Bunyan Burgers," and is soon feeling a lot better,
burgered-up and topped-off with a couple of brewskis while chatting
it up with an attractive barmaid, name of Amy, the old Lexington
charm comes through again, always does, hell, he's almost forgotten
about last night, almost ... and then it's off to MacArthur for what
will undoubtably head a page in his peripatetic journal as The Big
Stake Out.

MacArthur looks less bleak in the bright daylight though there's
still no more of it than there was before, the dilapidated house and
what might have been a barn behind. On the other side of the road
are the very overgrown remains of the tiny store, the roof of which
had collapsed probably more than a decade before, this structure in
much worse shape than the house, apparently not having been kept
up at all after its initial fizzle, out here in the middle of nothing,
it's not surprising. ... But there is a tiny bit of interior—rotted

72

weather-bleached boards sheltered by a corner of broken-down roof, with a west-facing paneless window that might be perfect for Kowalske-watching. It's no problem to pull the bike into the weeds either; it's a good blind. Before settling in, he checks for fresh tire tracks, the spoor of a lost Ferrari, but there are none, the rain of last night having washed away the ones he had seen yesterday, so all he can do now is wait. . . .

*   *   *

Synandra sits atop the hill on her favorite heart-rock, the one with a comfortable seat and a good view of the windy bay. She is thinking of nothing, head empty as the breeze, sometimes it's like that when she's up here, all that's necessary is *to be,* seems like there's really nothing else . . . just her and the earth, wonderful, sitting quietly, prudently, here in the backwaters, deliciously tangential to the epicenter where the current flows so strongly; it's like having her back to a fire, gently warming her spine, but with not exactly heat, no, instead, luxuriant squiggles of energy. . . . Could this rock she sits upon have been somehow *placed* in this spot, so absolutely perfectly for her? Sometimes she wonders if it *is* just her, just she who is able to partake so avidly of the vibrant flow. . . . Perhaps there are others, but either they do not come here, or they do not stay long enough to sense the power. . . . Anyway, she always thinks it will be a girl, much like herself, although there was a time about five years back when a tourist, a young boy about nine years old, seated himself in the exact center of the hilltop and promptly went catatonic. It was a strange scene, his parents afraid to move or even disturb him, sending a sister running down to the Wasson house for help, for a doctor, but Synandra answered the door and somehow knew (surprising even to her) exactly what to do, running back with a pitcher of water to douse the boy—if that's really what he was, a frail creature so fair of skin and face and hair that Synandra when she saw him thought that she must have misunderstood the sister, this had to be a girl, but it was not—and immediately the drenched young androgyne roused himself, but appeared so lethargic Synandra had to pull him to the edge of the hilltop and then warn his parents

73

to keep him away from the hill entirely, explaining that sometimes people get "dizzy" up here for no apparent reason. . . .

She's not all that startled when she hears someone walking up the side of the hill and turns to find Dr. Bo. He's someone you never expect to see, but then are never surprised when he appears, either. "That was quite a storm last night," the doctor smiles as he strides over, sits beside her.

"Yes, it was." Synandra can't help smiling too. There's a certain smugness she feels about the whole thing. She never actually thought about the storm arriving when it did, it simply *did*. The time was right; it was here. She smiles again. This was power, so sweet, so simple. She is silent for a moment, then she sighs, "Well, he deserved it." She knows he *knows*.

"Oh, did he?" the doctor's eyes are shining.

Darn. She also knows what he is thinking: that she has done it again. It seems that in one way or another she always managed to scare off any potential suitors, ever since she had been old enough to be noticed by them, and she had never looked back. Perhaps in a way it was her pride, a sense that she was awfully damned special, she and her hill, or perhaps it was that she was so selective, not one of those yahoos from Wasson's Bay and environs ever seeming right for her . . . but finally, perhaps it was the prophecy, delivered by Dr. Bo himself, shortly after she had come of proper age, and had learned the secrets of the hill. The *prophecy*. Well, maybe it was a little too heavy for italics-of-the-mind. It was just something Dr. Bo had casually told her. But it was something, parentless serious girl, that she took quite seriously. And besides, he was never, ever, wrong. "Yes he did," she answers. "He was so obnoxious."

"I see," replies the doctor. "You seem to have a predilection for attracting obnoxious young men."

"Well, maybe I shouldn't have been—quite so nasty. But I didn't really know—"

"The hill," interrupts the doctor, "is a strange and powerful friend you have. It attracts thunderstorms seemingly from nowhere. The indiginous ones, the true early Americans, believed that such storms were caused by huge spirit birds, thunderbirds, they called them. And they were absolutely correct—in the most literal sense. Three of those big birds, sometimes more, often circle the hill. Up there." The medicine man points skyward.

"Yes, you've told me ... but I always thought that it was just a story that you—"

"And when have I ever told you 'just a story?' Those birds surely exist. They are your friends and they protect you. And I believe that soon you will be able to see them."

"Really? How? When?"

"Soon, I should think. But how ... I think it will be quite interesting to find out."

8

Time has been dragging by, it is five days now and Captain Jimmy has not shown at all. Basil is starting to get a little worried here, like maybe his detecting has not been all that accurate, and it's not hard to start doubting oneself, is it? hunkering down like a–a gnome in this decrepit hole across the road from the MacArthur hovel . . . so much for the glamorous life of a private investigator. He has been keeping watch on the house in staggered six to ten hour shifts with burger and beer breaks in between and it is *bo*-ring as all get out. . . . He has brought in some supplies, a couple of cartons of Camels, giant-size bags of barbecue chips, and in a cheap styrofoam cooler increasingly replaceable six-packs of a beer he finds he favors, *Heinenstuber,* a northern Wisconsin brew from the town of Eau Claire. To pass the time he listens to Brewers' games on his Sound-Pac, tries some bird-watching with the binocs, leafs through a *Playboy* magazine he has picked up along the way, and idly plots revenge against one, Synandra Wasson. Yeah, it's so ironic too, it really pisses him off, the one thing, the only thing, really, that still gives him hope, makes him think that maybe he wasn't wrong about Kowalske is that witch-girl's terse pronouncement that Kowalske was actually there—or had been there, at that house across the road, his

76

stake-out. He actually *believes* in her, her—intuition, or whatever. And he must, he has to; right now, it's all he's got.

During off-times Basil skulks around Wasson's Bay afoot or blasts through on the noxious motorbike, either way avoiding the now sinister perfumery and herb shop, Ars Aromatica. One morning he found his ripped-off clothing on his doorstep, laundered and neatly folded, his precious Zippo tucked into a pocket. But no note, no her. Which has taken the form and force of a fantasy: abject girl appearing at his door, tears streaming down rosy cheeks, begging forgiveness for pulling such a dirty low-down rotten trick on him. Perhaps the offering of her unworthy, yet delectable body might provide a meager start in the long round of restitution she must make . . . but still no her. Tiffany doesn't seem to be around either, but it doesn't really matter, the two are probably in cahoots anyway. In fact, until a day ago he started thinking that he would never see her, that Synandra, again, just do his job and get out of town, and that was fine, he knew he didn't really care about her anyway . . . but then quite unexpectedly—wasn't it? on his way to breakfast at a diner he's discovered that has a 99-cent early-bird special, the Heart Rock Cafe, he caught sight of her on her way to her shop, wearing a breezy T-shirt and cutoff blue jeans hitched up with gaudy suspenders, racing by on *roller skates,* zinging along clickity-clack over cracks in the mica-sparkling sidewalk, throwing long morning shadows, knife-edged in the crisp lake air. Basil had pressed himself into a shaded doorway across the street and watched her slice through that crystal dawn, her slender legs sunlit, golden. . . . Steadying himself, he felt something swell to a lump in his throat while another entity in his chest sort of—deflated, leaving him strangely empty, an undeniably good tight feeling . . . but what was it that wanted to perch upon those emptied shelves?

Well, one thing that intrigues him still is the way she tricked him. In retrospect, as the evil deed passes farther along into the great black pit of the past, he has to sort of admire her—but still of course hate her—and wonder just what kind of strangeness he's up against here. He thinks it's got something to do with that weird hill, a power center, to be sure. That's why it's called Mystery Rock Hill, right? And perhaps our favorite witch-girl Synandra holds the key to this mystery, and-and no one else knows? Again, he isn't sure, but did manage to putt-putt over to the tiny library in town in which he found a corner dedicated to the hill and indeed the Wassons' themselves, the founders of the burg. There were some old photographs of early Wassons', including the venerable Captain Milford, and other gray photos of the early frontier-boom period: old buildings and rutted streets, freshly constructed docks stacked with cubic acres of cordwood jutting into the mist-faded lake, eager groupings of young lumberjacks and their teams of horses, and the great gray hill itself, with the Wasson house easily identifiable before it. There was also a glass display case of Indian relics from the town, *The Wasson Collection*, no less. It contained numerous flint and chert arrowheads, several green-encrusted copper spearheads, pottery relics, bone drills, and other unrecognizable oddities . . . but nothing very mysterious—other than a printed card stating that none of the relics were found in the immediate vicinity of Mystery Rock Hill, only in outlying areas, presumably because the Indians considered the hill very sacred. . . . The librarian, an intense, cheerful middle-aged woman with an apparent enthusiasm for any tourist interested in "what makes the hill such a mystery anyway—besides the rocks?" was only able to provide him with a few references to it in books of local history, Sir Reginald Battlesea's hoary account, and another short monograph published by a professor at the University of Wisconsin, one Clyde Mortell, Ph.D., which said little more than he already knew. And no mention whatsoever of "power centers."

Now it's almost chowtime at the old stakeout and Basil yawns, checks his watch, time to call it a day, what the hell . . . catch some grub, but this time something other than burgers, he's getting a trifle tired of the same old—uh, oh, lookee here up the road, it's-it's a red Ferrari rolling up in a cloud of dust . . . holy Jesus! Kowalske! Basil scrambles around, kicking through the beer cans and empty chip bags and burger wrappers that have begun piling up around his feet, looking frantically for his binoculars . . . finally finds them and with shaking hands tries to focus in on his man. He's only able to catch a glimpse of him walking around behind the old MacArthur homestead, but the glimpse is plenty, it's *him*. Kowalske! For sure. He had been carrying something too, a cardboard box, it looked like, and something long and black, Basil suspects a crowbar . . . figures he's right, too, for seconds later he hears muffled thumpings and the faint whinesqueal of aged nails being forced from their moorings. And then, with binoculars focused tensely upon the front window where a couple of boards have fallen, he sees the gloomy interior briefly brighten and then darken again, as though someone had entered through the back door.

Well, there he *is*. Basil is elated. He has gotten his man. The Jack of Hearts Detective Agency can chalk up another victory. Basil pulls a can of beer from the cooler, cracks it open and celebrates. It's Heinenstuber time. Now all he has to do is get a few pics here of Captain Jimmy, for evidence of this job well done—just in case Kowalske decides to lam out again for God-knows-where. Then it's pack-up and hop on his Honda and wire Yates, collect some bread and blow this crazy burg.

Funny thing though, how Captain Jimmy came *here* to hole-up, he thinks as he clicks his telephoto lens into the Nikon body and sets up his miniature tripod to face the current hideout of the messiah of the Church of the Electronic Trinity. Maybe it was like Synandra said, he was running from the church hierarchy. Maybe things out there *had* gotten out of control for him.... Well, he sure picked one hell of an anonymous place to hide-out. Basil has to admire it in a way, it's *so* isolated, the perfect place to get away to; no one would *ever* have found him ... except for, heh-heh, private investigator Lexington, and now he has to turn him in. Jeeze, it's too bad, Basil sucks on his beer and thinks, listening to the scolding yee-yee-yee of circling Kildeer out in the surrounding fields, decides he really feels sorry for the guy, yeah, it's really too bad ... but he's got a job to do and anyway, goddamn, he's a good detective! What the hell. He will drink to that and does.

And does. About three hours and four, or five? progressively warmer beers later, Basil senses something amiss. He has been watching the house more or less steadily since Kowalske's arrival and there has been no sign, no movement, not even a change in the lighting within the house that he can perceive, nothing to signal the presence, the *existence,* of Captain Jimmy. Besides it's getting darker and there probably isn't enough light to get a picture anyway. Could the man have just gone inside and, uh, crashed-out? Or, jeepers, now Basil remembers back to, say, a quarter hour after Kowalske had entered the house, when he had heard, maybe, a faintly soft pop! as though a distant gun had been fired. This perception insinuates itself alarmingly into Basil's beer-basted brain, bringing forth the uneasy possibility, could it be? that Kowalske just might have *offed himself* in this empty corner of Wisconsin? Jesus, it just might be. The guy was probably really depressed. Maybe he'd better get over there, take the camera, pop some Heinies in his jacket pocket, you never know, and sneak a peek. . . .

The place looks empty. There are only four rooms to it and a careful peek through the windows reveals only the cardboard box on the old table, and on the floor the crowbar Kowalske carried in—and nothing else, like when he and Synandra had first looked inside a week ago. This is really weird, he knows he hadn't seen Kowalske leave . . . and the Ferrari is still here, of course, parked in front of the house. Basil is relieved that through the window he doesn't spot the man's body crumpled on the floor, but—where is the guy? He circles around to the back and decides to sneak inside for a closer look. He pushes open the back door and steps, cautiously, into an odd ozone-like smell and a strange *feeling,* as though the atmosphere is somehow—charged, or something, a sense of electricity in the air. Well, there is some blood, drops of it from the back door to the main room where there is a middling splotch of it, and the crowbar, also bloodied, lying alongside. But it doesn't really look serious, only as though he cut himself while prying the boards from the door. He's sure that's what it is; certainly not a form of suicide . . . and no corpus delicti. . . . But where the hell is he? Basil figures he ought to be able to dope this one out—after all, he tracked Kowalske to MacArthur. . . . But after umpteen circuits of the tiny interior and a few trips outside for observation and urination, Basil is truly confused—and feels strangely bushed, too, increasingly less interested in this very peculiar puzzler right now than he'd care to admit . . . Can't seem to stop yawning as he prowls yet again through the place, finding essentially nothing in the way of a clue, seems really weird, even the cardboard box is empty, Basil vaguely wonders what he might have carried inside it . . . needs to think straight but is just too drowsy right now, the ozone and beer an odd brain-numbing combination, and he hasn't eaten anything either, makes him want to just sit down here on the floor and wait it out for Captain Jimmy; he ought to come back sooner or later . . . feels good to stretch out too, he was so cramped over there on the stakeout. . . .

... funny how he never noticed the trapdoor before, sharp and square as a ship's hatch in the moonlight streaming through the windows. He can feel cool air rising through the crack alongside it too, aha! so *this* is where Captain Jimmy went. There must be a tunnel or something. ... Basil feels around in the shadows, finds a worn wooden handle, and heaves. The damn thing's heavy, but it creaks open and a cool updraft rushes against his face bringing the dank black scent of earth and stone, and water, perhaps, running far below. ... There's a ladder and—strange how he's not scared, no light or anything—he swings onto the damp top rungs and begins to climb down into this black black cellar, worries vaguely about the ladder not holding out, but it does and after a fairly long descent he finds himself in a damp corridor paved with worn slippery stones which he begins to follow toward some faint light up ahead, and ... Jeeze, now he hears drumming, weird, the cadence just like the one he remembers from not-so-long-ago, and he smells woodsmoke, too, turns a corner ... and finds himself in a vast underground chamber with a fire burning out there in its center and-and sitting before it two familiar Indians, one with long gray hair, reminds Basil now of Michael Ansara, Cochise in *Broken Arrow* on bygone TV, and the beaky one with the single-feathered fedora.

"Hi kid," Keno grins, "welcome back. C'mon over here . . ."

Basil is oddly grateful to be here with them after his long descent, sitting between them again (he's forgotten all about Kowalske), but still shudders as he gets the Big Eye (blue) from Dr. Bo, and is bid to watch someone out there in the firelight again moving slowly around, the intrepid dancer, up and over the twentieth century. It's the same old thing, just like before ... even his stomach growls again, loudly, this is getting embarrassing ... but there's no wonderful burger aroma in the air this time, instead Keno passes him a small clay bowl containing dark liquid.

"Drink it up man, it's good for you."

Well ... Basil does, quickly, as if there's no decision involved here, and immediately suppresses the urge to vomit—the stuff is wretched—and tries to keep it down, he *hates* to throw up.

Keno laughs. "Better than burgers, man?"

Not by a long shot decides Basil, trying to relax his constricting throat muscles, relax, relax, not-to-gag, it's so uncool ... and then, and then is rather pleased by the way things seem to be sort of

81

lighting-up! and his vision is punctuated by bright flashes now, it's odd, seems to be every time he blinks his eyes, or—no, it's more like each time his heart beats, it beats brilliance, far beyond this dark cavern, a flash that persists longer each time, brighter, and clearer ... and then, suddenly, it's that crazy endless junkyard again and that poor brave out there picking his way through it. Basil feels kind of gushy inside—must be the potion—like he *belongs.* And it sort of fits, the three of them magically somehow here, now in broad daylight at the foot of a glacier of garbage ... that brave still out there climbing, climbing. . . .

"Look closer," the old one directs Basil's gaze out and up towards the brave and—oh shit—Keno thumps him on the head again, and suddenly—he is now very very close to the dancing brave, who looks so *familiar* from behind here, turning around at this moment to face Basil, and—(gasp!) it *is* Basil, face to face with-with himself! and then he realizes he *is,* or *has become,* the Indian youth, *has been him all along,* in fact ... now finds himself standing rather unsteadily amid a clankcrunch of tin cans and garbage bags and old dishwashers and stuff ... with that peculiar liquid-burning glow inside him and the reeky garbage stench without. He isn't sure exactly where to go here, but a tiny glowing red light from below suddenly catches his eye. He looks down and sees an object snugged-up in the litter that looks *rather strange*, a mechanical or electronic whatzit of some sort, hard to focus upon in this strange daylight, but it's somehow appealing ... looks like one of those Japanese-miniaturized gizmos, like a geiger counter or something—the configuration of buttons and dials highly unfamiliar. Basil reaches down to take hold of that fascinating instrument when it suddenly jumps back, or actually sort of—*burrows* itself down into the trash a bit, there's a corner of it still sticking out. . . . He picks away a couple of empty bottles of Seagram's and Budweiser, some Campbell's soup cans, and reaches again for the weird box, and c'mon now, it jumps backwards again. Basil pushes away more trash, tries once more for the thing, which pulls back again, and hell, now it's behind an old RCA television set which Basil heaves away, revealing ... huh, a deep dark hole, what the heck, Basil in Garbageland here, kneels down to peer inside this otherworldly aperture, and spies—Jesus, a weird green glowing room down there, big as a warehouse with a huge pool of water for a floor, and brightly radiant within its depths green fluorescent masses of— Basil suddenly understands the scene, realizes these are hot hot radioactive wastes, the spent fuel rods of a nuclear reactor, effectively non-disposable . . . the stuff is at once the strangest, most unnatural, and the most terrifying stuff he has ever seen—ultimate garbage. The green glow is incredible, mesmerizing, in a way, terribly beautiful, to think that poor simple humans have somehow produced such strange radiant matter . . . but the stuff is pure evil, he knows it . . . and then suddenly the old refrigerator he has been perched upon gives way and—oh God!—he is now falling right into that bizarre pool of certain sickening death—falllling! And boom! He awakens, bathed in sweat, on the same dark wooden floor from whence he had left. But where is that? Was he dreaming? Is he awake now? Nothing seems real in this ozone atmosphere anyway, nothing at all now . . . and he's still really tired, rolls over and sleeps, or half-sleeps, doesn't know, doesn't care, doesn't understand what is what in this gray garbled crazy place.

*   *   *

"So our detective is staking-out the MacArthur house?" asks Tiffany as she pours more suntan lotion on her fingers, prior to applying to the hollow of her friend's as-yet seasonally fair back, especially amongst the small vertebrae that protrude so delicately there, just above her bikinied bottom, just where she liked it most— Tiffany well knew.

"Uh-huh." Synandra, lying on her tummy, raises her head above the blanket, lifts her sunglasses to squint up and down the brilliant beachfront before reaching back to untie the top—or semblance thereof—of the bikini she wears. Save for a couple of surf-strollers at least a quarter-mile away, they are the only ones on the beach this day, not surprising for a Wednesday afternoon in June—it not really warming-up on the lake-side of the peninsula until after the Fourth. "I haven't heard boo from him, either. I wonder how he's getting along . . ."

"Well, you don't really expect to . . . after that, uh, stunt, you pulled." There is a cool breeze blowing off the water today, and

83

gooseflesh crawls along the length of her arms as she rubs her friend's glistening back. Sitting cross-legged, she turns slightly to shield herself from the wind. They are in a favorite spot, a concavity formed by the dunes that encircle this beach, protected, for the most part, from the lake breeze—at least in prone sunbathing position. Later in the season, like most other such spots on the shore, it will house a covey of tourists, but now it is safe and secluded, perfect for lolling about in the bikinis that Tiffany brought up from Chicago—Brazilian imports—fairly scandalous for 1970's Wisconsin, and exactly what Tiffany liked.

Of course . . . Synandra remembered back to when they wore these things for the first time, several years ago, with the temperature fixed at 98 and all the tourists flocking to the lakeshore, Tiffany daring them to walk along the water's edge of the bay before all the boys on the beach, Synandra blushing terribly in the ridiculously scanty thing, heart tripping with, well—excitement, hyper-sensitive her actually *feeling,* like many exhalations of heated breath, the hungry eyes of everyone upon her ninety-seven percent exposed being . . . and Tiffany strutting in the surf cool as cress, haughty, defiant, as she always was . . . then a dizzying walk to her house or Tiff's, wherever elders were absent, and still sunblind before the neutral but omniscient mirror admiring each other in ways that they knew, even then, were secret and sacred, and would remain always so between them. . . .

"No, I guess not. . . ." sighs Synandra, heavy heart-heave with the acceptance that they are older now, dares aren't what they used to be in the summers of youth, and overall—the time's they are a changin'. . . .

There is laughter of old times, close calls, retelling of tales famous between them, only them. . . . It's enough to recount the highlights, the details they both know well . . . Tiffany, how she slept with the Illinois congressman in order to gain his support for a child day-care bill she cared strongly about and this corpulent conservative family-man not a whit . . . the big joke on him being the look on his face when she made her demand during an evening of highly illicit lust, reaching underneath a pillow, proudly pushing her driver's license into his horrified face at the singular moment, it screaming SEVENTEEN! and then the even bigger joke on her, he keeling over with a monumental heart attack (turned out it was his third—

and last), and her attempts to revive him a desperate failure, calling hotel security before bidding a quick adieu. . . .

Well, the ending of that incident always brings a somewhat sickly smile (the bill failed), not unlike Synandra's oft-told tale, which goes back even further, to when she was about fifteen and dying, really, to capture the attentions of "Big" Jim Junger, a super-handsome high school senior at the time, star fullback, rock-combo guitarist, and all-around conceited jerk (who said love was blind?) who was at that moment daffy over a bosomy cheerleader, one Col-lete Cumberson, and would not in any way acknowledge the exis-tence of that gawky (and somewhat strange) Synandra Wasson. It seemed it would take a *miracle* to gain him, some sort of magic! So one night when the moon had grown full she was out in the woods at dusk, not far from the hill, surrounded by budding wild roses, seated in the grassy clearing, wearing nothing but a blue chintz cape she had fashioned from some old curtains. This was her first attempt at love magic, *any* kind of magic, actually, and she had only the most rudimentary idea of what to do, equipped with a kitchen knife and a wine glass, a small incense burner and most importantly, a comb of big Jim's with several precious hairs caught in the teeth— a fantastic piece of luck, having fallen from his pocket in the school corridor right before Synandra's eyes. It was enough to convince her to try to put together this "spell," which consisted of burning the in-cense—a dubious combination of cedar, yarrow, frankincense, hen-bane, and belladonna—the latter notorious poisons—that she had raided her herb collection to concoct, pricking her finger with the knife, mixing her blood with Jim's hairs, and then reciting an "incantation" she had scrawled consisting of repeating her name and Jim's and some other wording she came up with: mostly mysterious passages from *Finnegan's Wake,* a book she had found in her grampa's study, the nearest thing to magical mumbo-jumbo there was in the house.

By the time she had finished fooling around with the para-phenalia she had gotten quite a snootful of incense, and, oh my! what a difference then! everything: bushes, trees, the tops of her toes were ringed with marvelous pulsing auras, tiny hearts bursting out all over . . . the twilit atmosphere itself taking on an odd violet cast (like maybe the same shade that passes before the eyes of a poison-ing victim, eh?) and she had to force herself to concentrate on the last step of the "ceremony" which consisted essentially of tantric

85

trivia and thoughts of Jim Junger, including the specific wish that "he come to her," and then ... and then came the climax of the spell ... with her opening her incense-stinging eyes to find—Big Jim Junger! amazingly in front of her! in the flesh, to be sure, apparently directly, miraculously delivered from a concert, a rock and roll performance, still carrying the smoking pink guitar with which he serenaded Collette....

Well, after shaking-off the shock of his life (the visage of curvaceous Collette strangely, suddenly, displaced by that of skinny Synandra Wasson ...?!) he had immediately run away, out of the woods, and never mentioned it to her, or to anyone, thank goodness, as far as she knew. It was the last time she had seen him, his graduation only a week away, and it was absolutely the last time she had ever tried her hand at structured magic. She never dreamed the spell would work at all, let alone so fast, or so *literally!* But it certainly taught her about the incredible powers that were there for the taking.

"Didn't you tell me once that your grampa, er, you now, I guess, actually *owns* the MacArthur homestead?" Tiffany asks.

Synandra flinches, whether from the question, or the fact that Tiffany is now applying the lotion to the backs of her knees, always a ticklish situation, Tiffany can't tell. But, yes, Synandra admits that her grandfather had purchased the place on the advice of Dr. Bo. Many years back, around the time she had been found on its porch after a two-day absence.

"It's a power center, like the hill," she explains. "In fact, it's sort of a sister-center to the hill. I've dowsed there. Three underground streams cross directly below it, which results in a lot of energy centered there, which is fine for, ah, metaphysical endeavors—but very bad for average people to live above. The MacArthur house was sited very poorly—which resulted in a lot of misfortune for them. Several of them died of cancer, and there were reports of poltergeists when they occupied it. Eventually they—and everyone else who tried to live there—abandoned it. Dr. Bo says that some places on earth are simply not good for people to live upon. That's why my grampa bought the place, so that no one else would ever occupy it."

"Why didn't your grampa just tear it down, then?"

"He wanted to, but Dr. Bo said to let it stand, that it would be destroyed in due time—"

"No kidding."

"Uh-huh. He said that he foresaw that it had some purpose for us, the Wassons ... I guess now, for me."

"Well, what do you know ..."

"Yeah, it sort of looks like things are beginning to happen ... but what, I'm not exactly sure. All I know is that that house is a strange place. I hope he doesn't get into any trouble."

"Well, he's just watching it right? You don't think he's actually going to go inside?"

"No, of course not. ..."

9

It might be morning; inside the old house it is dusk. Basil is awake, groggy, and stiff from lying (sleeping?) all night—if it was night—on the wooden floor. He thinks he dreamed, vaguely recalls the shape and texture of gray mysteries . . . of meeting strangers, of dangerous situations . . . that, and a sort of stenchy garbage odor. . . . But it's all long gone, no use trying to track it down. He feels utterly alone and out-of-it here, like clinging to the fantail of a great gray wooden ship that is receding rapidly from port, home, friends, the familiar crazy jangled essence of L.A. . . .

Well, his heart sinks as he remembers the Troubling Thing, reality striking after the first moments of post-awakening confusion: Kowalske's disappeared again. From right under his nose. Damn! But then, suddenly a spark of hope flashes in his heart—wasn't there a trapdoor? Yes, he seems to remember one, begins pacing around the house, looking for the trapdoor . . . that damn trapdoor . . . damn, it's not here. Not in any of the rooms, not anywhere. He feels like he might cry. Tired, hungry, thirsty, unwashed, and so groggy—the atmosphere in this place might best be described as *potent*—he wants to leave . . . but knows he can't, not yet, feels oddly about this, as though something is *so close,* as though he might break the spell or something, and never be able to find Kowalske ... and then suddenly there is a sharp POP! behind him in the main room and a brief gust of wind washes through the place as though someone opened a window. He steps cautiously over, and right there before him is "Captain" Jimmy Kowalske, the new messiah and leader-on-the-lam of The Church of the Electronic Trinity. It is as though he has appeared in the proverbial puff of smoke.

Except that there is no smoke, proverbial or otherwise. He has simply appeared! looking like the pictures Basil has seen of him, though perhaps slightly younger, more like an early 5x7 black and white glossy the lawyer Yates had provided Basil with, but here his blond hair is tousled, and his eyes are wild, blue, and penetrating, and Basil, without consciously apprehending it, instantly understands his charisma. He is in fact using those electric eyes on Basil right now, standing with a surprised look, which fades slightly as he relaxes from what appears to be great tension. He is breathing pretty hard, too, apparently the process of instantaneous materialization not an altogether carefree event. ...

"Hello there," Kowalske mumbles as he slumps heavily to the floor.

"Oh, hi."

"What are you doing here?"

"Oh, nothing much I guess. Just planning on leaving actually."

"I guess you're wondering what this is," says Kowalske defiantly, referring to a box-like object he is cradling in both hands. It is somewhat smaller than a breadbox, appears to be made of wood with a curving polished brass handle and small brass levers, or something, protruding from it.

"Oh, yeah, I guess so." It is in fact the first time Basil has really noticed it.

"Damn, I knew I should have looked through this whole place before I returned."

"Returned?" Basil feels like a desert straggler viewing a saving, yet troubling, mirage. He is relieved to see Kowalske here—the first thought flashing through his weary mind is to get a quick photo of him and then get out—but now there is something really *strange* going on here ... where, exactly, had he come from?

"Yes, I returned, from another, er, place," he manages a weak smile.

89

God yes, Basil now truly understands that Kowalske has just *appeared!* He looks hard at the strange object he holds and asks, "Yeah, what *is* that thing?"

"It is the sacred cask of Shaman Nabokoff, as Mr. Kowalske well knows!" a voice booms behind them.

Both Basil and Kowalske start at the sound. Kowalske jumps to his feet, and they both turn and look toward the back of the house.

A man dressed entirely in black, wearing a brimmed hat also in black, is standing largely in the doorway. He looks to be about fifty years old, has a long beard and is wearing horn-rimmed glasses. His voice carries a thick European accent, German perhaps, he pronounced Kowalske as Ko*val*ske. Through a missing window-board Basil notices something new outside, an old black bicycle, kickstand-upright on the porch, apparently this fellow's. The man seems angry, smiling menacingly at Kowalske as he walks in.

Kowalske smiles calmly back. "Ivan Ivanovich, so we meet again."

"As you can plainly see, *Cap*tain Jimmy." The emphasis sneering. "And you know why I have come."

"For this—toy, Ivan?" Kowalske indicates the box in his hands.

The man nods grimly. "The sacred cask is no toy, as we both know."

"How did you find me?"

Ivan Ivanovich shrugs. "How did he?"

He means Basil. Basil gulps, thinks he's suddenly in over his head here . . .

"Yeah, Ace," says Kowalske, "what *are* you doing here?"

Oh hell. They are both looking at him now. He can't think of any lie offhand, he's so tired anyway, hates being on the spot like this. . . .

"Tell him, my boy," the man commands gently.

"Well . . . I'm a private investigator. I've been hired to find you."

Kowalske's eyes widen by many angstroms, emitting beaucoup blue quanta in Basil's direction. "By Ivan?"

"No, no. I don't know him. It was by the church. Your church, The Church of the Electronic Trinity. They, a lawyer named Yates, hired me."

"Yates." Kowalske breathes the name thoughtfully. He seems genuinely surprised by all this; his brow wrinkles, weariness clearly apparent. "So, they're after me too, now."

"Of course," says the black presence, smiling smugly, "what did you expect? Your business is worth millions, to them. Your—toy, is worth even more, to me. See, if not me, them."

The man turns toward Basil again. "You don't even know what that object is, do you?"

"No, I—"

"Then leave. Get out!" Kowalske barks.

"Let him stay!" the man shouts back. "I think he should remain here with us. I would like very much a witness should you try to outsmart me again. And besides, Jimmy, think! What would he do but go and report on you, bring the police perhaps."

"Let him. Let him," yells Kowalske. "I'll be long gone by then." He smiles thinly at Ivanovich.

"No. You must stay and listen," the man says to Basil as he eases himself into the house's only chair. "We have time. Time, ha, is something we all certainly have enough of right now. And I wish that someone, this Mr. Detective here, if it is to be ... someone, besides Captain Jimmy, hear my story."

Basil settles gratefully to the floor, while Kowalske, having placed the central object of controversy, the odd box, before him on the floor, shrugs, looks impassively on.

The man begins to recite a tale that one day will perhaps head a passage in Basil's journal as

THE OLD RUSSIAN'S STRANGE STORY

"Long ago I was an apprentice to the very great shaman Arcady Nabokoff who lived near the town of Vanavara on the banks of the Podkamennaya Tunguska river in the central Siberian wilderness of Russia. I was born in the year eighteen hundred and ninety; I was a youth of eighteen years at the time I refer to. This was the early summer of nineteen hundred and eight—" The man pauses for a second and looks calmly, somewhat expectantly, at Basil. And though he is tired, Basil realizes this can't be right; the man would have to be eighty-some years old, and he doesn't look more than half that.

Picking-up on his perplexity, Captain Jimmy says quietly, "he *is* that old, sport."

"Yes, I am," Ivan sighs heavily. "You will presently understand.

"So ... in that time our village was fortunate, or perhaps unfortunate, as it has turned out, to be the home of that great and all-powerful shaman. There was a village gathering in the spring of that year, and two other shamans arrived to visit with my master. During the festivities, however, much qumys—fermented mare's milk—a most exhilarating beverage—was drunk, and the two visiting shamans made the grave error of ridiculing shaman Nabokoff. Yes, they mocked him, undoubtably because of envy, as it was known to all that my master possessed greater powers than they, but also because of some troubling pronouncements my master had recently made. You see, during his spirit-journeys of that period he often found himself in an odd, seeming land of the future, where there were huge cities of steel and stone, and strange swift wheeled vehicles that traveled across endlessly long roads stacked one on top of another, and metallic flying machines in the shape of great birds that roared across the skies. He told the villagers of these visions, and pronounced that the time of their way of life and even of the shaman himself, would soon come to an end. As might be expected, this revelation was not an especially welcome one, and not many truly believed my master, but neither did anyone dare dispute his prophetic powers. Perhaps this was the primary reason for his derision by his fellow shamans. Yes, I am certain it was. But still the error was made and it was up to my master to right the wrong or lose his standing in our village.

"That very night shaman Nabokoff summoned me, and informed me that he, with my assistance, would bring to the villagers proof of the coming changes, as much to help them prepare for the future, I believe, as to maintain his venerable reputation. And so ... the next day the great shaman and I set out on a journey into the Yenisei taiga, the vast forest north of the trading post Vanavara. For ten days we travelled through the dense taiga and open swamp, over snow-covered hills and swollen rivers until, near the base of the mountain of two peaks, Shakrama, we came to a particular clearing in which there stood a single straight birch that had been split by lightning. This was a sign of power. Here we were to conduct our business. My master and I constructed a yurt around that birch, with the tree as the central post, representing Tuuru, the tree of life, the axis upon which the world turns.

"For the next forty days and forty nights, my master took upon himself a fierce regimen of fasting and purging, terribly stringent purification ceremonies during which I attended him. And each evening he would undertake what he called "little journeys," in which he sought knowledge preparatory to his major quest. Again it was I who served as his anchor upon middle earth; it was I who beat the sacred drum. During these journeys he wore a pouch of wolfskin, and each time he would 'return' something would be in the pouch: an object of wood or brass or gold, a gear upon a shaft, a lever, a dial, a small portion of the cask," Ivan Ivanovich's voice shaking here, raising from somewhere around a fairly constant *mezzo piano* to a level very *forte,* pointing over to placid Captain Jimmy, "that very cask which this false messiah holds at this very moment!"

To which der Captain smiles and nods, even yawns here.

"And from these sacred objects, which were gathered by sacred means by a sacred man!" (*ff*)! "I, an earnest unsuspecting youth was instructed by my master to carefully construct the cask that this, this, unworthy holds now!"

Ivan Ivanovich's eyes circle the room but are focused beyond, past them, the walls, the present world.... Then he begins again, "Finally, near the end of June, the sacred cask was complete, its innards a magnificently-wrought vessel of crystal, lead, copper, and pure gold. The awesome power it was soon to hold would be directed by means of clever, hah! ingenious! mechanisms my master, through his spirit aides, had devised. Now Arcady Nabokoff was ready to attempt the final journey, one in which he would venture far beyond the fourteen magical spheres of heaven, as far as his power would take him. It was to be the ultimate task.

"I will never forget the night before we parted. It was a fine summer evening, a magnificent sunset, but my heart was heavy. I felt I would never see my master again. It was also the first time I ever detected within him, even briefly, a trace of fear. I believe he also felt that it was our last time together. But he did not show it. You see, he knew that the capture of this great power would be an unspeakably difficult task; he knew that it would be most dangerous for me to attend him on what would be his most fearful, and, as it turned out, final, expedition.

"He left the next morning at dawn, taking with him, of course, the sacred cask. He left instructions for me not to follow him, but if he should not return in five days, to seek his body at the very least, and at the very most, the cask we had so carefully constructed.

93

"And so he set out. Due north. I very much wished to follow him, but knew his displeasure would be monumental were he to learn I had disobeyed.

"Well, as you might expect, I was exceedingly anxious to know the fate of my master. By the evening of the fourth day I was beside myself with worry, and with dread. I could not sleep, I could not eat. I felt I just could not remain at our humble yurt and wait for his return. And so, after a thoroughly sleepless night, I arose before dawn and set out for the foot of Mount Shakrama. As the sun rose on that beautiful cloudless morning I climbed the lower slope of the mountain so that I could watch for the return of shaman Nabokoff. I found a perch on the slope that afforded me an excellent view of the taiga to the north. I believe I was able to see as far north as the river Khushmo. Yes, truly an excellent view. I settled down to watch. But the climb and sleepless night had exhausted me, and, although it was contrary to my plans, I laid down in the shade of a great tree to sleep for just a few minutes before continuing my vigil. As it turned out that short nap was what undoubtably saved my life.

"You see, the next thing I remember was being awakened by a ferocious roar, and a terrific rush of scorching wind, the earth shaking terribly beneath me and everywhere the sound of the forest around me being uprooted, trees crashing to the earth by the hundreds, the thousands! The very tree I lay behind was pushed violently backwards, but caught upon ones behind it. I was protected by it, I was saved!"

The man's voice here drops to a near-whisper. "The sight before me was incredible. It was, it was like a vision, you know, of the apocalypse. Of the day of judgment. The sky was a cauldron of fire, the earth itself was set ablaze, the taiga all around, all over, everywhere! knocked down, uprooted, blam! blam! blam! smoke, fire, and astounding destruction. I was struck with terror and awe, and at that moment I realized that my fears had come true; my master had surely been vanquished. His great power, an immovable force of the earth, you could say, had met an irresistible object of the heavens, and there it had ended.

"I was in a state of shock. My head was reeling, my ears ringing from the terrible roar of destruction. The forest below me and, in fact, all around me was so devastated from such an incomprehensible force that I could only sit and stare. I slept little, ate next to nothing, but continued to watch that terrible and yet fascinating spectacle, hoping always that somehow my master would emerge from it. . . .

"Black billows of smoke flooded the sky and fire blazed beneath for several days. Then the wind shifted from the southwest and huge thunderstorms rolled up and quenched the fires, leaving only blackened steaming wasteland before me. And still I sat and watched. Before those awesome forces of nature I felt truly tiny and helpless. And yet . . . I could not help but feel great pride that all this was something that my master Arcady Nabokoff, with my humble assistance, had initiated! Remarkable power!

"I stayed at my perch all those days and nights. Hah! There hardly was a night! The sky remained amazingly bright for many nights afterward. I wondered truly whether my master had in fact altered the heavens and the earth—the actual cycle of day and night itself. Finally, I could rest no longer; I had to find the remains of shaman Nabokoff, or failing that, the infernal device for which he had sacrificed all. My progress was difficult through the tangled and scorched taiga. I traveled for three full days and brilliant nights for perhaps twenty kilometers until I reached the center of the destruction, a sparsely forested area, a large bowl-shaped depression. It was, I believe, a peat bog. But it looked like nothing, like the center of nothing, an area hideously choked by death, by the nothing which is death, the apalling result of the clash of immense powers. . . . And it was there, in the midst of that sea of black and gray ash that I spied it, yes, I spotted the gleam of the brass handle of the accursed machine. It, as my master had hinted, had survived, and he . . . well, I found nothing else there, no body, bones, nothing. I could see nothing else; it was as I might imagine the surface of the moon.

"All I was left with was the sacred cask, the incredible machine which my master had given his life for, so that we all might know more . . ." The man's voice begins rising again in anger, "Except that some of us desire to use it for their own selfish means!"

The Russian is silent for several moments; Captain Jimmy raises his eyebrows at Basil, half-smiling. Ivan Ivanovich begins again, softly: "So I had it, but what did I have? Alone, a mere youth holding the incredible object of shaman Nabokoff's design. And I knew that it had *changed,* it now held *power.* I knew this, you see, because it had lightened, it was almost—buoyant! Before it had been oppressively heavy, and now it was wonderfully light, light with remarkable energy!

"Such power! The sacred device my master had conceived could sweep us across limitless distances, whisk us through the barriers of time, allow us, even, to fly! I only wish he could have seen the fruit of his labors. . . ." The man trembles now as he speaks. "My first use, my first task, you might say, was to get out of that hellish area, out of that place, out of that time! And so I did. There was certainly nothing more for me there. . . . I pushed a lever, the one of the dimension of space, ever so slightly. And then just a *tiny* bit more. I directed myself to the west, actually slightly southwest, for Europe." He sighs. "I had heard about the wonderful cities and civilized people of the west and there I desired to go! And then, I pushed the other lever, the one of the dimension of time!" he whispers hoarsely. "Just a bit. To the future! Oh, I was a foolish boy. But the power I held. The power was intoxicating. . . . And then I *pushed* the final lever, just as my master had instructed me, and held on."

Basil realizes he is leaning forward, straining to hear through the man's thick accent and hushed voice. Even Captain Jimmy across the room seems interested.

"Well," says Ivan Ivanovich, "I ended up in Germany, in the town of Wiesbaden, in the year 1938. It was in a beautiful little town park. It was warm, just after a rain shower, there were puddles in the street, many flowers blooming in the gardens. And I had just *appeared!* Imagine. I had travelled over three thousand miles distance and thirty years time in an instant! Imagine! Wiesbaden in the spring of 1938! And there in that park I met Anna. Anna. A chance meeting at a particular time on a particular day . . . ah me.

"There is no time now to recount to you the depth of joy created by our love—suffice it to say that, the relationship between I, a poor peasant lad from Central Siberia suddenly possessing untold powers, and speaking not a word of German, and she, a fair, fine Jewish girl oblivious with cheer and love to the looming menace of the Nazi atrocity, was quite wonderful. Ah, but what strange differences youthful, wonderous love can overcome. . . .

"But I told her nothing of the sacred cask. It was just as well; the knowledge of such saving power may well have been torture. As of yet, I cannot know. Know this, however, that I used it only

96

enough times to learn to use it properly, and then I used it improperly. *Improperly!*" the man shouts, pounding his fist into his open hand.

"I will tell you. I found inexpensive lodging, you see, in what was a tiny storefront attached to a *Bierstube* on one of the town's main thoroughfares. Ach! Such a place. It was vacant and cheap; I blocked the windows with paper. I served as the janitor for the tavern next door. I assumed it was only temporary until I became fantastically rich through my use of the cask. I never dreamed I would become—enslaved, to the machine for the next thirty years. Of course, of course ... when we are young we are eager, we are carefree, and then ... we make a slip. And that is what I did."

The man pauses here, sighs heavily. "There are, you see, two certain controls on the cask; one is set for travel in time and the other is set for travel in space, distance. I had the cask on the table in front of me and had moved forward the lever for time travel a small amount—I was so excited I was trembling, for I had not attempted to view the future since my original journey. There was more than enough to digest with that small leap, sufficient to understand that shaman Nabokoff was telling the truth—and now I was ready for more! But then as I excitedly, foolishly, stood up with the machine, I dropped it. I let go of it, and as I tried to catch it, I accidentally bumped a lever. And what happened? Poof! It vanished from my sight. Gone! Gone! And there I was ... stuck." The man sighs mightily.

"For how long? Well, it was hard to know with exactitude, the device is controlled by levers—analog calibrations, not digital—interesting, is it not, that the spiritual powers guiding shaman Nabokoff's construction considered time to be a continuous entity, rather than discrete? From this we could perhaps all learn.... But I lose myself in speculation.... From my previous use of the machine, I figured it to be somewhere between twenty-five and thirty years. As it turned out ... such a long, long time to wait.

"Well, in the time that passed in Germany and all of Europe in those years, much happened. Cursed time! That autumn came the *Reichskristallnacht,* a horrible pogram, the beginning of the end. To think! If not for my stupidity I could have escaped with Anna, skirted its terrible, tumultuous crest! If I could have only looked, peeked, behind the curtain, and *seen* the future ... but I could not.

Events passed by us, frightened us, apalled us, tumbled us along like dust before a frightful vicious wind. Times became very difficult for Jews ... that was understood, but who ever could have conceived the inconceivable...?! Anna and her family were sent to Poland, for 'resettlement.' I begged her not to go, to run away with me, but she would not leave her parents—after all they were only going to a camp for a while, *ja?* Who else could have known but I ... and I failed to look when I could! Ah, besides, it was only a matter of time for me anyway. If not military conscription, then the camps ... unfortunately at that time it was a curse to even *look* Jewish, which I did. At least it helped to disguise my Siberian heritage, which was no help to me either. So soon after Anna and her family were shipped out I fled to Switzerland. I determined it would be safer to wait there until the insanity was over and I could be reunited with my precious Anna. I certainly didn't think it would be more than a year or so until ... but of course we all know what happened. I returned to Germany afterwards; Anna and her family did not survive Auschwitz."

The man stops talking and silence surrounds the three of them, along with the sorrows and fears of thirty years past. A breeze kicks up outside, blows dust through the cracks in the window boards. Basil glances over at Kowalske who doesn't return the look, remains staring straight ahead, also avoiding Ivan's tortured stare ... and eventually the man begins to speak again.

"So there was only one hope for me, to return to that tavern in Wiesbaden, to the small storefront attached, and wait. Wait for the cask to reappear! The building had survived the war and a family named Berghoff owned the building at that time. Of course it was in the storefront alongside that I had to keep my vigil, and luck of luck, it was vacant at the time! I had saved some money in Switzerland, working at odd jobs, living like a miser ... not a lot of money, but enough to open a small business in the shop. I did not particularly care what type of business it was, just so I controlled that particular *space,* you see, the particular area where the cask would return. I enjoyed music very much so I started a small record business. In the center of the store where I knew to be the exact space of the cask, I placed a large cabinet which I always kept empty. Nothing could violate that space! And there I waited, making a paltry income, living in a meager room in the back. ...

"All went relatively well—considering that I was sacrificing the best years of my life for such an oddity—until the year 1968, exactly thirty years after my fated arrival in Wiesbaden. At that time—cursed luck!—the Berghoff's spoiled hippie granddaughter expressed an interest in my poor storefront. It seems that she fancied herself a mystic, a–a fortuneteller, if you can believe that! She wanted a small place for her business and her doting grandparents decided that the space they rented to me for my always almost-failing business would be just perfect. They cancelled my lease. Ach! Can you imagine? I was beside myself with grief. I had spent thirty years of my life waiting for that infernal machine, and then, when I knew it would not be much longer, when the time was nearing . . . oh woe! I was beside myself with anticipation, thinking each and every day that perhaps it would be this day, and then . . . well, perhaps tomorrow. Then, then I would be free! Free to go back and forewarn, rescue, my beloved Anna. And then this! I begged, I pleaded, but I could not sway their hardened hearts. Even to her, this Charlotte, their granddaughter, did I go. I told her I was hopelessly attached to that little store, that it had great sentimental value to me, that I was a poor, humble merchant with so little else. . . . Alas, all I could gain with my entreaties was to remain living there and become the unpaid janitor of the little place. Because of my extreme reluctance to leave during the times she was open, I also became sort of an assistant to her, the shuzzly Fraulein. But I knew I was close, I knew it would arrive soon. I prayed that it would be at night, that in the morning when I entered the room, always before her—she kept deplorable hours!—that it would be there.

"Oh, fate was cruel to Ivan Ivanovich. I encouraged her to keep that space free, the area of the machine's return. I even gave her the large wooden cabinet to preserve the area, but she moved it carelessly to the side and placed her table, her idiotic fortune-telling table in that very area! Precisely at that point! I would always move it in cleaning, hoping that she would prefer the new placement, but, stubborn Charlotte (who, ach! had taken to calling herself Madame Carlotta!) would always move it back to the room's center. Oh, did I watch her fortune-telling sessions from the back of the place with terrible fear, always wondering if *this* would be the moment. But I never relented; I kept my terribly taxing vigil. I chewed my nails; I developed an ulcer. But also, within the depths of myself, I gained hope, for Charlotte played a terrible mystic, her predictions if not ludicrous, were banal. She dressed each day in foolish Gypsy garb, keeping ever more irregular hours, and I began to see that she was tiring of it, of the farce. And then one day when my hopes and terrors were each in themselves immense, it happened. It came. It *arrived!* From whatever peculiar limbo held it for all those years, the sacred cask of shaman Nabokoff dropped from mid-air to the center of Madame Carlotta's table!"

Ivan Ivanovich looks around sharply at Captain Jimmy, his eyes scrunched in a sort of satisfied sneer, wipes saliva from the corners of his mouth. Then he turns to Basil and sighs. "As you might expect, it was not an opportune moment. For the first time, perhaps the only time in her entire brief career, Madame Carlotta spoke the truth. Do you remember, Jimmy?"

"I do indeed, Ivan."

"Yes, he was there," Ivan tells Basil, "at that very moment, having his fortune told by Madame Carlotta, the all-knowing."

Kowalske chuckles. "Well, she was right wasn't she?"

"Ach! Right!" the man sputters. "She is looking in her idiotic crystal ball and tells Jimmy here that he is about to receive a gift. A great and wonderful gift—I am still amazed by that, she must have sensed it, it was so—near. But anyway," he sighs, "at that moment *it* appeared, thirty years after I had lost it, before the very eyes, of this *zhlub!*"

"Hey, hey now. It fell right into my hands. I didn't know what it was. In fact, I thought it was some kind of hokey trick. It scared the hell out of me. It sure freaked poor Carlotta, though. Hey Ivan?"

"Yes, it did." He immediately falls silent, along with Kowalske.

Basil, more awake now, detects their somber mood. "Uh, so what happened?"

"She screamed and ran out of the shop," Kowalske tells him, "and into the street, where she was killed by a car, an old Packard, as I remember, something foreign in a foreign land."

"I take no responsibility for that," Ivan loudly protests. "If you want to blame someone, you might as well blame shaman Nabokoff. I begged her to let me have the shop. Begged her."

"Well relax," says Kowalske, "what's done is done."

As if he feels it is up to him to continue the tale, Kowalske begins to speak in Basil's direction. "I was in the army at that time, a Captain, from which derives my nickname, as you might have guessed. Anyway, I was on leave just before returning to the States and a discharge when I wandered into that old resort town as a pure tourist and decided to have my fortune told by a pretty gypsy. And what did I know about Madame Carlotta?

"Anyway, after this thing drops from thin air into my hands, from out of the back room or somewhere this crazed man comes running up to me. Tells me that the sacred cask is his and that I should go now, and thank you, goodbye, and God knows what else. He was practically foaming at the mouth. Of course I didn't have the foggiest what was going on at the time. And I sure as hell wasn't going to give him the box. After all, Madame Carlotta told me I was going to get a gift."

"She was a fraud!" shouts Ivan.

"Maybe not, pal, maybe not at all," says the Captain. Then, turning to Basil again, "So to finish this episode of incredibility, sport, after the commotion with Charlotte's accident is over and I leak out of there with the machine, which nobody seems to have noticed, I find that Ivan here had followed me back to where I'm staying and tells me about what you're hearing right now. I listened to his explanation of how the crazy machine worked—"

"You tricked me!"

"So what. You were dumb enough to ... ah, so anyway, pal, after he shows me how it works I try it, and bye-bye! That's the last old Ivan here ever saw of me." Kowalske breaks into a laugh.

"And you took it! Took it!" Ivan screams. "My Anna bound for the death-camps and my hands tied because of you!"

"That was thirty years before that!" Kowalske shouts back, but then, for the first time Basil has noticed, he appears contrite. Perhaps the man's story has moved him, as it has Basil ... along with everything else that has taken place here. He actually pinches himself to see if he might be dreaming; but he is not.

"Okay, *okay,*" says Captain Jimmy. "I'll return the machine. To you here. After I've gone. I won't need it anymore anyway. In fact I'm damned burned-out on it." And then as an aside to Basil, "Traveling with this crazy thing is a pain in the ass, pal."

"And just where are you going to?" asks Ivan Ivanovich.

"There's a place ..." says Kowalske quietly, "I've found a fine place to go to ... a place, a time ... an *earth* that I can best describe as similar to this one, yet—different."

"How do you mean . . . different?"

"Oh—very. It's . . . it's a world that seems to exist in the past, in a time, a–a dimension, if you will, that seems to be the earth in an arrested stage of development, about one or two hundred years ago in the past, say. But it's not that either, really, it's so strange, it's—"

"You've seen, Jimmy?" asks the Russian. "Far ahead?"

Kowalske looks him right in the eye. "No. Not *far* ahead. I-I couldn't do that. I wanted to, many times, but . . . when it came down to setting the damn lever . . . I just couldn't. I didn't want to know. I always figured I'd get around to it later."

"I understand. I, in the short time I had it, never was able to either. But perhaps this time, perhaps if all else would fail . . ."

"Uh, what," Basil hates to interrupt, but, "what was it you couldn't do?"

They both stare. "Look ahead, pal," says Kowalske. "Into the far future of this place where we live, this planet. We couldn't do it. It might not be so pretty. . . ."

"Oh. I see . . ."

"But this place, Jimmy . . . ?"

"Well, as I say, it's like where we live now, it's definitely planet earth, the same air, plants, trees, but that's about all I can tell you. . . . It's as if the world took a different turn somewhere along the way. It's a totally agrarian society there, no industry, no cars, no guns, no war. It's a version of the world that seems to have missed the industrial revolution. Like ancient Greece or Rome. Yet it's not any of those places; it's more or less a modern society—but without any of the mechanics that we associate with modern times. Or any of the angst. The people I've found there are kind and loving, very peaceful, very non-agressive. . . . It's incredible. It's like— I've found *Brigadoon!*"

"But why go, Jimmy? I am grateful that you will return the sacred—the machine, of course, but why go there, then?"

"Well . . . it's simple, uncomplicated. Life is hard there, but it's honest. Besides, life is hard anywhere. And there the earth is so pure you can breathe the air, drink the water, watch the sun and the moon, feel the changing of the seasons. Man, I should have done this long ago, when I had first gotten this thing.

"I tell you, since I've had the machine, started the Church, and observed how people have lost their minds over simply the, the *promise* of power, nothing more, I've learned a great deal. I've been idolized as the new messiah. I've been worshipped as a kind of god! And I can't say it didn't go to my head. I wanted the adoration. I needed it. I reveled in it. But in the end I discovered that it wasn't exactly right for me. It's funny, but I think all the time after I'd gotten the Church started, I'd been searching for a way out of it, no kidding. A way out of what could have been the most powerful position on earth. Hundreds of people loved me, maybe thousands, millions soon enough, but not for what I was; it was for what I represented to them. Their leader into the New Age. Their guide to salvation. Their guide out of this troubled world. Their guide to the Electronic Trinity. Which I had all along—and never let them in on. Man, now I look back and wonder how I could have done it all." Kowalske slowly shakes his head. "But, but, the machine was just too powerful for them, for really anyone. Even for me. I never could figure out how to deliver it to them, you understand.

"Well, maybe it's all for the best ... now at least I've found a place where I can be happy. Funny how in the end all it comes down to is looking out for number one."

"But why *this* place," Basil asks, "why here, MacArthur?"

Kowalske turns toward him. "Well sport, it seems to be a unique place, there's a strange kind of power here, I think, something maybe related to that Mystery Rock Hill down yonder. I found this house years ago when in a fit of extravagance my parents sent me to a summer camp just about a couple of miles north of here. I went for a hike and ended up at this place—it was practically in the same shape then as it is now. A thunderstorm had come up pretty suddenly and I pulled off a couple of boards and crawled inside. And I fell asleep. Well, I had this terrific dream of a wonderful, peaceful, uncomplicated land—it was absolutely vivid—somewhere that I realized could be gotten to somehow from only here, through this place, this house. Of course I didn't think much of the dream at the time, I was just a kid. But I never forgot it, either. In fact, maybe it did kind of impress me back then; I brought my campmates here and we broke in and smoked some cigarettes or something—kid stuff, you know. And then we stole the MacArthur sign. I just had to have it; I smuggled it all the way back to Bakersfield in the bottom of my camp footlocker. The one thing I was sure of was that someday I would go back.

"Well, then, as you probably know, the Church—the company, actually—really started taking off the past couple of years, and the bigger it got, the less control I had in it. My executives began to do end-runs around me, and if the truth be known, I hardly objected. I was only concerned with my Church-folks and my Sound-Pacs, and besides, I had the machine all the time anyway, even though I hardly ever used it—I was actually too damn busy, not enough time, ha-ha. . . . And it all still seemed like a lark. A very big lark, as it turned out. But I guess in the end, there's no excuse for poor leadership. I was being undermined there, and my workers were being made to look like slave-laborers by the media. They were starting to be called 'Trinnies.' There were rumors that we were putting subliminal messages behind the music on our workers' Sound-Pacs. True or untrue, I don't know . . . but we were starting to look like just another crazy cult, and in retrospect, I guess that's what we had become. . . . My believers were becoming more fanatical than I had ever envisioned, and I realized I was losing control of the whole thing. I was getting tired of dealing with the company on the one hand and the Church on the other. It was really wearing me down. I guess I was just frazzled. And then one night I had a dream, one just like the one I had right here nearly twenty years ago, of that wonderful far-out land. That dream brought me back so much peace and contentment—I could almost taste the fresh air, feel the bright sunshine. I was, I was, being called. I knew it. I dreamed there was an old gray-haired Indian chief telling me that I had to come here. And then I knew it was time to head for MacArthur. My time to return had—"

"Did-did you say an old *Indian* told you to come here?" This jolts Basil. He can't quite place it, but something about that Indian sounds awfully familiar, as though it were part of his dreams too.

"That's right, pal. An old Indian with—get this—blue eyes! I can't tell you why I dreamed *that* though . . . can you tell me?"

"Uh, no, I guess I can't . . . it just seems sort of familiar to me, but I don't know why."

"And so you are going back to this time, this place, Jimmy," asks Ivan Ivanovich, "never to return?"

"You got it, Jack. That's going to be it for me. That's where my happiness lies. I'm sure of it. I don't even know exactly why I came back here now ... probably for a last look at this screwed-up world as I know it ... or maybe you guys just put off some heavy vibes ..." he laughs.

"I never really expected to have an audience for this, but if that's the way it is, so be it. I'd appreciate it, sport, if you wouldn't tell Yates anything about our meeting here—I'd rather just simply disappear forever—but it's up to you, you'd have to do the explaining. I know they've got some heavy life insurance on me they'd hate to have to wait a long time to get their hands on. Not to mention my share of the company itself. At least maybe all those poor people who believed in me and in this," Kowalske looks down at the machine he is cradling, "got something, some hope, if even for a brief time, but I'm sure it really wasn't meant for them. I'm not really sure it was even meant for me, or even you, Ivan. Maybe it should go to the kid here—"

"Captain Jimmy!" Ivan Ivanovich pleads.

"Don't worry Ivan, I'll send it back to you in good shape. I know I won't need it anymore. Well, gents ... To simplicity. To peace. To sweetness!"

Kowalske apparently has already made the settings he wants, for all he does is throw a brass lever atop the machine, his body for an instant grows fuzzy, there is a sharp pop! and he is gone.

10

The Captain's exit from this world affects Basil profoundly. Whether it is the mind-shock of watching a human actually dematerialize before his eyes, or perhaps something that he detects from deep within, a kind of vibrational backwash that accompanies the man's departure and probably accounts for the ozone acridity that fills the small room—whatever it is, it is debilitating, like a sudden fist in the pit of his stomach. Basil lies quietly, tries to relax until the feeling passes, the atmosphere loses its heavy charge. . . . Ivan Ivanovich seems to be affected not at all. Or perhaps in some subtle way he is, sitting in his chair, eyes cast downward, expression inscrutable. . . . After a while Basil rouses, isn't sure if he slept, thinks by the light coming between the window boards it might be dawn. He is terribly thirsty, reaches for one of the Heinies he has brought along with him. The Russian is still sitting in the chair. He appears not to have moved. Basil addresses him. "Uh, say, you thirsty? Wanta beer?"

The man moves slightly, clears his throat. "Yes, that would be nice, I think."

Basil passes him a warm beer, and after popping the flip-top from his and taking several long swallows, attempts conversation.

"Well, it seems you've had an interesting life."

"Bah! A life wasted, spent waiting for something ... something powerful, necessary ... that was lost again as soon as I got it."

"Huh." Basil, in his weary, yet heightened, state, is touched by this, feels moved almost to tears.

"Now Jimmy Kowalske," the man continues through a swallow of beer, "there is a smart boy. Imagine creating an entire religion, a company too, just for the fun of it, he says. Ha! Just to understand what it was he had. That is why he did such."

"To understand what he had?"

"Yes, the sacred cask, lad! The miracle machine! What I am again patiently waiting for!" He sounds upset.

"How does it work, anyway?" Basil asks, as much to change the subject as from any real curiosity.

"Internally, I do not know, exactly. I never did know what was to be the source of its awesome power. I do not believe my master did either, other than that it would *be*. And that, and that," he whispers fiercely through stained teeth, "it would be tremendous!"

"After all these years I scarcely can remember the mechanisms within, other than that as the levers on top are manipulated, shields of various metals and minerals slide one upon the other.... How they interact ... I do not know if my master would have known."

"Huh ..."

For several moments the man is silent, then he smacks his lips and announces, "I will, however, describe the operation of the device to you. If, perhaps, something should happen to me, I want someone else in the world to know...."

The Russian spends perhaps half an hour explaining to Basil what of the machine does what, Basil managing to jot a few notes with a pencil stub and candy bar wrapper he finds in a pocket. The man finishes precisely as a sharp pop fills the room and the machine suddenly, amazingly, *appears* about a foot above the table, and then drops to its surface with a sharp clunk.

"Ah, ah, ah!" Ivan Ivanovich jumps up, knocking over his can of beer. "He kept his promise! He has kept his promise! He sent it back!" Ivan takes the brass handle of the machine greedily and pulls it to his chest, silently embracing the sacred cask as though it were a long-lost child, home, safe in his arms once again.... Then he lowers it to the table-top and carefully sets the levers, humming softly to himself. Basil watches intently, understands that after all these years of waiting the man must know exactly what the settings should be to go back to wherever—and whenever—he wants to be. Finally, Ivan looks up, smiling broadly. Tears are streaming down his cheeks. "You see, I have waited. And now here it is. I am to go back and do what I must—what I can! I have waited so long! And now, goodbye my friend! Farewell!" He pushes a lever, and, poof! he, like Captain Jimmy, suddenly reduces to a soft blur, and then is gone. And Basil once again falters in the unleashed ozone wake.

The passage of time becomes uncertain, ceases to be Basil-linear, cheekbone and eye so close to these rude gray floorboards, the numbness in his body and the electrical atmosphere of this small weird wooden spaceship warping everything into, at times, near-nothingness. . . . Here, hours, days, may pass unnoticed, each fading into the shadow of another . . . the weather outside unknowable, dumb, distant. He hears rain come and go hollowly on the roof, watches the violet glow of sunset paint the walls . . . but there is still this pressurized underwatery ambience, warping to infinity in the unapproachable corners, this silvered impossible space. . . .

Basil awakens, was he asleep? to a somewhat familiar atmospheric ejaculation by now, a sharp pop! He looks up and there in the center of the room is an old gray-haired man, holding *the* machine, braced as if against a stiff wind, and then, as though the wind has suddenly stopped, the man pitches forward and collapses to the floor. He is sweating fiercely, breathing hard. He is, Basil recognizes with a shock, Ivan Ivanovich. But he has aged considerably. He is an old, old man now of perhaps eighty or ninety years. It's frightening. He looks tremendously sad, says nothing, doesn't even glance over at Basil, who tries to rise, but can't, feels terrible, can't find his voice, can't think of anything to say if he could. All he can do is watch as the man slowly manages to stand up, shuffles to the back of the house, and pushes open the door. Basil feels fresh air wash the room. Bright daylight hurts his eyes, startles him. He pulls himself up to the window, watches the man shakily mount his black bicycle, pedal through the weeds to the road and ride off.

Basil finds tears streaming down his cheeks, realizes he is weeping profusely here, body shaking, unable to pull it back together, and isn't really sure why . . . other than, perhaps, the fact that reality, once a steadfast friend, has deserted him. Or at least transformed into something barely recognizable, now an act of faith more than anything else . . . a terribly hard, sad feeling. A cool breeze and almost unbearably bright sunshine streams in through the door. He knows now that it is time to leave, to gather up his gear, follow the old Russian out into the world, begin a new life. It seems there never was that much to the old one anyway.

Basil's journal:

Now that I've had some time to think about it, I've narrowed the whole weird twisted thing that happened back there down to two basic facts, both good and bad. One, I've got the machine now, the crazy sacred cask of Schuman Nabokoff, or whoever. That's the good thing. Carried it out with my own two hands. The bad thing is that I never got a picture of Kowalske to give to Yates, but then I don't really care now, either. The fact that I have the machine makes that, and a whole hell of a lot else very, very unimportant.

Also, Kowalske's Ferrari is gone. When I came out of the house it just wasn't there. I suppose someone must have stolen it when I was so out of it. And I know that I'm not going to report it missing. That's for sure. I just hope Kowalske is happier in the weird place that he went off to. I don't know how I'd ever report that back to Yates. Anyway, what I did was phone his secretary, telling her that I lost Kowalske and I'm off the case for good now and just send me my dough for time spent, what I figure to be $2,000. I think, for my time and trouble, that's pretty fair. I'll just have to wait and see. What I'm going to do right now is write down here how this machine works. Just what Ivan told me. It really is damned strange. I don't think I'd believe it myself if it wasn't sitting right here in front of me. Even still, I don't know if I believe it, it being the actual Electronic Trinity *of Jimmy Kowalske, all in one, a gizmo that actually beats-out time and space, and even the force of gravity. If it really works.*

There are these brass thingamajigs on the top of the box that supposedly control it. One lever swings from far left to far right, over a distance of about six inches across the top of the box. This sets the time dimension. Right is future, left is past. The center

109

indicates the present, or NOW. It stays in the center, and is sitting there right now. To the machine and myself, I guess, it is NOW, which makes sense. It is after all, the telechronos, *right? There is another lever that travels only about four inches and lies vertically on the left side of the machine. This is set to determine how "far," in space, one desires to travel. You face the direction you wish to go. Then there is another lever, a switch, actually, to right of that, with a throw of about two inches that is supposed to finally take care of business. Pushing it up to the middle position causes the machine to take you* wherever *or* whenever *the other gizmos have been set up for, but not into the actual reality of the moment. The machine holds you in what Ivanovich called the "ghost-dimension," some kind of weird nowhere-zone, so that intrepid travellers can view where—or when, they are before appearing there. Then, if all looks cool, another flip all the way forward on the old lever, and shazam. According to Ivan, there you are. Flipping that switch the opposite way will bring you back. So he says.*

So there it is. As for the anti-grav component of Kowalske's "Electronic Trinity," Ivan Ivanovich only told me that it was somehow a part of the other two functions. That's all he said. Also, he warned me that it was a very powerful device, to be used wisely. And carefully. Sounds like the ultimate understatement, hey? Oh yeah, he told me two important things about the machine, too. One, that I should be careful to never let go of the handle when I'm using it. Makes sense. And second, that the thing is very sensitive to the energies generated by the user, and that thoughts are energy, so my thoughts and desires about where and when I want to go influence it greatly. He also said, and it's hard, at this point, to really understand this—that it is, quite simply, the ultimate machine. This I hope to find out.

Midnight. Up on top of Mystery Rock Hill, Basil takes a fitful drag on his Camel, looks down upon the lights of Wasson's Bay, watches a solitary car puddle-jumping through creamy pools of the village's few streetlamps. Not much doing down there. Synandra's house is dark. Eastward the lake is vast and black, the minute red and green lights of a far-away freighter glowing in the night. To the west a gibbous moon slinks into a nacreous cloudbank, and high

110

overhead floats the ice cream cone of Bootes, stars akimbo above the twinkling orange giant, Arcturus.

A trace of a breeze rustles Basil's hair as he sits upon a heart-rock, takes the machine from the brown grocery bag he has carried it up here in, and holds it carefully before him. In the kitchen of his cottage he has preset the brass leverage for a trip backward in time for what he estimates to be about seven years; the space coordinate remains at zero. He wants to check out Mystery Rock Hill and environs at a time in the past, hopefully to find out the secrets—the actual *mysteries* of Mystery Rock Hill, from which Synandra Wasson derives her pride and her powers. The time of seven years is arbitrary; he realizes he may have to travel back hundreds or even thousands of years to discover the actual *origins* of the Mystery Rocks, but that can wait till later, and besides, he has to start somewhere. Seven is his lucky number anyway, and it would also put him back around the time of Synandra's onslaught of puberty—which, it has occurred to him, might be the time a woman would begin to address whatever powers she might one day attend to.... All of this possible if the machine actually works—or if it works right. Yeesh! He cares not to consider the cosmic calamities possible, here at the Moment of Truth, but understands them to be truly awesome. Time is something he has always considered ever-flowing and absolute, certainly nothing to be messed-around with, but then such a feat had never seemed possible before. Before now. Good God, could this thing actually, really work? He saw it, hadn't he? Basil once again goes over in his mind the events as he witnessed them in the old house, decides they had happened, and now really gets worried. This thing is actually going to send him somewhere!

His hand shakes as he stubs out his half-smoked cigarette upon the rocky ground, mouth is dry, too. This is it. Basil stands up, holding the machine's brass handle at chest level, feels the night breeze riffling his hair. He is shivering now, the only sound his heart pounding mightily in his ears. He takes several deep breaths and then gently, cautiously, pushes the significant lever to its center position—which it snaps into, terrifyingly, with a firm click. And nothing happens. Gripping the machine's handle with both hands, Basil feels a wave of disappointment crash over him—oh boy, what a fool! But then, suddenly, an electrical tingle shoots up his arms,

111

his shoulders, followed by another, and then another, the pulses growing rapidly stronger, quickly merging into a terrific rippling force
rushing through him until he is shaking violently, hanging on for
dear life in a vicious windstorm that has come up from nowhere, ob-
scuring everything into shades of swirling gray, of vastness, of nowhere, and then a sense of contraction, a brief jangled brilliance of
blinding colors and then ... and then it suddenly stops.

Whoa-ohhhh. Basil feels like he has just jumped off an amazingly fast roller-coaster ride, the wicked, death-defying Timebender.
Everything is spinning like crazy and his stomach feels as though it
wants to return the spaghetti supper Basil had foolishly filled-up
with before his voyage ... maintain, he thinks ... maintain....
The whirling gradually slows and Basil, clutching the machine's handle
tightly, like the handbag of a little old lady who has just stepped off
the bus in an unfamiliar part of town, looks around. He is apparently
still on the hill, upright, but—hot damn!—it is daylight! He has
made it! He has—no shit—he's done it! He's actually traveled *somewhere,* hopefully about seven years *back in time.* Or at the very
least, night has suddenly become day—*something* has happened—
although things are indeed a bit, uh, strange. The ground, the heart-
rocks, the forest, the very air around him shimmers brightly as if
part of a gigantic mirage. The world is softly vibrating in remarkably strong sunlight, with an oddly elusive quality, as if an ill-timed
eyeblink or shake of the head might shatter it. Occasionally a brilliant rainbow wave, redyellowgreenbluepurple, vibrates sort of, di-
agonally, across the scene like a television disturbance. He feels as
if he is viewing the world as a fragile three-dimensional picture, a
world under glass. He assumes he is in what Ivan Ivanovich described as the "ghost dimension."

Looking downward, Basil sees that his body appears quite solid.
Has the whole world changed and not he? He would have guessed it
would be the other way around. Well, he decides to try movement
in this ghost-world, and takes a tentative step. The sandy sparkling
earth beneath his foot seems to yield slightly; it is kind of spongy.
Basil determines that he feels oddly light and bouncy, as though
gravity had lessened somewhat—of course, the *anti-grav* function!
He takes a few more steps and feels that he could fly! God, yes, if
he would just *push off!* Basil impulsively jumps upwards and—omigod!—he reaches—must be seven or eight feet!—and then suddenly

loses his equilibrium and—oof!—crashes sideways onto the ground, letting go of the machine with one hand, quickly grabbing hold again, whoa-boy, understands that he'd better be careful here, good ol' gravity was still in effect—to what extent he isn't yet sure—and the ground isn't *that* soft.

From his head to his toes, Basil vibrates along with the rest of the ghost-dimension, a state of more or less constant trembling—unsettling, but tolerable. The vibrations seem to emanate from the handle of the machine, and because of that he has the odd perception that he, along with the machine, might actually be *creating* this crazy, glittering world. But the thought is too complex to deal with at the moment; he is lightheaded with excitement. He may have actually reached his destination, a bright day seven years in the past, in say, the month of June. Wow. Well, what now? There isn't much going on up here, and he wonders how to carry on his explorations when he suddenly hears something off to his left. Faint voices and crunching footsteps carry through the ether. Looking around, straining his ears, Basil determines that someone is ascending the northeast side of the hill. Uh-oh. He wonders if he should run or hide, but it is already too late, breaking the demi-horizon of the hill is the craggy countenance of a tall dark Indian and someone else, a skinny dark-haired girl, Synandra! It has to be. Oh man, she looks only about eleven or twelve here, oh man, oh man—is this too much?—he has definitely, actually, really, made it into the past!

Basil backsteps to the edge of the hilltop as they approach, crouching down in a ludicrously futile effort to hide. But it isn't necessary, they don't seem to perceive him, he is apparently transparent, *invisible,* in this ghostland. Oh god, invisible. This realization comes on hard and fast, suddenly, along with everything else, becomes too much to really deal with here, finds himself hunkering down in despair, almost beginning to sob, but manages to get a grip on himself . . . maintain . . . maintain . . . and sniffling slightly, forces himself to step a bit closer to hear what this vaguely familiar Indian and the young Synandra are saying.

"I just can't stay here too long, that's all." Synandra's voice is all little-girl, high-pitched, almost comical. But also somewhat muted, along with all the other sounds of the ghost-dimension, as though coming to Basil secondhand, once removed.

Synandra is wearing shorts, her legs and hips still possessing the boyish angularity of prepubescence, youthful breasts budding beneath a summery blouse. She is standing in the center of the Mystery Rocks, before the stern gray-haired Indian. "See, I-I'm shaking here. It's too much. It's too *strong!*" She suddenly bounds away to the edge of the rocks. She is giggling. "But it's kinda neat, too, the feeling I get, Dr. Bo."

Dr. Bo. Now there's a name. Basil must admit that this is one dude who certainly looks *consequential,* also: ancient. In his chestnut hand he holds what looks to be a slender forked tree branch. "We have already discussed something of the nature of power—in a general way. Today I wish to tell you about the more subtle aspects of the energies that issue from the hill and the peculiar affinity you have for them."

Basil nearly cackles with glee. Great! This is exactly what he wanted to hear! He has to believe now what Ivan had said about the machine being sensitive . . . it's perfect! But, uh-oh. The doctor suddenly shifts his keen eyes around as though looking for something— or someone? At one point he stares directly at Basil—yeesh! But the focus of his eyes is through him, Basil thinks, hopes . . . beyond. Yeah, Basil is invisible! What a fantastic machine!

The doctor is speaking now in a lowered voice, difficult to hear in the ghost-dimension, so emboldened Basil edges closer, in time to hear him explaining to Synandra that Mystery Rock Hill might well be thought of as a geographic representation of earthly life itself, understandable and beneficial to a sensitive person attuned to its subtle powers. And that person is she, the doctor gravely tells her, handing her the forked branch and adding that today she is going to attempt the ancient art of dowsing.

He instructs her to hold the stick at waist level, a hand on each fork, and asks her to attempt to seek out the faint, yet sublime, telltale vibrations that indicate flowing water. He motions her to begin walking around the mound. Synandra does as he says, but none too seriously, giggling and prancing until the doctor frowns and directs her to walk to the center of the mound, inside the rocky heart. She quickly becomes serious, as the branch immediately begins to visibly twitch downward. Synandra looks back at the doctor, beaming triumphantly. He motions her forward still to the precise center of the mound, and after two or more steps the stick suddenly bends downward with such force that it actually twists free from her hands and embeds its point in the earth! All of them, Synandra, the ghost-Basil, and even Dr. Bo, stare in shock at the quivering branch.

"Gosh, I couldn't hold on!"

"There is a great amount of flowing water there—and power," says the doctor solemnly. "And you are a very good dowser," he smiles, "a natural." He explains that the hill is actually the cap of a huge aquifer that starts some three or four hundred feet below ground level. The water pushes upwards in an artesian flow into the center of the mound until it finds a stratum of porous rock where it splits into four approximately equal flows which channel down and out-wards, about four to six feet below the hill's surface. The Indian walks over and retrieves the embedded dowsing branch and hands it back to Synandra. He tells her now to take it again and walk slowly around the perimeter of the hill. She does so, slowly at first, then increasing her pace as she quickly discovers by less dramatic, though profoundly insistent dips of the stick, that there are indeed four such flows, each running underground precisely in one of the four cardinal directions: north, south, east, and west.

"You see," says Dr. Bo, smiling softly, "that is why there is such power here. The alignment is perfect. I find it hard to imagine that one would ever encounter another formation as beautifully appointed as this. Here the great mother earth expresses herself most exquisitely. East is the direction of the rising sun, of beginnings, light, life, vitality, the purest ideas. South is the direction of heat, dispersal, passion, the true heart. North is representative of cold, the intellect, gatherings, the very distant. The West is the land of the setting sun, of endings, darkness, mystery, the unknowable. The cosmos is mapped by these directions; from them a man—or woman—can determine their destination, if not immediately, then ultimately.

"Now this," he continues, "is your hill—in a most pragmatic sense. It could, of course, be anyone's, but through the truly unfathomable inner workings of the universe, your, ah, being, is in perfect harmony with these energies. It is also very curious to note how such affinities have expressed themselves upon the surface of your life: your inherent predilection for hearts, and the heart-shaped formation here on top of the hill. Some would call it coincidence, but of course we know better; there is no such thing." The doctor then taps a boulder with a moccasined foot, "How or when these rocks were originally placed here, I do not know. I suspect that a seer

115

many centuries ago recognized the power here and decided to immortalize the hill with this monument. Or perhaps it was fashioned by great power, in a very short time, in an instant. It really is not important in the end, to us now. All that matters is this, the essence. The heart shape is a universal one; it is most powerful, even in ancient glyphs that symbol is representative of love and the feminine life force. Perhaps long ago there was a girl too, one like you. . . ."

Dr. Bo has Synandra sit on one of the boulders next to him, tells her that all of the universe is simply energy, the earth, the sky, the beings that inhabit them, and all are inextricably interrelated. There are channels in the earth through which these currents of energy flow; in Britain they are called leys, the Chinese know them as *feng-shui,* or wind and water currents, and the practical Americans, of course, have no name for them because they do not know they exist. But they certainly do exist, and Mystery Rock Hill here is a conjunction of many flows, a veritable plexus of energy lines, manifested in the physical world by the tump of the hill and the miraculous flowing waters beneath it.

Also—and this is most important, the doctor tells her—and most miraculous—it seems that each of the four underground streams has generated an energized node some distance out from the base of the hill, detectable only via the uniquely calibrated vision of seers—or the peculiar sensitivities of a certain girl. Holding the dowsing rod like a conductor's baton, the doctor points to a small clump of cedars growing due north of the hill. Inside them, he says, is an energy center that focuses directly upon the intellect. "That spot is an optimal place for you to solve problems and generate ideas. I suppose you might have already encountered it in your ramblings through these woods. . . ."

Yes, she had. In fact, she knew well the limestone boulder there with the garish countenance—she called it her "thinking rock"—and found, she didn't know why, it a good place for concentrating on problems, for doing after-school homework. It always seemed quite special; in the winter it was always surprisingly warmer than the surrounding air, and in summer, always maintained an aura of coolness. She is now not too astonished to learn that it was *meant* to be that way. . . .

Dr. Bo then points to the east at a huge Bur oak tree, a giant in the woods, that sprawls between the hill and the shoreline road,

116

farther out. He says that it grows over the energy center that most directly affects Synandra's life force. And she immediately recognizes the ferny, mossy area beneath the great tree as a favorite place to play, sit, relax, simply *be,* in the wonderful Wasson woods, where she always felt peaceful and happy, revitalized maybe, though again, she had never really considered its meaning. He also mentions to her the essentials of a story that she had heard many times before, about a time during the winter of her second year, when she, a normally robustly healthy toddler had been stricken with pneumonia, a high temperature, and hovered frightfully near death. Her young parents and grandfather were determined to take her to the hospital in Sturgeon Bay, a good twenty miles away when, catastrophe! from the gray clouds of despair a blizzard suddenly came up, immediately ending any thoughts of travel, and yet—more of the supernatural—out of it also appeared, calmly rapping at their front door, the Indian doctor with the name of Bo, at the time a considered, yet still mysterious, new friend of the Wassons. He came bearing hope, in the form of a strange suggestion: take the sick child outside in the storm, to the foot of the huge old oak tree in woods surrounding the hill. While the Wassons debated the merits of this apparent idiocy, the doctor calmly examined the girl, administered what he could of an herbal tonic, and then flatly stated that she was beyond hope. This was the only way. Synandra's grandfather was the first to agree, then swayed the others—this Indian man probably knew a damn-sight more about curing than any doctor he had ever known ... and besides, what other hope had they? So soon a troupe of four and the bundled girl plodded through the driving snowstorm for the significant tree. The men cut a lean-to while her mother held her daughter, shivered and prayed, and then the sick child was placed on the spot the doctor indicated ... and then, after several long minutes, the miraculous occurred. She roused slightly, opened her eyes and smiled, just enough to let everyone know that this was right, she would be better, *she knew.* They huddled around her in the swirling storm for an hour more until her fever broke, her color returned, and the relieved Wassons understood that they had found a real man of medicine. A true friend.

"Go there," the doctor tells her, "when you feel ill or simply wish to lift your spirit. The power there is very helpful." He adds that the well for the Wasson house had been dug over a century

117

ago, quite unknowingly, into a branch of that flowage. The well was only ten feet deep and never went dry, even in times of severest drought. "That water has nourished your family for over a hundred years," Dr. Bo tells her, "and hopefully it will continue to nourish you."

Now the doctor directs her attention to the south at an open area to the right of a cluster of white birches. Down there grows a bed of wild roses in the center of which is an open grassy tump. Which Basil immediately recognizes as the place devious Synandra had brought him to, where she had played that dirty, rotten, low-down trick. . . .

"That spot," says the doctor, "is the center affecting your passions, your, ah, sexual energies." He loudly clears his throat. "It is nothing to be ashamed of; it is as natural as flowers blooming and going to seed. . . . The power, I suspect, would tend to be latent until a certain age and cycle of the moon. It makes no difference to me whether or not you have already discovered its power. If you haven't yet, you soon will. . . ."

Synandra is blushing terribly, Basil sees it as quite a rosy glow in the ghost-dimension, and the doc himself even turns his penetrating gaze away from her. . . .

Trust him as she may, the young Synandra could never tell the good medicine man about the time a month or so ago, when spring had warmed unnaturally early, and she had awakened one Saturday morning—or at least she thought she was awake—to the sound of a trumpet playing somewhere outside, a passage from "An American in Paris," a piece her grampa had played on the hi-fi the evening before. She had gone to the bedroom window and saw standing atop the hill, in the incredibly bright morning sunlight, a beautiful curly-blonde youth, bare-chested, with a cloud-white mantle swathing his loins. He was playing a shining golden trumpet, spilling Gershwin's sweet notes to the sun. Synandra was thrilled, imagining his clarion song was somehow for her . . . and then . . . and then she awoke for real, humming the tune to herself as she brushed her hair with more concentration than usual, then donned a light cotton dress in lieu of her customary bluejeans—it was spring!—and ran outside, barefoot through the trees overloaded with buds and warmth and sunshine.

She marveled that fine morning how everything seemed so *alive* after winter's long siege, the woods peppered with thousands of yellow and purple violets, trilliums, hepaticas, and sunshine freight trains of marsh marigolds down by a little rainwater brook. Playfully, she stalked a beautiful brown and orange butterfly, newly arrived into the bright spring world. It flitted from bud to leaf to flower and finally into a patch of wild rosebushes that were still a good month away from blossoming. Synandra followed and watched as the iridescent creature fluttered in loops and spirals above the thorny shrubs for many minutes, seemingly neglecting its reproductive duties. Thinking its antics odd, she stepped into a grassy circle almost totally enclosed by the bushes, and as she did so, the errant lepidopteran, as though losing an updraft, dove and air-danced away. She was about to follow when suddenly there was the strangest sensation . . . as if Pan himself rose up under her breeze-billowed dress, caressed her soft thighs, blew gently on her blushing downy bottom, and whispered, *get to know me.* . . . And so she did, entering quasi-consciousness for the first time, initiating the first of many scintillating tete-a-tete's with the shaggy old fellow upon this spot, her body no longer her own, and yet totally her own, exquisitely abandoned to the tune of the earth itself in this wonderful pulsing magical arena, sun-red hearts exploding with a hitherto undreamed-of violence behind her twittering eyelids . . . no, she couldn't bring herself to tell him *that*.

But Dr. Bo has already begun to describe to her the fourth center, aligned to the west, the land of the sunset. It is an area of what might be called negative vibrations, nothing sinister or evil, but a spot whose power was opposite to the positive vibrations of the others, a necessary balance in life and of energies. "The structure of power here would be incomplete without it," the doctor tells her. "With it the energies of the hill are in perfect equilibrium."

He goes on to say that the center to the west is overgrown with brambles, making it, if not quite difficult to find, nearly inaccessible. Synandra says that she has never encountered or even suspected the existence of the center, but Dr. Bo tells her that at the age of three, after she had impetuously gobbled a mouthful of red-domed fly agaric mushrooms and then wandered off, it was in that spot that her frantic grandfather had found her, tangled in blackcap thorns, unconscious. And, yes, she did remember that incident, or oft-told-tales of it that had become ersatz memories—what a little dickens she had been! Dr. Bo had handily shown up with an emetic that time too—but she didn't remember being at that particular spot. Now she understood. . . .

Basil has been taking all this in like a great evil sponge; it is so fantastic, it is exactly what he had hoped to find out. The medicine man and Synandra continue discussing power centers but invisible Basil isn't listening anymore; he is coming down with a bad case of the ghost-dimensional jitters.

Though he finds he can shift the machine from hand to hand, they, along with his wrists, arms, and shoulders, have begun to sorely ache. The steady electrical vibrations coursing through his body are making him sick to his stomach, and the constant shimmering that obsesses this crazy land is starting to give him a headache. It is obviously time to either *materialize* into the reality of this world of seven years past, or to return. He certainly isn't about to pop in here, so ... his finger tentatively touches the brass lever that will (hopefully) take him back, but he suddenly becomes stricken with ghost-dimensional madness; he can't quite bring himself to leave this incredible colorful world. Everything here is so-so fantastic! Like the sky, for instance; there it is, yet it looks so *unreal,* like a pure blue fabric stretched above him, billowy clouds printed on in white fluff-ink ... complete with three great big birds up there, eagles, he thinks, white head and tail, circling overhead, soaring perhaps on the vortical power currents of Mystery Rock Hill. He determines to do just a *little more*, really wring this baby out. Why not? And he gives just a teeny, tiny nudge to the time-set lever, leaving the other, of course, in ghost-dimension status—and zzzippp! The jolt is not nearly as bad—nor as long—as the first time, but the world does a sort of gigantic *blink*, Synandra and the doctor vanish like a flipped photograph, and the day changes from sun and color to dismal gray. It is raining. The suddenly slate skies are depressing and he can feel the raindrops as tiny zinging shocks that seem to go through his phantom body—a weird, vaguely unpleasant feeling. Undaunted, he nudges the time-set a hair more, and ... another jolt, another rainy day, or perhaps even the same one—Ivan told him that the thing was quite finely calibrated—for it is almost dark now, the skies are deep purple and gray of last light, and again the tingling raindrop sensation ... aargh! He has to get out of that rain! Like the petulant last act of a dying emperor, he taps the time-set ever-further. At last. Blue skies again; the hilltop, surrounding forest, and lake beyond bright with chunky golden sunshine that he bets never danced and wavered like *this* on any tourist's eager retina or camera film. Well, he's out of that goddamned rain anyway, maybe he should go back now, the strain really getting to him ... but he detects some fleeting sounds, voices distant and tinny carried from the south, it seems, the high-pitched chatter of young girls. Hmmm. Quite machine-mad by now, Basil goes where his insanity takes him, bouncing down the side of the mound and through the birches to the, oh boy, the rosebushes, in which standing waist-deep are two girls, Synandra, adorably bare-breasted, though his view of her is mostly blocked by, unmistakably, the young Tiffany, gangly and beautiful and yet clothed, her golden hair even longer than she wore it now.

Maybe he has become, ah, slightly schizophrenic in this ghost-dimension, but his suddenly heightened sensitivity detects strong energies bouncing between them, is certain he can actually see a faint rubicund glow surrounding the two. What does this mean? Well, it looks to be ... interesting, as the voracious voyeur approaches ever-closer, trying to make out snatches of their giggled conversation through the ether.

"Your grampa told me you were out here somewhere, but ... gosh, I didn't think ..."

"So just come over here, huh."

"Okay, okay, but this is so dumb ..."

"No it's not ... just ... now ... "

"Gee ... I don't know, but ... gee, it—is, uh, that why you've got all your clothes off?"

"Uh-huh ... c'mere, now ... right here ... there ... wha'dya think?"

"Oh ... wow ... gosh, well, it sure is weird—"

Boyoboy, Basil figures to get much closer now, Mystery Rock Hill here is about to spill its watery *guts* of secrets ... but suddenly the sky seems to darken briefly as a black shadowy something passes fast and low over Basil's head. What was that? He looks up in time to spot—my God!—the biggest fucking bird he's *ever* seen swoop away, and then, holy shit! here comes another! a–a monster eagle or harpy or whatever swooping down—right for him! Agghhh! Basil ducks, hits the ground. Uh-ohhhh, here comes another, again from the south, they seem to be driving him away from the girls but, hey, that's okay, time to go anyway, hey, hey! he ducks again, can feel the evil needle-talons just missing the nape of his poor neck....
And then he is bounding back towards the hill for dear life, it's

okay, he's leaving, he's leaving ... trying to watch out for the crazy birds, trying to take a good look at the bouncing machine-top to hit the saving return lever ... then suddenly finds that he has run, bounced, flown? back to the top of the hill somehow, not exactly a good place to be during a bird attack, but a familiar reference point, essential for the harried time-traveler-on-the-go ... sneaks a peek skyward, spots three of the evil fowl not far overhead, starting downward, looks like another fearsome death-run, uh-oh, here they come!!! Basil unlocks his white-knuckled grip on the machine long enough to stab the return lever, hears girlish laughter to the south rise and fall, and holds on as that wild windstorm comes up again and sweeps him awaaay....

Ohhhhhhh-agggggghhhhhhh ... the agonies of time-travel. Basil lies like a crumpled dishrag on the moonlit mound, retching the final acidic traces of vile orange spaghetti-and-enzyme broth from his twisted stomach. Slowly, slowly, he releases his death-grip on the machine. His hands and arms are numb, his body aching in a thousand places, but-but he is back! Back to the real world, silent, steady, cool ... and solid. He turns his throbbing head up toward the moon, filtered by clouds, but the same moon, still the same rounded gibbous, same angle in the sky.... Tears rise joyfully in his eyes, run down his cheeks into the acrid puddle beneath. He is back.

11

It has taken Basil a whole day to recover from the effects of time travel. Not only from the obviously debilitating physical effects of the machine, but also the mental confusion, the incredible sensation of the ghost-dimension, of invisibility, of the ability, perhaps, to fly! yes, along with the understanding that reality, good old reality, which he thought he knew and trusted, might be, perhaps, *problematic?* Yes, all this and the awesome realization of *what he has done* is what Basil dutifully records in his journal this late evening at the kitchen table in his little cottage, along with a careful recollection of the secrets of Mystery Rock Hill. It seems he can't write fast enough; this is knowledge of the first degree. All he has to do is think of a way to use it in a manner that will be most dazzling—shocking, actually, the effect he most desires here—to that smug witch-girl, Synandra Wasson. That, he decides, is his final mission before blowing this hick burg for whatever wealth and fame awaits him and the magnificent machine.

There is a sudden rapping upon the screen door. He gasps—the machine is sitting in the middle of the table.

"Bazz-il it's me, Tiffany."

"Just a min-ute." Oh, Jesus. He quickly opens a cabinet underneath the kitchen counter and stashes the machine and his journal inside.

Tiffany is on her way back from a late date, apparently on foot. She is cheerfully swinging a magnum of champagne like a cheer-leader's megaphone, and she is somewhat tipsy.

"Just thought I'd stop in here and see how Mr. Detective is get-ting along. Did you ever catch the Captain?"

Basil lights up a Camel. "Er, no, I guess he got away from me. I'm sure I'll never be able to find him now. So, I'm off the case now, for good. I'll probably be leaving town soon . . ."

"Noooo . . ." coos Tiffany, wrinkling her nose in comic sadness. "You can't leave now. What about Synandra?"

"What about her?"

"Well, I thought that you two . . . I mean I thought that you and she would . . ."

"Would what?"

"Look, be a dear and get us a couple of glasses so we can have a proper drink here, okay?"

Basil fetches two water glasses—the fanciest glassware Mrs. Frost has seen fit to furnish the cottage with—and Tiffany pours cham-pagne for two. She takes a gulp and starts giggling, "Yes, I felt that you two might actually get along, despite your—stormy, past en-counter."

"Are you kidding? After what she did? No fucking way. She'd have to come over here, get down on her hands and knees and beg me for—"

"Oh, dream on, Monsieur Poirot. She's just as stubborn as you are. But, you know," she says, squinting seriously at him across the table, resting her chin on her hand, "I am kind of worried for her lately. I mean, now that her grampa's gone she could use someone like you around here. To help her. Being a detective and all . . . heck, the ol' Peeper wouldn't let her down, would he?"

Basil takes a drag on his cigarette, exhales slowly, thoughtfully. "What do you mean? What kind of help?" The idea of Synandra in need of help is immediately intriguing.

"Well . . ." Tiffany waves away the smoke cloud, sploshes more champagne into their glasses, "she's got a big problem with this pain-in-the-neck college professor. His name is Clyde Mortell, Dr. Clyde Mortell. He's an archaeologist, also an obnoxious swine, and he's decided that he's in love with Mystery Rock Hill, Synandra's hill, and that he has to investigate it and understand all its mysterious, uh, mysteries."

"Oh really," says Basil coolly, closely inspecting his cigarette, "and what's so wrong with that?"

"I mean, he *really* wants to investigate it, like make it his major study: probe it, dig into it, *ex*cavate it! You know . . . archaeologically. He's obsessed! Syndy's convinced he'll ruin the the whole site, and she's right. He will. He'll ruin it completely. Forever. For her. For everyone. He's convinced that the whole hill is just a great big Indian burial mound, chock-full of bones and pottery and arrowheads and whatever—"

"Isn't it?"

"No, of course not. It's—" Tiffany stops suddenly, bites her lip.

"It's what?" pounces sneaky Basil.

"Nothing. It's—I can't say."

"Why not? What can't you say?"

"Nothing. Look, just trust me."

"Okay." Basil eases off smugly, feels powerful with his knowledge and the incredible machine, just hidden out of sight; he knows anyway—why be a total jerk? "So what's she so worried about? It's her property, isn't it?"

"It is, but the state can legally authorize the excavation if they feel that it will, 'significantly enhance the body of knowledge of the early history of Wisconsin,' or some such rot. Anyway, they're having a hearing about it, people from the state and the university, in a few days, down in Milwaukee. Synandra's going to be there, to protest it, of course."

"Do you think she has a chance?"

"I doubt it. This year Mortell has managed to get a big grant from the National Science Foundation to make the dig, around fifty thousand dollars, I guess, so that's like a stamp of approval in itself. Poor Syndy, all she's going to do is look unreasonable."

Basil sighs a smoky speculative cloud, wonders why these women around here don't understand anything. Synandra pulls an extremely dirty trick on him, almost kills him—really, and now he's supposed to be sorry for her? Well, he manages to get the approximate time and place of Synandra's Milwaukee meeting—he's planning on being a real bastard here—before Tiffany begs a ride home on his motorbike while actually having the nerve to refuse his offer of breakfast tomorrow and, uh, bed tonight. Says she has an early rehearsal *manana*. Well, he's *such* a sucker for a pretty girl, and, she left the rest of the champagne.

*   *   *

Stinky Harrison. Old Stink. Basil's best buddy in the whole world and he doesn't see him much at all anymore. It's a shame that when he has to see him now it's to ask a big favor, but maybe that's what friends are for. Stinky Harrison, now quite the successful southern California businessman, who even as he aged remained cherub-faced, diminutive, the most serious sign of the years passing being thinner hair and progressively thicker eyeglasses, making him, in terms of prosperity and post-show recognizability, the most- and least-changed member of the original cast. But of all the actors that *Those Doggone Dawsons* spelled the kiss of death for in the biz, Stinky Harrison was probably the most tragic of the lot.

But then no one ever knew that the name would stick as indelibly as it did. It had nothing whatever to do with actual odor, being—as Basil vaguely recalled—a conjuration of the show's creator and early scriptwriter, the zany and brilliant, and also terribly troubled, Cash Cahill, before his well-publicized suicide. But the malaromatic connotation certainly, unpleasantly ... lingered, his actual name being Henry Harrison, but during the run of the show no one, or almost no one on the set, ever called him anything but Stinky, at first in jest, but then as a sort of common-law name, with the cloying encouragement of his parents, both pitiable alcoholics, just showed how anyone would do anything for money and some sort of weird fame out there in camera-land, eventually going through *all* his money, even cashed the insurance policies, father dead last Basil heard, mother pretty sick now in a private hospital somewhere out in L.A. . . . Still Stinky dutifully tends for her, a story in itself how he struggled, endured the awful name to build up his business to make the seemingly endless amount of cash it took to pay the bills, long gloomy itemized invoices ... Basil had seen them. There wasn't anyone who loved his mother more than Stinky, and after the way she had exploited him. . . . Basil always finds it a little hard to comprehend, still has to come to terms with his own folks retired now very comfortably and remotely in Palm Springs . . . yeah, whenever he thinks *he* had it bad, parentally pushed into being America's Peeper, all he has to do is remember his big-hearted pal and his always-smiling (always half-loaded) parents who pressed him into the service of millions of TV-watching tykes nationwide as that big stinkeroo, the Peeper's lovable little buffoon buddy.

There was only one person who would call him Henry—never, ever Stinky—when they weren't filming, and that was Jack Dougherty, who played Pop Dawson. Basil can still hear his strident, tobacco-enriched voice, "Hen-ry," which he thought at the time a joking formality, only later understanding that the old man was showing the earnest ten-year-old the only real respect from anyone on the set he was ever to receive.

The business Stinky had built up in his post-series years is now called Harrison Printing, Inc., a string of rapid-print stores, and several larger publishing operations, including the flagship Harrison Press, all in the Los Angeles area. But in its first struggling years as a tiny photocopy/offset press shop hugging the UCLA campus the shoestring business had to trade on the dreadful Name: Stinky's Quick Prints. It was also quite a success, students always needing cheap copies, and then there being the opportunity to meet old Stinky himself, and sometimes even the Peeper, for Basil at the time dabbled in studies and coeds at UCLA, his small estate a fortune compared to Stinky's near-pennilessness, aggravated as it was with the care of impoverished sick parents. Basil would visit the shop often, to cut class, help with the work, lend money or food, whatever he could.

Now it is time for a visit, for there is something he urgently needs printed and Stinky is just the guy, actually the only guy, who can do it for him. The trip is to be made with the incredible machine, why not? it's a good chance to really wring out the distance-traveling capability of the beast . . . and besides, he can't see blowing all his cash on an airline ticket for simple revenge, even revenge as satisfying as this fiendish little caper is going to yield. . . . So Basil stands unsteadily in the small cottage kitchen, a couple of beers under the belt for courage and—he thinks—stability, and checks his settings. He has levered the distance more or less for Los Angeles, but it's almost a joke here, who knows? There are fine lines

127

etched into the brass dial, but there are no numerals, no way to tell how far he might actually "go." There is, after all, an ocean out there into which he might possibly overshoot.... But blithe Basil worries not, feels that odd sense of power he receives when in contact with the amazing machine, plus, a couple of beers don't really hurt ... providing a sense of confidence as much as anything else, that he can do no wrong. Same with the time coordinate. He has set it for what he guesses to be about a dozen or so years in the past, or about the time of the filming of the show.... Yes, sentimentality, that warm and fuzzy beast, has crept up on him here while thinking about his old buddy and the rest of the cast ... and as long as he's going to be in the neighborhood, in terms of, uh, space, and now that there is a way of fixing the heretofore Unattainable Coordinate—why not drop in for a ghostly little visit, hey? So here goes. He is really anxious, he realizes, to see his old pal Stinky Harrison again, chuckles to himself as he throws the essential brass lever, hears in his mind's-ear Pop Dawson's voice rasping, "Peee-per," once again, and the vicious wind from nowhere comes up and he is taken with it.

It seems like a long, or at least, longer, time than he remembers from before that the ruthless buffeting persists, as though the two thousand odd miles it is to Los Angeles might take longer to "travel" (yes, and it is also odd how quotation marks have begun, more often lately, to bracket certain of his perceptions ...) from Wasson's Bay, Wisconsin, than it did to skip back seven years in time ... but this thought is really all there is room for within the terrifying swirling tornado-wind that has taken him up ala Dorothy and dropped him off here, or, there, or, uh, wherever.... Because it is definitely not Los Angeles in which he finds himself, nor Kansas, either. In fact, it takes him several long moments to realize this, but with a heart-stopping gasp of suffocating gray breath he knows, in a sense, where he is.... It seems impossible, but as defined by the gossamer graininess of the ghost-dimension he seems to be, well, actually *within* the stark black and white TV confines of a *Those Doggone Dawsons* program, not a spacetime leap back to the Hollywood soundstage of more than a decade past, but, somehow ending up *within the actual program,* as if it is itself a very definite, very tangible monocolor subset of reality. Too, too freaking much! Basil, still reeling from the machine's terrific kick, is beyond himself with amazement. He clutches the brass handle tightly; he knows it is his last precious link with apparent reality because—what in God's name is this? He keeps turning around in the familiar Dawson living room set, subtly vibrating now in silvery shades of gray, looking frantically for cameras, lights, other cast and crew, the rest of the cavernous soundstage. But it is not there, only the other half of the set, with the front door, windows, curtains, same occasional table and lamp he remembers, because it appears to be an actual contiguous room, *as if it had always been one.* He had never seen the sets together before, funny how small everything looks now . . . with an actual honest-to-God ceiling over the whole thing! Yes, he is actually *within* the program, which is no longer itself even a program but something that might even be *real* . . . yet he recognizes the story line immediately: it is the one in which the Dawsons host a formal dinner party for Pop's cranky boss and friends, except that goofy Pop has somehow managed to enclose within el bosso's invitation a card from a previous affair proclaiming *masquerade* . . . and guess who decides to come as a leopard-skinned caveman, and to bring along his buddies, the mayor of Mapleton and snooty wife, Marc Antony and Cleopatra, no less, one of the early, wacky lighthearted shows.... And true to ghost-dimension dogma, Basil seems to be quite invisible here, scrunching back into a corner of the room, real tears coming to his eyes here as he sees his old TV family— almost a real family, in a terrifically heart-wrenching sense—moving about in this strange, yet wholly familiar interior, reciting the old lines . . . and then he gets a great big lump in his throat as in walks himself, the Peeper, and his little buddy, Stinky. They are making for the kitchen, beginning their customary whine for milk and cookies, prior to their sizing up the situation as usual.

Although he has seen the shows rerun many times in the past, knows all of them, this one too, very well, he knows that there is something incredibly wrong being here, inside of something that shouldn't really even exist . . . but it is the crazy machine that has somehow brought this to life—or whatever. The prospect of materializing here is intriguing, but, of course, totally out of the question. He understands that he is a kind of humble explorer here, and if he actually *could* surface in this odd reality, there is the possibility that he might get sort of stuck here, because *this* really isn't anywhere, is it? and, and what would happen to his gray younger self out there were he to—? No, no, he is a stranger in a very strange land now, which carries with it the sadness of old friends from far away and all the oppressiveness of his black and white dreams. . . . But still, this marvelous enormous apparition is not to be denied. His interest focuses upon the windows and the door of this set, or actually, room. He can see gray light out there through the chenille curtains, and he wonders, *what is outside?* A bit of ghost-dimensional madness overtakes him here as he walks over to the door, and tries to grasp the heavy steel-gray doorknob—remembers it from long ago as deep bronze—and finds he can't do it! His hand actually *passes through* its oddly fragile surface with a tingling jolt, as though the surfaces here, though opaque, are as unreal as anything else here, and this seems to snap something inside of him—reality be damned!— he rushes blindly forward, feels a thoroughly chilling body rush, brief peripheral blackness, and pushes, yes, right *through* the door into brilliant gray daylight.

Oh wow. There *is* a whole outside world here! He finds himself out on a street that he immediately recognizes as the one they used for exterior shots on the show, turns around, and he finds the familiar facade of the Dawson house, just like all America saw it every week at the beginning of the program. Jesus, it is hard to believe that right now, inside that house, a pseudo-family of ghostly actors is going through its inane paces. . . . Of course, all of this is pretty hard to take, Basil considers as he wanders along the gleaming gray-white sidewalk. Good thing he has no tendencies toward madness, as this would surely put him over the edge. But, heh-heh, that's nothing to be delving into now, is it? . . .

He hears something up the street, the soft purring of an automobile engine in the ghost-dimensional distance . . . and here comes a gray-white car down the street, a sort of scaled–down Cadillac convertible, and he is interested in who, or what, might be inside of it . . . turns out to be more *what,* a party of small dwarf-like beings, the men with-with tiny sunglasses and shirts open down to the navel and supremely fine gold chains strung over hairy little chests, the women in tight lame gowns and blonde wigs looking like miniature Marilyn Monroe's, braceleted wrists holding champagne glasses, smoking cigarettes in slender black holders . . . Hollywood gnomes. Jesus, it looks like they are also passing a joint amongst them. They all smile and wave to him as they glide by, and one of them, cackling wildly,

130

heaves out what looks to be a–a newspaper . . . splats neatly at his feet—it's an L.A. *Tabloid*—and there's a headline in letters six inches high that makes his head reel: KENNEDY ASSASSINATED. Of course the date is *that day,* November 23, 1963, the beginning of the great American odyssey into truly Modern Times and the end of so much for young Basil, the run of the show, pampered stardom, childhood itself . . . and he figures that it is time to go. It's bad enough that he has to be in this monochrome weirdland, and that the creatures inhabiting it are, uh, really weird—he probably looks pretty strange to them, too—but when they start *mocking* him like this, that's just damn well enough. You bet. Onward to Stinky's. He slides the "time" lever dead upright, to the present, he ventures, and holds on tight—

And he is presently flashed back into the real world, where there is an abundance of wonderful color—at least it looks real, as much as the ghost-dimension parody allows. He recognizes it as the street in front of Stinky's biggest operation, Harrison Press, on an honest-to-God busy street in L.A. All right! Wonderful how the machine seems to know just where, exactly, he wants to go. Yes, he is coming to realize that the machine actually seems to be able to *tap-in,* sort of, to his thoughts, and, even a bit more than that, it seems to be able to go *beyond his consciousness,* yes, actually retrieving its multi-dimensional coordinates from somewhere behind that thought-curtain, from something purer than thought itself, from, say, *central desire?* It is incredible enough to plot those four central coordinates: x, y, z, and the essential t, but to *add-on* a fifth, and maybe a sixth, and perhaps even more, it's got to be what happened there before in that strange gray TV-land, had to be. . . . But, well, the crazy vibrations are getting to him again, and it is now it is time to, ahem, materialize. Forget the theories, Basil loves the fact that he is actually doing this, and just for the hell of it (machine-madness has taken hold again) decides he will appear in a phone booth, you bet, just like his old comic-book buddy Superman. Why not? There is one a little ways off the busy intersection there, so it won't be too conspicuous . . . and, oh, this is going to be good, a man is leaving the booth at this minute—it's not, heh-heh, Clark Kent is it?—and a woman is plodding up, apparently to use it, she thinks, next. Basil hurries over, the man leaves and Basil slips in, squishing right through the glass-panel wall, and here comes the woman. This should be good. He watches her closely, grimly now, hoping she'll look away for a moment, just for a moment ... she doesn't, maintaining a dull bee-line for the booth. God, he can't just *materialize* right in front of her, he'll have to abort, and just then a car out in the street honks and she looks over and Basil hits the switch.

Apparently there is quite a report when he does this, for the lady turns suddenly toward him and the booth and sort of yelps! Oh man. He feels his guts turn over from the zap into reality and has the slight presence of mind to put the machine down below the opaque panels of the lower part of the booth. Superman would have never been so stupid, he realizes as he turns to face the incredulous woman who is presently demanding, "Now where did you come from? I was right here, I was next!"

Basil manages to flash the old Lexington smile at her, usually a winner in difficult situations, a real toughy this one, a real dumb one too ... but all she really seems interested in is her dibs on that booth, strident about it too, knocking, even kicking now on the door, "Hey, you get outta there! I was next!"

Okay, *okay*. Basil pauses only long enough to shove the machine into his backpack before staggering humbly out of the booth and into Stinky's building. But before he goes inside, promises himself that no matter how tempting it may be, he won't reveal to his friend the existence of *le machine*.

"Hey, Stink."

"Yo, Bas."

It is a warm reception, as always. Basil's business is immediately Stinky's business and it doesn't take long for his old cohort to understand exactly what it is that Basil wants, which is a printed-up something that graphically explains the secrets of Mystery Rock Hill in a manner that would be most shocking to a certain young woman.... Stinky sorts through the diagrams and tourist brochure pictures of the hill Basil has brought along, and knows immediately just what to do. It just so happens that the Harrison Press prints up an interesting little magazine called *Impossible Destinies,* a periodical that investigates all sorts of strange phenomena: UFO sightings, hauntings, Bigfoots, and the like. Why not make a fake issue with a cover story of: SOLVED! MYSTERY ROCKS OF WASSON'S BAY!

authored by Basil Lexington, none other than.... Basil agrees that this is a terrific idea, Stinky calls in his best layout artist and copy editor, and work is begun.

Even as a rush-job-for-the-boss it will take a whole day to finish the bogus mag, so Basil accepts Stinky's offer of dinner and a room for the night, and over some steaks and beer they reminisce. Basil learns that Jack Dougherty is in the hospital again, felled by a stroke, his second. Stinky's been to visit him, but was barely recognized by the old man, doesn't think there's much hope.... Basil feels very bad about this, the man being about as much of a real father as he has had, and the same, he knows, is true for Stinky too, yet neither of them will admit it.... But Stinky informs him that visiting hours at the hospital are until eight, it is almost seven right now, and after a certain unspoken message has passed between them, the two sitcom castaways find themselves racing the busy freeways in Stinky's Porsche, as if they could by their presence at this appointed hour, somehow save the grand old man. Deep within though, these two almost-brothers know it is not the man himself they are trying to save. . . .

Walking along the muted corridor, Basil remembers again that he has always hated hospitals, their tile and linoleum, ghastly fluorescence and aromatic antisepsis ... as upwards they glide now, in an wide elevator of glistening doom until they arrive at Pop's floor, the fourteenth, although Basil notices that there is no thirteenth. Pop is in a semi-private room, the other half unoccupied. He looks as Basil had imagined from Stinky's description: bad—gruesomely pallid, and thinner than Basil had ever seen him, so that his always-craggy face looks unreal in the white lights, an odd complex of angles that Basil finds hard to recognize as one he once knew.

"That's him?"

"Shhhh," Stinky admonishes, for the man seems to be asleep, but in some sort of elaborate animated dream: sighing and sputtering, grumbling and growling ... and then, miraculously awakening, even speaking coherently as he sets his wild eyes upon them: "Peeper! And, and, Stinky! By God, come to see your old pop through this, hey? By God, I knew you'd come, was just telling that to Martha when she was here a minute ago ... dunno where she went now ..."

Basil and Stinky exchange looks, Basil less shocked by the man's mental state than hearing him address Stinky as Stinky.

"By God, by *God!*" the aged TV-thesp chortles on, "come to see your old Pop . . ." and then squinting up towards Basil, "Say, you wouldn't happen to have a cigarette on you now, would you, my boy?" His face something the years of acting readily assemble: humble, hopeful expectancy, an old dying man's last request.

"Oh sure," Basil automatically retrieves his Camels from his shirt pocket, feels Stinky's immediate arm upon his.

"No, he can't—"

"What?" Basil feels anger flare instantly within him. He has quickly assessed that one more cigarette is going to do the man no harm, and besides, he hasn't had one himself for about an hour and a half and this is not exactly an unstressful situation, and, well, he looks forward to lighting-up with his old smoking coach, there's some very strong camaraderie amongst smokers, as much as between others brave and bold or very foolish: soldiers of fortune, smoke jumpers, kamikaze pilots, possessed with a kind of paranoia that one might decide to leave their ranks, those who don't could never understand. . . . "What, so what?" Basil sputters. "The, the poor guy, what's it gonna hurt?"

"He can't! Just look at him!" Stinky whispers harshly, looking squarely, severely at Basil. It's intense. His diminutive balding old buddy, blue eyes behind practical steel-rimmed glasses so penetrating at this close range Basil has to look away. But he's wrong.

"Sorry, Stink, he'll be kicking the habit soon enough . . ." Flips out cigarettes for both of them, helps Pop guide his to his lips, the man's hands shaking terribly. Lighting both of them up with Pop's lighter, Basil nearly regrets his decision, feels like the Angel of Death here, a real skull-bones-n'-scythe image, but shakes it off, tries to enjoy this moment of affection and tobacco with the magnificent raving old man. For the first time Basil notices that Pop's fingernails are stained nicotine-yellow, and his teeth are very brown. He involuntarily rubs his tongue over his own teeth, looks at his own fingers. They aren't that bad. Not yet they aren't. Isn't sure about the teeth.

"Ahhhh, now that's being good to an old fellow," says Pop through a grateful cloud of exhaled smoke. "Just because they got a sick man in here don't mean that they can deprive him of the pleasures in life. Ha! I've got connections, you know, the producer, the mayor, the governor—by God, now there's a fine man, Ronnie

Reagan, an actor, finest profession there is. Hell, with acting you can do *anything,* now he's the governor of California, can you imagine, a fine, fine man, he'll be president some day, you watch, you watch . . ."

Basil rolls his eyes toward Stinky, who after being overruled on the smoking issue had walked over to stare out the window at the twilit Hollywood night . . . he turns to Basil and shrugs, maybe Pop *did* know him.

"Listen, son," Pop is speaking to Basil, "just tell me what's going on out there, outside, hey? What's happening?" His eyes are pleading, very yellowed, too.

"What's happening, Pop? Why, uh, just the usual, life rolling along out there . . ." doesn't really know how to answer him, can see the humming freeway from here through the yellow-gray smog, the weary tired world just rolling along. . . .

"And that's it, huh." The old man's eyes are wild, disappointed.

"Yeah. I guess that's it."

"That's too bad," says Pop, frowning, taking a feckless drag on his cigarette. "Too bad. I'd hoped that maybe it'd be different some-how . . ."

A nurse appears, cheerily informs them that visiting hours are over, and then, outraged, "Who said you could smoke in here?!"

Pop has been flicking ashes wherever he gesticulated, the floor, the sheets, the water glass. . . . Basil, tipping his upon the tiled floor, discretely rubbing them to gray smudged nothingness with the sole of his shoe, but it's sort of a bad scene.

"Mr. Dougherty is a very sick man!" she bellows, taking the butt from Pop's mouth, drops it, a quick death-sizzle, into the water glass. "You should be ashamed of yourselves! You get out of here. Now!"

Basil can't look at Stinky directly, and they both try to offer goodbyes to the old man but it's no good, with nothing of the feeling or respect Basil had imagined. The nurse is not to be denied, and they have to slink out in shame. Basil feels terrible, and as they leave the hospital Basil tosses his nearly-full pack of Camels into a trash barrel. It's a decision long-time coming. Stinky sees this, puts a kindly hand upon his old friend's shoulder and no more needs to be said.

135

12

I t is early evening when the woman comes. It can be anytime, morning, midday, midnight, but whenever Synandra encounters her, it is a meeting of significance. Now as the sun fires the sky behind the hill in carmine and gold and the time becomes magical, Synandra sits somber beneath the huge oak and feels the otherworldly presence off in the gloaming; it is she. As always, her approach is heralded by distant footsteps and the rustle of leaves ... then an extraordinary silence that deepens widely around Synandra's alert ears: all birdtwitter, insect-flit, even the wind in the treetops is strangely muted ... it is only the old woman's movement through the woods and Synandra's hushed breath that, for now, truly exist.

"I-I'm glad you're here. I need to talk."

"Of course, dearie," comes the voice, surprisingly close in her ears although the woman sits a good several yards away. It is like that, however—a strange nearness. It is hard to perceive her, really, although she is readily visible. Her face is old, lined, wise, her hair long and unbound, dress dull, feet obscure. But her aura is kindness and her scent is rich, sharply of the earth itself. And her knowledge is immeasurable.

"Well, I guess I just don't understand. I mean about the way

136

they want to wreck my, er ... our hill. Why? Why? Why?" She is close to tears.

"It is simply their way. The men. They cannot understand a thing until they have destroyed it. And even then they cannot understand. It is a pity."

"But can't we do something?" Her eyes blur with tears and pale-pink hearts. "I mean there's great power here. I know it. I can feel it. Beneath my feet. All around. If I could just use some of it, guide it, like, like ..."

"Like a witch, dearie?"

"Yes, yes ..."

"Such powers are the result of calculation and utmost determination. You are not bidden to proceed in such a manner. I know you know that. Your magic here is without structure."

"Well then what good is it?"

"That is something you will have to determine for yourself." Synandra feels very low, so dispirited by the old woman's admonition that she can't reply, doesn't even want to look up.... The hag continues, "Remember this, that a man's power lies within his penis, his guns, his sword. It is forceful and direct: shooting, piercing, jabbing. It is quite potent, terribly destructive when it finds its mark. But it is subject to deviation.

"A woman's power lies within her womb, circular and contained. She is given to snares, entrapments, enclosures. She creates deviations, enticements. When challenged, she is cunning, when angered she is ruthless. She is the spider within the web; man is the fly she lands."

Some of this begins to sink in. "I think," Synandra sniffles, "I think I see what you mean.... But, but I'm so rotten with men, especially older, pompous university types that I can't even stand to—"

"There is another, though, a younger one you greatly admire, even though perhaps you will not admit it to yourself."

"Oh!" Synandra gasps as the old woman's recognition becomes her own, "You-you mean Basil? But he's such a–a ..."

"He possesses tremendous power, just as much as you yourself possess but of a greatly different kind. However, his power is much more usable ... helpful to you at this time."

"He does? But how in the world ...?"

137

"You will see, you will see," the hag whispers as she shuffles away into the darkening woods, into—Synandra can imagine this— the magic hill itself, silhouetted now by a sky of deep purple touched with cloud-wisps of rose-red.

*   *   *

Milwaukee, four in the morning on a midsummer night, and Basil steps out of the bus with a backpack of magic. It is apparent that this midwestern, mid-seventies city of the heartlands can use some. No *Valkyries* ride its caustic air, no *Nixen* swim its darkened waters, their playful giggles in the night long ago given way to foamy gurgles and bottleglass tinkling as the third shift rushes to supply the nation with tomorrow's quota of golden beer. It is from here that flow America's amber waves of grain.

Basil stretches his legs, it has been a long ride on the bus. He really hated to take it, but his motorbike is simply not up to the long drive and the machine ... well, after returning from Los Angeles via electronic trinity express, he was so totally *wrung* that he felt it best to proceed like a normal mortal, at least for a while.... The ride wasn't so bad either, he slept like a baby almost all the way ... yawns now, scratches himself and pokes around in the backpack for his caramelcorn.

Well, yes, caramelcorn. Since the swearing off of cigarettes— it's been about a week now—it seems another addiction has rapidly insinuated itself upon the hapless ex-smokeroo—caramelcorn, it's sort of embarrassing, he can't seem to get enough, finds himself plotting its purchase in large quantities, even dreaming about the stuff, fluffy white kernels flocked golden-tan sometimes still warm from the carameler, the rich mouth-watering burnt-sugar aroma wafting into his nostrils ... well, whatever it takes. So he chomps down a fix, a few crunchy mouthfuls, steps outside the bus terminal, takes a deep breath, and—yecch!

"Man, what *is* that smell, anyway?" he gasps to no one in particular.

A huge black man in Oshkosh B'Gosh overalls steps out of the darkness, "Prosperity, son, dat's de smell of prosperity."

138

The man stands in acute shadow before the downtown elemental glitter of mercury-vapor, sodium-iodide, tungsten, neon . . . "Oh," Basil smiles politely upwards, "didn't know . . ."

"S'all right, son. See, here where de Great Plains reach a no'east terminus on de shore of Lake Mich'gan . . . wheah cahloads of grain meet acres of water, de breweries inevt'ly sprung up, de ah, hops-flower, so t' speak, of German-American collab'ration. They be in the center of the city, near-bouts, whilst all 'round," the man spins gracefully about, a massive pirouette, "is lotsa other industry, you know, cy-nide steel whammin' and a-clangin' in de night. It be paht of," here the man smiles, gestures broadly with monster baseball-glove hands, "an in-dustrial ca-coph-o-ny!"

"I see."

"Yessuh, and on warm nights lahk dis de vapors rise upwards in gaggin' thermals of brewer's yeast, mos'ly, an' somethin' lahk batt'ry acid. Dat's what you be smellin' in dis heah Cream City. De actual pollutants demselfs pour into de sacrificed rivers, ult'mately de depths of dat sad ol' great lake. Out 'dere. Wheah de silv'ry lake trout no longuh be safe to eat." The man points eastward where the city glow diminishes in the midsummer darkness.

"Prosperity," says Basil.

"Dat's de ticket, son."

"Gotcha, thanks." Basil smiles and walks into the city, toward the place where he and Synandra will meet once again . . . but then remembers something he wanted to ask. "Say," he yells back, "why do they call it Cream City?" Because of the milk, he bets, America's Dairyland.

But no.

"It's on 'count of de brick dey used to make de buildin's," the voice comes back in the night. "It be of a cream coluh and de name stick. You be comparin' it wif St. Looie to de south, wheah the buildin's be of red brick."

"Oh, yeah. Makes sense, I guess . . ."

"It all make sense . . . somehow . . . someway," the voice chuckles deeply like a river in the night, "ever'thing allus makes sense e-ventually. . . ."

The hearing concerning the University's right to dissect (or vivisect, to Synandra's thinking) Mystery Rock Hill is being held in a meeting room in the federal courthouse, an impressive ornamental edifice on Wisconsin Avenue, Milwaukee's main drag. Wind has shifted off the lake—the smell is gone—and the day has come in sunny and clear, the city looking bright and very clean in the daylight, very, uh, mid-American, decides Basil as he skulks around the downtown, looking for a suitable place for, well, actually, a dematerialization. His plans are to attend this meeting invisibly, courtesy of the ghost dimension, so ultimate detective Lexington sneaks down a suitable alley outside the courthouse, and no one's around, so here goes ... and he's about to throw the brass lever, steeling himself as best he can for the terrific gut-wrenching shock ... when he stops, wonders, just what *is* he doing? Reflecting momentarily here about how really lonely it is up on the pinnacle of Awesome Power. In a way, jeeze, it really is too bad he isn't doing this in a sanitary well-lit place before galleries of skeptical scientists ... instead of hiding-out in a garbage-strewn alley. But, he sighs, it is no doubt the way of men-possessing-terrible-secrets everywhere. Though the comics never showed it, Superman must've metamorphosed in some pretty vile phone booths, hey? (*But of course, Basil, if the comics never showed it, then it never really—*) Gahhh! Okay, forget the idle speculation—Basil never big on the stuff anyway—just flip the damn lever and ... he is gusting helplessly again into the void—amazing kick this little box has, whooooooooooooooooooooooooo!—until, after interminable seconds he can relax his clenched teeth, open his eyes and ... here he is. Yes indeed. Wobbly but here in Beer City as the world comes out of a slow spin into crazy daylight, the alley now brilliant, shining, wall-bricks gently wavering in weird diagonal patterns, here and there dazzling rainbow spectrums rippling by, and the sound, faintly, of-of singing, in German, it seems. . . . Basil whirls around and there at the far end of the alley, boisterous around several oaken beer kegs is a party of roly-poly little men decked out in lederhosen and Tyrolean hats. Wow. Milwaukee gnomes. He smells sausage cooking and the amber fragrance of beer. And, and they are calling to him now, little pudgy-pink hands waving him over, yes *him,* for a brewski! Yeah! Well, it is a bit early, but then this is Beer City right? It's Heinenstuber time—or time for whatever ancient brew these characters from the Other Side prefer. Sure enough, one of them winks and shoves toward him a big tankard of brew which Basil gratefully accepts. The *Bier* is strong, on the bitter side, but cold. For that he is grateful. The other fellows take only moderate notice of him and jabber on amongst themselves—Basil can't understand a word—miniature eyes rolling above great bushy moustaches and red glowing noses. One thing strikes Basil, though, all the guys' shirts have words embroidered on the backs in what must also be German, *Die Meisterkegler von Milwaukee, Gnomen der Brauer und Wurster, Die Würstchenschauunger,* oh, he gets it, these are bowling shirts! The man who has given him the beer seems to have taken an interest in him, has the legend *Meister Karl* sewn above a breast pocket flap, and through a series of comradely gestures, smiles and winks, seems to be inviting him to a game of *kegeln.* Well sure, not that Basil has done much bowling, really, hardly any at all ... but the little fellow bends elbow and hand in recognizable kegling motion, points over where some of the boys are setting up the carved wooden bowling pins ... or, uh, maybe nine-pins, what was it that—who was it—Ichabod Crane? played in the story with those guys? Hmm, uneasily shifting the machine in one hand, Basil warily eyes the fresh brew he has just accepted into the other, having downed the first pretty rapidly, just nervous and all, but now feels a trifle edgy, some of the little fellows in the back becoming a bit rowdy, laughing, back-slapping, singing and stomping around in a sort of jig ... someone is playing a concertina and another has begun oompah-ing upon a battered miniature brass tuba.... The crazy music jangles through the ghost-dimension and Basil begins to think maybe he had better move along here, as friendly as they seem to be—ah! it was *Rip Van Winkle!* that was the name Basil had been trying to recall, the guy who supposedly slept, *Himmel,* twenty years after drinking something.... Oh boy, Basil looks hard now into his mug which he has already drained halfway, sort of Milwaukee-automatic here, it's catchy, and wonders how he can remove himself from these krazy keglers, some of whom have now gathered around him in an effort of *gemütlichkeit,* edging him over to the bowling, er, alley, when suddenly a wild Tarzano-Teutonic scream pierces the ether, and Basil looks up in time to catch a blurry figure streaking toward him, one of the more inebriated bungholers swinging dangerously in on a rope he has rigged somehow from a lamppost, beer mug in the other hand, yelling something in German: *Was ist Wirrrrklichkeit?!!* and the impact a terrific WHACK! that knocks the marvelous-machine-that-makes-all-this-possible from Basil's hand with a great WHOOOOOSH and a shower of brilliant blue sparks and everything sort of shudders and flashes first pitch black and then into sickening gray as if a dense fog has suddenly closed-in but Basil is moving fast, leaving the beer mug behind in mid-ether as he leaps headlong into the instant mist toward the trail of sparks, sees the brass handle of the machine just about to vanish forever, stretches out, genuinely flying now, reaching desperately for the brass handle, which has just passed through the stone wall of a building and Basil follows right along, feels the peripheral heavy cool damp of stone-block and wooden beam as he passes through, simultaneously feels the handle in his palm—Thank God!—clutches it hard, and shazam! suddenly finds himself in what appears to be a cavernous room, darkened except for a brilliant white eye of light ... which, after some orientation, turns out to be the light from a slide projector that is at this moment displaying upon a screen across the room a view of Mystery Rock Hill. He has found the meeting.

As his vision clears, he makes out Synandra herself, in a white summer dress seated bored on one side of a large oak table centered in the room, a half-dozen people on the other side, five men and a woman who looks a lot like—must be the ghost dimension—Margaret Dumont, university/government types all, wearing suits of blue and gray.

Tuning-in, Basil hears a voice droning nasally, veddy British, "... actually, you see, Mystery Rock Hill is really quite a remarkable site. On first look it appears merely to be a simple mound like so many others I have researched in the British Isles. But of course the rocks atop it are arranged in that peculiar heart-shape. Imme–diately brings to mind the historic heart-shaped Bury Wood Camp mound in Wiltshire ..." A slide, a line-drawing of a very recognizable heart-shaped mound appears on the screen. "But of course that is the shape of the mound itself, not of the pattern of huge boulders which we are dealing with here ... and that is what makes the Mystery Rock Hill so unique in this part of the world. I mean just the fact that it is a *mound*, is clearly not quite enough to fuss about. There are literally hundreds of earthworks formed into distinct shapes, effigy mounds, they are called ..."

A click-clacking series of slides project onto the screen across the room, of old surveyors' maps and aerial photographs all depicting mounds in various shapes of animals, recognizable deer, bear, fish, snakes, birds, and even man.

"... yes," continues the Britisher, who Basil takes to be professor Clyde Mortell, "these earthworks are very common in the Midwest, in Ohio, Illinois, and particularly Wisconsin. Why, the diversity of these mounds is truly remarkable, but none are so striking, so large and distinct, or so, ah, mysterious, as that of Mystery Rock Hill."

"Have any of these other mounds been excavated?" asks a florid, heavy man pointing at the screen.

"Er, some of them, a couple of dozen in the state I would venture, but you see after about 1840, as more land was cleared for farms and towns and roads—"

"And was anything found in them?"

"Oh yes, flint and chert arrowheads, potsherds, bones of animals and humans, some of the mounds being gravesites, but not what we could call an 'official' gravesite, in that perhaps one of the prehistoric workers died during construction and—"

"But anything that could be considered significant?"

"Ooh ... not *really* significant, but, but, at another site, in a mound near the Ohio River, the *very* significant Grave Creek tablet was discovered, a stone with some quite unusual markings that have been variously interpreted as ancient Greek, Etruscan, Runic, Gaelic, Phonecian, and I don't recall what else ... I wish I had a slide of it here to show you ..."

"And what is the possibility of making such a find in the area of Mystery Rock Hill?"

"A scintillion to one," smirks Synandra.

"Well, that's just it," says Mortell, "we just don't know. But the possibilities are absolutely delicious. Yes, just delicious. At any rate, we can be very pleased to know that we shall finally have a definitive archaeological study of the premier mound of the American Midwest."

The projector click-clacks and another hill, an earth-mound similar to Mystery Rock, but *sans* forest, and apparently much larger, appears on the screen.

"Now, this hill, as I expect you should all know, is Silbury Hill in North Wiltshire, the largest and most famous neolithic monument in Europe, in the world, I should think. It has been thoroughly explored, poked, prodded, and the like, as our young lady of the hill of the Mystery Rocks so thoroughly abhors . . ."

"And nothing, nothing at all," says Synandra, "was found in it, right?"

"Er . . . yes, that is correct, that excavation proved fruitless," tsks Mortell. "But-but, as you all can see, it still stands, *proudly,* I might add, like Mystery Rock Hill shall when our excavations are complete."

"Like hell," mutters Synandra.

"Er, yes," sighs the professor.

"Now, Miss Wasson . . ." starts Margaret Dumont.

"Quite alright, quite," interrupts Mortell. "I can understand her apprehension. After all a great many, a very great many, I should say, of the ancient works of Britain . . . cairns, dolmens, barrows, stone circles, and the like have been totally destroyed by farmers, shoddy 'self-styled' archaeologists, and just plain boorish clods— farmer Robinson, one of the most infamous in Britain, comes to mind. . . . But you must understand that it is precisely because such sites are subject to destruction, that it is imperative that we study them now, while there is still something to study!"

"My dear," Ms. Dumont addresses Ms. Wasson, "Professor Mortell here is an expert, and he has assured us that the, ah, dig, would be conducted most carefully."

"Yes, of course," says Mortell, "as we told you many times before, Synan—, Miss Wasson, the excavation will be performed in a comprehensive manner, yet with complete restoration. I daresay you won't even be able to tell where the excavations were made."

"I'll know," says Synandra lowly. "And I can tell you right now that there are no 'artifacts' in or around the hill. You'd just be wasting your time. And money."

"And how, pray tell, would you know that?"

"It's so obvious. The hill is clearly a sacred site and has been since, since, forever. The Indians, who understood the earth's sacred sites—areas that are naturally the focus of earth energies—knew that such places shouldn't be tampered with. They sought their visions and they left. They never would have camped, as a tribe, on, or even very near the hill. It would have been the ultimate sacrilege. And what you intend to do is even worse."

"Well, I hardly think that is a consideration here, in the twentieth century . . ." observes Ms. Dumont.

"But, it's the *only* consideration! It-it's—"

"Excuse me for interrupting," says one of the gray suits, "but could you please enlighten us as to where you've received this information?"

"Well, from an Indian shaman—a doctor, actually. He—"

"A *shaman?* Really, now?" Mortell smiles triumphantly.

"Yes, but he's a Harvard graduate, too. He's a bona-fide—"

"I really didn't know," chuckles Mortell, "that Harvard offers a course in practical shamanism. Perhaps as a minor in their demonology program." Laughter all around the table.

"Goddamn it!" rages Synandra. "You're not listening! It's not just excavation we're talking about here. You just wouldn't understand, you stuffed-shirt limey creep! It-it's desecration! You've got to believe me. I know."

"Yes, of course," snaps Mortell, his anger rising to meet Synandra's. "Of course you would. You would because the-the 'vibes,' is that what you call them, wouldn't be just right after we're done? Or, or that the *ley lines* that I'm sure you figure connect the hill with all other points of the bloody earth wouldn't be just right? Or, or, *I* know, it's that the bloody stinking UFO's, the bloody *flying saucers,* that take-off and land during the new moon won't be coming around there any more!

"Oh sure," Mortell looks righteously at his university cohorts, "it's always that way with these granola-ingrates. Sitting pretty atop one of the most significant megalithic sites in the new world, easily as spectacular as the Great Serpent Mound of Ohio, and it hasn't even been properly excavated—yet. Well, if it has to come to this, it has." Mortell turns significantly to Synandra. "You know that we have legal authority now to excavate and that we shall. We have funding and we are ready to go. We shall be *in situ* and digging, in approximately three weeks. And no bloody hippie-girl is going to stop us now. It's taken some precious years, but now you see we've won this time. Maybe it's time you tried to eat some good honest red beef like the rest of us instead of all that bloody granola, hey?"

And at this point, Basil, who has been invisibly watching the juggernaut of academia roll over the now subdued girl, takes a handful of the caramelcorn he has been quietly munching upon

145

and tosses it at Mortell. What the hell. And with tiny pinpricks of blue light, the golden-brown kernels pass through to the Other Side, gaining, from Basil's perspective, an amplitude of ghost-dimensional brilliance as they fall in a small shower on the incredulous university folks on the far side of the table.

"Really!" gasps Margaret Dumont, lurching backwards with the rest from the onslaught. "Really, Miss Wasson! I hardly think that you must resort to . . ."

"I say . . ."

They think she threw them. She was reaching into her purse for a hankie at the moment, and she did jump, startled, along with the others. But Synandra, wide-eyed, is easily as surprised as them at what has happened. "But I didn't . . . no . . ." bursting into tears as she flees from the room. Basil feels a lump in his throat the size of a Mystery Rock as he rushes after her.

Outside, all is sunshine and brilliance, even more so in the ghost dimension. It takes some time for Basil's eyes to adjust and Synandra is moving fast, so he steps clumsily along busy Wisconsin Avenue like an idiot alien, dodging radiant humans, fire hydrants, lampposts—doing all he can to avoid going through them—trying to follow the pitiable girl. He feels terrible, ashamed at himself for plotting to cause her even more anguish. . . . But at the moment he is not feeling terribly well in a physical sense, either. In fact, he is tending toward a case of ghost-dimensional nausea. The constant vibration flooding every nerve and cell has taken its toll. This is the longest he has ever spent in the ghost-dimension and fast-chasing after this girl is not doing him any good . . . talk about your bad vibes. . . .

She finally stops on the sidewalk to catch her breath, quietly sniffling, apparently having expended a parcel of rage . . . but still looks so somber that Basil's plan of shocking her with the-secrets-of-the-hill-published-for-all-the-world-to-see now seems a trifle tacky. He has the bogus magazine in hand and decides to throw it and his whole nasty scheme into the dumper. There is a sidewalk trash basket nearby and Basil casually tosses it in as he strides away with a heavy heart and a churning stomach, knowing now that he absolutely must *get back*, before he becomes violently sick in the ghost dimension. Metaphysical puke. Certainly not a pretty sight. . . .

"Bye-bye Syndy," he thinks, Mr. Magnanimous here, casually

turning to glance back, and seeing with a shock that the little magazine has been caught by a breeze as it passed into reality, and has blown to the very feet of Synandra. Who spots it, looks hard at its provocative cover and curiously picks it up. Oh hell. Well, Basil simply can't stay any longer, sighs as he walks rapidly away; it was meant to be. And surprisingly, noble as he had felt before, he is not all that distraught at her no-doubt distressing discovery.

13

Even the air seems metallic, so base is the atmosphere, so gray in this land where the shadow is reality and reality is ... simply as it always is here, pallid silvertone of the set, one of the later shows, at the very end of the run, yes, the very end. Basil senses this acutely in the oneiric smaller-than-he-remembered Dawson kitchen, and that probably because of everyone gathered here together, Pop, Stinky, Martha, and of course, himself, the Peeper. He is suddenly panicky, unable to remember his lines, unable even to distinguish the plot of the episode—other than an inherent understanding that this is the *very last one*. But he is able to breathe easy for the moment, as Pop appears to be winding up for a speech. My God, yes, he is really going to let us have it, meaning ALL of us ... the Peeper understands, relaxes more, even finds it hard to stifle a beaming gasp as Pop winks, pulls a Pall Mall from a pack in his shirt pocket, something that he certainly has never done before on the show, and lights up, and then from somewhere below produces a bottle of, ye Gods! Wild Turkey, pours a good two or three fingers into a glass, and takes a righteous swig before their incredulous eyes. The Peeper expects at any moment to hear the director scream, but by now the set has disappeared and they are simply a family enclosed within four gray walls, a situation similar to one he has known before, but cannot quite place at the moment. . . .

"Well, it's about time, we might as well be finished with it, all of it . . . it's over," Pop suddenly proclaims in his throaty voice, ending up smiling at them in a fatherly, yet sheepish way, as though realizing that he might be a trifle embarrassing. He tosses back another belt and coughs. "I know that we don't often get to talk about a whole hell of a lot of things, I mean with every god-damned word planned out for us, it ain't easy I know, but as this is the end here, I've decided to tell you, extemporaneously, as it were, that while we've been here doing what we've been doing, acting our roles, speaking our lines, we've been missing what's really been going on out there." Pop's eyes go big, the look terrifies the Peeper, all of them, and Pop points to the windows. "I-I've looked out there and, and, there's something bad, really bad, gone by . . ."

Cautiously, the Peeper walks over to the windows, over to the constant pale glow beyond which he knows there never really was a beyond . . . and looks out. And all around as far as the eye can see are endless piles of garbage; they are surrounded—their kitchen, themselves—by a huge, huge dump, which again he finds vaguely familiar—and terribly disturbing. And out there . . . he has to squint, in one of the valleys formed by the trash-mountains, sits an Indian, one he thinks he knows, with long hair secured by a headband, and though he is distant, perched cross-legged atop an old console television, the Peeper can tell that he is looking directly at him, knows it, it's spooky, but . . . it seems that someone is, uh, at the door—

KnockknocknockKNOCKKNOCKKNOCKKK!

". . . mmmph . . . who's there?"

"It's me, Synandra."

Oh. Basil finds himself, hmmm, napping on the dim side of a latched screen door . . . yeah, seems like he's been sleeping ever since he got back from Milwaukee, and all the way back on the bus, too. The damned machine seems to wrench out every last bit of energy he has and sleep is always the best way to recharge—

She knocks again. "I want to talk to you."

"About what?"

"About what . . ." a pause. "About—who told you about the hill? And, and the centers?"

"No one."

149

"Tiffany?"

"No one."

"Well, dammit!" The screen door rattles furiously. "Will you—unlock—this thing? Honestly, how could you actually *pub*lish that, that . . . ?" Her voice breaks.

Basil smiles . . . at last . . . imagines the streaming tears . . . but at the same time feels bad about the whole thing, wants to let her in, comfort her, tell her that the joke's off. . . . But then, he suddenly remembers why he originally constructed such an elaborate prank, flashes back on the rainstorm and she stealing his clothes and his nakedness and the humiliation and the cold, and his stomach contracts with sudden anger as he recalls it all . . . and then relaxes with a certain satisfaction. Things are coming around his way very nicely indeed. He tells her to meet him for a drink at Maxwell's. Saturday night. Around eight.

"All right, all right . . ." comes the clenched reply, "but you're gonna tell me then—"

"That all depends . . ."

"Depends on . . ."

"On how famously we, ah, get along . . ."

"Argggh!" The door shudders from a kick and then is silent.

Basil's Journal:

Time to reflect. So much happening in the past few days that I feel like I've left my brain on hold while I go off ringing up some of the strangest numbers in this crazy directory which has been unlisted for me until now, and the thing is I can't tell when I've got a wrong number or not. Maybe they're all wrong numbers. Or maybe the equipment's off. Or maybe I'm just nuts. After this last trip I feel weird and hollow and tired and burned-out and really like I've been kind of crazy all through it. I mean, how do I deal with the fact of partying it up with a bunch of zany little gnomes in Milwaukee, and catching a beer with them? Where do I begin?

Ever since Kowalske lammed-off to who-knows-where-ville, and I get the machine things just haven't been the same. I mean here I have a contraption that I could probably make a trillion clams with, give or take a few billion, and be set for life, and then it's Easy Street, Moneyville, U.S.A. So what do I do? Go check out the future stock market or the lottery or winners at the track? No, I just burn to get back at that hippie-girl Synandra with a fire that's straight out of Dante's inferno, if I remember my college right, running off to here and there to pull a fast one on her like she pulled on me. Like that's the most important thing in the world. Like I'm just a sap. Well, that'll change soon enough.

Personal notes to myself:

1. Maybe I haven't had the time to really feel it, maybe because I've been too busy, but Pop Dawson's illness, his not being really all there, has left me awfully empty. It's like no matter where you ever were in the world you knew that there was someone really special out there somewhere, even if you haven't kept in touch, and now

2. Congratulations to myself for having stopped smoking cigarettes for over a week now. I promise myself, upon the lighter of Pop Dawson, that I will never smoke again.

(signed)   *Basil Lexington*

P.S. Have weighed myself on a scale at the bus station. Gained 5 lbs. mostly on caramelcorn, I think.

*   *   *

"Well ... you know what this means," says Tiffany, sitting at the dressing table in Synandra's bedroom, fumbling with matches to light a small onyx pipe, the bowl of which contains a sandy button of hashish.

"Uh-huh," Synandra sighs, standing behind her, watching in the circular mirror as she brushes out Tiffany's long golden hair. "I just can't figure out how he knows ..."

"So ... how do you feel?" passing the thinly smoking pipe overhead to Synandra.

"I'm not sure ... better than before, of course. Before we discovered his little scheme." She can't help smiling. Her heart feels strangely full and good. She tries to frown in the mirror at herself but can't, and catches Tiffany looking at her. They both giggle.

After Tiffany had received the call from distraught Synandra, and before going over to see her she had stopped at the magazine rack in the Wassons' Bay Superette and purchased the current issue of *Impossible Destinies* magazine (the magazine racks of Wasson's Bay, like those of most other towns in the peninsula, are often very complete, catering to the tastes of sundry and many tourists) and was unable to find anything about Mystery Rock Hill in the whole issue. And upon comparison with Synandra's supposed current issue of infamy, same month and year, it became apparent that skullduggery was afoot. And thence, in the larger sense, came relief.

Synandra's bedroom is upstairs in the venerable Wasson house. Beyond windows east and south the afternoon sun is on a brassy rampage, but inside, the room is cool, smelling faintly of sandalwood and vetiver and the tang of fine hashish, while celadon shadows sigh faintly in the farthest corners. "Oh, what a lovely afternoon," murmurs Tiffany, putting down the pipe and reaching out for a long-stemmed glass of champagne, "a fine day to be inside, hey?" She walks over to the big double bed and stretches luxuriously out, balancing the glass on her silken tummy.

"Um," Synandra finishes dabbing on perfume, her own concoction, *Tarde Deliciosa,* and walks over to the window. Each of the girls are wearing ridiculously expensive handmade dressing gowns Tiffany has brought up from Chicago for them, pure extravagance, a more or less essential component now of a regular event evolved during the last several years of their friendship, a social statement, really, a piece of performance art, exquisitely subtle, played out in the outer-reaches of the magical hill's emanation and influx. Now that the savage sixties have dissolved into something softer and more individualistic, they feel it necessary to express the *Zeitgeist* with this luxuriant style of lazy lounging, complete with something smokable and, yes, champagne icing in a tub. Two old friends and delightful decadence. Outside, fronting the lush Wasson lawn beyond a mass of red and purple peonies and snow-on-the-mountain, is an ancient bed of orange day lilies. Synandra stares out through old distorting window glass at their violent color, their interlaced fronds. Tiffany's voice distracts her.

"He sure went to a lot of trouble, though."

"Yes. He did. Why do you think—?"

"Because of what you did, Syndy, to him, when it stormed. It's perfectly clear."

"I see. But—"

"You're thinking about what the old woman told you, right? God, I wish she'd appear for me like she does for you. You just have a way with the world, you know, that I can't ever—"

"The woman, yes, but—"

"You like him, don't you? A lot."

"Yes, darn it" says Synandra, turning and blushing as she smiles. "I don't know why ..."

"So ... how are you going to handle it? Your—big date, tomorrow."

"Well, whatever happens, happens ... but first, you know, I'm going to go out there ..."

Yes, making the best of things, Synandra comes naked-underneath her silk dress out to the hill this evening before her rendezvous with Basil. She dares, under acres and acres of jolly orange pumpkin-clouds dotting the sky, to sip in some of the deliciously dangerous energy of the hill, lingering delicately on the fringes of the strange vortex in a sort of dance-of-daring upon the rocky summit with the streaming vibrations that so peculiarly affect her, as a sort of blushing organic satellite ... the music here none other than Schubert's 8th, the *Unfinished*, daring and taunting, withdrawing, then chastening ... and then daring again the adorable girl ... whose breath is now near pant-rate, heartbeat rapidly wanton as she decides to head recklessly south, through wild lily-of-the-valley, stodgy may apple, and parchment-peeling birches to the soft patch of green surrounded by the wild roses where—she knows this is the devil's work itself—she will find the silken vignette of panties dangling from rose thorn ... they are there, just as she had hung them this morning (shivering in her flannel nightgown, crystal spheres of dew breaking upon her bare feet, precisely as the sun had risen above the crimson lake), but now—her own strange magic—to be slipped on under the blush-pink dress she has chosen for tonight, sweet and minimal, along with a perforated silver heart-shaped locket

153

stuffed with crushed patchouly leaves.

Such daring. Sucking a deep breath, she now lowers herself slowly dead-center onto the grassy tump, pulling her legs into a tight lotus, and feels ... so much ... really ... that it is all so rounded, really, the curve of the earth, of the universe, of it all, really, all there is, so gigantic, awesome, all there could ever be....

After undefined momenta (there is really no sense of anything else in this place) she has to jump up. It is *way* too much, she has to gasp for breath here, heart trip-hammering, the earth truly a potent drug for her, head gone helium balloon and legs rubbery, her whole body alive with twitches and tingles, sensitive as a safecracker's fingers. Her skin even seems to glow in the grainy twilight, she notices, or thinks she does, and so she does—or does she? the old Heisenberg uncertainty, always with a hand in everything—as she pulls on her sandals, smooths her dress with trembling hands, and begins threading her way through the trees to the path, the road, and Maxwell's.

Straight ahead, an enormous full moon hangs just over the lake, blood-orange and awesome. She stretches toward it, feeling something uncertain open up inside of her, and a stream of tears moisten her cheeks. The moon urges her onward.

Basil shifts on his bar stool, glances at the clock, sips his Heinenstuber. She's late. There's a good crowd in tonight, a lot of vacationers, Illinois people mostly, it seems, FIB's, which, as Betsy the bartendress has told him with a wink, stands for "Friendly Illinois Buddies." Basil sighs and smiles, Wisconsin is such a friendly state.

So there is a general midwestern murmur in the cozy tavern tonight, which perhaps causes his mind to wander, flashing back now to how he ever got here to begin with, to Captain Jimmy and the old Russian and, uh, Tiffany, and, God he's horny tonight; she was his last, uh, piece, truly a master-piece, one might say ... and she, veritable apotheosis of the soft and round delights, was in fact here tonight, stunning in a crimson voile dress, but only long enough to grab a quick drink with her date this evening, a young black veteran in a wheelchair, Michael Davidson Plato the third. Tiffany had introduced them.

"Howrya doin' brother," Michael had drawled. "Better than me, as I can see. Vietnam got me, got me goood."

"Oh. What a shame. I'm sorry . . ."

"Not a shame, not a shame at all . . . jes a pain. You white boys are always so' sorry. Make me wanna cry." He laughed.

Tiffany was one big grin. "So a heavy date tonight?"

"Uh-huh."

And over her shoulder a big wink for Basil as they had left together, she walking, Michael wheeling alongside.

Basil's next beer arrives at the same time as Synandra, breathless, cheeks flushed, beautiful.

"Well, hello."

"Hello yourself."

A tall, heavy-set young man with long hair pulled back into a ponytail, a large red nose, and vaguely scented of marijuana greets her from behind the bar. It is Maxwell himself. "How-do, Syndy. You two are, uh, together?"

"Oh, for the duration." She orders a vodka and unsweetened cherry juice. "Seen Tiff tonight?"

"Uh-huh, was in earlier with that black guy in the wheelchair again. Mike somebody."

"Michael Davidson Plato the third," says helpful Basil.

They both look at him.

"I met him before . . ."

Maxwell leaves them after a particularly disrobing glance at Synandra, and Basil, swiping a goodly look at her himself, feels, more than he particularly sees, something very, arousing, here, casually turns his head to look around the room and notices that people, well, it seems to him that people, some people, are kind of looking over here . . . aren't they? After all, as she had walked in it seemed that something had cracked its silent whip and set every beer-vapor molecule in the room a-bobbing . . . something . . . as conversations lowered, men and women hemmed and hawed, respectively, no one daring to voice, "I *say*, Sybil, what is it that has so subtly, yet unmistakably, charged the ambience so?" And only one tangible addition to the milieu, that girl coiling and uncoiling her slender legs around the bar stool, in the pink-to-colorless dress that seems to flash, yes, amazingly iridescent in the peripheral vision, that girl that seems, somehow, to glow. . . .

"Well, so here we are," Basil nervously clears his throat.

"Yes, so we are."

"Looks like you got some sunburn, or—"

"Yeah, maybe."

"Sooo ... how was Milwaukee?"

"How'd you find out?" flashing her eyes, suddenly, electrically, toward him.

"Uh ..." her demand, her look, startles Basil for some reason, like someone who suddenly discovers that he might be treading in an area he is wholly unfamiliar with and which just might be rather dangerous ... so he doesn't immediately answer, signals instead for another drink for her.

She is ready for one too, has nervously sloshed the first right down while playing with the swizzle stick, shredding the napkin into origami snow, rapping out fingernail tattoos on the bartop in primitive rhythms, anxious and undecipherable. ...

Her drink is brought by Betsy, a pretty auburn-haired girl who immediately begins chatting with Synandra. Basil wishes she would leave, but Betsy hovers across the bar top, eyes glimmering, talking about absolutely anything, "... what's that perfume you're wearing, Syndy, musk?"

"Patchouly leaves." Synandra flashes the silver locket.

"Umm, they smell great," Betsy says, leaning over, and she oddly, foolishly, places her hand on Synandra's arm.

It happens in an instant, but long enough for Basil to notice gooseflesh erupt the length of her arm before the violent jerk, sending her already half-gulped drink flying, smashing behind the bar. Forty heads instantly turn her way.

"Oh ... oh ..." Betsy is clearly shocked. "I-I don't know why I ... I'm sorry, I'll, I'll get you another—"

"No, no, it's okay," she turns to Basil, eyes enormous, "let's go now, okay?"

Outside, the cantankerous couple stroll rapidly away, not quite arm-in-arm through the moonlight, absolutely brilliant tonight, past people on porch steps actually reading newspapers by its glow. Basil turns to look up at the man in the moon, inscrutable heavenly head up there laughing back down at him ... thanks pal. He is really more of a sun-person anyway, predisposed to warmth and dazzle, a splendor you can't look directly at without blinding yourself. ...

But this night is the archetype, has to be, of all others before and after, explicitly for Synandra, moon-daughter that she is, casting a glance herself up at floating ancient mountains and seas, and receiving in turn a bit of moon-madness, passed along with the argent shadows furrowing the countryside. It affects Basil too, he practically dancing on the old gravel-relief sidewalk, very happy to be with this exciting girl tonight, dirty tricks forgotten now, dropping a step behind, sizing up that bobbing silken rump for a grab—not a pinch, mind you ...

She squeals, and wonderfully, *laughs*, skipping sweetly ahead, not even looking back, whilst Basil increases the dance, zeroing-in to cop another sweet handful ... and very quickly they are both skipping, trotting, *running* sleekly through the luminous breeze, Synandra turning to smile at him, racing with the moon!

The Wasson woods have become Diana's huntland. The mosaic of shadows conceals a silvery unicorn and other fabulous beasts with jeweled eyes, watching the moonstruck kids blunder through the trees. Well, at least one of them. Basil follows Synandra's deft lead through the shadowy forest although they both know their destination. The scene of their last encounter. Seems like so long ago now to Basil, the woods eerie, a regular Hollywood day-for-night scene as she runs ahead, skipping into the rosebush enclosure like a silvery moth in the moonlight. Basil gives playful chase and catches the liquid fabric, pulls her to him, plants a kiss to ballast her, brusquely at first, then tendering out ... and with this single first kiss he is unbelievably aroused, God, to have her so warm and close like this ... soft, and, well—frenzied, grinding so tightly, immediately, against him it seems they might *merge*.... The music welling up now is Rimsky-Korsakov, *Scheherazade*, they both hear it and smile softly at each other, understanding its portent. Leaning forward, Basil helps the dress transform to a moonlit puddle. Magic. His clothes follow, and slowly two glowing forms sink down onto the dewy bed, become one. This is really something, Basil's feeble last solid thought as her face, contorted somewhere between a laugh and a cry looms hugely before him and then: ohhhhhhhhhh as petals unfold and more magic floods endless fertile acres ... both suffering an attack of dream-time here, he a sort of hairy yet dignified animus, Druidic in character, lascivious in tone, hovering nastily, brutishly, competently, above; she, his nubile bride, pubescent, virginal, sacrificial, an instrument of the vast energies of the earth, setting sap flowing, bees

157

flying, buds bursting ... and soon their pace is obscenely electric ... frantic ... wild dogs ... bonecrack carnivores ... canine teeth gritted, eyes nowhere ... the earth and sky an enormous free-fall void, the only singular shared reality, a tremendous shuddering vibration. . . .

Through the woods and down the road in a candle-lit bedroom, Tiffany L'Oreal is similarly engaged, or about to be, tent-like beneath a gleaming silver satin sheet and above Michael Davidson Plato the third, about to make good use of a more common earth-energy, gravity, when ... "What the hell is that?"

"F-feels like an earthquake," chuckles Mike. "Don't pay it no mind."

"Earthquake?" Sure enough, windowpanes are rattling in their frames, candle flames flicker and strobe, a string of ornamental brass bells hanging on the wall begins a steady jingle. The vibration lasts for an approximate minute, then all is silent. "I-I can't believe it," mutters Tiffany, jumping off the undulating waterbed.

"It was only a little quake," groans agonized Mike, stretching to the bed's perimeter for cigarettes. "Nothin' to it. I felt 'em all the time when I was stationed in San Diego. . . . That whole state's gonna fall in the ocean one day. Y'see it's the crust which is so unstable out there ... hey, Tiffy-baby, whatsa matter anyhoo?"

But Tiffany doesn't hear him, kneeling on a chair before the window, absently scratching beneath her garter belt, staring out into the darkness. "My God . . ."

14

B asil's Journal:

Wow.

      *   *   *

Next day Synandra has to be at the shop, so there is only time for one more frenzied round of lovemaking (besides not getting much sleep last night after coming in from the hill) and a quick breakfast before she must roller-skate off to work. But it is time enough to clear the air between them, except, maddening to Synandra, he won't come out and tell her exactly how he learned all about the hill, says he's got to *show* her, and he can't do that until he gets something he's got stashed back at his cottage. ... Which leads him to hint that if he were to, ah, spend the night over here again he'd better bring over some clothes, and his toothbrush, and ... Synandra jumps on it so swiftly it surprises him, tells him, sure, might as well, to bring everything, all his stuff over ... and then, suddenly, across her eyes flickers a trace of cautious alarm that Basil picks-up on and is fairly touched by, coming from this supposedly tough cookie, a tiny sensory shock of what it must be like for her living alone in this big old empty house. Yes, Basil suddenly understanding that maybe more than the old Lexington charm is operative here, that maybe it is not only for himself that the world revolves, maybe not by a long shot. ... And so it is decided, by both of them, to stay together for a while, in a sudden and yet not-so-surprising instant.

Now Basil has Synandra's bomb, the black 1966 Chevy with the weird clatter in the engine and some trouble getting into third gear, but with hopefully enough life in it to get him over to his cottage to pick up his stuff and then a swing down the peninsula to the general delivery window of the Green Bay post office to see if that check from Yates has come in yet. Mrs. Frost does not seem very surprised when Basil checks out with the rent still good for another week. In fact, the lively lady appears not only to approve of the fact that it is Synandra he is moving in with, but to be extremely pleased by it, and oddly, somewhat awed. "I noted you were gone last night, son," she says, wiping her glasses. "It was a beautiful night to be out, too. I can't remember when I've seen a moon so bright ... maybe a long time ago now ..." and, romance seemingly heavy on her mind, goes on to tell him how people got married a lot earlier in her day, she having wed Mr. Frost (God rest his soul), in fact, at age fifteen. Times were hard then, but not as "damn crazy" as they are now.

They are standing in warm sunshine in front of her blue-shuttered house, gulls coasting lazily above the lake-murmur beyond the trees. She suddenly excuses herself, goes inside, and emerges with a small pot containing a single mauve African violet blossom. She also has a newspaper, the *Peninsula Gazette*. She gives the plant to Basil, tells him that it is a descendant of one she was given after her wedding, over sixty years ago. And then she has him examine a peculiarity of the petals, which turns out to be a tiny heart-shape centered on each one, of a darker shade than the rest of the flower. "Isn't this strange?" she asks him, looking into his eyes.

"Yeah, I guess it is."

"Just bloomed this morning. I know Syndy has a fondness for hearts. You take it to her for me."

"Now let's see," she says then, holding the paper at arm's length, adjusting her glasses. "Ah, here." She points to an article, hands the paper to Basil.

He can barely conceal his shock as he reads:

QUAKE JOLTS PENINSULA

TREMOR MEASURES 3.2 ON RICHTER SCALE; NO DAMAGE

Sturgeon Bay — A minor earthquake that registered 3.2 on the Richter scale shook the length of the peninsula last night, rattling dishes and windows, but causing no apparent damages or injuries.

Peninsula sheriff Mortimer McKee said that he received several telephone calls about the tremors from residents and resort owners concerned for their vacationers, but no reports of damage.

Felt by residents as far south as Green Bay, the quake lasted less than a minute, said Marvin Denning, geophysicist at the University of Wisconsin-Green Bay. The quake was centered in the Wasson's Bay area, he believes. Denning said that earthquakes are very rare in the peninsula, though not unknown. He said that a quake measuring 3.2 on the Richter scale is a "minor quake, definitely nothing to worry about." Denning also said the peninsula is "geologically very stable," and that there are no major fault lines in the area, though there may be some minor faults. He did not expect any aftershocks.

Basil's mouth suddenly goes very dry, "My God, an-an earthquake, it's incredible."

"Awfully damn strange to have an earthquake around here," says Mrs. Frost. Behind her glasses her eyes are bright and quite moist.

"Yeah, I guess it is . . ." says Basil, handing back the paper with a now slightly-trembling hand.

"I never . . ." she begins, but stops short. Then, "You know son, I had worried about that girl, with her grandfather being gone, and her so young, and there so many rascally folks around. . . . Well, you be good to her now. Stop by sometime."

An earthquake! A goddamn earthquake! Basil can't get it out of his mind as he drives down to Green Bay. There's a big smile plastered across his mug, and he has dialed in on the car's radio the 1812 Overture, of all things, and is whistling right along. It's true that their climax was incredibly—intense, okay, but Basil is sure that that's the way it is for a lot of women their first time with him, and then when (as she let it slip) it's also HER FIRST TIME, well . . . but an-an earthquake? Man, that's something that only happens in books, right? No point in dwelling further on it now, though, another of those things he'd never dope out on his own, but they'll certainly have something to talk about when he gets back.

Right now he is cruising down the southern stretch of the peninsula, blue skies above and verdant bay off his right shoulder all the way, a really nice day. He wishes he had some more caramelcorn, having just shoveled into his mouth the last couple handfuls of his current bag . . . maybe he'll be able to rustle up some more down in Green Bay. But it can wait, right now he's in a sight-seeing mood, and just on the outskirts of the football-fabled town he turns impulsively off on a small road he thinks might take him northwards, a little closer to the water. And it does, in a circuitous fashion, leading to a small park that is situated at the affluence of the river that flows through Green Bay the town, and the great Green Bay itself. Basil pulls into a gravel parking lot that seems to be the sight of some activity today.

Off to one side are station wagons with canoe racks, and out in the river Basil sees a troop of Boy Scouts paddling around together.

A solitary woman sits on a picnic table watching them. On the other side of the lot is an old pick-up truck with a camper in back and behind it a rotund little man standing before a smoking grill. Boy, can he smell that sausage cooking! Basil gets out of the car and the man behind the camper waves, beckons him over with a big smile. "Hey, sonny! You hungry? C'mon over here!"

Hungry? Since he gave up smoking, Basil always is. The man greets him with a rumbling belly-laugh and an ice-cold can of beer, just out of the cooler, Heinenstuber, in fact, and Basil unconsciously smacks his lips in anticipation of one of the big bratwursts the man is busily attending to. Basil gets a better look at the guy as he does, notices what seemed kind of funny to him before. The guy is dressed entirely in green and gold, Green Bay Packer colors, has a dusty "Packer Backer" jacket on and a stocking cap with the Packer emblem and a green and gold pompom on top. He also has a huge gut, no wonder, from beer and brats at this hour . . . but hungry Basil is not one to be critical, the smell of those sausages is driving him crazy anyway, pervasive as it is.

The man seems to notice. "That what you smell sonny ain't all from *these,*" indicating the sizzling wurst. "Hell no, that's from the mills, up-river, the paper mills. When the wind is blowin' up here we get that smell. Kinda like sausages cookin', ain'a?" he squints and smiles puffily at Basil.

"When you live here you learn to love it, that smell. Comes from the river out there, too. That's the Fox, runs right by ever' paper mill in this here valley.

"Yep, good steady jobs. I worked in them mills for twenty years before I got out," the man smiles at him, pops the tab on another can of beer. "Would've got out sooner, but that's how long it took me to learn how to read," he leans toward Basil conspiratorially, with a beery whisper, "the T.P. Ticker."

"The T.P. Ticker? What's that?"

"The T.P. stands for toilet paper, boy, wipe!"

"Toilet paper?"

"You bet, that's the way that this here river valley figures in on the economy of the whole dang United States. Once I learned that, damn, it didn't take me long at all to make my bundle. Hell, sonny, I'm"—he belches loudly, grins—"I'm a millionaire, twice over."

"You-you are?" Basil belches himself.

"Oh, I know I don't *look* it," he gestures at himself, the truck, "but, well, look here at this . . ." With some effort he pulls up the lower part of his jacket, sucks in his stomach somewhat and reveals to Basil what has to be the gaudiest belt buckle he has ever seen, a massive gold disk in the shape of a football helmet in profile with many green and white gems configuring the Green Bay Packer logo, a white "G" with a green border. The thing really sparkles.

"It's real," assures the man, grunting as he lets his gut plop down over it again. "Fourteen carat gold and emeralds and diamonds, cost me over thirty thousand. I don't let many people see that, but," he gets dreamy-eyed, voice reverential, "I love them Packers, everyone in this town does. They're the greatest. Or at least they were . . . when old Vince was still around . . . wish they'd win some more. . . ."

"Yeah, I guess you would," says Basil, impressed at the man's investment.

"But what the hell, they serve their purpose, hey? They've had their day, and it'll come 'round again, just you see. Their contribution to the survival of the human race can't be underestimated, no sir, and we've all got Vince to thank for that."

"Er, survival of the human race?"

"Damn right, boy. It was the Green Bay Packers who taught the country what a war—what *winning* a war—is all about. Leastways since W-W-two. Hell, I mean you can take your West Point and Annapolis and you can just play their theory against theory and all their namby-pamby ideas of doing battle and you can just cram it. All they get, see, is theory and wimpy war games, bangbang, nobody gets hurt, nobody cares. Well, professional football *is* war, by God, and people do care, and the players, the warriors— gladiators is what they are, by God—they do get hurt!

"See, here's the way it is. Professional football gets going strong and it gets to be a real big thing on television in the sixties, people start watching it every weekend, see. And who takes charge? Who shows 'em that by God we're not just fooling around here, we're playing to win, we're playing for keeps? Why Vince Lombardi and his Packers! He tells his men that you get out there and fight and you better fight to *win* or else your ass is gonna be in a sling, he told 'em. By God, what a general he would have made! What a man he was!" Tears are forming in the man's eyes, beginning to leak down his florid cheeks. "We-we made it through them cold war years okay because of professional football. Everybody got to watch a little war every week, got to root for their own local army, the Packers, the Redskins, the Eagles, the Browns, the Bears, and all the rest. Kept us out of a big one, a real one. 'Course there was Vietnam, that was a bad joke—somethin' we shoulda *won!* Johnson got us into that one, and then never made it to the last quarter! Should of sent old Vince over there, by God, *he* would have won it for us! They should've untied Dick Nixon's hands and let him win it. He watched pro ball, he loved it, he under*stood!*"

The bratwurst are ready, and the man plops a big one in a bun for Basil, who slathers it with mustard and warm kraut (the man thoughtfully has a can of the preserved cabbage sitting on the grill) and chomps down! With the cold beer, it's delicious. God, Basil wonders, why doesn't the whole world eat like this? "So, how'd you become a millionaire," he asks between chomps.

"Oh, that!" the man gasps through a mustardy mouthful. "Nothin' to it, once I learned the way, as I said, of the T.P. Ticker. Well, hell, that's what I call it anyway. Tell you what it's all about," he says, draining the last of beer from his can, effortlessly crushing it, and reaching in the cooler for another. He tosses one to Basil too, who isn't quite finished with his first, but takes it anyway.

"See, I worked for one of the biggest paper companies in the Fox valley here, made toilet paper for ever'body in the country, the whole United States. Ya know what our motto was? 'Your shit is our bread and butter,' unofficially, of course, son, unofficially!" he guffaws.

"Now I worked in shipping, on the dock actually. I was the shipping supervisor; I made sure that the tons and tons of wipe that we would ship each day got routed to the right places, which, as I said, was all over the country. Well, after doing this for a number of years, I began to notice things, like the way that certain areas of the country would sort of react to things. See, as soon as people sense something's wrong in the economy, start to feel a little uneasy, just before they panic, what's the first thing they do? Why, stock up on the old T.P., right? You can live without beer and you can live without brats, but, by God, you can't live without wipe! I swear that America's greatest fear is not of nuclear attack, but of running out of toilet paper! At the height of the Arab oil embargo we shipped so much wipe, I thought people were papering their walls with it! Anyway, long before that I began to notice that certain fluctuations would occur in the usual quantities we shipped-out, and that it would tend to precede an economic occurrence in that region. Maybe a calamity, maybe a gold rush, whatever, it was the inverse of what we shipped. Like, when all of a sudden there was a big upward trend in the amount of paper we were shipping to the Pacific Northwest, and Seattle, specifically. And, by God, if it wasn't before that big, big layoff they had in the aerospace industry there! It started out slow, just a slight up-tick, you know, but consistent it was . . . and then as weeks went by it grew and grew until the actual lay-offs themselves!

"I think it's that people can sense these things, but unconsciously, you know, they're edgy, just toss in an extra couple o' rolls of T.P. with the weekly groceries, don't know why . . . and no one notices right? But *I did!* Sitting pretty up here in the beautiful, unassuming Fox River valley. . . .

"So I start charting all the orders we ship out, and I start to get graphs going for all parts of the country, and soon I can spot trouble coming for a steel town in Pennsylvania, or predict layoffs in Detroit, or can tell the outcome of a strike at a textile mill in North Carolina just as easy as a fortuneteller with her crystal ball! By George, I had created the T.P. Ticker! And from that I began to play the stock market, buying and selling as the shipments of toilet paper told me. They were never wrong. In a strange way I had tapped the, whadyacallit, the collective un-consciousness of America! And that, by God, is how I made my fortune."

Basil is impressed, gratefully accepts another bratwurst from the toilet-paper tycoon who also fixes up one for himself, takes a big bite and sighs, looking out over the dark slow river before him. "I like to come out here, son, and look at this river. In a way, it's kinda symbolic of things, this being the butt end of this area, all the wastes flowing out into Green Bay and then Lake Michigan and, after a while, the ocean and the rest of the world. Kinda makes you feel you're a part of something really big."

"EEEeeeeeeeiik!" someone shrieks farther down the riverbank. Both Basil and the man turn immediately, see that it's the lady Basil had noticed before sitting on the picnic table. She screams again and they dash over to see what's up.

The woman is thin, with long brown hair and wire-rimmed glasses that she adjusts non-stop with nervous bony fingers. She is extremely upset. It seems that her son, one of the Boy Scouts performing canoeing maneuvers out on the river, has somehow fallen in.

"Oh dear God, dear *God*," the woman is frantically chanting, "I was afraid of something like this! I warned him not to horse around out there!"

"Can't-can't he swim, ma'am?" asks the Packer-backer, puffing mightily after his run over.

"Of course he can swim!" snaps the woman. "You think I'd let him out there at all, if he couldn't swim?"

"Well, then ... ?"

"It's the *water*," says the woman, "it's-it's so *polluted!*"

"Yes ma'am," says the Packer-backer, respectfully removing his stocking cap. "That it is. That it is."

The woman screams out to her son, "TRY NOT TO SWAL-LOW ANY, BILLY!" The scouters have quickly gotten the boy back into the canoe and are now heading toward shore.

"Th-this river is very bad, I wish they never would have practiced their boating here," rattles the woman. "This beach was one of the first in the United States to be closed for swimming, you know. That was in nineteen forty-four, can you believe it? And it hasn't reopened since."

The scouts reach shore and the woman runs up to retrieve her boy. "Billy, Billy, you didn't swallow any, did you? Tell me you didn't ..."

An older man, the scoutmaster, comes up, booming heartily, "No harm done, no harm," but he looks concerned. "Just get him home, get him out of these clothes, wash him off good. Then give him some ipecac, get him to throw-up any of that river water. I wouldn't worry ... but if he gets a fever, I'd get him to a doctor straight away...."

"Mebbe take him right to the hospital, right now," says the Packer-backer. "You don't want to take no chances with that water. That's a fact."

167

Yates, Yates, Barrow, and Ivener, Attorneys at Law. That's in the upper left corner of the envelope Basil has handed to him at the general delivery window. Oboy, a check! he hopes, figures he will rip it open right here, but ... hmm, he suddenly gets kind of a chill, sort of like he's being watched here, sneaks a peek around, and ... way over there, across the marbled post office expanse are, Jeeze, two sinister-looking men in suits who seem to look away as soon as he looks over—didn't they? Wee-el, maybe, just to be on the safe side, Basil decides to go back out to the car ... and then, outside on the sidewalk sneaks another look around, and, oh shit, the two men are out there, watching him while talking to a couple of other guys in a big white Buick, one of whom Basil recognizes instantly—Yates! Yikes! The black Chev is still a half block away and Basil breaks for it, boy, heart in his throat, fumbling with the keys to unlock the door, get inside, start the engine, get out of here! He makes the light before they do and there's a cop waiting at the other intersection so the Buick waits, gives Basil a chance to get away, or at least a start on it, doesn't really know which way to go here in the residential area he finds himself in, turning up alleys, running stop-signs, zig-zagging from one intersection to another, trying to stay on a more or less northeasterly course, the direction of Wasson's Bay. He breathes a bit easier, coming out of town through an industrial park, seems to have lost them somewhere back there ... and ends up amongst big fields and farms on a long country stretch of asphalt heading northward towards the bay. Then, he figures, bearing right should take him to—uh-*oh,* in the mirror he spots the big Buick behind him coming up fast. Shit! Basil jams the accelerator to the floor and the engine whine-clatters terribly as he pushes the car to its limits, still some life in this old road-horse perhaps approaching now its finest hour, he's got it up to almost eighty, c'mon! let's ... go for ... eighty-five, and the Buick is still coming smoothly up behind, Jesus, it must be going over a hundred miles an hour ... and then he hears what sounds like a–a firecracker going off behind him or, no, it's a shot! Oh God, they are *shooting* at him! And a glance back confirms this, a guy on the passenger side, his arm outstretched with some kind of small cannon aimed at him and he hears it again, *pop! pop! pop!* oh God, spare his miserable life, Basil has begun rocking in the seat trying to, uhm, uhm, uhm, make the car go faster by sheer will, his foot's to the floor, can't seem to get it over eighty-five, when KEE-Rashhhh! what the—? windshields front and rear seem to have—exploded! shots hitting, blowing them to smithereens, he nearly runs off the road, glass shards all over, Jesus, they must be using an elephant gun or something . . . and, uh-oh, all of a sudden in front of him there's a white wooden guardrail with diagonal black striping, oh Lord have mercy, he's at the end of the road, a cliff ahead, the bay below, and he *can't make the turn!* He ducks, smashes through the railing and feels the pit of his stomach drop to the floorboards as he realizes he is in a free-fall, and this is the end, it has to be, what can he do? he needs a miracle! . . . And then he spots the machine, the-the electronic trinity, on the floor through the half-open zipper of his knapsack, it's his only chance, the car going down into the bay, nothing to lose, he grabs the box, pulls it over onto his lap, snaps the lever up and holds on to the brass handle . . . and suddenly the vibration takes over all, seems like everything is shifting, the falling sensation suddenly amazingly amplified, intense, sickening, stomach twisted into a nasty knot, and Basil finds himself working his will again, *uhm, uhm, uhm, UHM, UHM,* trying as much to end the awful sensation of falling as to cause what really happens: the now ghost-dimensional car begins a graceful swoop upwards above the rippling green bay dotted by a few boats on the horizon, gulls floating by . . . yes, he is actually able to *will* the car up from the waters and around to the clifftop from whence he had just flown. Yes, by God, even if it is in the ghost dimension, he is *flying!* Flying! So the damn thing actually is the anti-grav too! He's saved, thank God . . . feels etheric air rush through the shattered windshield against his face as he swoops, silently, invisibly up over the brink of the cliff . . . and there sees, as only those who have passed over into another phase of being are ever able to see, the scene of his accident, from about one hundred or so feet above the long lonely road, the broken guardrail, the white Buick stopped and four men looking over the cliffside, in the aftermath of what they had done.

Well, Basil now isn't quite sure how to land, but thinks it is probably the reverse of flying, starts thinking, down, *down,* sure, the thing responds to thoughts all right, and it actually works, but yraaaammmmmmm! he suddenly seems to be in an awfully steep dive here, uh-oh, starts thinking up, up, uuuup, pulling back on the steering wheel ... and sure enough, finds himself in a steep climb ... there's a lot more to this than meets the eye. ... By relaxing somewhat he is able to level off, and then determines he will try to control things by thinking easily, lightly, of a soft graceful descent to mother earth, which seems to work, finds himself easing downward in a lazy lowering arc ... going to land on the road at least a mile away from the men and the Buick, far enough, but it won't matter anyway, he's in the ghost-dimension, all he has to do is relax and let it happen ... but as he gets closer to earth, twenty feet, ten feet, about to touchdown, it strikes him how the road looks like a runway, yeah, and all of a sudden the thought insinuates itself of he being a fighter pilot coming in for a landing, and, oh hell ... he starts speeding up again, but at least he's still coming down, and he bumps the earth once, then again, reaches for the lever to materialize so he won't break *through* the road surface, but bounces as he does, bumps the horizontal *time* lever a smidgen, the whole car shudders and reality strobes around him again in the too-familiar flash-bang of time-travel, and when it settles down, the road is gone, there's suddenly a lot of trees around him and, omigod! he seems to be headed right for an-an Indian village!

Yes, in a clearing he is bouncing rapidly toward is a cluster of primitive huts, smoke rising from campfires, people—Indians, milling about. He has surely reached the ancient Wisconsin past, and in fact is headed right for the center of the village! He reaches frantically for the box, hits, damn! the wrong lever and BOING! *materializes* suddenly right in the middle of them, throwing up a whirlwind of dust, bouncing past screaming buckskin-clad folk, women, children, dogs, scrambling to get out of his way, Basil trying to steer the crumpled demon safely through the primitive melange and at the same time flip the stupid switch back to the ghost-dimension ... just before he crashes into the largest hut in the village, in front of it an old, old Indian man, the chief, no doubt, caught in *the way* staring motionless with huge unbelieving eyes ... what a way to end a lifetime of bear and deer, nuts and berries, campfires and canoes ... scenes no doubt passing so swiftly before the ancient one, along with this onrushing evil entity from the forges of the underworld, manifest destiny incarnate, headed straight for him—and then Basil finds the right switch and he and the car suddenly vanish! rising invisibly upward into a steep, sharply-banked climb outta there!

*　　*　　*

"Good morning."

Basil jumps. He is in the Wasson house, Synandra's bedroom. Synandra is sitting at her dressing table, pouring a cup of tea.

"Oh. Morning. Up early."

"Well, you were asleep when I came back from the store. You must have slept over fourteen hours."

"Mmmph . . . long day."

"Basil, what-what happened?"

"Happened . . . ?"

"What happened to my car? The front and back windshields are completely gone. And the left front and side is smashed—it looks like you ran through a billboard or something. I'm surprised you're still alive. Have-have you been drinking?"

Basil has to chuckle, settles back into the pillow. "Nope, well, except for a few beers down in Green Bay. And some brats."

"And what is this thing Basil, this box-thing?" She is holding *the machine,* and is about to take a poke at *the switch.*

"No!" shrieks Basil, sheets exploding, leaping instantly out of bed over to her, probably about ten airborne feet, and grabs it out of her hands.

"Basil! What the heck . . . ?"

They have much to discuss.

The earthquake is what Basil really wants to know about. It sure has turned him into a believer about power centers, and about this girl here too, bye the bye. . . . But the sacred cask of shaman Nabokoff, the embodiment of the THREE of Jimmy Kowalske, and now the amazing power-box of Basil Lexington, inevitably takes center stage. Of course she doesn't believe him at first, wholly apparent by the vapid expression she presents as he describes to her his adventures with Jimmy Kowalske and Ivan Ivanovich in the old house, but begins a slow fade as he tells her how he learned the secrets of the hill, spelling out the details, more or less, of her and Tiffany's encounter in the rosebushes so many years ago. . . .

"How do you *know* that?" she demands, stricken.

"The machine, sweetie, I'm telling you . . . it's for real."

171

"My God, why, it's incredible, amazing . . . the old woman was right. . . ."

"The old woman?"

"Oh nothing . . . what else have you done with the machine?"

He tells her over breakfast, includes his misadventures of the day before. . . . "Sorry about your car," he says through a mouthful of toast and elderberry jelly. "I guess the power struggle for the Church has taken a nasty turn. I suppose they wanted to erase any connections between me and them and him."

"So they tried to kill you—"

"And probably think they did. I'm the link. Or I *was* the link. Maybe that'll keep them away from me now."

"And, and, you *flew* away from them . . . in my car. . . . God, that's awfully hard to take. . . ."

"Yeah," Basil yawning, "I guess it is. But that's the truth. I'll have to give you a demonstration."

Which is going to be a tiny trip into the future. Just a short hop, Basil figures, of maybe a month or so with the main purpose being to check out big gainers on the stock market, future lottery numbers, horse race winners, maybe bring back a future *Wall Street Journal.* . . . Synandra feels uncomfortable about such a mission, telling Basil that she doesn't think it is a good idea to use the machine to try to make money . . . as money, after all, is only so much dross, necessary in moderate, life-sustaining amounts, of course, but in the proportions Basil contemplates acquiring, nothing but trouble. She feels strongly about this and tells him so—that money, in its varied forms, is the purest embodiment of the material plane, as the absence of it, or poverty, embodies the spiritual. The coefficient of money is, of course, desire, so varying degrees of money and desire create all the possibilities of life in the material world. And because the vibrations of money are extremely powerful, expanding perhaps geometrically as the amount of wealth increases, it requires strong character to control the desire that money begets. Any weakness of which (she looks sideways at Basil here) leads to excess: in accumulation, in greed, in depravity . . . it is indeed powerful and dangerous stuff.

Of course Basil believes nothing of the sort. He has opened the envelope from Yates and found only a short cozy note requesting they get together to discuss his fee. Real cozy. So now money has become something of a necessity. And anyway, the idea of anyone rejecting the opportunity to make some big bucks seems suspicious, really un-American to him. "You've gotta be crazy, people would kill to have this kind of opportunity," he declares.

"All the more reason to question the merit of your plan. Money, lots of it, creates a force of its own. Very rarely a good one. I'm not sure we're ready for it. Just ask Tiffany."

"Oh, brother. Look, we're going to the future. And if I happen to see a newspaper there I'm going to bring it back. Do you want to come or not?"

"All right. But I'd rather go back and visit those Indians you ran into. . . ."

Basil sets the *time* lever ahead just a smidgen, hardly at all, a couple of months he figures, enough to calculate untold riches. Plus, it's a nice short hop to demonstrate the thing to Synandra. They will launch from the Wasson house, her grandpa's study. Basil briefly describes to her how the machine works, about its tremendous kick, about the crazy ghost dimension . . . reminds her to hold on to the brass handle at all times. And then he throws the switch and the awful buffeting begins. Basil is more or less used to it by now, but a glance at Synandra next to him, face distorted, teeth clenched, holding onto the machine's handle for dear life, doesn't let him forget they are on one hell of a cosmic roller coaster ride. And then, suddenly, it stops.

"Oh wow," gasps Synandra, at the amazing change the machine has brought about.

"Jesus," Basil gasps too. For it is not, he is pretty sure, the Wasson house, two months hence, they are in. No, definitely not. But, where then, are they? Well, it appears to be, actually, a long, long hallway, the ambience: dusky, with tiny spectral waves running through the ether, the primary color: none.

"Damn!" Basil grunts, but softly. A near-whisper seems to be appropriate. "It-it didn't work right."

"It didn't?" Synandra whispers back.

"No. It's the ghost-dimension—I think. But we should've stayed in your house. At the least. I don't know where we are."

"Everything is so gray."

"I know, dammit. I think it's me."

"What?"

173

"Never mind right now. Let's see where this takes us."

They step carefully toward the light at the end of the corridor. It leads to a great vaulted room, very sparsely furnished. Here it is obviously daylight, though quite colorless. A huge chandelier hangs from the ceiling at least fifty feet above them. To the left and right of the time-travelers are marble columns before a wide veranda that overlooks acres of lawn and gardens, pools and fountains. Basil and Synandra stand silently overwhelmed by the magnificence of wherever it is they have come to. It looks like a cross between the Taj Mahal and a Maxfield Parrish illustration . . . but in relentless monochrome, grainy old-movies black and white.

"Wow . . ." they both sigh in unison.

"Do you like the view?" someone speaks behind them.

They turn instantly and confront a tall aged man in a dark suit. And just as they do, he leans forward and with an ancient hand deftly flicks the switch on the magical box—before Basil can yank it away—and they pop! into whatever reality this is. Color returns to everything, except, oddly, this man. The materialization is a shock, and though reeling, Basil manages to protest feebly, "Hey!"

Then he realizes who they are facing: William Randolph Hearst. But not the actual personna, no, the familiar man in the movie, *Citizen Kane,* the old, old, I-have-been-through-so-very-much-in-this-unforgiving-heartless-world, dome-bald version of Orson Welles in the cinema classic is standing very quietly, patiently, before them.

"I asked if you like the view."

"Er, yes, yes," Basil is able to reply.

"Good. It is very pleasant here, don't you think?" his gaze falls upon Synandra.

"Yes," she whispers.

"Say, uh, where are we?" musters Basil.

The apparition's eyebrows arch. "Why, where you want to be. Your destination. Your goal. The land of plenty. Where anything you want is yours."

"Anything?" asks Basil.

"Absolutely," Hearst replies and snaps his fingers. "Music . . ." And a string quartet instantly appears, begins playing Bach, in a corner of the room. "Food . . ." Another snap and long tables laden with meats, fish, fowl, fruits, pasta, pastry, pate, wines, beer . . . an endless spread worthy of Roman orgy-feasts or the most lavish bar mitzvahs appears in the room. "Oh ... pardon me," he looks crookedly at Basil, the faintest hint of a smile crossing his face, snaps again, and a huge table appears piled-up and grossly overflowing with mounds of golden caramelcorn. The caramel scent is overwhelming, practically nauseating. "Or perhaps it is beauty you desire ..." Another snap and the room is filled with works of art, the walls with paintings, the floor with sculptures, a most tasteful and gorgeous collection. Basil and Synandra, as though drawn by the sheer magnitude of all this excess begin wandering around the now quite-full room. Basil grabs a huge Oktoberfest mug of dark beer, then swipes a handful of caramelcorn; it is delicious, he takes another ... while Synandra sips a glass of wine, stands meditatively before a stunning ancient fresco by Giotto ... *la dolce vita,* it is all quite overwhelming.

"Well, say ..." Basil inquires of his grayness, after he and Synandra have completed a circuit of the *galleria,* "What does one do around here, anyway?"

"Why ... one simply enjoys," says the rigid apparition, and snaps his fingers again. Suddenly, before Basil appears an incredibly gorgeous woman with the most sensuously sculpted lithe body he could ever imagine, minimally attired in diaphanous finery, standing easily six feet tall, oboy ... and before Synandra, the beautiful blonde youth of a bygone (but never really forgotten) post-pubertal dream of hers, stunningly handsome with a white mantle at the waist, terrific chest rippling with waves of perfect muscles ... well, uh ... Basil and Synandra exchange awkward glances here, pausing for one perilous moment before they both respond to the monochrome man, "No ... no thanks ..."

"No?" A snap and the two are gone. "What else can I get you?"

"Well ... we just came for a newspaper, actually. But we didn't think we'd end up here...."

"Here ..." says Hearst gravely, "is precisely where you will end up. Here where there is everything ... and nothing."

As he pronounces the word nothing, he snaps his fingers a final time and all that he has conjured in the room instantly vanishes, leaving it as it was when they had first entered. His face reflects deep sadness. Basil is more moved than he'd care to admit, sees that Synandra is also, staring intently at the man, and then is surprised

175

when he sees—or thinks he sees—a whirling halo of five or so tiny pink hearts glow brightly over the man's pallid bald head, and then fade away.

"Good day," says the apparition as he walks slowly, stiffly, out of the room, footsteps echoing emptily behind.

Basil feels terrible, suddenly very young and very foolish. This wasn't supposed to happen. He looks over at Synandra. She is fighting back tears. "I-I think we ought to leave now," she says. "While we can."

15

The house, the Wasson home, the wooden whitepaint edifice itself, exudes a certain wistful happiness lately. It might even be heard at times softly intoning to itself old melodies it has picked-up over the years from ever-more-distant voices: raggedy child-sopranos and merry alto-tenor-baritone conglomerations that would accompany the player piano at family get-togethers and warble the likes of "Bill Bailey," or "Darktown Strutter's Ball" long after the beer keg had run dry. It liked the swinging music from Bernard Wasson's extensive record collection, enjoyed creaking along to the beat of Count Basie or Duke Ellington, or *swaying,* ever so slightly, to a sultry number by Peggy Lee. Essentially, it is the wood that has taken these sounds, along with myriad other perceptions, into its rigid cellular memory, lumber logged a century before from the magic forest behind, tempered all its growing life in the energies of the hill, giving it perhaps an edge over its sylvan cousins in remembering the life it surrounds.

The interior oak of door moldings, baseboards, and kitchen wainscoting, the laths behind the rough plastered walls, the footworn staircases and perfricated floors have absorbed much: babies bawling, adults arguing, pork and cabbage cooking aromas, children laughing, playing, crying ... carefree chatter floating above a friendly game of sheepshead, business dealings of land and livestock, the great 1911 parlor-brawl of the hotheads Evan and Forrest Wasson, after which Evan nursed a broken hand and Forrest a broken heart ... grave low-toned discussions by kerosene lamp-glow ... new-born infant squalls, lively quilting bees, chilling death rattles, the inky shuffling of bats in the attic....

When Bernard Wasson left the home for the last time, carrying a cased fly rod as carefully as a magician would his wand, the hypermnesic house didn't know that it would be The Last Time, the memory of the man destined to become just another pattern of warming touches that have soaked into its furniture, its patinated woodwork, like so many other vanished Wassonites. The house is neither clairvoyant nor precognitive, its gauge of time roughly the same as ours, though measured in terms of rain in the gutters, smoke in the chimney, snow on the eaves ... and when it sensed that he was not going to return again, ever, something went out of it, left the sacred space as a great gasping sigh lost in the encompassing blow of a passing spring storm. And then it quieted down, glumly anticipating the time when She, the bouncing, dancing, singing girl would also be gone.

Until now.

Yes, contented creaks and wood-swell sighs can be heard once again by the architecturally attuned ear (along, perhaps, with occasional fleeting melodies when the wind blows just right), for the house's venerable soul has detected the presence of another being within its protective walls, definitely male, and it seems to be staying awhile ... a long-awaited complement to the girl's vital aura, the potential for offspring toddling across its floors again, another family growing beneath its expansive ceilings. It perhaps might have known, after the way its rafters shook, during that freakish earthquake not so long ago....

Basil says he's sorry about the car, but Synandra tells him it's really okay, it was falling apart anyway, and ... there's another one in the garage behind the house, her grampa's old car, one he drove in the summer, mostly. Well. A spare car. How fortunate indeed ... and throwing back the big old doors on their rusty hinges ...

Lord have mercy, it is an old *woody* car, a super Chrysler Town and Country convertible, black with a white top, dusty as hell. A 1948 or '49, he thinks, with tons of chrome and real wood framing and leather seats and wide whitewalled tires and a front end that possesses all the arrogance of Charles de Gaulle. He immediately understands that this has to be the zenith of his unworthy life, this sacred consort between man and metallic beast, all else must proceed downhill.... Turns out that she never wanted to drive it, not with her grampa gone, it wouldn't be the same, really doesn't get into machinery anyway ... but maybe with Basil behind the wheel....

Basil's Journal:

It was all I could do to stop from proposing to her on the spot. The car is the most beautiful hunk of iron I've ever seen, on the road, in a museum, or anywhere. It makes me believe in America all over again, in a real corny way, that maybe there is some kind of goodness at the heart of all its excess, if there's some part of it that can come up with a machine as terrific as this.

The other machine, though, that sucker is one big puzzler. I just can't understand what happened, or where we went. I told Syndy that the machine seems to follow your thoughts, like it's somehow linked-in to your feelings. She said that maybe, with the two of us, it got mixed-up somewhere in our collective subconsciouses, a place where her negative feelings about unlimited wealth and my show-biz background got kind of jumbled and the result is where we were. But the problem now is I don't know if I can trust the machine. Syndy says she knows *she doesn't trust it. For these reasons we have agreed not to use the machine for a while. On one hand this depresses me, and on the other gives me great relief. At least it gives me a chance to take it easy now and figure out just what to do. I don't think that it's going to be safe to go back to the Jack of Hearts office right now. Maybe not for a long time. The rent will run out at the end of August and there's nothing in it except an answering machine. That I can get Stinky to take care of. The whole thing is is that I'm not sure I'm cut out to be a private eye. It's sure not all it's cracked-up to be. And anyway, now I've got the machine, which is going to change my life, you can bet on it. For the better I hope. When I get around to using it again. But for the time being I'm pretty content here with this very cosmic chick, and thus begins a whole new life for me. She doesn't have much interest in machines anyway, tells me that it is the earth and the hill and her gardens that gets her attention. Well, to each their own.*

*   *   *

Yes, things have turned-out pretty well, Basil has to admit to himself, not on paper perhaps, but sometimes it seems like he's found the rainbow-end of the twisted, goofy trail he's been traveling for quite a ways now. Enough for an essentially simple guy who has been trying to make his way through what is left of the twentieth century, hoping that it won't self-destruct in the meantime. And while he sweats it out, it is not hard to be happy living with this mystical girl in a peaceful woodsy land, distant as Timbuktu from the rat-race he has left behind.

But all is not idyllic idlesse. Synandra has the Ars Aromatica shop to attend to, and Basil, other than simply infusing the relationship with trust-fund cash, tries to be useful on a more practical level. At first it was only building some new shelves for an expansion in her line of herbs (as precise an undertaking as he has ever made in the mechanical realm, resulting in a fairly acceptable job; he not the handiest with her grandpa's set of tools), but then actually helping in the store itself from time to time, feeling like a latter-day apothecary, weighing out ounces of precious ginseng, or goldenseal, or parsley, sage, rosemary, and—whatever. He was less skilled in handling her line of potpourri blends: colorful mixtures of aromatic flowers, herbs, and oils that she had created in scents of lavender, bitter orange, patchouly, sandalwood, and so on. Even more nebulous were the perfumes she had concocted: Midnight in Kenosha, Sheboygan Fantasies, Musk at Dusk ... not to mention her extremely popular *Caliente y Frio* massage oil—he let her handle that stuff.

Oh, and speaking of that oil, one hot night a couple of weeks after the incredible earthquake, Basil, aided by a most creative application of the *Caliente y Frio* and a few glasses of wine, managed to persuade the gaga girl to slip Out There, to the southern power center, to, heh-heh, "shake things up again," requiring more convincing (the medium being the massage) than he had anticipated because it turned out that that quake had bothered Synandra more than she had at first admitted. The hill is, after all, a fragile structure (she told him) like all of our fair planet, and with its wonderful complexity of water courses, undoubtably more so. And with the earth responding so violently, to their, ahem, violent, union, she wasn't sure if it could stand such a shock again—if (she had conjectured, over her third glass of wine) the shock would even actually occur again . . . oh, probably not, it was just some freaky kind of thing . . . had to be, and anyway, if it *had* been them . . . well, there wasn't exactly a full moon in the sky now, and then, maybe it was just the pent-up lust of their first time together . . . she could never be *that* hopelessly excited again—could she? Oh God, could she? Tiffany was always fantastic with the oil, but this guy, God, he got her so *revved,* running, half-stumbling through the woods at midnight in a (now very oily-clingy) bottomless baby-doll nightie, her one concession for, ah, dignity's sake, and he totally naked behind—what the hell—wild unicorn prodding her along to a very rosy crucifixion, which is what it was like, she dragging him down upon frenzied her at last, upon the grassy earth, not caring at all now if . . . if, as they made their frenzied love, the one thing, the only thing there really ever was, ever would be, everEverEVER could be . . . if the earth, again, really would . . .

And the next day Mrs. Frost had knocked on their door, carrying a basket of still-warm homemade doughnuts. Looking somewhat—jolted, her eyes bright and liquid as the day when Basil had moved out. And she again, as a sort of scorekeeper in this crazy game, had the morning paper: 2.7 on the Richter scale. "My, my," she had said, again obviously awe-struck, "another quake. Strange, isn't it, strange as strange can be. . . ."

So that was the last time—out there—for a while, anyway. Until they knew more about what was going on—and about any damage they might provoke, during, perhaps, an even more inspired encounter. Disappointing, but not the end of the world; the bedroom was still seismically safe . . . as was just about each and every other room of the house, including the kitchen table—and, uh, the big desktop in her grampa's study . . . also certain of the mystery rocks atop the hill, and, well, quite a lot of other areas of the magical forest. Not to mention anywhere within the gardens surrounding the house (preferably moonlit) . . . and that's really where Synandra—when their exploits range far and wide—seems most at ease. . . .

Basil isn't surprised, because when she's not working at the herb shop, or whipping up something vegetarian and delicious in the kitchen (bolstering Basil's growing respect for the tasty terricolae), it seems that the first thing she does in the morning and the last thing at night is work in those gardens. There are an approximate dozen of various sizes, from small singular beds of peony or day lily, to big vegetable groupings, like the monster at the back of the property containing tomatoes, peppers, beans, potatoes, eggplant, zucchini, and, she vows, "the best damn sweet corn you've ever tasted." Although there is no great distinction, roughly a third are devoted to flowers, the rest to vegetables and herbs. Basil, whose concept of vegetables has been limited to the pale wilted lettuce and pinkish tomato slices he might pick off of a jumbo-burger prior to consumption, has had absolutely no experience in this area, but is willing to learn, begins one warm late-afternoon by helping her plant a second start of spinach.

"Blecchh!" says he, half-seriously, "What do you want to even grow this stuff for? Who eats it?"

"You do. It was in your salad last night."

"It was?"

"The dark green leaves."

"I thought that was a different kind of lettuce."

Well, even as her eyes roll in comic-mockery, Basil can't help but feel a vague thrill as he carefully follows her directions and makes a finger-line depression in the loamy soil, spaces the seeds along the miniature valley, then covers them up. That's it.

"That's it? I mean to get vegetables that's all you do?"

"Uh-huh, that's it, except for watering. And weeding."

"No. . . . C'mon." Basil knows he's being jerked around here. Just seeds, dirt, water? And that's all?

"Well, there is something else," Synandra tells him.

"Fertilizer?" guesses Basil. His conception of growing things, of gardening, farming, is a tangled confusion of bags and bottles of sprays and chemicals, tractors and tillers and other incomprehensible implements.

Synandra recoils, almost spits. "Fertilizer, you mean NPK chemical fertilizer?"

"Well, whatever. . . ."

"Honestly Basil, don't you know anything?"

"Hey. This is not my area of expertise."

"This is an organic garden," says Synandra righteously. "All of these gardens are. The only fertilizer that goes into this soil is natural compost from that bin behind the house. Where we throw the garbage. And also where we put leaves, grass clippings, weeds, anything natural to decay into humus, organic material we can return to the soil. That's what organic gardening is all about. Taking what you need and putting back everything you can. Some of these gardens have been in the same spot for over a hundred years, and they're better now than when they were first dug. Gardening, and for that matter, farming, is actually a very simple process. The chemically synthesized fertilizer you're talking about, in various nitrogen, phosphorous, and potassium ratios, causes the plants to suck up those three chemicals to the exclusion of all the minute quantities of minerals that they would naturally take into themselves—and them into us, when we consume them. And those are most anything naturally occurring in the earth's crust: zinc, calcium, magnesium, manganese, tin, silver, gold—"

"Gold?" Basil perks up. "There's gold in that thar soil?"

"Sure is, in tiny amounts. Scientists are finding that very small amounts of these trace elements are necessary for good health, elements that we miss we when we consume only foods grown in soil doused with chemicals, specifically NPK fertilizer. But that's not the worst of it. For one thing, because the soil is not being rebuilt as it is in organic farming, it requires more fertilizer every year to sustain the same high crop yields. For another, because the soil is no longer healthy, the plants aren't either and are much more susceptible to disease and insect infestations. And that requires spraying with insecticides, which leads good innocent farmers further along the path of chemical farming, to finally what I think is the ultimate tragedy, the use of herbicides for weed control. Isn't it crazy, now we have farmers spraying a poison, a plant-killer, albeit a selective one, on their *plants,* in their poor overworked fields so as to save them from tilling and to increase their yields a bit more. These herbicides, which eventually end-up in our groundwater, by the way, are very bad stuff, related closely to the carcinogenic defoliants they used in Vietnam. Very bad. And of course who suffers in the end but the consumer, who buys unhealthy food raised on unhealthy soil . . . and then wonders why they aren't healthy."

"Huh. Never knew that before . . ."

"It certainly doesn't get big press. Or is often discussed in polite company. It's always amazing to me how defensive people are about what they consume. Religious fanatics pale in comparison to people who will defend their trashy eating habits to the death, and often do. Anyway, looks like you've done a good job with those spinach seeds. We'll plant another row in a month or so."

"So this is the way we plant our garden?" says Basil, feeling rather pleased with himself, dusting off his hands like an old sodbuster.

"This is the way."

"Well, what was that 'something else' then, to get the plants to grow. If it's not fertilizer."

"Oh," she says, "you have to talk to them."

"The plants? I've heard of that."

"Yes, the plants, of course. But that's not exactly it. . . . See, it's really the spirit of the plants that you talk to. Little entities that sort of oversee the growth of the plants. They're like little elves, or fairies; at least that's the way I like to think of them."

Basil has to laugh. "And maybe pixies, brownies, guh-nome-ees?"

"Shhhhh!" Synandra very serious here, shooshes him. "You'll hurt their feelings." Then, to the plants they are kneeling before, she speaks. "Don't mind him, guys. He doesn't know what he's saying. He doesn't understand. He's just a big dumbhead—"

"Hey! Now cut that out . . ."

"Well, you're a fine one to talk, after the guh-nome—now you've got me saying it—the gnomes you told me about seeing. With the machine. Or maybe you just made them up."

"Hey, I did not, I saw them as plain as day. Whatever they were . . ."

"Well, what's the matter, then," she smiles devilishly, "afraid they'll realize you *are* a big dumbhead?" And at that she jumps up and playfully bounds away.

Basil follows, chuckling as he chases her barefoot around the big Wasson lawn in the late afternoon light. Around and through her gardens already thick with vegetation although it is only the end of a northern Wisconsin June: onions with two-foot spikes, tomatoes and peppers and zucchini bearing almost-harvestable fruit, and in the back of the big plot, sweet corn well above the proverbial knee-high point. Basil has to admit that the stuff really does grow here. They finally square-off in a flower bed, a spiky line of gladiolus swords between them.

"So," puffs Basil, "so, where are your little buddies to protect you now, huh?"

"They're always around . . ."

"Yeah, well I don't think they're big enough to—" And suddenly Basil senses an odd *tickling* sensation on his left ankle, which translates to something like an itch, it's irresistible, he has to bend down to scratch, just for a second. . . .

And in that pause she's off again, laughing, "I told you, I told you so . . ."

She races into the woods, but it's a short dash, verily calculated, and they make love under the soft shade of some quietly tsking birches, dusty, sweaty, crazy, out there in the late summer light, no one else around. . . .

Afterwards, idly picking grass-shreds from her hair, looking up at a patch of very blue Wisconsin sky she asks, "Would you like to see them?"

"See who?"

"The fairies, the elves, the spirits that tend my gardens."

"I think I've seen enough gnomes for one summer."

"Well, from what you've told me, I don't think these are anything like what *you* saw. We won't really *see* these guys, anyway, only their energy fields. But that's fantastic in itself. You'll see. There's an herbal preparation Dr. Bo once helped me whip up, I think there's enough left for the both of us."

Later, fresh and showered, clean, but not fed—Synandra wants them to have empty stomachs for this, to Basil's extreme consternation—they are sitting on the big swing on the back porch looking out towards the biggest gardens with the woods behind. The top of the hill looms massively beyond, the summit still backlit by the last faint glow of the setting sun. "Oh, by the way," she casually says after Basil has gagged down a cupful of the ugliest-tasting brown liquid he has ever had set before him, "I hope you don't get too sick to the stomach. One of the ingredients in this is fly agaric mushroom, a very deadly poison."

"Oh God, no . . ." mourns Basil, looking around for someplace to be sick.

"Now, don't worry, it's not enough to hurt you—I don't think—but anyway that's the way these things work, you know, a bit of the death in life, something to break through the walls we build around ourselves . . . it's liberating, is what it is."

"Jesus, I don't know . . ." mutters Basil, wondering how he lets himself get caught-up in these situations. Synandra's exuberance isn't catching; she apparently really wants to show him something here, but garden spirits, fairies? and-and via deadly *toadstools?* No way, boy. Basil starts to get up, to get to the bushes at the edge of the yard perchance to puke, else perchance to die—

"No, wait Basil," Synandra pleads, holding him back. "You won't really die, honest. Listen, I went with you to God-knows-where with that weird machine and I trusted you right? Now you've got to do the same with me. As much as anything I want you to know that my plants and my hill can show you some interesting things too, maybe things a shade more subtle than your high-flying machine can show me."

"Well . . ." as long as she puts it that way. After all she drank it too, and at least they'll die together. . . .

They snuggle closer as the evening deepens around them. Synandra tells Basil that when she was very young, about five- or six-years-old, she was out wandering in the gardens just about this time of year when she chanced upon a very small man, about four inches high, standing alongside a zucchini plant. He was dressed in tiny work-clothes: plaid shirt, overalls, miniature broad-brimmed hat, and he seemed to be inspecting the prolific squash. When she came upon him and gasped, the little elf (that's what she figured he was) whirled to face her with a surprised look, but paused long enough for a wink and a smile before disappearing into thin air.

"Wow, did you ever see him again?" Basil is impressed by the story, remembering again his own strange encounters with gnomes—or whatever they were. Of course those were big fellows, compared to what she's talking about here, weird metaphysical subspecies, per-haps . . . but, he has to admit now that maybe her notions aren't all that strange. In fact, the whole concept is taking on much more a cast of believability as the punchy potion has ever so gradually begun asserting its own version of reality, beginning with a buzzing in his ears, a tingling in his inner elbows, and a peculiar clarity to his night vision, as if the darkness had slightly lessened. . . .

"Nope," says Synandra. "I never saw him, or any of them, again. Not in that form, anyway."

"Well, then exactly what form—"

"Oh, Basil, look, out there, do you see it?"

"Uh . . ." Basil does. He sees *something* pretty weird out there by the glads, a strange glowing ball of light bouncing around like the biggest firefly he has ever seen! "Oh my god . . . what *is* that?"

"It's an earth-spirit attending to the plants . . . look there's another, oh! and another . . . oh, they're all coming out!"

Yes, Basil sees more and more of these lights, dozens now, floating through the gardens in pale hues of gold, blue, green, red . . . some hovering bee-like above the plants, others seemingly earthbound, winding slowly around the rows of beans, peppers, potatoes, cabbage, corn. . . . Synandra takes him by the hand to step off the porch and stroll around the gardens . . . and as they do, speechless, awestruck, Basil finds he can discern subtle differences in the tiny glows—the ones attending the carrots do seem to have a definite orange cast, those around the peas very green, and so on. He can't believe it, feels as if he's in some kind of Disney movie, expects to see Tinkerbelle fly by at any moment. . . . Yes, there's a whole other world out here, hundreds, maybe thousands of these little glowing buggers flitting all over the place. They're on the lawn, the bushes, in the trees too. The sight of all these busy lights is quite dazzling, like an enormous firefly convention. He turns to look at Synandra, who is grinning really big with an I-told-you-so-Mr.-Smarty look plastered on her face.

"Wow, that's some potion," Basil whispers to her.

"Let's go up on the hill, okay? I'll run in and get a blanket."

From up here, the woods appear alive with tiny, busy, glowing lights. It's incredible.

"I-I just never could have believed," says Basil. "All this going on, but unseen, unknown to us. Tending for plants everywhere."

"Not exactly everywhere, I don't think" sighs Synandra. "Here by the hill, it's thick with them, there's so much energy around. That's why the gardens do so well. I haven't witnessed this for sure, but I feel that the spirits have pretty much left the crazy chemical-doused farm fields ... it's not their way, you know what I mean?"

Basil nods. He does; he believes her.

"These beings understand that weeds, insects, even diseases are a part of the scheme of things. If a plant succumbs to something like that, it's a tribute to whatever took it. Maybe it's a sign of the health of the soil, or of moisture, or the climate. The early farmer was incredibly sensitive to such things; he or she had to be. Their ability to survive through the winter depended upon it. But now, gosh, farmers are more and more becoming businessmen-with-plows than tenders of the soil. Just buy some new chemical to slop on the earth if it doesn't produce what you want. God, it's nuts. The earth-spirits won't stand for that."

Basil nods again. She has to be right.

The sight is fascinating, dazzling, but as time passes, increasingly ethereal, until either all the faeries have gone home to bed, or the illuminating drink has worn-off, or both. Synandra yawns, snuggles closer, says that it's the potion that's left them, not the spirits. They're always there. Basil looks up at a sky velvety black and yet moonless, a bottomless bowl of stars.... He yawns himself, and then starts as he notices someone watching them off the edge of the hilltop. It appears to be an old, old woman ... and at the same time he detects an earthy aroma, not entirely disagreeable.

"Hey," he whispers, turning slightly to Synandra, "who's that?"

She seems to have picked-up on the scent too, albeit unconsciously. "Where?" she asks, delicately sniffing.

But as he looks back and points—it is only an instant later—the woman seems to have vanished. "Huh, she's gone!"

"What-what did you see?" whispers back Synandra, now very awake.

"Looked like an old woman. Like a bag lady. A hag."

"Oh my God. You-you saw her!"

"Saw who?" asks Basil. "Who did I see?"

"The old woman, the one who comes to me here."

"What do you mean—*comes* to you?"

"Well, at certain times. When I need her."

"I don't get it."

"I guess I might as well tell you ..." she sighs, then explains to Basil about the woman, how she seems to appear whenever she, Synandra, is in need.... Then, after a moment's consideration, decides to tell him about the last time the woman had appeared, when she was so upset with the archaeologist Clyde Mortell, and about the advice the woman had passed on to her about Basil.

"Me?" says Basil after what Synandra tells him sinks in, "you think she meant me?"

"I'm positive. See, the absolute worst thing that could happen is for that stuffed-shirt of a professor to dig up the hill in search of bones, artifacts, whatever . . . and I didn't know what to do. And now you're here . . . with me . . . with the machine. . . ."

"The machine," echoes Basil thoughtfully.

"It's the power we need to stop him," she says. "The old woman knows. . . ."

"But how?"

"We'll think of a way."

16

One morning Basil is awakened by sounds, sleep-muffled at first, then louder, of drawers opening and closing, the creaking of footsteps on old oak floor boards. It is early, the roselight of a budding summer morning fills the bedroom, and bustling through the tinted atmosphere is Synandra, getting dressed.

"Uh . . . what's going on?"

"I have to see Dr. Bo."

"Mmph . . . why?"

"I can't explain it," she says, zipping up bluejeans, "I just know that I have to see him today. It's a feeling I get."

"Hmph."

"Would you mind watching the store today?"

"By myself?"

"You can do it—"

"Aww . . ."

"It's a snap. You know what to—who's that?"

Someone is rapping at the front door.

"Mrs. Frost with doughnuts?" says Basil hopefully, trying to remember exactly what they had done last night—and where—while Synandra goes over to the window, looks down.

"Oh, it's Tiffany. Haven't seen her in a while . . ."

That is true. Tiffany hasn't been around lately, having discretely stayed away from the two lovebirds . . . although Synandra had mentioned that she had dropped into the Ars Aromatica shop after the quakes. Gushing.

Basil has just about drifted away again, a dream coming up about the hill and him together with the girls, it's in black and white, of course, looks to be a *good* one too, but is interrupted by a voice from Out There, Synandra calling him to come downstairs for a moment, please. . . . Then pouring him a cup of *mate* tea as he slumps, wearing her grampa's mandarin silk bathrobe, into a chair at the kitchen table.

"Hi Tiff. What's up?"

She looks tired, but gorgeous in a rather tight-fitting T-shirt. "Oh, not much," looking at her fingernails, "I just deprogrammed a Trinnie."

"You—what?"

"Deprogrammed a Trinnie. Isn't that what they call it?"

"Up here in Wasson's Bay?"

"Uh-huh."

"One of Kowalske's crazies?"

"Yep."

"Well, what the hell? . . ."

She tells them. How the day after the earthquake, the, er, second one (Synandra can't hold back the blush, Basil the big grin, Tiffany the awe) she found this guy hitchhiking on the road between here and Sturgeon Bay. She didn't know why she had stopped, there was just something about this guy that seemed to latch on to her (he was pretty good-looking, too), it's happened before. . . . Anyway, he seemed very intelligent, though very confused . . . and also, as it turned out, incredibly horny. It seems that Trinnies, single ones, are expected to be celibate. Apparently to help them avoid the temptations of the outside world, retaining members a function of restraining members . . . and Tiffany simply couldn't resist a challenge.

"So, uh, he's been with you ever since?"

"Yeah, we've hardly left the bedroom . . ." Tiffany's turn to blush. "But my parents are coming up for the Fourth of July, and I've got to get him out of there. Besides I've got a part in our next play, and rehearsal starts next week. I thought taking him up to

191

Dr. Bo would be the best thing. The poor guy is still awfully confused. I don't want him to try to go back to that stupid church."

"How bad is he?"

"Pretty bad, he feels really guilty about being with me, for some reason. Plus, he thinks he killed someone. I don't know whether to believe him or not. He says he ran a car off the road, off a cliff into Green Bay somewhere south of here."

"What?!" ask both Basil and Synandra in unison.

Tiffany tells them that this Trinnie, by the name of Rudy Godwit, is apparently a privileged member of the Church of the Electronic Trinity. Almost an associate of the controlling hierarchy itself, but probably not, according to her, a sure bet to advance into it, he being too much of a *believer*—wholly dedicated to the coming of the Three; he was a graduate student in physics at Stanford before entering the church, and possessed an unusually keen interest in the alleged extraordinary machines. . . . But at any rate, he could be trusted by them, and ended-up serving as a flunky for three church heavies who were after someone they suspected knew something of the whereabouts of Jimmy Kowalske. They had almost cornered him in Green Bay, at the post office, but he had gotten away in his car, until they found him again on a road leading to the bay, and in a high-speed chase the poor slob went over the cliff. The only thing was, they couldn't see any trace of the car below. The heavies decided that it was underwater, even though the bay at that point was quite clear and not very deep . . . but unless the car had disappeared into thin air, Rudy Godwit feared that he had aided in the murder of the man they were after.

"Who was it?" both Basil and Synandra ask, in unison, again.

"I guess they didn't trust this Trinnie with everything, and they used a code word for the guy. They called him the 'Jack of Hearts.' Say . . . wasn't that the name of your detective business back in L.A.—" She frowns and slaps her forehead. "Ohh, of course, boy I *am* tired. That was supposed to be you, wasn't it, Basil? But-but, wait a minute, you're here, and he said that the car went over the . . . said he saw it . . ."

Basil and Synandra exchange appropriate glances here, and then Basil puts on his best smirk, "Heck no, he's been caged up too long, I think. As you can see I'm right here, safe and sound." He hates to lie, but he can't tell her about flying around with the crazy machine, hardly even believes it himself. . . .

"Well, he said it was an old black car, a Chevy, and-and that's like your car, Syndy, and where is it now? You've been driving your grampa's car around—"

"Hey, hey calm down," says Basil, "we had to junk it, didn't Syndy tell you, it blew a dipstick. In fact, it blew both of them."

"Oh. Well, I guess I am a little tired . . ."

"Sure. After all nobody's going to survive a drop into the bay like that . . . er, where you said, it must be a hundred feet straight down . . ."

Synandra cuts in here, reminds Basil that the reason Tiffany has come over is to take Rudy Godwit up to stay with Dr. Bo. Since he ran away from his companions—literally a mad dash from the motel room they were staying in, taking the car keys along—the Trinnie was afraid that they would catch up with him.

"Besides, he's practically a basket case," Tiffany adds, "in need of some wise counsel. . . ."

"Well," Basil yawns, nods at Synandra, "I guess your feeling about heading up to see the doc was right on target."

A faint smile. "It always is."

Later, six o'clock-ish, novitiate herb-slinger Basil is flumped on the sofa after a long day at the shop, surprised at how really tiring taking care of business can be, even such a simple one as this, his hands telling of it, like Synandra's when she comes home, reeking of lemon verbena, peppermint, lavender, rosemary, sultry patchouly, with sandalwood, vetiver, sticky styrax under his nails—it's almost a dirty job. . . . Well, he can take it easy now, turns on the TV, waits for the news, thinking that this herb stuff, though about as far from his line of work as you can get, wasn't really all that unpleasant, something maybe a guy, even a tough dick like himself, could get used to, maybe do a little P.I. work on the side. . . . And anyway, business was brisk today, kind of fun watching the register drawer fill with money, selling so direct, up-front and immediate . . . no major problems to contend with, fortunately . . . and even more fortunately no sign of Yates and company. He isn't quite sure if they are *still around*, or if he should worry about them or not, guesses not, it's easier, and chomps down on a big handful of caramel corn as the news finally comes on: A rabid congressman whining about why the United States should build bigger nuclear missiles in order to maintain parity with the Soviet Union. The congressman has with him plastic models of each country's missiles to help him illustrate his point. He waves around the Russian model, which is about a foot long, thick, and sleek shining black, says that if one of these babies scores a direct hit it's bye-bye time for sure. The news host, David Brinkley, counters that the American Minuteman missiles are more accurate than the Russian missiles, and thus could be smaller, gesturing toward the American model his guest has brought in, barely six inches tall, thin, and very white. The congressman sniffs that we should build *more* missiles to stay ahead in the arms race. David Brinkley tells him that we already have the capacity to destroy the planet twelve times over.

It's too depressing. Basil switches channels and blunders into a commercial for Morning Candy Crunch, the L'Oreal breakfast confection. It's a dozen or so cartoon elves dancing around a toadstool, each carrying enormous spoons heaped with *le crunch,* red, green, yellow, orange, and blue stuff, looks exactly like sugar-encrusted gumdrops, enhanced here with animated sparkling stars . . . when suddenly an old, white-bearded elf elder appears, poof! atop the toadstool and in a sort of high-pitched Gabby Hayes drawl informs the gang that a boy and a girl are in trouble over yonder—thataway. The elves zip-zip-zip-zip-zip at blur-speed into the woods, to a glen where a purple-cloaked crone has a small boy and girl locked in a cage. Getting serious, the elves tip-toe behind the witch's back, and shovel-toss their spoonfuls of cereal into the children's mouths. With each spoonful pink balloony muscles pop up on the kid's cartoon bodies, and in no time they are strong enough to smash the cage, which explodes, blowing the witch off-screen, apparently killing her. Then, as a large box of Morning Candy Crunch slowly fills the screen, the muscle-bound tykes inexplicably *fly* away while all the happy elves wave bye-bye.

Wooo. Time to turn off the tube . . . time really to push it out of the window, way past time maybe. . . .

Yes, and it's nod-out time, too. Basil, big-yawning, not really used to putting in more than a full eight all in one place, the detective work an entirely different thing . . . not since the Dawsons' days anyway, really goddamn happy days as he fondly remembers

194

them now . . . times like this when he would drift-off in the dressing room between takes, not so far removed, really, not at all . . . waking to Jack Dougherty's throaty chuckle, cigarette bobbing amusedly from the corner of his mouth, kindly aura filling the room and the boy's heart with good-natured humor and warmth . . . except that now the man is oddly pale, colorless actually, but still there as he is best remembered, not as he looked the last time, but—

POP! The sound fills the room, along with a hair-blowing, curtain-billowing gust, rousing a confused Basil, blinking at Synandra and Tiffany who have just . . . appeared, in the middle of the room here. Oh shit . . . as The Realization strikes Basil, angry and sudden, the girls collapse together onto a rug in the center of the room, each still clutching by a hand the brass handle attached to the sleek wooden box of the infernal machine. They're exhausted, but obviously happy, each beginning to chuckle in a certain private way as they slowly open and close white-knuckled hands, bend elbows, stretch slender bluejeaned legs, hmm. Tiffany turns to Basil, beaming, speechless. Aw, he can't really be mad at them . . . waking fully now, releasing the sweet-sad memory of Pop as the old man was, back then . . . even that . . . the past rushing always behind you, always so rapidly away, so certain, so inescapably linear no matter what they say. . . .

"So, where'd you go?"

"Oh, the future . . . nineteen eighty-four."

"Nineteen eighty-four? The-the future?"

Yessir. Well, at least that's where they decided to go after Synandra "slipped" to Tiffany that, yes, they possessed the marvelous machine. The actual embodiment of the THREE. Seems that on the drive back from Dr. Bo's Tiffany went on and on about how Rudy Godwit, her trembling Trinnie, was absolutely captivated by the coming of the THREE. And she had been trying to tell him how absurd it was for anyone to believe in some devices that could not ever exist, not ever, no way, no how. . . . Poor Synandra. It had to come out; after all, she had been friends with Tiffany since practically *forever*. . . .

But . . . 1984. That prophetic year, that Orwellian touchstone that, in the seventies still looms ahead, awaiting the western world's smug summation of itself. It isn't quite so distant anymore, but with times so touch and go right now, Basil can pretty much understand

195

why they chose it. He is actually quite impressed, as that year had, in fact, crossed his mind as a future destination, but an especially dark one, owing to the warnings of Captain Jimmy and the old Russian, and the memories of the book remaining from Modern Lit. 101. But he wants to hear their version, "So . . . why then, nineteen eighty-four?"

"It just seemed like a good time to go to to see if it was even *there,* first of all," says Synandra. "And then, if it was, what it was. You know, Orwell's book made it out to be such a bad scene. Jeeze, you can't even set the dumb thing, the machine, anyway, Basil."

"Yeah," says Tiffany, "that's what I don't understand, how does it know exactly where, or when, you want to go? There's no numbers or anything. . . ."

"I don't know. It seems to just know. But sometimes you're not even sure where you are. Like when Syndy and I—"

"I know, I heard all about it," Tiffany waves him off. "Gives me the creeps. And you guys too, I gathered. But anyway, we ended up in New York City, Times Square, in November—I'm not really sure of the day—nineteen eighty-four."

"Hey, you didn't bring back a paper or anything? A *Wall Street Journal,* perchance?"

"No, I wanted to, but Syndy wouldn't let me. Said you'd waste your time with it."

"Damn! What's the big damn problem with you guys anyway? We could be rich!"

"I am," Tiffany smiles, "and it's such a bore."

"Oh Basil, is money all you think about? Then you'll fit right in, in nineteen eighty-four," says Synandra. "That's all *anyone* thinks about there. It's a totally materialistic world where everyone is a–a what's the word, Tiff—a yuppie?"

"Yup."

"A yuppie? What's that?"

"Stands for young urbane plutocrat, or something like that." Then to Tiffany, "Should we tell him who's president?"

"Might as well. Basil, we got there right after elections and . . . guess who it is?"

"I give up."

"Here's a hint," says Synandra, "remember that old movie we

watched last night on TV?"

"Uh, the one with the monkey, Bonzo. A monkey is president?"

The girls burst out laughing. "Practically. It's—you won't believe this—Ronald Reagan!"

"The actor? The *old* actor from the borax TV westerns? No, c'mon . . ." Basil smiles along, shows them he can take a joke.

The girls can't stop laughing, between gasps for air keep insisting that, yes, he *is* the president and what's more—they begin shrieking now—he just won *his second term!*

Basil is laughing right along too now . . . but the laughter is sort of an over-layer here of something inside kind of troubling, the realization that perhaps they are not kidding here. Maybe the old geeze really *is* president. He's known Synandra long enough now to know just how long she will carry a joke, and when she stops for a breath, wipes her eyes and says in a semblance of deadpan seriousness that yes, he really is president—or, actually, *will be*—Basil knows she is not kidding. They all quiet down somewhat and Basil says that he just can't believe that the man has made it to the top, although he can sense a certain kinship there, after all, he himself was an actor at one time and, besides, Reagan was governor of California. But, that was back when just about everyone he knew had become a hippie, the times laid-back so much that someone like Reagan, a hardcore Establishmentarian, appeared to be an aberration.

"Times have really changed," sighs Tiffany, rolling her eyes. "You should have been with us. It seems like absolutely *everyone* has gone completely retro. The kids especially. It-it's like everything's reverted back to the fifties. Girls are wearing poodle skirts and bobby socks, guys have crewcuts and black leather jackets, and their fondest dream is to get into a good business school. *Bowling* is back!"

"No . . ." Basil is truly horrified. It can't be. They've got to be jerking him around again. . . . But Synandra has *that look,* nodding seriously that, yes, it is all true. All of it. Basil wonders what the hell happened then, to, to America's youth? Where are their values? What burning issues do they believe in now? *Crewcuts? Bowling?* "Are-are you guys sure you made it to nineteen eighty-four?"

"Absolutely."

They didn't stay very long but have managed to learn a few odds and ends. One thing is that little home computers have become big stuff. Everyone, it seems, has one. Exactly what for, though, the girls aren't sure . . . to turn on the coffeepot in the morning and the lights off at night, most likely, and probably so that people can work right out of their home. They can even tell old "ticker-tape" Lexington here that IBM is a maker of the little computers, of course, but there's another one with the funny name of a fruit, they think, banana comes to mind, but they can't quite remember, maybe peach or apple. . . . Other than the future being an essentially retrograde time, there's really not all that much change, Basil learns as they talk long into the night, at least with what he always considered the Big Issues: war and peace, love and death, haves and have-nots— they all still exist in varying degrees, but one thing is very hard to take: someone, some psychotic murdered John Lennon, the bodacious Beatle. Around 1980, they think.

"No . . ."

"Afraid so. Wish it weren't . . ."

"No . . ."

This is very bad news.

For Basil the Beatles were much more than a musical group, they were part of the cultural juggernaut that rolled him and everyone else his age into and through the sixties. The best of times, and, at times, the worst of times, in which he expended his precious youth. It was that pivotal year again, right after Kennedy was killed, after blushing, skinny-tie, Boy-Scout America forever lost its innocence, burying visions of Camelot and the carefree fifties, it seemed, together. A rude awakening. And that was when THEY came on the scene, as though according to some Grand Design, transmitted right into all of America's living rooms, immediately into that sacred space, amid the plastic-encased sofas and hi-fi's and Pat Boone albums and the dreaming young minds of this quivering age. Sunday night; The Ed Sullivan Show; February 9th, 1964.

It didn't really matter that they didn't know what they were doing, no one else did anyway, or that they were probably more a function of the *Zeitgeist* than a precursor . . . but they were out there, they were public domain, they were a *force,* with us through it all: Woodstock, Vietnam, love-ins, peace rallies, psychedelia, spiritual questing, back-to-the-landism, chamomile tea . . . until, in 1970, they disbanded. Suddenly: no longer together; the Lennon-McCartney genius had split, as though yin had left yang—neither alone possessing the brilliance of the two, the amazing creativity that had turned rock and roll on its head, produced the music of the era, the background force, the rhythm, the beat, the pulse that seemed to unify us all—that spark was gone.

Again, it wasn't THE END, but it was the warning shot that it was near, rolling across the land as a very slow shock wave, gradually overtaking and splitting apart the what-was-it? the Movement, the Force, the strange counter-cultural whirlwind that had swept so many good hopeful folks along with it, humble electronic-age settlers who now look around and find themselves a dozen or so years older, wearier, harder, perhaps wiser, but all wondering where they are going next. Where? Back then, it seemed that It, the movement, would end *somewhere,* some sort of pleasant, blissed-out free-love Nirvana-land, somewhere ... the seeds planted in the Haight-Ashbury, the communes of northern California and Michigan, the extended families of Boston and New York, the fabled Farm in Tennessee ... *somewhere* ... or at least keep on moving.... But not so. The bubble burst, the Vietcong won, Geronimo's Cadillac stalled. There was no one left, certainly not Richard Nixon, who could put it all back together again.

And now a peculiar rootlessness has spread across the land. People are not *together* anymore. *This* is truly the lost generation. The Beatles, as much an embodiment as a symbol of what was truly going on with the youth of this country, have drifted apart, along with the whole big rolling movement. The national *I Ching,* cast by the great alabaster hand of Uncle Sam himself, comes up with the hexagram *Po,* symbol of dispersion. It's depressing. The baby-boomers are no longer babies. Everyone is getting old.

Basil, poor aging Basil, has sensed this more or less subconsciously along with, he believes, everyone else of these muddled times, and wishes for something that could bring it all back again. One thing is, or was, the hope that the Beatles would be reunited. Together again. Going somewhere. And then, somehow, maybe it would be like all of us *were* back together again. But now even that dream has apparently died, along with the man, the poet, the dreamer who could make it so.

Of course they discuss it. It becomes an argument of sorts as the night becomes later, the hour earlier. Lennon is not at this time dead. He can be warned. He can be saved.

Basil is all for it, Synandra is against it, and Tiffany is unde-
cided, thoroughly confused, actually. The only thing that gets decided this pivotal evening is that they can't decide and that they
need sage advice. That, indeed, of a sage, Dr. Bo. Perhaps after the
holiday rush, they will be able to visit him.

*   *   *

The Fourth of July celebration blows into the peninsula like a
hot wind, carrying along with it a stream of tourists, steamy days,
sultry nights, and, as it seems to Basil, having recently encountered
in Bernard Wasson's study the incomprehensible might of *Finnegan's Wake*, great Joyceian thunderrrolllerumrummummummummu-
mmummrngngngrollllllrollllllshkhkhkshhazambmbm-a-zamm-a-zamm-a-
zzzammmm!bBoommmbBoommmCRAKCRAKCRAKBOOMCRAK-
BOOMBoomerollllbBoombboomerers echoing through greattowering
bottomdark anvilclouds between shore and hill, cliff and meadow,
inland sea and roaring sky . . . with business at the store very good
(the showers driving tourists inside, Basil learning), he becoming the
(relatively) handyman of the operation, tending to the yard and the
gardens of the Wasson homestead, puttering around the great house,
helping with customers when she needs it . . . tiller of soil, purveyor
of herbs, mower of endless lawn . . . surprising how good it feels to
do honest hard work . . . really satisfying, healthy . . . considers himself to be an actual non-smoker, too, even doing some jogging with
Syndy along the dusky village backroads, after a veggie dinner and
before a warm shower together and the evening's lovemaking . . . hot
nights lately outside somewhere in the woods with a shared bottle of
wine, she convincing him to allow her to sit quietly in the center of
the blooming roses beforehand, earth-princess soaking in amazing
earth energies . . . while he watches intently, excitedly, limicoline
dweller before these uncharted seas (her color deepening, breath rising, nipples distending before his eyes—always amazing), before taking her, flushed and trembling, to—any place but dangerous there,
often devilishly up on the hill itself if no tourists lingered after the
sunset, ending up atop one of the heartrocks, the longish flat one,
the energy strong there, but purer, safer, quakeless, becoming a

rhythmic silhouette, a strange shadow pantomime before the light of the moon ... yes, all this and even time enough for Basil to reflect during odd moments on how it's such an awfully long way now from the southwestern sun-baked land from whence he had come: perpetually dry, asphalted, and jagged-cacti-angular, atmospheric carbons layering on palm fronds and jade plants and the heated brittle soil ... so unlike here of profuse and fragile greenery, sky-blue waters, clean air and rain, warm blessed rain, tonight again, perhaps, pattering on the rooftop, on meadows, on gardens and trees, so pure, so sweet ... and away again, the celebration, the tourist surge, and the firecracker weather blows out of the greening jutland.

Last night it stormed. Tonight they have recently finished love-making atop the hill, naughty Synandra having wished that it would, er, actually *thunderstorm* while they were so engaged, Basil more than a trifle edgy at the thought, lightning, you know.... But tonight's storm passed farther south and a cool wind has come up to clear the remaining night clouds away. Wrapped in a blanket, they watch lightning flicker silently to the south and east out over the lake. The moon has not yet risen and Synandra points out the stars and constellations to Basil. They are really bright tonight and she knows them all: Bootes, Lyra, Cygnus, Hercules, Corona Borealis, Draco the Dragon ... her grandpa taught her. The only one Basil knows besides the Big Dipper is Orion, the bright-belted hunter, but he can't seem to find it ... because, Synandra tells him, it's a winter constellation, of course, and isn't around right now. Oh, of course. . . .

"I love watching the sky," she says. "It always reminds me of how truly tiny we are ... in relation to all this ..." her slender arm sweeping the universe. "For example, Vega there is the really bright star in Lyra, the brightest star in the sky," she says. "It's only twenty-six light years from earth, a light year being about six million million miles long, it's about, um, one hundred fifty-six million million miles away. But of course, that's no big deal, Deneb over there in Cygnus is fifteen hundred light years away, or ... nine thousand million million miles, and the M13 cluster in Hercules is *thirty thousand* light years away, or—"

"Hey, what's that?" asks Basil, who was checking out the milky way, that softly magnificent cross-section of our galaxy, one of *billions,* he has heard, and we're talking *galaxies,* unbelievable, never really understood it so clearly before as here, the incredible *vastness* of it all, the ancient ones, primitive people, *cavemen,* probably understood more about all this than most folks today ... but closer to home, to the east there's this unusual white cloud glowing and actually, sort of *pulsing* out over the lake. "Jesus, what *is* that? A nuclear plant meltdown?"

"I think it's ... the northern lights," says Synandra, turning to the north. And there, just above the treetop horizon is an eerie swath of luminescence, celestial footlights before the big show. Suddenly a spire of light shoots upwards from the glow, followed by another, and another until dozens of polar rays shift before them, gradually becoming a towering spectacular of gossamer pale curtains flickering pink and white and green across the northern sky. Basil has never seen the northern lights before and they're truly a strange sight. There are moments when the display nearly vanishes, leaving only white ghost-clouds glowing in the west and east, then reappearing in a gigantic surge of glimmering streamers draping all of the starry vault from horizon to zenith.

Synandra says she can hear them crackle.

Basil says he can't.

They sit back and watch the dazzling display, neither of them speaking ... but there's always a vaguely palpable current of energy surrounding Synandra, especially while they're up here on the hill. Basil can feel it slightly, along with other growing sensitivities he has noticed since being with her, and it seems that there is some perceptible modulation of that energy occurring now that he is picking-up on, perhaps through some function of the aurora they are watching, enough to ask her, "So, what's up."

"Oh, it's not that I'm not happy or anything; I am with you, I really am," she says without hesitation, as though she has been speaking to him all along. "But," she sighs, "I guess what bothers me is that it was so darn inevitable."

"Inevitable?"

"Yes, you and me—I know it's going to sound terrible, but it seems we really had no choice. I didn't want to believe it myself but then ... that day when you first came into the shop, I understood. You see, Dr. Bo had hinted that someone—you, it turned out—was going to show up that day. I think I even tried to discourage you a tiny bit, remember? That night it stormed? I guess I was rebelling against the powers of the prophecy, to no avail of course. . . . But then that day in Milwaukee when I saw that magazine I knew it was true."

"Huh? What was true? What are you talking about?"

Synandra hesitates, then rushes on, "About a prophecy that Dr. Bo had made years ago when he told me the secrets of the hill. He made me promise never to reveal them to anyone . . . although I did tell Tiffany, but she's a girl, and—"

"Wait a minute. What about this—prophecy?"

"Well, that word is so profound, but it's what I've always called it. It's just something he told me a couple of times. Of course everything he says is so profound, and he's never wrong . . ."

"But what is it?"

"Well, I didn't want to tell you this so soon—"

"What? What? What? Tell me what?"

"Okay. All right. Well, Dr. Bo told me . . . that whoever, whatever man . . . would describe to me . . . the true nature of Mystery Rock Hill . . . that man . . . would be the one . . . the father of my children, my husband." She is sniffling, tears big in her eyes.

"What?! That's crazy, crazy," Basil shaking off the blanket, standing up, pacing around the hilltop. "Why is everything so crazy around here?" he shouts to the silent neon sky. He has that terrible helpless feeling again, of being a pawn in a colossal chess game that's always *way* beyond his control.

"It's not *that* crazy," retorts Synandra between sniffles. "American Indians have been arranging marriages for ages, and not just for political reasons. They simply know when two people are meant for each other—wherever and whoever they might be."

"How do they know?"

"I'm not sure. It's just something the elders, the wise ones, know . . . through divination, I guess, visions, dreams. Dr. Bo never elaborated . . . of course he rarely does."

"And so it's me, huh? Us?"

"I guess so. Are you—disappointed?"

"Aw, jeeze, Syndy, of course not . . . but it's just so weird . . . isn't there any free will left in the world anymore?"

"I honestly don't know, and I've thought about it a great deal, believe me. How do you think *I* felt, never knowing what sort of Bluebeard—or if anyone at all—would show up to claim me? I had always hoped, at first, that the prophecy was just a joke, but the more I learned from Dr. Bo . . . well, it didn't look too good . . . and anytime I would ask him about it he would just chuckle and turn away . . . or tell me not to worry, the powers of heaven and earth wouldn't let me get stuck with a–a lemon."

Synandra begins crying harder now and Basil comes over to her side, feeling awful again—and suddenly, strangely, thinks he spots a tiny shower of pale pink and blue, ah, *hearts,* momentarily flash and fade before her bowed head—probably lasts less than a second. Huh. "Jeeze, Syndy, I know I'm not the greatest guy on earth, but I can't be *that* bad, hey?"

A laugh bursts though her sobbing, she puts her arms around him. "Oh Basil, you idiot, of course not. I love you, you . . . big galoot! It-it's just . . . what I was always afraid of was that it would be that pompous jerk, Clyde Mortell. With his digging and probing I thought that . . . once he finally got permission to dig here . . . he would be the one who would know the true nature of the hill. It seems that it really was a miracle that you came along . . . with that machine . . . to me that really is a miracle."

"Yeah, I see," says Basil, feeling better. Feeling really good, actually. "Hey, uh, when is that guy supposed to set-up camp here anyway?"

"I don't know. Any day now, I'm afraid. I think I've been trying to put it out of my mind. Somehow, we've got to stop him. But we've got the machine," she says firmly, brushing tears from her cheeks. "We can ask Dr. Bo's advice tomorrow."

"Tomorrow? Are we going to see him tomorrow?"

"Uh-huh. I feel the time is right."

Basil has to smile, shake his head. "Jeeze, I don't know if I can ever get used to the idea of your just—knowing."

"Well, it's just something we have to do. It's—I don't know— *right,* what's happening, inevitable. We just have to go. I can't explain it. . ."

"I know you can sense a lot more than me, I guess. But I just hate the feeling of being so—manipulated."

"Well, manipulated by life—or fate maybe. When you think about it, are they any different? Really? You know, I didn't ask to be born into the legacy of the hill. And-and you, Basil, did you *ask* to have that crazy machine dumped into your lap? Did you *plan* on coming to Wasson's Bay to meet me? You know, my grandfather used to quote something in Latin, by Seneca: *Ducunt volentem fata, nolentem trahunt*. It means, 'The fates lead him who will, him who won't, they drag.' "

"I'm beginning to think that's true," he says, silent for a moment, then, "Wherever you go, there you are."

"You've got it," says she. "The center of the universe is everywhere."

They lay back against the protective hill, pulling the blanket closer against the cold, two tiny figures gazing up into the enormous dancing sky.

17

B asil's Journal (excerpted):

*. . . One of the strangest things about the machine is the presence
it seems to have, as though the energy inside it creates what Synandra would call "vibes," and I would normally call "bullshit" except
that I think I can feel it too. Of course Synandra also says that
all machines give off some sort of vibes because, in fact, (she says)
they actually have souls, being purposeful assemblages of raw matter
and therefore just below living organisms in the structure of life on
this planet!*

*Man, sometimes she's just a little too far-out in left field for
me, but one thing—when it sits upon the dresser in the bedroom and
I wake up in the middle of the night, I know it's there and it's okay
and I feel kind of good about it. . . .*

The next day Basil, Synandra, Tiffany, and the incredible machine—it sits contentedly on the back seat—make the trip up to see
the Indian doctor, and on the way Tiffany tells them that the LoFoCo
breakfast foods division is planning a new atrocity, an ostensibly
"adults-only" breakfast cereal that they secretly hope children will

clamor for. It is to be called: *Dawn,* but the company joke is that it was developed under the working name: Sex Flakes.

"Can you believe it?" sputters Tiffany. "'Dawn, the sexy cereal for lovers,' is how the ads are going to read. God, this time daddy's just gone too far. And the thing is that it's the same old grain mush pressed into flakes, heavily sugared, and shot with the usual synthetic vitamins. But on this one they're going to throw in more vitamin E, the supposed sexy wonder vitamin," Tiffany groans. "And those grains *have* vitamin E in them before it's refined out."

Basil says that he thinks it might be a gigantic seller: sex, sugar, and an adults-only mystique; kids—older kids, anyway—will really want to check it out. "What they should do then, see," he jokes, "is put little pornographic picture cards in each box. Ha-ha."

"Oh, be quiet," sighs Tiffany. "There must be some way to stop them . . . but they're too big. Daddy won't listen to me, and the project is practically complete. If we only had some kind of magical something-or-other that . . ."

Uh-oh. Both Tiffany, and Synandra, who hasn't really said anything yet, are looking across the Chrysler's front seat at him. It's a set-up. Synandra knows all about this. Both of them start giggling. "Are you guys kidding?" fumes Basil. "What do you think we can do about it? Even with the machine?"

"Well," Tiffany smiles at him, "we do have a little plan. . . ."

Which they briefly outline to him . . . following which Basil informs them both to find another sucker. There's no way he's going to do *that,* boy. No way. And a kind of ugly silence insinuates itself between them.

To change the subject, Synandra tells Basil what she knows about the venerable medicine man they are about to see. Which is really not that much, in that there is not a lot that is known about him, even by Synandra (in the manner of all shamans, mystery shrouds much of his personal life), though a few facts have sifted down during the course of the enigmatic Indian's association with the Wasson clan, most notably she and her grandfather—and with the Wasson real estate, most assuredly, Mystery Rock Hill. It was, of course, the hill that brought them all together. Once, when a young Synandra asked him why he was a friend of the Wassons and (as far as she knew) no one else in town, he smiled and said softly, "I am a friend of the earth first, and those that inhabit it, second. One of my

207

missions upon this planet is to watch over the hill—and consequently, those who are watched over by it."

He was an orphan (so the story goes) found literally in the horse-trodden streets of Green Bay at the turn of the century, adopted and raised by a wealthy family in the town, Petroski, given a white man's name: Nicholas, and sent away to a succession of private schools (his blue eyes and father's money overcoming the aquiline curve of nose in gaining admission—and then his keen mind and superb athletic physique keeping him there), ultimately graduating from Harvard Medical School, class of 1929. But he was not long for the establishment medical world, perhaps understanding that there must be something *more,* some greater knowledge attainable (which would make 1920's Harvard medical school seem primitive) and the brash young doctor one day disappeared, to where, no one really knew . . . some said to the witch-doctors of Amazonia, others, to the toadstool shamans of the Siberian tundra, still others, to an apprenticeship with a Lakota Sioux mentor in the Black Hills—perhaps all three, but returning years later as someone quite different, still a medical man, but now also a *man of medicine* with an understanding of the real thing: of the delicate relationship between man and earth, plant and planet, how they become unbalanced, and how that balance can be restored. He returned to the northwoods of Wisconsin in the hungry teeth of the depression and began ministering to needy rural folk, Indians mostly, and whatever white people came to him, pay as they could, whenever they could, however they could.

Basil is fairly nervous about meeting someone he had seen, or observed, actually, seven years ago—or one month ago—depending upon your time-frame, although it's really funny . . . he somehow feels that he has already formally met the man.

It is midafternoon when they bounce down the logging road to the doctor's digs, a small two-room shack in a large clearing on a hillside in the Wisconsin northwoods. The medicine man greets them with the slightest nod of head, the faintest of smiles. He doesn't even seem to notice Basil, first taking each of the girls' hands in his—a sort of customary welcome, it appears. Basil recognizes him instantly, there's no mistaking the steel gray hair, the headband, the chestnut arms and hands . . . but the deja vu's are coming in fast and strong . . . he can't shake the impression that he's been with the man before, as though on a long journey together, but when? Where?

Synandra formally introduces him to the doctor, a solid handshake, a piercing look, and Basil is taken aback (again?) when he meets those blue eyes; they surely mean business.

Rudy Godwit, the cult-shocked Trinnie, is notably absent. The medicine man explains that his has been a tough case, the young man in need of a total break with his church—indeed, all civilized attachments. So the doctor has prescribed an authentic vision quest for him: naked, fasting, and crying to the four corners of the world for guidance. He has been gone for two days now, and the doctor thinks he will be gone for two more.

"Ooh, alone and naked," sighs Tiffany. "Where is he?"

The doctor almost smiles. "Out there. In the forest at a power spot I know of. One something like the Mystery Rock Hill. Keno and I keep watch on him."

Keno . . . another nagging familiarity. Basil wants to ask who exactly *that* is, but immediately the doctor takes them on a walk through the forest surrounding his homestead, ostensibly to gather plants for Synandra, which he does, Basil notices, with extreme reverence and care, softly chanting as he cuts twigs from a shrub with a sharp knife, or deftly unearths tubers with a digging stick. Along the way he points out certain plants and flowers and trees—more for Basil's benefit it seems, as Synandra and Tiffany politely look on— the doctor mentioning the medicinal properties of one, the food value of another. He takes them to a clearing in the forest, where there is a spring feeding a clear pool.

"This is the source of it all," murmurs the doctor, a sharp look at Basil.

"Of what all?"

"All."

"Oh."

"This is the earth mother's purest manifestation. She provides this to us, this gift of water. We defile this gift."

They sit silently in the afternoon sun filtering through the trees, gazing into the gently burbling pool . . . no one speaks, the girls seem quite content, Basil restless, as usual . . . hates this kind of thing, wants to get up and walk around, climb a tree, anything other than just sit here and look into a stupid pool, though it's a nice one—as far as springs go—very clear, about a foot deep, a brown-green bottom and, uh, what's this? in the water, what looks to be a

... *face,* seems to be taking shape, yes, a silvery face, colorless as his dreams ... and it looks here to be, er, *James Dean,* yes, it's unmistakable, the hip young 1950's embodiment of Troubled Youth, as Basil remembered him from, say, *Rebel Without a Cause* ... and here is this tragic sneering face looking directly up at Basil, and then—winking! makes Basil's heart skip a beat, maybe several ... the communication between him and Dean so direct, *ojo a ojo,* seems to mean something. ... Basil looks around, Synandra and Tiffany don't seem to notice anything, each gazing into the clear pool, perhaps lost in their own visions, but, uh-oh ... over there Dr. Bo is staring intently at him, *he knows,* Basil has to look away, back at the water, the image gone now, thank goodness, Basil not exactly one for *visions* here, decides to keep his mouth shut, eyes too, just sit quietly, relax, meditate, take a few deep breaths. ...

They leave the spring as the sun begins to set. The doctor leads them back, passing by giant oak trees edging a clearing in a stately rustic row, firey skies beyond touching the upper limbs into so many silhouetted golden boughs.

It is twilight when they return to the doctor's homestead. Another Indian, wearing a battered fedora with a large feather in its brim, is there when they return, greets them all, even Basil, by name. Basil breathes hard at the sight of him, knows he's seen this guy before too, his bright bulging eyes, it's eerie ... and the man introduces himself, of course, as Keno.

He has been busy while they were gone; a small fire has been built, and a pot of something is simmering upon it. Good, Basil thinks, food. It's supper-time and he's famished ... maybe a little venison stew, hey?

Well, not really ... it's an herbal potion, and these things are best done with an empty stomach, Keno explains.

Aw ... no, not this again ... Basil begins to protest, but Synandra and Tiffany quickly shoosh him; it's truly an honor to be able to partake of one of the doctor's magical brews.

"But ... why?" grumpy Basil wants to know.

"Why not?" laughs Keno, lifting the clay pot from the coals. Synandra pulls Basil aside, whispers, "Dr. Bo's doing this for you. I don't know why, but don't complain. You're incredibly lucky—"

"I am?" agonizes Basil.

"Yes, just try to ... prepare yourself ..."

"Oh God . . ."

"Hey, what about this thing?" Tiffany calls from the car, holding up the magic machine by its brass handle as if it were a forgotten picnic basket. Basil's heart skips a beat at the sight of it, he truly has forgotten, brain-circuits presently overloaded with double-time deja vu's of the enigmatic shaman and his single-feathered cohort, and also, James Dean. . . .

Tiffany brings the machine over to a circle of log sections where they are sitting, an open flat area between the doctor's cabin and the fire, and places the machine on an empty stump between Basil and Keno.

The doctor speaks to it, "Welcome, friend, to our little group."

They all chuckle, though neither the doctor nor Keno seem to wonder what the strange wooden machine-like object is; in fact, they already seem to know, as Synandra begins to explain their current quandary: how exactly to use this thing?

Keno begins laughing softly, shaking his head back and forth, "Man, there's your friend Rudy out there and all those crazy Trinnies just waiting for this thing to start a 'New Age' on earth, and you've got it right there, pal. Right there!" He laughs harder.

Basil feels sheepish, doesn't know what to say.

Synandra speaks, "Well, listen, we came for some advice. We've got some important decisions to make. Do you know that some psychopath in the future kills John Lennon, the Beatle?"

Keno's jaw drops a foot. "What? No . . . when?"

"We're not sure; nineteen-eighty, we think. We've got to decide whether or not we should, or even if we could, save him. I-I mean there's lots to consider, lots we don't understand . . . like . . . for example, my grandpa . . ." her voice breaks, tears fill her eyes. "He-he could be saved, too. I'm just not sure, you see—"

Dr. Bo snorts loudly, stopping Synandra in mid-blubber. "What we must first understand here is that all is vibration, you, I, everything; what we think of as reality is merely a collection of agreed-upon vibrations, or pivot-points, we might say, each of which branches to another, which branches to another, and so on, infinitely. Therefore there is a reality in which this . . . John Lennon, is alive and one in which he is not. The same is true for your grandfather. This is what you had trouble understanding, is it not?"

"Er, yes," says Synandra, "but if that's so then why—"

"Why anything? That is what the world is, that is fate, that is the pathway of the reality which we follow."

"The doctor is talking about parallel universes," says Keno. "You follow that don't you?"

"Well, yes, of course, but—"

"So," continues Keno, "this machine here simply allows you to go back and take another path if you want."

"Then," blurts Basil, "we could go back and—"

"But *should* we?" asks Synandra.

"That is up to you," says the doctor, "but be aware that in doing so you are simply following another path; at the moment you choose it may be the one you desire, but ultimately, will it? Will you choose to change it again, and again, and then again? For example, your grandfather's death. Believe me, there is no one I would rather see back in this world again. Nor you, I imagine. But then at some future time you will again have to deal with his passing . . . or perhaps he with yours. Remember that reality changes continuously. We are sitting here together now with our thoughts, our perceptions, of what has happened, who is alive and who isn't, what exists and what doesn't, and all are simply memories, some more distant than others, gathered along that path we have followed. It is just that we normally don't have such a formidable view of the process. Believe me that the path that has unfolded for us, for whatever unknowable reasons, guided by an infinitely greater power than ourselves, is truly the path of least resistance. Think of that. Any other path will have obstacles strewn before it.

"What I think we are truly discussing here is knowledge. When you use this machine, what you obtain is knowledge: of what was, what will be, what might have been. Then you must choose. In the end, it is yourself you must live with."

"Yes, yes I guess I see . . ." sighs Synandra.

"Well, then what can we do with it?" whines Basil.

"Anything you choose. Something you can live happily with. Something the world can live happily with."

"Oh, I know something we could live with," pipes Tiffany. "And it would do some good in the world. But he," pointing to Basil, "won't do it."

"Aw c'mon, that's a crazy idea," Basil smiles. "Just listen, doc, to what they want me to—"

But the doctor raises his hand for silence and nods to Keno, who skims scum and woody shards from the soupy brown potion that has been cooling by the side of the fire. Keno pours out three cupfuls, carries one each to Basil, Synandra, and Tiffany.

Basil sighs, it's useless to protest, the doctor's presence is overwhelming, the three of them each choke down a cup of the still-warm liquid, Basil noticing nervously that the doctor and Keno abstain, busy themselves bringing wood to the center of the fire circle, proceed to build it up as the darkness increases around them.

Basil feels decidedly more uneasy as minutes pass, a gentle buzzing wells up in his ears, a now-familiar tingling in the inner elbows, mouth suddenly very dry, breaths coming unusually cool into his rising chest, subtle heightened patterning of the darkened forest all around ... finds his thoughts becoming more disjointed as they sit silently, wonders if the girls are feeling the same ... when suddenly the bonfire leaps up before them and a strong drumbeat begins solemnly from behind ... or is it ahead? It's difficult to tell, but Dr. Bo and Keno are sitting along roughly the same plane, same oblique angle, facing the last orange glow of the sunset, but neither is playing a drum. Where does it come from? Is it even a drum? Or just his tripping heartbeat? And-and, now slowly welling-up, a murmuring chorus, rising and falling rhythmic chanting, eerie, aboriginal ... not really all that frightening ... but still, seems like it's coming from nowhere, or everywhere ... and then slowly the medicine man lifts his arm, points out beyond the fire where they all turn to look, and amazingly the scene before them is one of murky graylight, of-of an endless expanse of ... trash, an impossibly colossal garbage dump, hills and dales of piled-up junk, seems all too disturbingly familiar to Basil, a sort of never-ending deja vu.... And out there, in the midst of the stinking mounds, is a lone Indian in breechcloth and headband apparently picking his way through this grotesque conglomeration, movements attuned to the drumbeats, the chanting voices, as though it is a kind of solemn dance, a vaguely purposeful progression through this vast waste area.... Increasingly, Basil finds it difficult to resist the urge to, uh, *get closer,* yes, he feels strangely drawn toward the lone figure, appearing larger now as he zooms outward like the lens on his Nikon, until yes, he again *becomes* the Indian out there ... again? Yes!—and with a terrific heart-stopping rush he suddenly remembers when and where all this has happened before: during the thunderstorm, and in the old house in MacArthur. He understands it all, simply and with great clarity, like a dark and dumb curtain has fallen away, because *he is right here now, he is now and has always been the dancer,* and feels no fear or sense of confusion, only that of mission, of a need to push ahead! To see, finally, what it is that lies beyond the greatest peak of this bizarre refuseland. . . . The incessant drum, the chanting, guides him, smoke and stench fills his nose as he climbs upward over junked avocado refrigerators and snowmobiles and electrical transformers and air conditioners and smoke detectors and microwave ovens, and thousands of bottles and cans and papers, and multitudinous stinking disposable diapers (wants to steer clear of those, you betcha), and plastic, lots and lots of plastic containers of all colors, shapes and sizes, everything in the world's made of plastic nowadays . . . trudging higher up the looming pungent peak, to look out over, finally, to see. . . .

The summit. Just ahead, the now-darkened sky above gaining a swath of deep orange . . . and there, as he plants his feet unsteadily in the shifting conglomeration and looks out . . . the sight takes his breath away . . . for the trash continues onward for miles and miles rolling eventually up before the sunset city, "Golgothapolis," a whisper in his ear, an immense blackened bustling plain of gigantic beehive domes, elevated tramways, belching stacks, squat fortifications, and a continual movement of tiny aerial lights against the smoky black-mud-orange sunset, swirling departures and arrivals of aircraft of some sort . . . the terminal dark city . . . yet pulsing in Basil's heart of hearts with a strange inherent radiance, something terribly truly fascinating about it.

"Haw-haw, got you too, does it?"

He jumps. Unmistakable throaty laughter. He looks over and . . . it's Pop. Jeeze, Pop Dawson. It's incredible, wonderful. The old fart is sitting slightly below the broad summit of the trash-mountain here in a greasy old recliner, a bottle of Pabst in one hand, a smoking Pall Mall in the other.

"Gosh, what-what are you doing here?"

"Don't know. Same as you. But one thing I'm pretty sure of is that *there,*" pointing a yellowed finger toward the smoking city, "is where we're headed."

"Yeah, yeah," Basil murmurs in agreement, gazing outward. "It sure seems like it . . . that's the place. Never knew how to picture it before . . ."

"Me neither. I've just been trying to figure out how it, how everything, got this way," with a broad gesture to the conglomerated landscape surrounding them.

"Any ideas?"

"Well, other than the goddamned industrial revolution itself," the old man chuckles, "I know *that* didn't help any . . . I think a big part of it might be . . ." he points now to an old television set in a nearby trash-crest, a *Doggone Dawsons'* program flickering grayly, eerily, across its screen.

"Television? Uh, us?"

"Sure, one and the same. Living's become easier in the twentieth century. The electronic age, the push-button age. Maybe too easy. Too easy on the old *noggin!* People don't *think* anymore! And we're to blame." The old man pauses, coughs mightily, wipes his lips with a quivering hand. "Yep. Us. We come into their homes in that funny little box there and we showed 'em what their lives should be like, how to live, what to buy, how to talk, how to *be,* we showed 'em! By God, we misled 'em is what we did! We made 'em think that by tuning-in to that magical box that they knew all that they had to know. We made illiteracy easy. Who reads anymore? Who *thinks* anymore? But that's not the worst, no. Maybe the worst is that we kept 'em busy with us night after night, little play after little silly play, one after the other, half-hour, hour at a time, Ozzie and Harriet, Lucy and Ricky, Beaver and the Peeper, we kept 'em so busy, no one stepped out to see what was piling up outside, *this!*"

"Jeeze, maybe you're right, I never realized . . . the terminal city, Golgothapolis . . . it's out there, waiting for us . . ."

"Son . . ." Pop's look is acute.

"Yes, Pop?"

"We did what we had to do. To put food on the table, to make a buck . . . like everyone else . . . we didn't know . . ."

"No, we didn't, no one knew. . . ."

"Son . . ."

"Yes, Pop?"

"Oh . . . nothing, never mind."

"Sure, Pop," he understands, seems like there's really nothing more to say, maybe there's never anything really to say.... It's enough just to be here in this strange place, at this strange juncture, with the old man....

Basil turns to look around; he has been gazing so long at the dark city he forgets what lies to the east, the direction from which he supposedly has come. It's really black that way ... but there's a pinpoint of light out there, flickering, the light of a fire, it appears, someone else camping out in this crazy wilderness? And as he gazes, he is surprised to find the light rapidly enlarging in his vision, as if he were being, uh, *pulled* toward it ... and he is, very quickly rushing forward, the sound of drumbeats increasing too, it seems, much, much louder ... and suddenly he is back. Standing upright, between all of them and the campfire.

"I-I've seen it, I've *seen* it ..." he croaks hoarsely. And then he collapses.

18

B asil opens his eyes to daylight, feels like a wreck. He's slept late, Synandra and Tiffany are lolling out in the sunny meadow, the doctor and Keno nowhere in sight. Basil's stomach growls, and as though they hear it, though they are probably a hundred yards away, the girls both look toward him and start on over. Dream-fragments float upon the backwaters: he trying to throw the awful machine away, but he can't, it won't let him, he can't let go ... it's dark, scary, and he ends up following it over a cliff, a terrifying dream-cascade ... finds a curious goatlike horned being presiding at the very bottom, and it, the creature, seems *terribly sad,* disappointed in him for some ought-to-be-obvious reason, the drift Basil catches, the last pre-awakening dregs, the horned one becoming the doctor's face as Basil last remembers it, glowing jack o'lantern orange above the embers of the fire....

Really creepy, shakes it off as best he can as he rolls up his sleeping bag ... a glance at the girls tells him they have all seen something profound last night—undoubtably the same terminal city— but he will confirm his vision with their's in due time, probably isn't necessary anyway, at least not right now, and so they drive back mostly in silence, grabbing some food at a diner along the way

217

(greasy burgers with everything for Basil and the girls don't even look too revolted). . . .

They arrive in the early afternoon to discover the southeastern corner of the Wasson woods suddenly transformed into a busy little encampment of a dozen or so brown canvas tents, tables, picks, shovels, and other implements of desecration, along with a modest sign:

Archaeological Excavation of Mystery Rock Hill
University of Wisconsin
Dr. C. R. Mortell, Ph.D.

Clyde Mortell's archaeological team, himself and an eager young crew of graduate students, attired in khaki and cutoffs and overly-serviceable mountain boots, has made the scene. The court's decision allowed the team to occupy the site, and they surely have, much to the distress of one already very stressed-out crew.

*   *   *

Basil's Journal:

Outside the sun falls bright, clear, and very white upon the waters of the bay. It is very hot, even for Wisconsin in the middle of July. A breeze is blowing up from the southeast and whitecaps form about one-half mile out and then die before reaching the shore where I sit, feeling strange and sad inside. Seeing Pop again like that, in that junkyard that rose out of an Indian potion, surely saddens me. He tried to tell me something about where we are all going, and how we got that way, and I think I understand. For that I am glad. It is that city of darkness out there that awaits us, terrifying and fascinating all at the same time. And we are all a part of it. This I know and this I understand. So many of us have been a part of things which cause other things to happen which might not be as harmless as the thing we only thought we were doing to begin with so I am not bothered by that, and also it only was part of the Indian potion to begin with but it still leaves me feeling sad and

218

hollow inside because I know it is all so very true.

I have learned now that there are such true things in the world. True as the pure sunlight, as the love I have for Synandra, as the good Wisconsin beer I am drinking now, as the books by Ernest Hemingway that sit on the shelves of Bernard Wasson's study. I have just finished A Farewell to Arms *and a collection of his stories. These are fine books with true words. Synandra said that her grandfather told her that no truer words have ever been written. Perhaps he is right. They help to take my mind off the problems which confront me, and all of us.*

Synandra could not speak to us when she first saw the archaeological team. She was very sad, and I tried to comfort her and Tiffany tried also but it was no good. All she could say was that she felt sad and empty and that the end was near and that she could feel it. I did not know what to do except to tell her that we had the machine and that with it we would somehow stop them. Tiffany told her that she would sleep with the local magistrate to get him to issue a restraining order against Mortell. And this she has done. Which is why we are breathing a little easier this bright morning. But I still feel the sadness.

There is the machine, of course. It is the machine, I am sure, that troubles me. Machines are what they will be. This is to be expected. But I have always lived with machinery and have learned to trust it. I have never doubted its place in the world at any time in my life, until now. This is because I possess the ultimate machine. There is absolutely no farther for the world to go, nor is there any reason to stop now. I am sad because the rest of the world does not yet know this, and yet, without a doubt, this is where it is headed. To create precisely this machine. And there is no way to stop it. There is only a way to shorten it, and that is to give it to them now. This is just what Captain Jimmy expected to do, but in the end he could not just as I cannot either.

The girls understand this in their own way. They are very practical. This is to be expected. Women have long endured the infernal machinery men have created. This machine, they believe, is simply another of all the other machines, and they intend to make the best of it. Perhaps they are right, and perhaps it is all for the good.

219

The magistrate himself has told Tiffany that it probably won't be long before his restraining order is quashed—the University's lawyers would be working on it immediately—but it would buy them a little time, maybe a week, maybe two. In the meantime Basil has agreed to help them with the LoFoCo Caper. The dark vision of the terminal city has affected him profoundly, it obviously the doctor's idea to show him that which he might have had a hand in creating (along with, Basil figures, the rest of western civilization) and perhaps priming him to help to forestall, in some small way, our inevitable journey there. Besides, Tiffany has a more or less interesting plan cooked-up and Synandra wants very much to do it and she is so morose, and, well, he is *such* a sucker for a pretty girl anyway. For two of them he's an absolute patsy.

They make Chicago about an hour before noon.

Tiffany wanted to arrive at LoFoCo at lunchtime when less people would be around, so to kill time she treats the intrepid team to soup and sandwiches at a favorite vegetarian restaurant in Evanston. There they make final plans and coach Basil until it is time to head out into the industrial sprawl.

The L'Oreal Food Company's corporate headquarters is a long six-storied stretch of dark windowglass and stone, a neo-neolithic lodge. An American flag lolls on a central pole against the hazy July sky. Nondescript industrial park shrubbery dots the short plain that separates the building from the heat-shimmering parking lot. It is very hot. Basil parks the Chrysler in the lot at the end of a long row of Mercedes, Porsches, Lincolns ... Kingston's Kadillac gleaming in the first space.

"There, on the top floor are the executive offices," says Tiffany breathlessly. "The boardroom is on the other side of the building. Let's get going before somebody spots us."

She leads them away from the main entrance to an inconspicuous steel door at the side of the building, pulls out a plastic card and inserts it into a slot in a brass plate mounted alongside the door. Electronic lock. The door buzzes and they file in, Basil last, carrying a heavy leather suitcase which contains their implements of deception. They find themselves at the bottom of a concrete gray stairwell, steel steps leading upwards for six flights.

"C'mon," whispers Tiffany, "we don't want to run into anyone here." They begin to run up the stairs, the suitcase heavy as hell, but the adrenalin's working here, Basil skipping two steps at a time, it's weird how buoyant he's become, maybe they could've teleported themselves here, but the three of them? None of them wanted to take the chance, maybe a bit of machine-shyness setting in . . . although, Jesus, with what they were going to try to pull off—a stunt worthy of the pages of *Impossible Destinies,* easy—maybe it would be best to just be able to zip-zap right out of here, but it's too late for that now. . . .

At the top of the stairs is another steel door that Tiffany opens slightly, peers down a long carpeted hallway. "This is executive row," she whispers. "There's a vacant office we've got to get to. Right next to the boardroom. Everyone's at lunch now, except for daddy's team—they send out during these meetings. There's a receptionist we've got to watch out for, but she doesn't seem to be at her desk right now. Let's go!"

The hallway is deserted, but just as the door closes behind them, midway down the corridor a young man in a gray suit steps out of a door and glances their way. They freeze. But if he sees them at all, he takes no notice; he turns away, straightens his tie, and walks through another door.

"What the heck?" Tiffany hisses. "I know him, he's a junior exec. He came out of *our* office, too. Well, c'mon."

Basil and Synandra exchange a glance here, but commando Tiffany is already fast-walking down the hallway and they have to rush to catch up . . . stopping at a door of which she slowly turns the knob and peeks in . . . and then silently hustles them inside.

"Hi Christy." Tiffany smiles at a pretty young woman standing at a window in the dim office. She is startled, in the process of buttoning her blouse. Her skirt is unzipped.

"Tiffany! Wh-what are you doing here?"

"Oh, I'm just showing my friends around the place. But I didn't think they would get such an interesting tour."

"Oh, well, I was just . . . er, well, you know Dick and I . . . he's separated from his wife now."

Christy turns away to finish buttoning up and Basil slides the suitcase behind the empty desk, out of sight. "Dick came up with the Sex Fla—, er, Dawn cereal concept, you know," the nervous girl continues. "He's done a wonderful job and, and he gets so excited at these meetings. . . ."

"That's okay, Christy," Tiffany smiles.

The girl tosses her hair and turns to face them, blushing terribly. "Your father's in the meeting. I could get him, if—"

"No, listen Christy, we're going to leave in just a second. Do me a favor and don't breathe a word to anyone that we were even here today, okay?"

"Oh, oh, sure, you bet. Sure thing."

"Are they in there now?" Tiffany asks, pointing at the wall, behind which is the boardroom.

"Yes, they just finished lunch, I think. Er, I'd better be getting back to my desk now. It was very nice meeting all of you. . . ."

Tiffany locks the door behind her and the team whips into action. Or at least the girls. Turns out they have skillfully stitched a canvas harness for the miraculous machine, which is intended to go over Basil's shoulders and around his waist, holding the thing at about belly-button level. It's slick but makes him feel a little like an organ-grinder. Then over that they both lower a black Franciscan brothers *monster* of a robe with big floppy sleeves and a terrific hood. Basil makes faces at himself in the mirror of Tiffany's makeup case. He loves it. "Wow, when did you guys—"

"A seamstress made it for us." Synandra giggles. "We told her it was for a costume party."

"Oh. And these slits here are for my, uh, hands."

"We cut those. So you can throw the lever on that thing."

"Oh, yeah. Say, you know, this might even work."

"Of course it'll work," says Tiffany, working up some vile-looking green face paint. "Here, flip back the hood, and let me smear some of this on your face. Your hands too."

Meanwhile, Synandra pulls off Basil's shoes and helps him pull on a pair of very worn high-topped deerhide moccasins.

"I never saw those before."

"They're winter boots, Dr. Bo gave them to my grampa. You can't wear your loafers in there."

Tiffany applies a few finishing touches, heavy black shadows around his eyes, flips down the cowl and . . . "There! You look like the creature that drank the Chicago River."

"And survived," adds Synandra.

Basil feels more like Merlin, doesn't say so, but with the machine secured to his waist and the sheltering burnoose, he knows he has become one hideously weird and powerful creature.

He looks at the girls beaming at him, at their handiwork. Synandra has tears in her eyes. "Be careful . . ." she whispers.

Feeling vaguely sea-diverish looking through the tunnel of the Capuchin cowl, he gives them his best *Morituri Salutamus* wave, then turns toward the wall through which he is about to pass, behind which are the executives of LoFoCo, before whom he is about to materialize! *en costume!* Too much. He reaches inside the floppy serape and stabs the lever.

The time is set for zero, this trip only a lateral one, but the power does not seem in any way diminished. His arms begin vibrating, then in a few seconds, the rest of his body, and he is buffeted again by that familiar losing-it-all rush . . . and then everything clears and the room is suddenly lit-up, sparkling with ghost-dimensional twitches and quivers. Basil shivers himself. The wall awaits. He takes a deep breath, steps forward and squooshes on through. . . .

And emerges in the boardroom, a bright spacious room paneled in shining ruddy mahogany. In its center, at a long dark table sit a dozen or so men, all dressed in various shades of corporate fear, grays, blacks, and blues. Tension hangs heavy in the air, Basil can feel it—more of the machine's uncanny heightening of his previously basaltic senses—but to these fellows it is just another day, the usual passel of decisioning, pressuring, posturing, squirming, scapegoating, and the like, everyone on this sultry summer day with get-out-of-the-scorching-city vacations on their minds—he somehow understands this as he wanders around the big table, a mad monk from the Beyond, past ostrich briefcases, soft leather chairs, glistening bald-spots, dandruff shining like stars on pinstripe shoulders. . . . On the table, amid folders and coffee cups and yellow legal pads, are several prototype boxes for their new breakfast cereal, Dawn. The packages are glossy black with a soft photograph of a voluptuous model clad in a white sheath dress. Beneath the Dawn logo, raucous in fluorescent pink, the legend, "Breakfast of Lovers." Below that, in bright yellow letters, "Fortified with Vitamin E."

Basil tunes-in on the discussion, which actually seems to be a spirited debate on whether or not to put pornographic picture cards in each box. Well, hell, Basil thinks, he could have been an executive all along.

Kingston Elliot L'Oreal sits at the head of the table, waves for order. "All right, all right! Rexberry, just what did you have in mind, for God's sake?"

Oho. He is asking "quickie" Dick Rexberry, who had just accomplished the inter-office tryst with Christy.

"Well, sir," answers Rexberry, "we weren't actually thinking about beaver shots—" The boardroom rings with laughter. "Er, we were thinking more of girls wearing swimsuits, bikinis, that sort of thing. Of course, we'd have the subliminal sex motifs embellishing each picture."

"Of course," grunts L'Oreal. "Well, you work it out. I want to see samples in a week."

"By the way," turning to two gray suits seated to his right, "how much longer do we have to wait for our spots?"

Both of them snap to attention. "We'll have a presentation for your approval in two weeks, Mr. L'Oreal," says one.

"We'll be concentrating on prime time with heavy saturation of pre-seven o'clock news," says the other. "Both children and adults will be watching."

"No saturday mornings?" L'Oreal grumbles.

"I don't think you'd want to risk it. Those bleeding-heart bitches' groups would really come down hard on us. We have to keep in mind this is a radically new concept. . . ."

"Of course it is!" snorts L'Oreal, leaning back in his leather chair with a smug smile. "That's the beauty of it. No one's going to beat us with this one."

"Er, Mr. L'Oreal . . ." says an owlish-looking bald-headed man with thick horn-rimmed glasses.

"Yes, Carbuncle . . ." says L'Oreal with an audible sigh.

"Er, that's Garfunkel, sir. Tom Garfunkel, from production. Er, we're still waiting on your decision about what, exactly, we're going to make the Sex Fl-, er, Dawn cereal, from. Now, as I had outlined in our report to you, whole wheat has the highest concentration of vitamin E, or alpha tocopherol, but we're not sure if you—"

"I thought," interrupts L'Oreal, speaking with forced patience, eyes rolled upwards, "that I had given you my answer."

"Well, yes sir, you had said you, ah, didn't care. But I thought that you were only joking. After all we are a *food* company and—"

"Goddamn it, Carbuncle, I *never* joke! Listen, I give you the color, the flavor, and the texture, and you give me a product! Is that

clear?! I don't give a damn what it's made of! What the hell
... whatever's cheapest. I'd make it out of goddamn *wood* if I
could get away with it!" smirks L'Oreal, obviously on a roll, smiles
warmly at the guffaws that follow, although some of it, Basil notices, is fairly nervous laughter.

Well, it is time for him to make his move—to appear. But it
occurs to him that he might cause more of a scene if he got up on
the table and materialized, yes, right in the midst of them ... for
maximum effect. No one is sitting opposite L'Oreal at the other
end, so Basil moves over there and climbs aboard, careful not to
push through, a definite hazard here in the ghost-dimension, matter
being not quite what it ought to be ... and steps invisibly to the
table's midpoint. This is it. Feeling with his hand, he finds the significant lever, braces himself, and flips it up.

The electric jangle stops as the room loses its fluid glitter and
dims by many candlepower into good old (corporate-style) reality.

And there, in the midst of a sudden gust of wind that tosses
around papers and legal pads, knocks over several svelte cereal boxes
and rustles the curtains across the room, he is.

From around the table comes a collective horrified gasp as wide
eyes reflect the gruesome apparition that suddenly stands above them.
Several awed "My God's" whisper above the generally open-mouthed
silence. Many of them tremble visibly, L'Oreal himself shaking like
a leaf, regressing to babbling, "Wha-wha-wha-wha-wha-wha? ..."

Basil finds himself also fighting against losing it, against a similar state that many of these immaculately-suited men have clearly
entered: shock. The jolt actually hadn't been too bad this time, but
now he is definitely center stage, before a captive, yet expectant,
audience, and finds himself paralyzed with stage fright. His heart
pounds so loudly in his ears that he can barely hear the whimpering
around the table. Looking downward through the hood, his eyes suddenly lock in on a solitary standing *Dawn* package and, as if in a
dream, his leg muscles contract and neatly place kick the box of sex
flakes into Kingston L'Oreal's terrified face. L'Oreal recoils and squeals
remarkably piglike, "Nya-nya-nya-nya-ya-ya! ..."

Boy, Basil realizes, are *they* scared! This thought calms him
somewhat, and he begins to remember his purpose in being there,
if not the exact words Tiffany had rehearsed with him on the drive
down. He attempts to lower his voice to what he hopes will be a

rich, menacing tone: "Healthy foods, natural foods, are ... what's happening." *Oh boy, don't blow it,* he thinks. "Uh, stop making your unhealthy foods." He directs his words to Kingston. "Stop ruining the health of children with your unsavory junk-food products." *That's better.* He begins to remember some of Tiffany's speech. "Stop putting excessive sugar and chemical additives in your products. The world is ready for wholesome natural foods. Make them good, advertise them well, and your competitors will be forced to follow your lead. In this way you will profit many, many times over ..." At the word "profit," some of the men stir; he is talking their language. Basil feels in high gear now, tunes his voice to a more sinister pitch, "I come from the ... the Great Wherever, a place you puny mere mortals cannot understand, and I bring with me power—terrible, terrible power to enforce my commands. I *will* be obeyed! Mark my words, if this company does not quickly change its despicable practices, it will henceforth be cursed! And from each of you ..." Basil turns dramatically around the table to look at every fearful face, "... I will exact a horrible, horrible price. Ah-ha-ha-ha-ha ..." Some of the men begin to edge away. "No one move!" booms Basil. The men freeze. "Heed my warning. When I appear again, I shall—" *Uh*-oh. All of a sudden, Basil feels sick. His sensitive stomach has apparently just now caught-up with the shock of de- and re-materialization and has done a righteous flip-flop. *Uh-oh.* Basil feels a heave in his gut, a nasty burning in his esophagus, and from under his cowl suddenly issues a stream of putrid vomit, roughly the same color as his face. Yes, vegetarian green pea soup, his choice at lunch, spews over the rich mahogany table and executive papers and pates and pinstripes as Basil lurches and pivots on the table-top voiding his poor stomach, feeling terribly helpless, sure that at any moment someone will dare grab him by the ankles. But when he's finished purging and coughing, when he manages to refocus his watering eyes, he sees that no one has even dared to move, having sat stoically motionless throughout the onslaught of verdant puke. Perhaps they thought that this was The Way of the Cowled Creature. No time to speculate though. He is getting out. Frantically he reaches inside his spattered robe, moves his sweating fingers to the magic lever and throws it, managing to croak out a final warning, "Repent LoFoCo!" before he vanishes in another sudden gust of impossibility.

226

The room dazzles once again. Basil never thought he would be so relieved to enter the ghost-dimension.

The executives sit stunned, glancing furtively around the room at the closed doors, the windows, tentatively eyeing the green vomit-like? substance oozing down their ties and lapels.

Meanwhile, invisible Basil has foolishly jumped off the table, falling to the floor, breaking its plane in several places, spends anxious seconds extricating himself from that thin-ice situation, then becomes disoriented, walks over to the wall and pushes through past a lot of sweating water pipes he hadn't noticed before into ... well, it seems to be a stall in the women's restroom, and right next to him here is cute Christy, humming softly, sitting on the closed stool, thoughtfully arranging four long lines of sparkling cocaine (iridescent as fire opal in the ghost-dimension) across a polished agate plate balanced upon her knees. Oh hell, wrong-way Lexington ... back again through the boardroom, looks like a war zone now, past executives murmuring, sobbing, milling aimlessly around, Dick Rexberry weeping openly, while Kingston L'Oreal tries to restore order, "Please, please, let's all calm down. I think, I think we are all agreed that we won't be mentioning this, this *incident* to anyone...."

But Basil barely notices, concentrating on avoiding executives, carefully stepping over one who has collapsed in a dead faint, until he reaches the opposite wall, pushes through its custard surface. Tiffany is sitting at the desk, Synandra in a chair before it, talking in low tones.

Basil shows up.

They fly to him at once. "Oh, Basil," ripping off the the boots, the green-splotched robe, "what *happened* in there?"

"Ugh ... later. Let's just get out of here."

19

That was a nice touch, puking all over them like that," says Tiffany as they glide northward, away from the bad craziness they had wrought.

"Ugh," Basil groans, sprawled across the back seat, "it wasn't planned."

"Yes, but it worked so well ... wow–oh–wow!" Tiffany exclaims softly, gazing at the gleaming rows of corporate headquarters lining the sides of the Illinois Interstate, "just think, just think ..."

Synandra can hardly speak, her eyes glitter like diamonds: What power! What fantastic power! What one could do! "Basil, what you did back there was just ... wonderful," she bubbles, "but, you know, there's so much more we could do. Especially when it comes to protecting the earth itself. Why, imagine, we might even be able to clamp-down on the—Army Corps of Engineers! That would preserve a lot of planet...."

"Amen," says Tiffany.

"But, overall ... when decisions are made by government and industry greedheads ... projects begun that can endanger the earth, who's ever there to change their minds? Who's ever there to shut them down—?"

"Us," murmurs smug Basil ... er, SUPERBASIL, protector of the planet, avenger of the atmosphere, defender of the depths. Yeah, he never really thought or cared about it before, but in pulling-off this stunt it's all come together for him now: the amazing power of the machine and Synandra's unflagging respect for the earth. Maybe her ideas aren't so corny or crazy at all. Maybe, hey, she doesn't go *far enough!* Yes, he's finally grasped the visions that the great medicine man had conjured for him, understands now that it's a small planet, our only home, and we damn-well better take care of it. You bet. He's decided he can't abide anyone who would defile or otherwise intend on debasing this fragile blue sphere. No more nonchalance. At least not from SUPERBASIL, ha-ha, the ultimate urban guerilla—who will haunt the bosses into honesty, morality, integrity, peace ... and whatever else is lacking out there....

In the meantime, companies that have encountered *the perverse presence* will hire exorcists, hang garlic at stockholder meetings, display the occasional silver crucifix in the lobby at company headquarters.... Executives will become *reborn,* sneaking off to St. Peter's to light a candle, mutter a prayer ... and no one, no crusty chairman or CEO or plutocratic pol who had recently doubled or trebled his Valium dosage would dare mention The Problem to anyone, never, nohow ... but ... perhaps ... it might surface ever so casually, during cocktails perhaps, the corporate transcendental hour, and an ear would go up across the room, some sweat from Allied Chemical would—did he *hear* that? That fellow from Dow on his third manhattan joking about a *spook* sabotaging their operations?

Ah yes, welcome to the haunted men....

*   *   *

Meanwhile, in the gentle Wisconsin northlands, midsummer has descended righteously upon the peninsula, cherries are heavy in the trees, alfalfa thick in the fields, sunflowers following the sun high across the sky, and vacationers everywhere in between, it seems, keeping Basil and Synandra very busy in the Ars Aromatica shop and the herb gardens at home (Basil understanding that he has rather handily stepped into the role her grandpa had served in maintaining

Synandra's small enterprise). Tiffany is busy too with rehearsals for the raucous musical production of *Lift to Heaven, Stairway to Hell*, an imported British farce in which a young tart, Heather, suspects that the upper floors of her apartment building might be inhabited by celestial tenants, whilst the basement (where resides the building's diabolic owner) is somewhat akin to the pit . . . and the eternal landlord-tenant conflict is to be resolved in her flat, in hilarious upbeat manner, the play carrying somewhat liberal political overtones of the sixties, an off-broadway hit over here, but never quite catching on in its homeland . . . with Tiffany in the role of Pamela, flighty girlfriend of the harried Heather. . . . One afternoon after rehearsal she drops by the shop, asks Syndy if she thinks it might be time to head up to Dr. Bo's to visit the Trinnie she rescued from the clutches of the Church of the Electronic etcetera.

But Synandra says that she does not feel that it is. When she does, the time will be right . . . as always, it is.

Such are the ways of this magical maiden, who has been, bye the bye, to Basil's thinking, remarkably stoic about the archaeological interlopers encamped on the southeastern corner of the Wasson property. She has been to her thinking rock, he knows, in the northern scruff of woods between the hill and the house, the one of the crazy laughing face, but says she hasn't really come up with anything yet . . . is just waiting for inspiration. . . .

Overall, she is confident they will be able to save the hill. They have that incredible machine, don't they? Maybe it is time, she declares, that a machine be used to spare something of the earth, rather than exploit it. Yes . . . time indeed. She likes the symmetry of the situation. As one who has long been given to signs and portents, this may appear as an opportunity unique upon the earth.

In fact, it is Basil who is uneasy. Every day he goes out to visit the site, watches members of the khaki crew pound stakes, stretch strings over grave-sized patches of the forest floor in preparation for excavation, while others dig, scrape, and screen dirt in areas where preliminary work has begun. They are digging outward from their camp towards the base of the hill, almost exclusively in the southeastern quadrant of the property, where—Basil learns through idle appreciative chatter with one of the graduate students, Rolf, a long-haired gentle giant wearing wire-rimmed glasses and a beard reminiscent of Walt Whitman—members of a Late Woodland tribe might most likely have camped, nearest to the lakeshore. Also, the current theory is that the hill itself was probably constructed during the Late Woodland period, between 400 and 1600 C.E., about the time of the famous effigy mound builders, those mysterious earth sculptors of turtles, bear, panthers, birds, lizards, and other earthly fauna. In this company the hill is just a simple conical mound, but extraordinary, of course, because of its large size and the most mysterious configuration of rocks upon its summit. Rolf also tells Basil that Professor Mortell is really *daffy* about this excavation, truly ecstatic that after all the legal wrangling, he is finally going to be able to do this dig.

"What is it," Basil innocently asks, "that you guys are really looking for, anyway?"

Well, the overall goal is to try to determine how the hill got there; Mortell's theory that the hill is mostly man-made, a type of burial mound perhaps piled-up upon a smaller natural formation, is in need of proof. And then there is the puzzle of the rocks ... another, ah, mystery that would require some determined excavation in order to attempt to solve. To find signs of construction, ancient timbers, stone tools, that sort of thing.... But Mortell knows that he's treading on some thin ice here, too, Rolf confides; the professor understanding that if he starts digging into the hill itself at the height of tourist season that he won't have much local support, and a full-fledged community protest is the last thing they need. So his plan is to begin more gradually, with smaller digs in the surrounding areas for more prosaic artifacts.

"Like ... ?"

Potsherds, for one thing, which would pretty well provide evidence of the Woodland period, also: bones, tools, shell beads, particles of ancient pollen ... stuff that could only warm the cockles of an archaeologist's heart. But Basil learns fairly quickly that what really would make a difference in the dig would be if they turned up something *very significant,* like, well, treasure. Gold. Jewels. Doubloons. The student sighs as he speaks, because it's not really what they would ever expect to find and extremely difficult to come up with theories to explain the presence of such booty, but they're flashy (like gold is) and it's what gets you in the news, it's what gets you funding, and it's what might get you tacit approval, university, community, and otherwise, to proceed more rapidly, perhaps

231

somewhat more extensively . . . with the excavation of said hill. And besides it's exciting as all hell. Seems that Mortell has let it slip during daily briefings that he secretly hopes the hill might contain some such goodies. . . .

"But, isn't one of the conditions of the dig that any excavation of the hill itself is to be of a fairly limited nature?" Basil inquires.

Rolf shrugs and says, "Even if we find something significant? Something . . . very valuable? It would be really tough to clamp on the binders."

Basil reports all—or most—of this to Synandra, who sniffs at the information. The hill, she knows, is much, much older, and of course certainly not man-made. The rocks, the heart of rocks . . . she is not sure about them . . . but overall she doesn't think they'll find much of anything, because no native peoples would have set up camp at the base of such a powerful center—would anyone ever have *lived* at stonehenge? But isn't it typical of the brittle minds of science, to think that anything so geologically imposing, so sweetly, naturally, aesthetically perfect was created by man! Her laugh is bitter and short. Although Basil coaxes her, she refuses to visit the dig site, partially because she can't bear to see their preliminary excavations (none—yet—thank goodness, near any of the significant centers outlying the hill), and also because she might run into that jerk, Mortell—and she knows that the time is not yet right for that, because when it is, that congress will be devastating, she knows, for at least one of them.

*   *   *

Basil the tinkerer. One Saturday he surprises Synandra with a bit of his handiwork, a merging of old and new, classic and contemporary, automobile and Electronic Trinity. Uh-huh, working all afternoon with some of her grandfather's tools and a bit of ingenuity the barely-mechanical kid has rather cleverly installed the magical machine up and almost-under the dashboard of the Chrysler Town and Country. The levers of the bracketed box might be taken for some sort of old-fashioned radio amplifier attachment, or perhaps an auxiliary heater—but whatever, looking vaguely purposeful.

232

Synandra is delighted and stunned. (Basil had told her only that he was going to change the oil of the great chromium beast.) If it works (and Basil, sniffing, assures her that it will), they will be able to voyage to wherever and whenever in much greater comfort and style than before. On the tip of Synandra's tongue, "It's, it's . . ."

"A timemobile," Basil grins.

She smiles back. "Yes . . . a timemobile. We'll have to put it to good use."

This is also the opening weekend of *Lift,* apparently a huge success, and Tiffany is elated, takes Basil and Synandra out for a late supper Sunday night after a rousing curtain call. She is stirred, and after hearing of Basil's tinkering wants to do something "really big-time" with the machine, er, timemobile. She proposes that they go right to the source, why not . . . a close encounter with the president? Of the United States.

Synandra's eyes brighten. Basil drops his fork.

"What, the main man? And-and all his bodyguards and secret-service goons, and we just—appear, poof! howdy gents, how's it going . . . ?"

"No, not our current leader, it's too late for him . . ." Tiffany's eyes glitter above the candle on their table, "I mean one who is *going* to be president!"

"Reagan!" smiles Synandra.

"Exactly. He's just sitting out there in California at that big ranch he bought. I don't even think he's still governor. It's the perfect time to pay him a little visit."

They more or less agree . . . Basil still not so sure, but after more wine the thing starts to sound kind of interesting . . . and they hatch a plan of sorts, and even a timeframe: tomorrow night.

Which arrives quickly.

"Now, we're all going to have to concentrate on where we're going," says Basil sternly, driving the big car down a little-traveled Wasson's Bay back road, silently praying that no other car appears. "I don't want to end up in the Pacific Ocean. This thing isn't going to float and we're not going to tread water very well in, in these crazy things. . . ."

He is referring to their garb, which this evening happens to be otherworldly *soigné*: Creature-From-Beyond-With-Two-Angelic-Attendants, Basil in the mad-monk cowl (*sans* makeup this time), and the girls wearing pure white robes and wimples that Tiffany has lifted from the *Lift to Heaven* wardrobe.

"Are you sure you know where this Rancho Bonzo, or wherever, is?" Synandra asks. "You're the one that's going to have to concentrate on getting us there."

"Rancho del Cielo. Yeah, I've been there lots of times, for dinner and laughs. Ron, Nancy, and me. We'd play bridge afterwards, the monkey makes a fourth. . . . No, but actually, it's northwest of Santa Barbara, on a mountaintop. We shouldn't have any trouble finding it in this baby," fondly patting the dash. "If it does work. . . . Well, ready for warp ten?" Casually reaching toward the new equipment with a slightly unsteady finger. . . .

There comes a jolt and, and, by God, yes, they're off, gliding upward above the road surface just like, like Fred MacMurray in that old Model-T in *The Absent-Minded Professor!* the car vibrating smoothly as much from the still-running engine as anything ghost-dimensional, Basil wonders whether or not he should shut it off, decides to let it run, what the hell, it's so incredible anyway, the moonlit bay slowly arcing off below them, village lights diminishing as they gain altitude, and Jesus, they're getting high, it's a little scary, time to proceed westward, a lean forward, a glance at the beaming girls, and with an easing of the steering wheel, the car responds very nicely Pacific-bound, then a push on the distance lever for about three thousand miles (actually—hopefully—slightly less), the timemobile shakes mightily, and it's whooooosh! three caped crusaders shoved backward into seat-leather, into hyper-drive or whatever, and onward to fulfill a mission of destiny.

Later, Tiffany would describe it as "rushing through a dark misty tunnel" and that's exactly how Basil remembers it too, like driving through fog at night, straining his eyes to find his destination, a little panicky perhaps—he doesn't of course know *exactly* where Reagan's place is—but the damn thing works like a charm again, they emerge from a cloudbank and looking down, appear to be gently circling above a regal mountaintop compound: Rancho del Cielo! el Rancho Reaganzo, it has to be.

"God. Look at that," he breathes thankfully as they glide lower toward the desert summit gently shimmering deep beige and ocher in the ghost-dimensional twilight. The view is breathtaking, a California Pacific dusk, spreading out through miles and miles of night lights and L.A. smog, and westward over the ocean to a dull red afterglow of setting sun.

"Omigod," says Tiffany, "is that him?"

She points excitedly toward a small figure standing alone on a ridgetop before what appears to be a tiny smoldering fire, a finger of smoke wafting lazily upward. . . . Some distance behind him they can see a tiled rooftop and faint lights, probably the ranch house itself. All this time they have been drifting lazily downward in a sort of broad spiral, just taking all of it in, near-speechless, this amazing thing they are doing, this amazing impossible machine. . . . But now, drifting lower, it is time to make a decision about landing. And as this idea begins to insinuate itself upon Basil's burning brain, the old jet-fighter flyboy fantasy takes over again, uh-ohhh, and they begin a fairly screaming descent, the girls moaning as they angle right for the ridge and the man atop it, the situation rapidly becoming desperate. . . .

"Basil, slow it downnnn!" yells Synandra through clenched teeth while stomping an imaginary brake pedal to the floorboards, which is what Tiffany is doing too—and Basil, he's got his foot on the real brake for all it's worth . . . which seems to work, this collective desire to stop, and the perceptive timemobile eases its descent gradually, gradually . . . gliding in for a landing about twenty feet from the person, who they can see is, in fact, Ronald Reagan, heir to the presidency, and quintessential cowboy, dressed in jeans, plaid shirt, boots, and Stetson hat.

"Get ready . . ." Basil warns, flipping up the hood of his cowl, the girls adjusting their headpieces, and Basil pushes the lever for materialization as they roll smoothly in, wheels just about touching the ground, he wants this to look good, thinking: *God, I hope the shock doesn't kill him—or us* . . . as they suddenly, quite out of nowhere, appear with a dusty thudding bounce—Basil's judgment a trifle off here—to casually drive up to the man himself.

"Well, hello there pardners," Reagan jauntily calls out. "Where in thunderation did you come from?"

"Er, hello," stammers head-spinning Basil as he and the girls manage to get out of the car and orient themselves, straighten their garb, brush-off desert dust. . . . *Boy, is this guy mellow*, Basil can't help thinking as he gazes at the man's weathered, yet undeniably handsome face, which looks calmly, bemusedly, back at them. Basil and the girls together breathe a sigh of relief. They have made it here, and, wonderful luck, have an audience alone with their quarry, with this photogenic fellow originally from the Midwest, from Illinois, in fact, one of the many who had pushed westward to the shining land of ego and opportunity, the camera coast, and made good. And now he stands here before a small fire on his expansive spread, at the end, apparently, of a long day of work. It seems fitting. The sound of a twanging guitar comes faintly from the ranch house behind him, must be some of the hands whooping it up after chow time.

"Say, that's a nice car you've got there, reminds me of better times, when, heh-heh, cars were cars!"

"Oh, thanks."

"You're welcome, pardner. Now, may I ask what brings you here? In those fancy get-ups?"

"Uh, well, we come from a place you cannot understand," Basil begins. "We are emissaries from the Great Wherever. We journey through time and space at the drop of a hat. We know all of the past and all of the future. Nothing is hidden from our—"

"Who's going to win the series?" Reagan asks.

"Beg pardon?"

"I said, who'll win the World Series this year? Surely you must know?" Reagan's face breaks into a crinkly, expectant smile.

"Surely, surely we do. But, ah, such trivialities are not to be dealt with at this time. We have much more important matters to discuss with you, matters related to the future and the hand you will have in directing the course of this nation and ultimately, the world. For you see, Ronald Wilton Reagan, you will become president of the United States of America in the year nineteen hundred and eighty-one—"

"I-I will?"

"Yes, you will."

"No kidding?"

"No kidding. And in that most powerful of earthly offices you will have the opportunity to do great deeds; you will have the ability to create a better country and a better planet—"

"Who'll I beat?"

"Beg pardon?"

"Who'll I beat in the election? Who'll I be running against?

Which Democrat? I-I'll run as a Republican, won't I?"

"Look, none of that matters," Basil's voice cutting a trifle sharp from beneath the cowl, "what really matters—oof!" an elbow-jab from Synandra catches him in the ribs.

"What he means to tell you, sir," she begins, "is that we will be entering a time of great struggle, a time of great adversity between man and earth, rich and poor, the flesh and the spirit—"

"And of course the greatest struggle of all time," interrupts Reagan, releasing a world-weary sigh that seems to encompass his true feelings about the nature of the great task ahead, "capitalism and communism ... the eternal struggle," he says, the deep lines of his rugged face catching the firelight as he gazes out over the darkened rolling hills of yesteryear, of this great capitalist country, of the West.

"But-but that's just an illusory thing, that struggle," pipes up Tiffany. "Really not all that important. That's just the reason we have come, you see—"

"From the Great Wherever," adds Basil.

"Yes, to tell you that you must focus on much larger issues, that the future will be in your hands, that our fair planet will not be able to withstand much more abuse. We are terribly polluting her waters, her atmosphere, her soil. We're destroying her once-abundant tropical forests at insane rates—millions of acres a year; we're destroying the fragile ozone layer in the upper atmosphere; we're causing acid rains to fall upon our forests, the last of which we are greedily clear-cutting in the Pacific Northwest; we're creating tons and tons of terribly radioactive wastes, which no one has any idea what to do with—"

"Yes, yes," Reagan sighs again, "I've heard it all before, and I'll hear it much, much more, I'm sure. But I'm certain that you must also know that God gave earth to man to use for his purposes. You can read that for yourselves in the Good Book. We must make good use of our resources, which includes our military might, otherwise the Russians could surpass us. That's my biggest fear. We must strengthen our defenses or end up living in a communist world. Surely you must understand that?"

None of them know what to say, watching this one-track cowboy peacefully leaning on his rake, tending his fire on this California summer night, totally missing the crucial message they have brought to him in (what they thought to be) a terrifically dramatic way. Talk about unruffled. Here they are, looking like refugees from the Monastery That Time Forgot, standing in front of The Car That Came From Nowhere, and the guy doesn't even seem to have noticed, or perhaps has already forgotten ... talk about dumb. But, along with his lack of depth, Basil can sense the man's inherent noble goodness, perhaps they all can, and he feels suddenly shameful, that perhaps they are pretty much invading this simple fellow's privacy. It doesn't seem that he could ever be elected president, not in a million years, the girls' perception must've been really wrong....

The wind kicks up a bit, shifting in the direction of the threesome, and suddenly three noses begin twitching, sniffing in unmistakable sweetish smoke: marijuana!

"You know," says Reagan, raking a twig into the fire, "I can't say that I don't appreciate your message from, er, wherever you come from, but the truth is whenever I hear that stuff it just brings me down a bit. Really, now what kind of talk is that on a beautiful night like tonight? Fact is, I find there's nothing better to lift the spirit than to put in a long hard day of honest work, like clearing brush here, and then start me up a little fire and look out over all this wonderful land—"

"Uh, what kind of brush is that?" Basil asks.

"Hemp. Grows like a weed out here. The cattle get into it so we cut it down as best we can. But it comes up mighty fast. Sometimes I'm out here burning it every night. But I don't mind. It's so nice and peaceful up here. The pure natural beauty of our land is just ... just incredible. Makes you wonder why kids these days want to get high on drugs when they can just step outside their own back doors and look up at the sky, where the stars twinkle like diamonds and the moon rises over the fruited plain like the shining face of, of George Washington, the father of our country, the United States of America, one nation under God...."

This last said in a heartfelt whisper as a plaintive harmonica carries up from the ranch house behind him, and a few tears actually begin rolling down his leathery cheeks. The breeze sends more sweet smoke into the cowls of the creatures from the Great Wherever, and tears begin to form in their eyes too. Perhaps not just from the smoke. They exchange somber glances, Synandra's and Tiffany's most telling, the marijuana seeming to intensify the feeling that their mission is a failure. That this is one cowpoke who can't be reached. It's time to go. Three dejected eco-warriors climb back into the front seat of the car.

"There now, d'ya hear that?" Reagan says suddenly, cocking his head in the direction of the ranch house. The strains of "Home on the Range," carry across in the smoky breeze. "Now there's a song that means something to me—to all of us here out West. This is what it's all about," he smiles broadly as the hands launch into the song. "Perhaps you could stay and sing-along?" asks Reagan. "No?" He looks disappointed. "Well, have a safe trip back to, er—"

"The Great Wherever," says Basil, starting the engine.

"Godspeed," wishes Reagan.

"Goodbye," they call, smiling. Even though they're disappointed, they can't dislike the guy. They wave goodbye and begin bouncing across the rocky hilltop prior to their takeoff ... and then it's up, up, and away, the cosmic Chrysler leaps into the moonlit sky, and as they loop away they look down to see Reagan standing erect on his mountaintop still waving his hat to them, a cowboy farewell.

"God, it's beautiful up here," says Synandra as they circle higher, in an approximate reverse spiraling of their descent. The air rushes softly past them, the luminous clouds seem friendly, and the moon sort of does look like George Washington, now that you really think about it. . . .

"You guys must be wrong about him," says Basil. "He could never be president."

The girls both look over at him, open-mouthed, smiling hugely. "Well of course he'll be president. Of the United States. We thought that was obvious. Didn't you?"

"Oh ... of the United States. Yeah, I guess I do see what you mean."

"C'mon Basil, drive, er, fly, us around a little," says Tiffany, pulling off her wimple. "God, this thing is hot."

"Yes," agrees Synandra, removing hers. "Let's go somewhere."

"Well ... where?"

"Oh, we don't knoow," says Tiffany in her bored-British accent, "anywhere," leaning forward to take a stoned-stab at the brass levers before Basil is able to intervene, slowed reaction time and all that, only manages a sluggish, "Hey!" before the car shudders sickeningly with what he knows to be a ghost-dimensional change, Whoaah!

from cool night sky to bright daylight, a shimmering flat landscape below them that Basil, hmm, thinks is still California . . . he's bringing the aero-auto down to orient himself, the earth shining in ghost-dimensional brilliance, rainbow-wave strobing on the horizon which at this altitude is something of greatness, the magnificent curvature of the earth itself, you know it's alive and breathing, from up here you just know . . . and besides it's exciting, fantastic, the doped-up girls laughing and whooping and bouncing around the car, Synandra dialing something in on the radio, Tiffany perched on the top of the back seat like a prom queen, Synandra climbing back to join her, it's a gas, and lower they go, about twenty feet or so above the ground where Basil spots a route sign, 466, which is strange, it should be 46 if they are where he thinks they are, somewhere north of San Luis Obispo, approaching the San Joaquin Valley and Fresno. On the car's sturdy AM radio comes some old Bill Haley and the Comets, "Rock Around the Clock," yeah! The girls begin rocking out, singing along, it's terrific, but Jeeze, this landscape, the route signs, the power lines running along the road, look so *old,* but not worn-old, just *vintage,* and holy cow, here come a couple of cars below them on the arrow-straight asphalt, a-a 1951 or -2 green Plymouth Coupe and an old '54 Merc, but it's not old, no, and Basil realizes that they have gone back to sometime in the fifties, all right! The girls realize this now too, and they pull their wimples back up . . . makes Basil suspicious because of course no one can see them in the ghost-dimension anyway, unless they were planning to, uh, materialize, but . . . uh-oh, damn, the girls scramble up front now and Tiffany's going to push the goddamn lever, he grabs her arm, says wait, we're pretty stoned here . . . but they're getting down to road level now, they do have a car that fits in perfectly with the times, and Jeeze, it would really be a gas to . . . uh, but look here, there's a fork in the road and whizzing up to it is a little sports car, looks like an old Porsche Spyder, a silver one with two guys in it—and suddenly something clicks in Basil's mind, on *this* road, at *this* time, my God could it be? Basil strains to see the driver as the little car approaches and it really looks like *him,* Basil yells to the girls, "Look, look, it's *James Dean!*"

"Well, I'll be damned," gasps Tiffany.

"Where did he—is this *it?*" asks Synandra. "Is *this* when he—"

"Look!" Basil points just below them where there is a black

Ford sedan slowing in the right lane, as though planning on turning left—directly in front of the Porsche. "That's it, I'm sure that's it. He slammed into this Ford."

"Oh my God. What'll we do?" wails Synandra. "Should we—"

"We've got to, we just can't—ah, screw history," grunts Basil, setting his jaw, "we've gotta get down there. Herrrrre we go . . ." the car angling down faster, running on pure triple mind-power here in the ghost-dimension, the big blackmobile in screaming descent, racing to the fork, beginning to level-off perfectly, it's beautiful . . . and they get there not ten seconds before the Porsche.

"Okay . . . now!" Basil releases Tiffany's arm and the car shudders violently, the wheels smoke as they hit the asphalt, his cowl flips over his head, and Basil lays on the horn. Three astonished heads look up at the suddenly appeared-out-of-nowhere Chrysler, a kid in the sedan, James Dean and his passenger—the timemobile now right in front of the Porsche—and everyone brakes, but Dean is going way too fast and slides out on all fours across the shoulder down into a ditch and miraculously out again, upright, into the desert in a cloud of dust, and sits for several long seconds before he starts gunning the Little Bastard again, that wild smile-sneer of his is for real, intense, incredible, Basil and the girls can't keep their eyes off him, and with fantails of dirt flying up behind the Spyder, the number 130 painted on its side, he manages to get it up on the road again, stare briefly at the strange occupants of the black Chrysler T&C, salute, and then zoom out westward on 466.

"Wow, it-it was really him," bubbles Tiffany.

"We saved his life. I think. Didn't we?" says Synandra.

"I think so," sighs Basil, slowly unclenching his hands from the steering wheel. "I really think this is when he would've bought it."

The sedan has also run off the road, apparently safely, the kid getting out, squinting curiously at the berobed threesome.

"Uh-oh," says Basil, "we better get out of here. Don't want to have to explain anything to anybody if you know what I mean."

"We do, let's go."

Basil steps on the gas and eases the big car eastward down 466, the kid starts yelling something at them, but there's nothing they could tell him—that he would understand—so it's a wave bye-bye and a gradual acceleration down the road until they reach the vanishing point, and then . . . they vanish.

20

B asil's Journal:

Now we have done it. We have altered time and with time the course of events of life itself. I swear that I, Basil Lexington, will never, ever, use that accursed machine again. Because now we have really done it. We have changed history itself. James Dean lives.

He lives! Yes! And the truly weird thing is that after we got back to Wisconsin, it seemed like he always was alive, *at least in terms of the rest of the world. Everything about him after September 30, 1955 (the exact date we saved him) that is common knowledge to everyone who has in the most minor way followed the career of James Dean is completely new to us. It seems that we've "surfaced" in another world, one that is exactly like the one that we left a week ago, except that in this one James Dean is alive and well in California, and in the other, he never made it beyond that day in September, 1955. In this, so far, small way we feel like strangers in a strange land.*

It's so weird, especially the horrible accident he had the very next day, October 1st, in the Salinas race: broken neck and back, both arms and legs fractured—he nearly died in that crash, was in

242

the hospital for nearly a year, and then there was a long period of rehabilitation. It is as if his death almost could not be denied! Rebel Without a Cause *was released three days after that crash—a cagey move by the producers—and his popularity just took-off. I have pictures in old* Life *magazines of him taped-up like a mummy in his hospital bed surrounded by mailbags full of fan letters. I can see now why he became so famous after his actual* death! *Which of course never happened now, which of course boggles our minds.*

It is incredible to think that you are possibly the only supposedly cinematically-sophisticated Americans who have never heard of the tremendous feud that raged between Dean and Brando in the late fifties and early sixties and that culminated in the famous fistfight between the two in a North Hollywood night spot in 1961. Brando put the wickedly drunk Dean in a hospital for two weeks with a broken jaw, broken nose, bruised ribs—but it seems foolish to go on with this as everyone, except us, appears to know all about it. I quote from photocopies of old Life, Time, *and New York* Times *articles that I have spent the last week collecting at the library in Green Bay. It has become an obsession for me, tracking the life of this indulgent, cinematic genius through all its ups and downs, from the pre-interrupted-death days of* East of Eden, Giant, *and* Rebel Without a Cause *to what most critics, including even Pauline Kael think to be the pinnacle of his career, the blockbuster epic* Nights in the Los Angeles Desert, *released in 1959, which many thought would win the Oscar for best picture that year, but was unable to beat out the extravaganza* Ben-Hur, *which took everything in sight. Of course it's a film neither Syndy, Tiff, nor I had ever heard of before, but there it is written-up in* The New Yorker *and the Los Angeles* Times *and everywhere else. Monster reviews and tons of commentary. We are going to try to catch it sometime. We're watching the late show listings.*

The really sad thing is that his life seemed to fall into such a predictable southern California young-rich-famous track: acquire so much wealth and fame that you can live any way you like, buy anything you like, indulge in anything—booze, drugs, whatever—as much as you like, and there's no one around you anymore to offer you any good advice—if you'd even listen—and then it's all up to you and if you're basically weak and indulgent, as we all are, you fuck-up. Which is exactly what he did—for five or six essentially lost years. People said that it got too heavy for him with the Marilyn Monroe thing and then the Kennedy family involvement, which was probably never true, but just might have been. And then there was There's No Cool Way Back, *the title, of course, of the best-selling account of his struggle for a new life. Followed by* My Voyage Within, *the amazing story of his surreptitious trip to India, where he wandered for five years as an unknown American renunciant—while headlines in the U.S. shrieked: WHERE IS JAMES DEAN?—and his meetings with some incredibly remarkable men, the Indian spiritual leaders from which he would receive his vision, and the message he was to deliver back to the rest of us.*

So there was some great good to come from it all, of course, the acclaimed recovery. To think that he could look as good as he does now—in his fifties—after all that. But that's the miracle of the man—when people said he had *something, they were right. If there's any real good that we might have done by sparing his life, besides providing the planet with what has become a truly classic flick, it is that his comeback seems to have been so spectacular, at least in the way the press has played it. His story (I have found no less than than a dozen books on it—including his own—at a library in Green Bay, Wisconsin, no less) is an inspiration to all of those caught in the southern California young-rich-famous track, or those addicted to anything, anywhere. It actually makes me glad that the acting jobs dried-up for me when they did—a fact I'd always pretty much regretted before.*

Who would have ever guessed he had such a spiritual side, though? I suppose it was pretty much there all along, but was something he really found during the trip to India. Anyway, as of this writing there are eleven chapters of the "James Dean Inner Space Institute," the seventh being right down here in Green Bay, and the first, opening in Fairmount, Indiana, his hometown, in 1967.

From what I can gather, the Institutes are primarily devoted to self-discovery, patterned upon the ashrams he visited in India, with a special emphasis for those recovering from alcohol or drug addiction, or for anyone trying to get in touch with their inner self. At least that's what I've read. They are into a lot of meditation and something called "vibrational therapy," based upon the teachings of his Indian masters. I've tried to visit the one in Green Bay, but they wouldn't let me past the lobby—unless I wanted to join-up, which

I'm not ready to do at this moment. So it's all pretty much secret stuff, but it seems to involve the use of drums, gongs, and, I have heard, quartz crystals—if you can believe that. Who knows? It might be worth checking-out sometime. Synandra definitely wants to.

Anyway, the fact remains that all this is something that we seem to have created. Or perhaps, made possible, *is more accurate, the last half of J.D.'s life. It's staggering.*

P.S.

Besides the Salinas crash, another reason I am so sure of the date is that in There's No Cool Way Back *he tells of speeding in his Porsche on the last day of September, 1955 on his way to the race in Salinas (he got a speeding ticket in Bakersfield) and escaping a certain accident with a truck because a "car full of angels appeared out of nowhere," forcing him off the road and out of harm's way. He only mentions the incident briefly, apparently not thinking it particularly important. Not as though it might have saved his life or anything!*

P.P.S.

So far this resurrection, if I dare call it that, is the only thing that we can find that differs with the world as we used to know it, but during our many discussions about it we assume that there are probably other more subtle changes with people, places, things that J.D. was more intimately involved with, particularly out on the west coast. It makes me wonder how many of the events of my past out west were in any way dependent upon the fact that the man had previously died in 1955. Synandra thinks that we might not find as much change as we fear, since it was our doing that apparently fashioned this "reality" and that, as Dr. Bo said before, it has probably followed the path of least resistance, that is, our memories of the past—except now one in which Dean exists—or something like that.

All I know is that, whatever the consequences, being there, at that time, in that place, we just couldn't have let the man bite the big enchilada. Some power greater than ourselves put us there at that time, at that moment—and we did what we had to do. It was meant to be. Besides, I haven't really told anyone about this yet—

not even Synandra—but the guy, or his spirit or something, winked at me from that pool when we were with Dr. Bo. So I know that it was the right thing to do. He let me know. Anyway, for now the only real before-and-after type differences are our three memories of a different past. Without them, there is no difference at all. At least to anyone else.

P.P.P.S.

As for our encounter with Ronald Reagan, it looks like pretty much of a failure. Though clearly good-hearted, the man is imperturbable and unbelievably dense. If he ever really does become president, I hope he gets a good scriptwriter, because he's sure going to need one. And as to whether we actually have made any impression at all—the nineteen-eighties, as they come, will have to tell.

*   *   *

"It's time," says Synandra, returning from the Wasson woods about a week after their California excursion. "I know that now is the time for us to act, but I don't really know what to do!" Her eyes are a trifle glazed, a look Basil has learned to recognize, one that follows her encounters with the powers of the hill, particularly after a visit to her thinking rock. He knows it's where she's been— every afternoon now after returning from her shop she's been going out to meditate (that area thankfully away from the targeted dig sites (by the same token, the rosebush center regretfully quite near)), waiting for inspiration, for a sign indicating when they should do something to prevent the ultimate destruction of Mystery Rock Hill.

Basil has kept up his acquaintance with Rolf, the long-haired graduate student who has been providing him with details of archaeological lore and gossip on the overall progress of the dig. Recently some strange things have been occurring, too. It seems that preliminary digs far from the hill itself though not very rewarding, were at least uneventful. But now that they have staked-out some trenches to be excavated much nearer to the hill, there have been problems. "The stakes are being pulled-out at night," Rolf has nervously confided. "Or are being moved around, or are disappearing completely!" Mortell quickly assumed it was Synandra or some of the townspeople, or even just neighborhood kids, and had set up watches. But every night no one, not even Mortell himself, saw anything and every morning something had been moved. Rolf tells Basil he had heard of similar happenings in the British Isles—the "little people" demonstrating their objection to molesting their sacred ground. He says that he had tried to tell Mortell as much, and the professor had flown into a rage, telling him that they were in America which had no bloody stinkin' *Leprechauns!* to begin with (Rolf's imitation of Mortell's accent quite humorous), and that they were on a *scientific* expedition that had taken a great deal of legal negotiation and common low-down power plays to bring about and that there was simply no room for such peculiar notions on this dig, and if anyone decided to entertain ideas about fairies, pixies, or other such bloody rot, they could leave the project immediately!

Whew! Rolf is close to his degree, what could he do—other than shut-up? But, by God, the stakes had moved. Even Mortell couldn't dispute that. Basil has to chuckle inwardly over the explanation of the elementals, after all, he has seen them, or something that seemed to be them ... and anyway, he has a really good feeling about these incidents, that something in nature itself could be aggressive, if only in a small way, when something threatened it.

But the digging is to begin in earnest now. They are already midway through August and time is running out for the team. The court delay has proved costly. They are going to have to speed-up things a bit, beginning serious excavation closer to, and possibly of, the hill itself. Mortell is going to request permission to continue the dig through next summer, and Rolf doesn't think he'll be denied, considering the limited progress they have made thus far.

Basil figures this is not going to cheer up Synandra, and it spurs him to ask Rolf something that has been on his mind for several weeks now, ever since he learned about Mortell's fascination with finding "something significant" in the course of the excavation. Since it would be so advantageous in terms of getting said continuation, greater funding, more prestige, and so on, was it possible that Mortell in say, a mad moment, might attempt to, ah, "salt," the dig with something of note?

For once, his good-natured informant is suddenly silent, and after exhaling a great agitated sigh, admits that he wouldn't put it past the impassioned prof. Maybe not before, but in all these weeks they have found little more than a couple of flint arrowheads—not the smallest shard of pottery, nor pipestone, nor anything. Which is one of the reasons Mortell is laying-out more dig sites, much nearer to the hill. But besides that ... Rolf came up behind the professor in his tent the other day and found him handling some objects that had the luster of ... of gold! Mortell had immediately covered them as he approached—Rolf hadn't really gotten a good look—they might have been anything, from fragments of a necklace to pieces of eight—but it certainly looked suspicious. Also suspicious is the fact that Mortell has been doing a lot of hands-on digging lately, in fact, leaving Rolf in charge of some of the coordinating duties that he normally would handle. Rolf thinks he's becoming unnerved by the strange happenings around the site, and also the fact that they're coming up so dry. He sighs again and says that, yes, it's possible that Mortell might be setting himself up to actually "insert" some such golden objects, something uncataloged, or essentially forgotten, that he might have come across somewhere, and saved for just this occasion—in fact, the more Rolf speculates before Basil, the more possible to him it seems. But, if so, Mortell's taking a supreme risk, for if his attempt failed, the site would be tainted. At least for that archaeologist, and a whole new attempt would have to be made, from team selection to permission and funding. But if he did a good job of "finding" it in the right position in just the right stratum—and the professor certainly knew his stuff—it would be equally difficult to challenge.... Salting was horrifyingly unethical, but Rolf knew the man was certainly desperate ... and, well, it certainly wouldn't be anything that *Rolf* would ever attempt ... unless, ha, ha, he could somehow go back in *time,* say, and put something there. Then there would be no way to dispute it. No way.

So when he gets back to the house Basil is not surprised to hear Synandra announce that it is now time to do something to stop Mortell. She's absolutely right. And they'd better act fast, Basil adds, relating to her Mortell's plan to speed-up—and possibly salt—the excavation. And then tells her that he just happens to have an idea about exactly what they should do ... Synandra listens to his plan and smiles, hugs him. This is it! This is exactly the kind of inspiration they had been waiting for. . . .

They spend the next day gathering up junk that will hopefully withstand the test of time, for about eight or nine hundred years, Basil figures. Synandra had learned from her grandfather, and Basil from Rolf, that archaeologists date artifacts they dig up by the age of the soil stratum that the object is found within. This process is called stratigraphy, and along with cross-dating (the comparison of similar pottery styles or like arrowheads) constitutes the most common method of archaeological dating. Basil and Synandra have to laugh at the cross-dating that will result from the comparison of the spongy plastic flipflop sandals she has collected (allegedly completely non-biodegradable) with the dozen or so used spark plugs Basil has found in the Wasson garage. Not to mention the old golf balls, light bulbs, mason jars, and a cheap set of plastic salt and pepper shakers imprinted with "1964 New York World's Fair."

And it's off to the timemobile with these sacks of soon-to-be-artifacts. So that there will be no actual "driving" of the great vehicle on this trip, Basil maneuvers the car around the garage and the back of the house and up an almost-overgrown double-rutted path that someone carved part way into the Wasson woods long ago, possibly to take out a tree or two, but it's in sight of the hill, and not visible from the road, a good place to take-off from. Basil has also precisely paced-off the distances from here to the three current excavation sites near the hill, has them written on the back of an envelope. But Synandra also has a good idea where to plant these things, Basil telling her that one of the dig sites is now directly east of the hill, between it and her power center to the east, and another to the south, an edge of the excavation centered on what would be a straight line (or watercourse!) extending from the hill to the roseate circle, insult to injury! yes, cutting through what has almost become a path beaten in the forest floor beneath the birches by the young lovers on the way to many an amorous rendezvous. The excavations are truly too close for comfort right now. This mission must succeed!

Synandra is hopeful and excited. Although they are not going *way* back (which Basil has promised her they someday will), they are going back far enough that it will be interesting to see what the hill looked like at this ancient time, during what was known as the Late Woodland period. The music playing in her head is the first movement of Dvorak's *New World* symphony, which was on the stereo just before they came out here, seems more than just a coincidence—Dr. Bo said there was no such thing anyway—but it's fitting as they're off to see what once upon a time, to those impatient ever-westward white explorers, was truly a new world.

The only coordinate set on the machine is that of time, about what Basil reckons to be one thousand years, or a hair less, it really doesn't matter, just as long as it comes out below the level the excavators are at, which is currently scratch-surface, geologically speaking, and above the pitch dark ripple of ancient watercourse. He glances at Synandra, she glances back, holding the armrest with one hand, her long hair with the other. Basil leans down and flips the lever, immediately grabs onto the wheel with both hands, clenches his teeth and waits for the shock.

It comes.

The car begins to vibrate in the usual manner, getting to be quite familiar by now, then comes the wild rushing gray fog, deepening to near-blackout, impossible colors, and then it all clears up and they find themselves in the daytime of a long-ago early spring, cool and windy, within the forest primeval. That the house, yard, and other trappings of civilization have vanished is not surprising, only awe-inspiring. The forest seems to be roughly the same, though perhaps completely rearranged. Everything, of course, is very bright, *intense,* in the ghost-dimension, normally a marvelous change, but Basil hates the sickening vibrations by now, even for a short time, and perhaps a bit impatiently hits the switch for materialization. There is the terrific shudder, and, there they are.

It is always so awesome to really *be there*. They shiver in the cold. Through the nearly leafless budding trees, the hill is visible along with the tops of one or two of the rocks ... and check this out, some upright poles have been stuck into the summit with several eagle feathers tied to the top of each, flipping and flapping in the wind. Damn, Basil hadn't noticed them before they appeared. Synandra grabs his arm. "It's someone on a vision quest," she hurriedly whispers, "an Indian brave, no doubt, with each of the four directions marked by those poles."

Indians. Basil feels a chill run up his spine, immediately wonders if they might be part of the tribe he encountered outside of Green Bay in the prototype timemobile. He suggests that they zap out of there, to another time nearby, as it were. But Synandra says they ought to stay, carry out their mission; as long as someone is seeking a vision here, no other Indian will come around, so they're actually safer now. Otherwise they'd never know who could be around the hill.

"But where is he?" Basil whispers.

"Probably lying down inside the heart—if it is a heart," she whispers back. "He might be near the end of his quest, exhausted from lack of sleep, fasting, wailing, waiting for visions."

"How do you know all that?"

"Dr. Bo told me."

"Well, hey, *we* might be his vision."

"Perhaps. If that's the way the powers of the Great Whatever have set it up. In the meantime, this is probably our best chance. Let's do it."

Silent as Indians—or a reasonable facsimile thereof—they stalk to the areas where one thousand years later an excavation will be committed to discover this time, and with garden trowels plant the implements of archaeological deceit. It isn't very difficult; the earth is soft from spring rains, and the job is over quickly. The wind is blowing steadily from the west, serving to mask whatever noise they may have generated, and it seems to have worked. Constant glances up at the hill reveal nothing—or no one. And they are back to the car before they know it. In a way it's disappointing. It's been almost too clean. Basil wonders what kind of visions the brave atop the hill is having, feels kind of jealous, actually. He sighs, what the hell, isn't traveling even a thousand years a thrill anymore? He glances over at copilot Synandra who gives him the high sign, then leans down to flip the lever to go back—and accidentally hits the horn. A brief BEEEP echoes through the ancient forest and they both hold their breath. Both their eyes are upon the hill and sure enough, a head, black hair with a leather band, appears above the rocks, peers inquisitively in their direction, pauses, and then the brave stands shakily, truly transfixed at the sight of the car, the strange visitors.... Basil can't contain his joy, hits the horn hard, BEEEEEEEP! and waves, Synandra muttering "omigod" reaches down and flips the lever herself, but Basil feels great, *they* are his vision, and as the car is buffeted by onrushing fog, he has a truly wondrous thought, that maybe, just maybe ... wouldn't

251

it be *something* if that brave was also, years later, the very same old chief that Basil blasted toward in the Chrysler T&C.... He will never forget the look on the old man's face, the great chromed grille reflected in those dark eyes, this black thunder-horse, *this vision,* reappearing in his old age.

This thought apparently rests more heavily upon him than his current jubilance belies, for by the time they return home he is morose, nearly weeping ... the power, the awesome power, what right do they have to mess with time, with peoples' visions and lives? What right at all? Synandra doesn't say a word, seems to understand his sadness, wonderful she, takes him inside, he's exhausted, sniffling, can't speak a word, tucks him into bed, lays quietly beside him, holds him until he falls asleep.

21

Every evening after supper Basil and Synandra sit atop the hill and watch over the darkening woods, waiting, wondering if today was the day, if today the "artifacts" were found. And, if so, whose? Their's or Mortell's? Someone plays the violin every night precisely as the first star appears, each time more exquisitely sweet and mournful than before, it seems to their anxious hearts. Hearts pale blue and shocking white to Synandra's weary eyes—this wait-ing game is wearing on her as every day the picks and hoes probe years deeper and inches closer to the ancient watercourses and their perfect channels of energy. It is getting to Basil too, Mr. Impatience here, worries that Mortell's golden hoard may show up before their future-relics, tells Synandra that he wants to play some suburban guerrilla, pull off a little disruption in the night that might make them think they're dealing with something a bit heavier than elves, hey. But Synandra says that the violin is a sign, if there must be one, that it would not be wise to proceed agressively against a group with such an inspired instrumentalist among them; this music is cer-tainly an omen of forbearance. They must wait.

To pass the time she tells Basil stories of her and the hill, one of them the time during her enlightened twelfth year when she had a hankering to know where, exactly, all the dead birds went. What happened to them? There must be hundreds of birds around them at any one time. Why weren't there ever any bird carcasses lying around? Her grandfather told her that he thought they flew into thickets or underbrush to die. Nope, said she, after an exhaustive crawling search through the local undergrowth: no birds, no beaks, bones, nothing. It was early autumn. Surely there ought to have been at least one, at least a skeleton. Dr. Bo happened by and she asked him, and *he said,* that unless they ran into a car, or were caught by something, birds simply disappeared when their time on earth was up by flying into a hole in the sky! The reason we never see it is because it happens too quickly for us to catch, plus, we don't know what to look for.

Of course she didn't believe him, but he just happened to have a certain potion along that might convince her, by helping her slow down the world around her ... and ... it ... certainly ... did, atop the hill then with the good doctor, watching blackbirds, crows, jays, gulls, flap-flap-flapping by, floating lazily around her in exquisite slow motion, a most incredible sight, as if the atmosphere had transformed aqueous, and the avians aquatic, the color aquamarine, swirling, intense—this truly was magic. Watching a particular bird, she could see each and every wingbeat with perfect clarity, almost able to discern the air currents swirling off the wingtips, the lilting empennage. Dr. Bo pointed out a big old crow circling the hill, told Synandra that it was soon to leave this earth. It was certainly old, its feathers ragged and lacking the sleek black luster of a younger bird. She could practically feel its age, its air-rush, its tripping heart. . . . Don't take your eyes off it! a fierce admonishment from the doctor, and she hadn't, watched it soaring, being teased by a gang of feisty blackbirds, when suddenly it performed an exquisite series of looping maneuvers, which to the ordinary observer might have seemed evasive, but Dr. Bo whispered in her ear that this was the creature's death-flight, its last voyage in this earthly blue sky. He needn't have told her. To sensitive Synandra the slowed gyrations of the old crow were nothing but. A magnificent aerobatic display that terminated exactly as the medicine man had predicted, with the bird flying into what appeared to be a black-black hole that had suddenly opened up in the sky! The crow had disappeared. She actually saw the bird pass out of this realm into something else!

Where, then, she wanted to know, had it gone?

The doctor had smiled at her, responded that that was another mystery, but one that she might also be able to investigate, if she were to align herself with the proper vibrations, those of the essentially negative, akin to the the undeniable masterforce itself: death. Such a flow of energy manifested itself at a spot to the west of the hill, a uniquely bare area in the midst of a bramble patch. This was only a few months after he had formally explained the true form and function of the hill to her, but she had obliquely known about this area, of course, as the site of her bout, many years ago, with poisonous mushrooms. In fact, ever since that time, if she was in the vicinity she bypassed it. It just didn't *feel* right.

But, if she would go there, right now, the doctor urged, she might be able to unravel the whole mystery. Although, he cautioned, one mystery ultimately led to another, and at best she would understand less than she saw, but undoubtably see more than she could now. . . .

"And you went?"

"Yes, the potion was wearing off, and I was terribly frightened to go there, but I had to and we both knew it."

"Why?"

"It was just an aspect of myself—and the hill—I had to learn, something I'd been putting off. . . ."

She went, pricking her way through the blackcap brambles that surrounded the particular area he indicated. She thought she could feel its power even as she approached. It had to be stronger than any of the others, even the southern one—really scary—but then the doctor was standing protectively up on the hill, and she was terribly curious. . . . The center was clear of brambles, grassy and a trifle damp, and she sat her bluejeaned bottom upon the exact center of the vortex, surprisingly sensual, almost like the southern circle, but different, as though a sword-sharp edge of sadness cut through it. The melancholy of the spot grew within her, became nearly unbearable until at its peak the vision came to her, or she to it . . . finding herself in what had to be the Land of the Dead, inevitably Egyptian, face to face immediately with the incarnation of intelligence there. Thoth, the keeper, body of a man and the head of the ibis, the bird that, when it sleeps, places its head beneath its wing, assumes the shape of a heart.

This creature gestured irresistibly onward and then she was in a tomb, a gigantic mastaba, endless hieroglyphics carved into stone walls, a barrow for departed fowl arranged in infinitely long rows: crows, sparrows, blackbirds, wrens, starlings, thrushes, tanagers, orioles, jays, owls, hawks, eagles ... *every single one* in here, yet not exactly *in,* there was light overhead, all around, an even graybright light that seemed to infuse everything here, to maintain in precise luminosity all those somnolent avians perched erect, eyes wide open and bright as if they could see her, were watching her, and they were all *dead,* yes, but in what strange world?

The realization struck that there was no way out, the birds eerily watching her knowing this ... and she understood then that there were *more* houses of the dead in this land, keeping other species, even—

She was rescued by the pull of the doctor's strong arms, lifting her away from the intense vision, the negative force of the circle, back into the realm of the living. . . .

"Pretty freaky," says Basil.

"You're telling me. But you know what—I just thought of this— that after I had taken that potion I should have tried to find those big birds Dr. Bo had told me about—the ghost eagles you said you ran into? I bet I could have seen them."

"Well, they must be in a different, uh, dimension."

"Yes. I'm sure they are. He always told me they were the protectors of the hill. I guess I never really needed them. Until now."

"Well, I hope they do their job."

"Me too. I hate this waiting."

Basil must be asleep, here's Synandra trying to place a call for him to his best friend, Stinky Harrison, walks in to tell him that she isn't able to, that no one ever heard of a Harrison Press in Los Angeles, or the Henry Harrison, aka Stinky, who she keeps insisting, is its owner ... it's, it's as if he *never existed!* Maybe saving the life of James Dean somehow altered—

Whoooaaah! This wakes him right up, heart pounding, sweating icicles as he shakes off gray phantoms, wades through chortling night-demons and darkness to the phone to place a desperate three a.m. call westward, gut twisted in a knot as it rings and rings and rings . . . and finally a sleepy Stinky answers—thank God! Basil never experiencing greater relief in his life, tells his old buddy he just called to, uh, see how he was. . . . Well, not much sleep this troubled night, which slowly evolves into a startlingly bright morning and an insistent pounding upon the front door. Synandra opens it to face one exceedingly grim-faced Clyde Mortell. Bearing gifts? In one of his hands are three small round black objects which Synandra immediately recognizes as the golf balls, now a thousand or so years old, their cracked skin revealing the withered black remains of rubber bands—nightmarish eggs from archaeologist's hell—and in the other the totally faded, yet intact plastic hulls of the New York World's Fair salt and pepper shakers, circa 1964 C.E., and dangling from his little finger a cracked, but near-intact plastic flip-flop sandal. The rubber strap has nearly rotted away but the sole of the sandal looks so good she almost can't believe it's one of theirs. Yet there they are, in his hands on this morning one thousand years hence—the "artifacts" had survived! The strain of the past weeks suddenly gives way and Synandra breaks up with laughter, can't help herself, whooping like a loosed loon. Basil comes up, looks over Synandra's shoulder at this angry Brit holding his goofy booty and has to start laughing too.

Mortell hasn't spoken a word yet, his face so screwed-up and purple that Basil fears he might be on the verge of a stroke, and then comes the torrent, raging like a North Sea storm, "I-I don't know how you did it, but I know you did it somehow, I'll wager, with that bloody goddamn hippie magic!" He almost spits on the word: magic.

"You-you probably don't realize the extent of what you've done, but I'll tell you. The stratum we found these in positively dates at one thousand years, possibly more, there is no explanation for how they could have gotten there, no explanation at all, the dig is finished, I can't explain it, can't hide it, the students uncovered them, they know, they'll report it, it's over, I'm done for, the project of my dreams turned into something in the bloody realm of *anomalies,* for Christ's sake!"

Basil, who had been smiling himself silly, nodding approvingly, especially at the mention of the dating at one thousand years, almost begins to feel sorry for the harried man.

"And this, this unholy rot! is all we've found anyway! We found absolutely *nothing* near the hill!" Mortell shrieks, looking like he is about to cry.

"I hate to say I told you so . . ." Synandra smiles politely.

"Well I can assure you," sputters Mortell, "that I will not be made a fool of so easily. I daresay you will be extremely sorry about this, this misdoing!"

"Hey now, take it easy," Basil feels it necessary to step forward, after all the last time he had seen him so angry was at the hearing in Milwaukee when the pompous prof was giving Synandra such a bad time. Now it's his turn. "How on earth could we possibly do, ah, what you said? Sounds impossible to me, pal. Sounds crazy. Now you get out of here. Take a hike."

Mortell glares as evilly as possible at Basil, but says nothing, turns on his heel and stalks away.

Later that afternoon Synandra excuses herself, tells Basil that she must go out to the hill by herself. There is something she must attend to. . . . Basil, surprising himself, understands immediately that she has to visit with the old woman, to whom she must give her thanks.

As the very last time, it is a good sign, a golden sunset, gorgeous beyond belief, as if the sun had not been shining in the past few weeks. She brings a nosegay of wild roses freshly cut from the spared southern circle, the last of the season, a willing sacrifice for one who truly understands the gesture. She has pricked her finger on one of the thorns and her blood drops onto the scarred earth below her. She stares blankly downward. This is the first time she has dared venture off the south side of the hill to where the earth has been lain bare. Tears, grateful, sorrowful, follow the drops of blood. Glowing hearts, golden and fire-red, fill the vibrating air, merge swirling with the burning sky. She proceeds eastward past the other awful excavation site, where she will find the old woman—or it's the other way around—at the base of the great oak, her tree of life.

All sounds decrease to nothing, a cocoon of twilight and silence envelops them. Time seems to stop. And then comes the voice like a strong whisper into both her ears, "Welcome, dearie."

"Thank you. I-I'm sorry, you were certainly right. I should have been more patient."

The woman chuckles joyously. The sound is delightful in the silent forest. "You were quite patient, certainly more than *him,* the boy," she smiles. "You did well."

Synandra wants to hug her, but somehow knows that they must remain apart, wholly separate entities, at least at this juncture in space and time. "It-it's been very strange. But I'm glad it's all over now, with the hill and the centers, anyway."

"I would not be so certain, dearie."

Is the woman frowning, sad?

"Oh no. What do you mean?" And Synandra suddenly thinks she hears the rumble of distant thunder.

"I fear that the storm has not yet passed."

"But-but, what else. . . . He, Mortell, told us that he was finished here. What would he—"

"Perhaps nothing. Nothing at all. But you must see that it is not only you . . . or this lovely place. The entire planet is in transition. Greater forces than you can imagine presently hold sway and I fear they do not bode well."

"But why here? What does all that have to do with us here?" And now Synandra is certain that she hears thunder, nearer . . . feels the storm in the pit of her stomach, rolling in.

"All are connected, intertwined with each other," says the hag. "Surely you must sense that. It is your great fortune that the hill is a gathering point for those forces, and also it is your great bane."

"But it's not fair."

"Fair that bounty is endless without dearth, power without weakness, creation without destruction?" the woman's hiss resounds in Synandra's burning ears. "It is indeed fair. This is something that you well understand." Thunder now crashes loudly overhead, the sky has darkened and the wind picked up quickly, but Synandra pays almost no attention to the change, it seems so much in tune with the mood here between her, the woman, the earth, the spared sacred hill. . . .

"Yes, of course," she has to raise her voice over the wind, "but we went to so much trouble—"

"And so you shall again."

"But, what will happen, what should we do?" practically yell-

259

ing, dust washing by them, lightning now flashing wildly overhead.

"Trust yourself. You will know."

And the hag begins to move rapidly away from her into the woods. Synandra wants to run after her but knows she can't, yells into the gathering storm the only thing she can think of that she really wants to know: *What will happen to me?*

If there is any answer at all, it is lost in the crash of the storm, which is suddenly and surely upon her.

Basil is waiting on the porch when Synandra runs in from the woods, drenched to the skin. He is ebullient, the quickly rising storm has charged him up, in fact, leads him to believe that this is nature's way of rejoicing, hey! Is he right?

He is holding her soaking wet against him, doesn't seem to care, and Synandra looks up at the lovable goofy guy, has to smile hugely, and pull him down for a kiss. Of course he's right. She can't tell him what the woman said, probably never will ... perhaps she will try to forget it herself. The world is so messed-up anyway. Everyone knows that.

Magic is incredibly sexy, Synandra remarks, after their heated lovemaking, Basil having carried her upstairs, throwing her laughing into the shower to warm her up, clothes and all. They were soaked anyway, and what fun to climb in too and peel clothing, vegetable-like, from her shivering body, seeking ripe fruit beneath. . . .

"So what did the old lady have to say?" asks Basil innocently, reaching starboard for a handful of caramel corn, blatantly a post-coital cigarette substitute.

"Er, nothing really, just accepted my offering of thanks," is all she can tell him, he's so certain that their troubles are now over and is so relaxed ... but then she tells him—so quickly that she's afraid he might suspect bad news—that she wants them to take the timemobile back to the placement of the Mystery Rocks. Tonight, if possible. Tomorrow for sure.

"Why so soon, all of a sudden?" yawns Basil. "You'd think that we didn't have enough, uh, time—"

"Well, it's just that now that we've done what we've had to with the machine, we should try to find out about the rocks, about how they originally got here. I can't explain it but it's something that I feel I've just got to do. And soon."

"You make it sound as though ... as though the machine isn't going to be around for much longer. ..."

"Well, all the prophecies have come to pass, I think, I hope ... but anyway, you remember what Dr. Bo said about the passage of events throughout the world, that their duration is generally related to their intensity: the bigger, the briefer? Well, you've got to admit that the machine is something awfully big."

"Yeah, but ..."

"One other thing. Today, after Mortell came over, I went into the study and consulted the *I Ching*. I wanted to get a reading on where we were at. And I got the hexagram: After Completion. So now I'm sure. We're definitely at the end of a cycle. Yet it's implicit in the oracle that there are still matters to be taken care of."

"What, I wonder," yawning again.

"I don't know. But it's interesting that the hexagram is the sixty-third, next to last in the great cycle."

"What's the last one?"

"Before Completion."

"Makes sense."

"Of course."

The time-travelers decide on tonight, and are off just as soon as it becomes dark enough to accommodate Synandra's strangely anxious sense of mission, on the usually deserted Wasson's Bay back road that Basil now favors as a runway into the absolute, getting the black beast going, sneakily turning off the headlights as they gather speed, then throwing the brass lever and holding on for dear life ... and to a casual observer, one walking quietly in the darkness alongside the gravel road (far from the misty isles of one's homeland), sorting out one's thoughts after all seems to be lost, swinging between the midnight poles of suicide and revenge, to such a casual observer a rapidly moving car, the car, the big black car belonging to the hippie witch-girl Synandra Wasson, would appear to suddenly and silently vanish!

Basil has set only the time coordinate for this trip, to take them back to the hill of, say, five thousand years ago, when hopefully they might learn the origin of the rocks of mystery. The timemobile emerges from the now all too familiar time-rush fog at a good altitude above the hill, above a clearing in the forest alongside the lake. It is daylight in the ghost-dimension and all they can see is amazingly green forest and glistening blue waters from horizon to horizon, slowly circling the hill below them just as they had circled the Reagan ranch, many, many years following this.... And there are still the black rocks, in a recognizable heartshape five thousand years ago, just as they are today. Synandra says that it's a tribute to the magic of the place that they have remained undisturbed for so long. Basil agrees, understands, feels humbled ... also kind of sick after such a long trip, this spiralling around in the ghost-dimension is wearying, maybe he shouldn't have eaten so much caramel corn.... But, whoa-oa, the vehicle lurches and shudders into the fog once again. And then out, Synandra having edged the time coordinate even further back, equal to another thousand years, she figures. Now that she's here it's imperative that she learn how the rocks got there.... "Basil, please concentrate!" she begs, "the thing isn't taking us where we want to—"

"Uh, I can't seem to get my mind together ..."

"Then don't think."

"'S a deal," and he sort of turns off his thoughts, lets Synandra run this show, she knows what she's looking for anyway ... closes his eyes, leans back and feels the car lurch again. Followed by an epithet from Synandra. And then another lurch. Ugh. And again. Hears Synandra mutter, "Christ, we must be back eight thousand years by now ..." and then in a whisper, "Oh, wow, Basil, look down there!"

He opens his eyes, looks over the side at what she has found. The hill, to be sure, but atop its sloping summit is something large, black and incongruous, what appears to be a single huge upright stone. Yes, that's definitely what it is, Basil decides as the timemobile slowly circles around, a solemn dark megalith centered upon the hilltop, casting a crisp shadow in the strong sunlight of a day long, long ago ... with none of the familiar heart-rocks in existence. And as they spiral lower it is evident that there is also something going on down there on this day in late spring, some folks involved in a procession of some sort ... looks like maybe a hundred or so, dressed in what would seem to be ancient Aztec garb, all robes and feathers and such, from pictures in books Basil has seen. They are marching up the hill, on the top of which might be a kind of table of lashed-together sticks standing at the base of the pillar, maybe an altar. . . . The hilltop looks very strange with this upright obelisk, without the familiar stones, but does have a kind of classic appeal, inspiring in an undefinable way, thinks Basil. But he is simply relieved they've made it—any further back in time and they were going to be running into the last ice age. . . .

"Oh, look!" Synandra now whispers, but Basil already sees what she is pointing at, very conspicuous in the midst of the procession below, someone, a girl, clothed in a sort of shortened white gown, a wreath of flowers crowning her dark hair, is being led up the hill by a thong tied around her neck; her hands are bound behind her. She is flanked by two huge warriors, holding her by the elbows. Basil and Synandra can see everything very clearly from here, hovering now only about one hundred feet above the megalith, descending no farther, fairly motionless in fact, as though held by a kind of tension, almost palpable, as they hang over the sides of the car gazing down at the strange ceremony unfolding below them.

"My God . . ." Synandra quietly gasps.

Basil straightens up, turns around to look at her, but suddenly a piercing scream, like an animal shriek, rips through the ghost-dimension, sends a chill up Basil's spine. It's the girl. The scene below has suddenly become very grim, a struggle among the berobed priest-types to lay her out upon the altar, and she's twisting and writhing like a captured tigress, fighting for her life! very clear and terrifying. There seems to be a murmur of disapproval coursing through the crowd, as though this is highly unusual, as though all good virgins should go to their sacrifice willingly. . . .

"Wow," breathes Basil, "so they *did* have human sacrifice." But immediately regrets saying it as Synandra, anguished, turns to look at him, her brown eyes glowing like coals. "Let's go," she snaps. "We've got to get down there."

"Yeah, but this far back in the—"

"I don't care. We've *got* to save her!"

"Yeah, we do," agrees Basil, grabs the wheel, wondering how exactly to get the black beast down there as there's certainly no time to lose, a glance below reveals that the priests have succeeded in tying the girl to the altar, one of them brandishing a huge shining sword, strobing rainbow-like in the ghost-dimension, another dipping his finger in a small pot of liquid and painting upon the bosom of the squirming girl's gown a heart. A heart! A rough valentine heart, the eternal glyph, in red—blood! it must be. They've got to get down there, got to move, Basil doesn't know if they will be able to make it there in time. And hell, he still isn't sure how to make the descent at all, as something, some sort of force seems to be holding them up there and they can't move—

"Oh, Basil, hurry, hurry, please hurry!" Synandra pleads, her voice choked.

"Yeah, sure, if I could just—"

And then, within the KA-BOOOOMMM! of a single sudden thunderclap from nowhere, the tension breaks. Their ears pop. The sensitive ghost vehicle has once again become responsive to their wishes and begins a fairly smart descent, but it doesn't look like they're going to make it in time, the head honcho has got his evil sword raised above the girl's bloodied breast, the crowd is chanting something rhythmic and dangerous and Synandra is whimpering hysterically, is going to, uh, actually leap over the side! but Basil reaches over, grabs the waistband of her jeans, they're still about fifty feet above the earth near the top of the great stone, she'd kill herself . . . and then both of them feel something behind and above them, the hair on the napes of their necks prickles irresistibly, and suddenly there is a brilliant white flash and a terrific roar: more thunder, they haven't noticed how dark the skies have been growing, both turn to look up and immediately have to duck, a great big dark bird-something suddenly swoops over them, scares Basil shitless, it's a ghost-eagle, a thunderbird! and Synandra turns, tears in her eyes, asks, "God, what's happening?"

"A storm, for one thing . . ." grunts Basil.

Meanwhile the timemobile has been charging down, now about headtop-level, and Basil has managed to steer it towards the main processional path—or that's where it's coming down anyway—right into the only free space atop the hill, right in front of the altar, the priests, and the girl.

"Wait, not yet!" Basil barks, they're still about a foot above the summit, but there's no time to lose, and she has already pushed the lever upwards, to reality, and it comes hard and fast, their graceful swoop-in quickly turning to a very serious ton-and-a-half drop of chrome, wood, and at least one bundle of very scared flesh.

They appear—and there is the to-be-expected gasp from the dozen-or-so priests and warriors crowding the hilltop, also from the throng surrounding the mound, Basil still bouncing on seat-springs, but Synandra is immediately out, brandishing like a pirate the red Swiss Army knife that she always keeps in her purse. Everyone, including the mean-looking fellow with the big blade, is totally cowed by the appearance of this strange apparition and the ceremony abruptly stops. Synandra is at the girl's side (wide-eyed and scared as anyone else) and is slicing through her bindings, the priest with the sword standing back but with a tormented look in his eyes, as if he isn't sure whether to intervene or not, Basil sees this and leans on the Chrysler's horn—BEEEEEPPPP! while pointing as menacingly as he can muster at the priest to back-off, buster, and the shocked swordsman does, even throws down his weapon.

In the meantime there's a storm blowing up, but good. Basil feels relatively protected from these befuddled—Aztecs? or whoever they are, standing a respectful distance away from him now, dividing their anxious looks between him and the increasingly angry skies. But he finds it hard to keep *his* eyes off this gigantic incredible megalith standing upright in the center of the hill, it's awesome, must be fifty feet tall, looks to be the same black rock of which the present-day mystery rocks are composed. And it seems to have a power of its own, almost seems to vibrate, as if it were *alive,* reminds Basil a lot of the monolith in the Kubrick movie, *2001,* he wants to walk over to it, wishes it was quieter, wishes that he had time to try and understand it . . . but of course at the moment he has anything but . . .

If these folk are big on omens, this surely has to be a *good* one. Synandra has gotten the girl free by now and as she helps her up off the altar, precisely as she grasps her hand, there is a terrific blast of thunder and lightning, brilliant and directly overhead, and—later, Synandra will say she will never forget the feeling she had when she looked into the girl's eyes: *"It was like looking at myself. She looked so much like me, and inside I knew we were somehow sisters. I knew at that moment that all of what was occurring was meant to be, that I had come to rescue her, that the time was right, and that it simply had to happen. There was no doubt in my mind. . . .*

Isn't it strange, I think I had found my true sister, one I

265

had wanted to find all my life—or more likely, my great-(to the nth power) grandmother. Saving her life probably saved, or maybe en- sured, the existence of my own."

And this: *"There was so much power there, at the base of that amazing stone—I'm sure both she and I could feel it—my hands were practically burning, although at the time I hardly noticed it."*

But right here and now Basil is beginning to get really edgy. The storm is increasing in intensity and some of the crowd begins drifting away for shelter, notwithstanding the amazing visitors from beyond. Looks to Basil like a good idea too, he bets this big megalith is a sucker for lightning bolts, even now thinks he can feel his hair prickling as the wind's velocity increases and thunder rumbles overhead. He's about to yell for Synandra, but just then the freed maiden stands up on the altar and begins solemnly address- ing the cowering priests in whatever passes here for language. She appears to know how to seize an opportunity, gesturing dra- matically up at the darkened skies and the great megalith behind her and then towards the Chrysler and the strange visitors. She seems to be admonishing the Aztecis, who certainly appear to be- lieve her, to a man dropping to their knees as she speaks. And when she finishes she pauses, then utters a single command to the men, sounds a lot like *schlemiels!* but whatever it is, it works, as they all suddenly jump up and flee down the hill. The girl turns to Synandra to offer her thanks, and then seems to warn her and Basil away, pointing overhead at the raging black skies and then at the megalith. She hugs Synandra, then looks imploringly into her eyes— a solemn last look between true sisters who realize they will never meet again—before shooing her back to the black vehicle just as the first sheet of rain begins to blow in.

Basil's already got the car rolling, turns it around on the hill- top, wondering vaguely if he should attempt to put the convertible's top up, when Synandra scrambles in next to him, panting, "We- we've got to get out of here! She's a seer, a prophetess, she thinks something terrible is going to happen here. On the hill."

"No kidding," says Basil, calmly jocular, stomping on the gas as they begin to bounce down the side of the mound, "what could possibly—?"

"I know she's right, we've got to go, right away, I can feel it too. Ready—?" Her hand poised to flick them out of here.

"In a sec. Just a little more speed . . . okay, now! Think *up*, think lift-off!"

The car shudders into immateriality and rises above the horde, the hill, the heroine . . . Synandra still waving to her, watching as she finally runs off the hill herself. "Thank God," she whispers.

"What's going to—?"

"I'm not exactly sure. We'll have to watch," as the car rises gradually up toward the black clouds, Basil pretty scared circling around in this crazy lightning storm, although in truth buffeted only moderately by the winds now, like being underwater, the rain hitting as tiny zinging shocks in the ghost-dimension, Basil feels as though he's looking out from the tornado-twirling house in *The Wizard of Oz,* expects at any moment to see the old witch on the bicycle pedaling by . . . but instead, swooosh! a *very* big bird suddenly buzzes them, oh God, one of the ghost eagles . . . whoosh! followed by another, soaring back into the clouds, then a third appears lower by the hill, accompanied by a steady CRAKCRAK-CRAKCRAKCRAKBBBOOOOOMMMMMM!!! of thunder, and blinding bursts of lightning now striking the black megalith below them like an anode in a horror movie, it's incredibly intense, they've got a ringside seat on everything, the storm and the spooky swooping eagles, this surely their element, birds of the storm, protectors of the hill. . . . And this is becoming one hell of a tempest, on the ground it must seem like a vengeance from one awfully pissed-off god. Basil is worried about all this lightning—are they immune in the ghost-dimension?—not to mention the big freaky birds, which at this moment seem to have gathered down below, circling just above the megalith.

"Oh boy," says Synandra, "something's gonna happen now, I bet . . ."

She's right. The wind begins blowing furiously, the skies churning like black smoke, and there is suddenly the biggest, brightest CRRRRAAAAAAAKKKKKKBBBBBBOOOOOOOMMMMMMMM!!! of lightning ever, has to be, exploding directly upon the megalith in a cloud of smoke, steam, and dust, throws the timemobile for a few good bounces too . . . and when the dust clears, the megalith is no more, the incredible bolt has shattered it into huge boulders, which have fallen into a surprisingly familiar heart-shape, yes, the blood-tracing of the priest's finger, and the present-day pattern of

267

the mystery rocks of Wasson's Bay.

All in one fell swoop.

"Wow," breathes Basil. "So that's how it happened."

Synandra can't seem to speak, moves her head slowly from side to side, "my god ... my god...."

"Wow-o-wow." Basil too is at a loss for any meaningful words, but understands the significance of what they have witnessed, vaguely wonders what would have happened if they *hadn't* been there for the timely rescue, but doesn't even know where to begin with that ... besides this kind of stuff is an incredible strain on the psyche—not to mention the body. "Hey, what do you say.... Time to get back now?"

Synandra nods, not taking her eyes from the hill, the scene of such awesome change, in a matter of seconds, from megalith to mystery rocks.

"Uh, the girl ... ?"

"She'll make it. I'm sure of it. She has her life as I have my own. We each must do what we have to do."

"Righto, yes. Well, time, ha-ha, to go...."

Synandra nods again, understanding that they have again intervened in the course of events that comprise the world, but knows, absolutely, that this was right, this was where they had to be ... what they had to do. Knows that now she truly understands the mystery....

22

I t's a rainy weekday night, no thunder, just a long soaking
shower, suits Basil fine, helping to wash his soul of remaining
smudges of southern California strife, soot, desperation . . . a welcome rain. Synandra is happy to see it too, the gardens need it, the
elementals out there no doubt happy atop swelling summer squash,
cucumbers, broccoli, cabbage . . . toadstools for umbrellas, acorns
for hats . . . just a rainy night a couple of days after a lot of weird
and crucial happenings and Basil, fairly calmed-down now, tells
Synandra he feels like a pizza.

"That's funny," says Synandra, "you don't *look* like a—" Ha-ha,
but she's hungry too, calls Tiffany, there's no performance tonight,
asks if she'll pick up a large veggie pie on her way over to hear
some . . . Very Strange Tales.

Very Strange indeed. The golden girl's eyes go big when she
hears how they foiled Mortell, "God, what a terrific job. I wish I
could have seen the look on that obnoxious creep's face. . . ." Then
she adds, "You know, when I stopped in at the pizza place, a bunch
of folks from the dig were in there, sitting out the rain, and I
overheard one of them say that they were pulling out in a couple
of days! So, isn't it wonderful?" She raises a Heinenstuber in a

269

toast, "To the eco-defense of Mystery Rock Hill. And its various and sundry mysteries."

"Hear, hear." They toast the hill, smiles all around.

Then Synandra tells her about their Big Adventure, what she has learned, and possibly, contributed, to the creation of the heart-rocks upon the hill, and perhaps even her own present-day existence—another of the troubling philosophical quandaries that always seem to emerge when they consider What They Have Done. And also coming out in the recounting, huge tears that have been secretly, surprisingly dammed-up behind the shock of the whole experience, really cloud-bursting down her cheeks here, Synandra can't help it, body shaking uncontrollably on Tiffany's and then Basil's shoulder, they're a soggy comforting team, exchanging empathetic glances over Synandra's gasping sobs, "that poor girl, that poor poor girl . . . what she went through . . ." and perhaps not a little of her grief is understood for whom it might really be. . . .

But Basil finds a way to cheer her up, attempts juggling with some eggs he takes straight from the fridge, he's not really that bad at it—Jack Dougherty taught him between takes—but looping the white ovoids recklessly faster, he finally drops one in front of Synandra, and it surprisingly *bounces* off the coffee table, they're white rubber, ha-ha, he's been waiting for this chance for a while now, picked them up in a novelty shop in Sturgeon Bay . . . and the prank works, shocking her out of the crying jag. . . . Then Tiffany tells a few jokes she has picked-up from the cast of *Lift,* Synandra begins chuckling a bit, and by and by the little party goes on into the night . . . and of course the subject, whenever they are together, the inevitable subject comes up.

The timemobile.

The big fabulous toy, it's Too Big To Be Denied, the incredible entity like a hugely potent drug, and like all such drugs—not to mention absolute power, ultimate sex, and, uh, caramel corn—dangerously addicting. And they all know it is only a matter of time before one of them, Tiffany, say, exquisitely stifling a belch, casually proposes that they go somewhere, sometime . . . in fact, why not right now, tonight?

"After all this pizza and beer?" Basil worries about his sensitive stomach for an instant, then gulps the last of his Heinie, "But what the hell, I'm game."

Two pairs of gleaming, slightly glazed eyes turn toward practical Synandra, who would offer any necessary objections, but she only smiles, "Well, Dr. Bo said that we should use it—as long as we could."

All right! Tiffany wants to zip over to merry olde England to the Globe Theater to see William Shakespeare's first production of Hamlet—and no doubt the bard himself. This has a certain life-and-times appeal and almost sways the group, but Basil's got an idea, one that he's been mulling over some time now, actually, and that is a trip to ancient Egypt, to learn how they built those pyramids ... gigantic blocks of stone weighing hundreds of tons and all fitting perfectly together within tolerances of hundredths of an inch—what precision! How did they do it? Why not find out? And then the Sphinx is out there, too, and King Tut and Cleopatra and the whole zany crew—why not buzz back about oh, five thousand years or so and check out that crazy Egyptian action, hey? Make that funky desert scene?

Well, why not? This is something exotic, something the intrepid trio can really sink their teeth into. And a couple of cans of Heinenstuber doesn't hurt either. It's settled rather quickly. And before there's any time for second thoughts, Basil pulls the cosmic Chrysler out of the garage. The top's down but it's stopped raining now, clouds parting overhead, a cool breeze coming off the lake, but busy Basil doesn't feel it, running quickly back into the house, returning a minute later with the girls, a big bag of caramel corn, and some more Heinies he's gathered from the fridge, provisions, just in case ... after all, they're going to the Egyptian desert, right?

But, ah, travel. By Tiffany's shaky flashlight beam in the dark driveway they set the time coordinate for around five thousand years in the past, but all of them know it's a relative formality, the machine takes them where they want to go anyway—more or less. And after the take-off drive down the dark road and then the seemingly endless tunnel-fog and multi-colored whooooooooooooooooooosssssssss-sssshnngnngnngngngngngngngngngngngngngngngngnngnngnnnggg-zzzzzznnnhhzzzzznnnhhzzzznnhhzzznnhhznzhznhhzzzzznnnnnz-zzznnnnnzznnznnznnzzzzzzzzzzzhhhnnnnnnnnnnnnznnnnnznnnnzzzzz-zznnnnnnnhhhh—ZZZzzzzip! of crazy spacetime defiance they find themselves flying fairly low, about twenty feet or so over the brilliant desert sands of, presumably, Giza. Egypt. It's incredible,

271

amazing, the streaking power in the ghost-dimension, awesome. Up ahead comes a row of mountainous rippled dunes ... they glide upwards and Ra be praised! is this a *sight*, all feet push brakes to the floor, the ghost-vehicle responds, and they come to rest on the crest of the dune and look out across a broad plain upon what must be the construction of the Great Pyramid ... being carried out by no less than three really strange-looking flying saucers.

Yes, well, not exactly saucer-shaped, but *some* sort of weird hovering aircraft ... appears to be proof positive that the pyramids were actually constructed by, ah, silver spaceships. But, Jeeze, these are unusual-looking things, like something out of a 1940's pulp forerunner of *Impossible Destinies* magazine, strangely aerodynamic contraptions of fins and antennae and jet blasters and hundreds of little windows—behind which sit what sort of beings? Well, whatever they are, they are steadily at work, slowly positioning the huge stone blocks onto the perhaps two-third's complete pyramid through some sort of light-beam technology. The blocks being lowered seem to be held aloft by a narrow cone of very bright blue-white light that surrounds them, emanates from the spacecraft above.

"Well, why the hell not. . . ." says Synandra blithely.

"Man, I just can't believe this," Basil smiles, slowly shaking his head. His concept has always been pretty much pure Hollywood, of thousands of extras chugging up and down elaborate ramps, ropes and log rollers, slave drivers with whips and the whole bit. Here there aren't really that many people involved, maybe a few hundred or so, casually watching the progress of the great tombstone.

"Maybe it's just a weird mirage, or the, uh, ghost-dimension," says Synandra.

"Maybe it's the beer and pizza," says Basil, belching mightily, hoping that he is not going to puke this time, the jangling of the ghost-dimension drawing him to the brink. "I'm going to, uh, materialize us. Maybe this ... weirdness, will go away."

"Yes," Tiffany agrees, "let's flip the switch and be here now!"

And they do so. It's the usual shuddering shock, the ghostly shimmering dropping by several lumens, and ancient reality, Egyptian-style, insinuates itself upon them. But the ghost-dimension has been a faithful reflection of what is before them. If anything, the sight of those crazy spaceships is more fantastic without the ghost-dimension's brilliant filter. And it is really hot, this vast silent desert is not by any means, imaginary.

Or, actually, all that silent. "Did you hear that?" says Tiffany.

They have. What sounded like a moan from, uh-oh, the back seat! They all turn and—oh shit—it's Mortell! pulling himself up, out from under a blanket. He looks like hell, must have sneaked in when they were running around before the trip. Looks like he's been through the wash 'n rinse cycle, hair plastered in straggles across his forehead, glasses cockeyed, the girls begin giggling after the initial shock ... but Basil's heart sinks—this is truly Bad Shit.

The brash Brit is of course looking beyond them, trembling, unable to take his eyes from the very strange sight before them. "My ... Gawd!" he whispers. "It-it can't be," looking around now somewhat panicky at the car, the desert, the spacecraft, "none of this can be—can it?"

"Well, noo, I suppose it just cawn't ..." Tiffany's voice affecting his own.

"It's real—we think," says Synandra, looking over at Basil, who is presently fuming.

"Hey, listen jerk, just what the *hell* are you doing here anyway?"

"I-I might ask the same of—us," says Mortell, regaining some of his composure. "This, of course, you understand is highly impossible, totally absurd. ... Well, it simply can't be, you understand, it has to be some sort of grand hallucination, mass hysteria, yes! It-it defies all our concepts of reality!"

"Of cawse ..." purrs Tiffany. "We understawnd."

"I-I saw the car vanish one night, you know. Or, at least I thought I did. Afterwards I couldn't be sure ... and-and then tonight I saw you all piling into the car, and I thought that perhaps I might just slip in ... you never noticed me behind the seat. I had to find out, you see. But this ... this...."

"Great," snaps Basil. "Now we've got him to deal with. Damn!"

"Well, I don't think we have any recourse," says Synandra, then turns around toward Mortell. "I think you are a thoroughly despicable person, but now that you're here, maybe you will be able to share in this experience with us."

Mortell nods vaguely, but doesn't seem to really hear her, he's transfixed, looking ahead at the crazy construction of the Great Pyramid, as, between witty repartee, they all are.

"Wow, then the pyramids were built by aliens, creatures from outer space, men from Mars," gushes Tiffany.

"They might be aliens," says Synandra softly, "but I doubt that they're extra-terrestrial. I think they're something that comes from other dimensions, right here on earth."

Mortell snorts, but weakly.

"No kidding . . . like us," grunts Basil, still disgusted that Mortell is on board, feeling down around the floor for one of the cans of beer he brought along, the stuff's probably warm as all hell by now, should've packed a cooler if they intended to stay and watch this for any length of time, glad he threw in the caramel corn though. . . .

"Of course," Synandra says, not taking her eyes off the bizarre construction. "Well, just look at us. I mean if someone from around here were to see us in this, this car, imagine what they—"

"You mean like these guys?" asks Tiffany. And Basil, Synandra, and Mortell immediately swing around to confront . . . well, it's some sort of nomadic party of desert dwellers, five dark kaftaned fellows leading a half-dozen heavily burdened camels, a trading party, perhaps, that has apparently just come up over the dune behind them. They're only about thirty feet from the timemobile now, closing fast, and have rapidly armed themselves, now five truly intent individuals, with five mean-looking spears cocked and aimed in their direction.

"Bloody Hell!" gasps Mortell, then reaches down and pulls up an equally mean-looking .45 caliber semi-automatic pistol, points it at the cameleers, draws a bead on the caravan leader's puzzled face.

"No!" shouts Synandra. "Don't shoot them! Please don't shoot!" She reaches out for Mortell's arm but he pulls away. "Bas-il!"

You bet. Time for action and Basil realizes being a little loaded doesn't really help the process. Or maybe it does. How else could the Lexington courage/stupidity threshold blur enough to enable him to casually retrieve a half-dozen or so cans of Heinenstuber—these guys look pretty thirsty in this heat—while giving one of them a surreptitious shake, then grabbing the caramel corn, quickly opening the car door, and stepping out onto the burning sands between them and Mortell.

He approaches cautiously, smiling like a gracious impresario, gestures grandly with the beer cans before the desert denizens, who are watching him, his gifts? with awed interest. And why not? thinks beery Basil. Hell, they've got spaceships building their crazy pyramids, why not a weird black chariot containing human-looking creatures with metallic beverages and golden grub? And the best is yet to come. Casting what he hopes is an imperious look at the armed Egyptians, he spouts gibberish at them—they don't speak English, he doesn't speak Egyptian, what the hell—gesturing from the beer to them to heaven above, to the car behind—

"Basil, what exactly are you doing?" asks Synandra through a clenched smile.

"I'm trying to impress them," Basil smiles desperately back. "Hope it works."

That's for sure, because the anxious men's arms are cocked now all the way back, shaking in anticipation of sudden release, eyes wild between sweating Mortell and this weird appeaser ... this is it; Basil reaches calmly for the flip-top with his free hand and pops it.

It's a veritable gusher, spraying warm brew over the astonished nomads—never before have they seen such a thing! and they all lower their spears slightly as Basil takes a big swig from the can, smiles hugely and then plows into them, popping flip-tops and handing out cans of Heinenstuber, handfuls of caramel corn to the incredulous Egyptians. And ... they like this stuff! Basil isn't surprised, there being something inherently universal about beer and caramel corn, almost wishes he had brought a grill and charcoal and bratwurst, so they could really get into it, partying it up—*tailgating*—during the building of the Great Pyramid—by spaceships. How far they had come, er, gone.

Synandra and Tiffany come out to join the impromptu party, Wisconsin beer in the Valley of the Kings—why not? But Mortell stays in the car, sweating, dividing his attention between the improbable construction of the pyramids and the desert *divertissement* with the now buddy-buddy ancient Egyptians. They leave him alone, at least he's put down the gun ... and for an incredible half-hour or so they eat, drink, gesture, laugh, and then Mortell barks that he wants to go. Figures, typical creep, won't join them and then has to leave early, and he's waving the gun again so he's difficult to refuse.... Synandra and Tiffany insist that they collect all the empty beer cans—aluminum having the potential to remain uncomfortably anomalous through the ages—but the nomads want to keep the flip-tops, wearing them like rings on their fingers . . . so what the hell, it's a cultural thing, they'll probably lose them anyway. They return to the car with an armful of empties and crawl into the front seat, Mortell gesturing from the back with the evil gun to get moving, then watches closely, incredulously, as Basil winks back at him before purposefully flipping the lever on the wooden box under the dash . . . and then, as the car begins its terrific vibration, they all watch the ancient Egyptians disappear into a gray mist as they begin their trip back to whence they had come.

The return voyage is not an especially easy one for the time-mobileers, the spacetime coordinates of ancient Giza apparently differing considerably from present-day Wasson's Bay, and it has left them essentially *wiped-out,* Mortell especially. It's all they can do after returning and parking the big Chrysler safely in the garage to leave him right there, breathing fitfully, but alive, sleeping sprawled across the big leather back seat, the three of them staggering into the house, the girls making for Synandra's bedroom while exhausted Basil, stifling waves of incredible nausea, only makes it to the living room couch before he peacefully passes-out.

He is also the first to awaken, from a great black hole of sleep, grudgingly pulled by an annoying irresistible force, a persistent knocking on the front door . . . okay, *okay,* stumbles over, swings the door open to greet sheriff Mortie McKee and deputy Thorson, who immediately place him under arrest for the murder of one James S. Kowalske.

Yes, handcuffs and all. This has got to be a bad, bad dream, but it's not. He pinches himself twice, hard. But it's no use. And then at the Wasson's Bay police station, tired as hell, he finds a handful of serious-looking men, among them Yates, the weasel-faced attorney from L.A., wearing an eight-hundred dollar suit and a thin satisfied smile. Well, why not. The son-of-a-bitch is *ruthless,* Basil thinks, screws him out of his fee (Basil realizes he didn't exactly keep his part of the bargain either—but how could one explain the inexplicable Machine?) and then tries to *kill* him by running him into Green Bay, and now faces him calmly, almost piously, hitting him with a murder rap. . . . Basil finds himself smiling despite the situation, at least this jerk is consistent, such a *pure* jerk.

During the requisite grilling, Basil learns that Yates has been in contact with the local authorities for some time regarding Kowalske's disappearance, the break coming when the repainted Ferrari was discovered during a raid on a cocaine dealer in Kenosha, the car seized, which led to the capture of the original car-thief, a peninsula punk of some local notoriety who admitted taking it from the deserted house in MacArthur. The very house with the telltale dried blood on the floor, where Captain Jimmy had cut himself with his crowbar. Then it was a job of matching the blood types and then matching the prints on the crowbar with those (Yate's helpful suggestion) of one Basil Lexington on file in the Los Angeles County Courthouse since the Dawson days when he was rather heavily insured and—they had their man. Although obviously no corpus delicti which is the topic of some rather heated questioning as Sheriff McKee and deputy Thorson attempt to break their prisoner before the state boys get a hold of him, and Yates is certain the F.B.I. will be in on it soon. . . .

Poor Basil, really hasn't had enough sleep to go through all this, though he understands the seriousness of the situation, has the sense to keep his mouth shut for the most part until Synandra and Tiffany can show up with a lawyer, and besides, it all strikes him as kind of funny, since he's got possession of the ultimate machine, the timemobile, the supreme getaway vehicle . . . makes him feel pretty smug, but the badgering of these two yokels who haven't had anything this big to sink their chops into since maybe something like cow-rustling way-back-when is starting to bother him.

Finally the girls arrive, are allowed to talk to him at least semi-privately in a corner of the Sheriff's office, and they tell him in hushed voices that Synandra's lawyer is on his way up from Sturgeon Bay, but he doesn't think he'll be able to get Basil released quickly, not with such a serious charge against him, in this neck of the woods.

"Oh great," scowls Basil. "Well you sure took a helluva long time getting here. What'd you do, walk?"

And instantly he sees their alarm intensify.

"Yes, we did," comes the whispered reply. "Basil, the timemo— the Chrysler, it's been stolen, it's gone!"

277

Mortell. Goddamn him, Basil knows that he took it, they all know that. It was really stupid to leave him sleeping in the car; hell, they were so wiped-out they didn't even think to take away his gun. Basil can't even remember if he took the keys from the ignition— apparently not. Terrific. Anyway, now Mortell had the miraculous machine; he had gotten back at them, just like he had promised. They can't even report the car stolen—if the authorities actually found it, closer scrutiny might reveal, if not immediately its true identity as a timemobile, at least that it possessed one very strange, very difficult-to-explain option. . . .

Basil mulls all this over while flat on his back on a cot in one of the two cells of Wasson's Bay's tiny clink. It's evening now, tomorrow he will be transferred, either to a bigger lock-up in Sturgeon Bay, or maybe even Green Bay, depending on whether or not Yates can get the federal charges to stick. The girls have had to leave much earlier, along with Synandra's attorney, a long-time retainer of the Wasson family, a specialist in real estate law who had represented them during numerous hill-preserving negotiations, a big florid man who was uncomfortable with criminal law in general, murder in particular, and with Basil, to boot. And he certainly wasn't very encouraging, didn't seem to believe Basil at all, and why not, incomplete and incoherent as his story is, omitting all parts of his encounter with Kowalske, Ivan Ivanovich, and of course, the miraculous machine. He even finds it hard to lie with a straight face anymore, too much like acting, never was that much of an actor as he got older, probably why he never tried harder to stay in the business after it all ended, to tell the truth. . . .

But the nadir has been reached. Never before has he felt so low, so absolutely bottomed-out . . . he just *can't* tell them what really went on with Captain Jimmy, it's impossible, they'd lock him in the loony bin for sure, unless of course he would produce the machine, which at this point is also impossible, even if it ever was a viable option—damn! He should have been more careful. He should have suspected Mortell might do something like this, especially after they ruined his dig the way they did. After all, he certainly wasn't a stupid person, if maybe somewhat driven . . . maybe totally driven. . . . Whoa! This is what really chills Basil, the fact that you've supplied a crazed archaeologist with a-a time machine, God, it's like giving a nuclear weapon to a terrorist, makes Basil break out in a cold sweat. Who knows what he's up to with it?

"Hey buddy!" comes a call from the other cell, a drunk driver from Illinois nabbed by deputy Thorson, a fat guy with freckles and short red hair, white knit shirt, plaid pants and white leather shoes— and still pretty drunk. "Hey, what're you in for?"

"Uh, murder."

"No ..."

"But I didn't do it."

"Oh sure, sure, sure, sure you didn't. I believe that. I'm an attorney, so you see, I believe you." He chuckles wildly.

"A-a lawyer?" Basil is surprised, figured him for maybe a used-car salesman. "Say, maybe you could give me some advice."

"Sure I could kid. You just push two hundred bucks into this cell and I'll give you some advice." He rolls over on his bunk, pulls the blanket over his head. "I've got troubles of my own, kid. Don't let'em hang you, ha-ha."

Well, fuck-you too, pal, thinks Basil. For a FIB, he's sure not very friendly. But what does it matter anyway? This is the end, there's no hope now, nothing, nada, nada, nada y pues nada y nada y pues nada ... that goddamn Ernie, could he put his finger on it? That's the way it is and that's all there is, nothing more, nada, it's true, it's eternal, even here where they leave a twenty-five watt bulb burn in the corridor, all night long he bets, thoughtless, not very clean, not well lit, but not dark either ... maybe that's good, the darkness holds real despair, all there is right now ... maybe he should try to get some sleep like that lawyer, do lawyers always sleep good? only when they're drunk he figures, wishes he were drunk right now, it would help him sleep, he needs sleep, it's been an incredibly long tiring day and then there's tomorrow, which will only be worse, the grilling will begin again, maybe by F.B.I. dudes, which he doesn't even want to think about. . . . It really was better when he was the Peeper, he can understand that now, when it was good, when he was the center of everything, when he always got his Pop out of trouble, and yet it was always Pop, only good old, grand old Pop Dawson who with a crusty joke delivered through a fog of Pall-Mall smoke who could knock him off that awful center, let him be a real kid, yeah, Pop, it's vivid but always in endless gray, where he is right now, where they always are now ... fond memories of so many years ago, like that time when Pop stole him away from the set in mid-morning, right between takes, the guy was crazy when you think of it now, but then it was exciting, playing hooky like that, just took him out and about in L.A., jumped on the freeways to anywhere ... to play some miniature golf, grab a hot dog and a soda, back in a few hours, but naturally everyone was totally out of joint about the whole thing, and Basil still sees Pop's face so clearly now, popping a Pall-Mall between his lips, and offering with incredible nonchalance: "We went out for a break. I didn't need it, he did. Kid works hard, and he's still a kid. Don't forget that." That darn Pop. He needs that guy now. Always got away with that kind of stuff, but always kept his distance too, never was able to get very close to the old man, frustrating, even in scenes where he got to hug him, somehow the man was always just too far away from him ... like now, appears silvery and silent, growing ever more distant, transparent, wraithlike, as though a good breeze might blow him away ... and WHOOOSHHH!

Something, some terrific wind nearly gusts Basil off his cot, pops his ears, blows dust all over, what the heck ... he must be dreaming, blinks his eyes open to something big and black right next to him: the timemobile! It-it has materialized right here in the jail cell, fills the whole damn thing with only inches to spare and the front seat is filled, Synandra is at the wheel, beaming, and next to her, Tiffany, with some guy Basil's never seen before. But sprawled jauntily across the back seat is someone he never expected to see again, "Captain" Jimmy Kowalske. It's incredible.

"Basil," says Tiffany, "I'd like you to meet Rudy Godwit, our ex-Trinnie friend."

"Oh, hi," says Basil, waves.

"H-hi," Rudy feebly manages, a big guy with light brown hair, looking all around at everything with incredulous eyes, the goofy smile reminds Basil a little of Wally Cleaver. "Oh, wow, this ... is ... so ... fantastic," he gushes.

"And of course you know Captain Jimmy...."

"Uh, sure. Hi."

Kowalske winks, raises his hand in a mock salute.

"Well, c'mon Basil, get in," says Synandra. "We haven't got all night."

"How'd you get it back?"

"Dr. Bo found it."

"No kidding?"

"Yeah, c'mon, get in before the screws show up."

Basil hops into the backseat with Kowalske just as a faltering voice rises from the next cell, "Oh . . . my . . . God!"

Basil waves. "So long, fella."

"B-boy, you sure got connections, kid."

"You know it," says Basil before, in another swirling cloud of dust, he disappears.

23

The Lexington luck . . . seems that it was this evening that Dr. Bo decided to return his Trinnie ward, Rudy Godwit, to Wasson's Bay, Keno driving them over in his old Rambler American. The doctor was on his way to administer to a patient of his farther up the peninsula and couldn't stay longer than it took to drop off the decidedly more *gemütlich* Godwit with the girls. Even the anxiously delivered news of Basil's incarceration couldn't stay the medicine man, although a back-handed wink from Keno indicated much: that the doctor was always aware of matters pertinent to Synandra and the hill, and as such, everything would be all right.

But in the midst of such despair! The doctor's solemn insouciance seemed inappropriate, even for him, until, just as they were leaving, he leaned out of the Rambler's window and asked if, by the way, wasn't that Synandra's car he had seen in front of Seraphim's hardware store? And just as soon as it took to dash down the main street, Synandra and Tiffany found the errant Chrysler T&C—a quick glance through the store window at Mortell inside, feverishly purchasing various implements of destruction: knives, machetes, guns and ammunition. They didn't wait to speculate about what deeds he might be planning to do with such dangerous items, plus a timemobile, just quickly used Synandra's extra set of keys to steal back the most incredible vehicle the civilized world had ever known—had it ever known about it.

But now, sitting with Synandra and Tiffany in the study of the Wasson home—Jimmy Kowalske and Rudy outside in the garden talking, probably freely for the first time—Basil wants to know about the retrieval of Captain Jimmy. How had they managed to get him back from the strange retro-land he had escaped to? He expects a timemobile mini-epic, but is shocked to learn that the marvelous machine was still missing at the time; Synandra had done it on her own.

"Once, long ago, I went to that land," she says, sitting in her grandfather's favorite leather chair, studying the back of her hand. "The one that Kowalske went to."

"You-you have?"

"Yes, once when I was very young, about four years old, I went there. To that house in MacArthur. You see, it's a window, a gateway to that land. That's why Captain Jimmy had to come here, to MacArthur, to get there."

"Tell me in plain English. . . ."

"Okay, as I said, I had sneaked away to the hill—my grandpa told me I always used to do that—and was up rambling around on its top and suddenly I found myself in a different place. I wasn't on the hill anymore, I was somehow outside the MacArthur house, which was in perfect shape—not the ruin it is now—as it existed, actually, in that world. Except I didn't realize it at the time, of course. There was a family there who found me and cared for me, a simple farm family. I told them I came from Wasson's Bay but they had never heard of it. I remember I thought it was funny that they had no car, and they thought it was funny that I thought they should have one. I wanted them to drive me back home. I was there two days. I think I cried myself to sleep the second night, terribly homesick after the initial adventure had worn off, and then awoke the next morning on the porch of the house, which had then reverted to its ruined state, a lot like you see it now."

"Yes, now you can see where that old story about the house, the MacArthur place, actually comes from!" Tiffany adds excitedly. "It's real! Or, unreal, I don't know how to put it. . . ."

"What old story? About it being haunted?"

"Sort of . . . maybe I've never told you this one . . ." smiles Synandra. "You see, it's a center, a power center on the earth, like the hill, but a little more, say, schizophrenic. That's why you had such a weird time in there. You met Dr. Bo there, more or less. . . . He's marvelous at manipulating the energy of centers."

"But what's the story?" This is a question that had intrigued Basil on the first day they had met—the cryptic jotting of Bernard Wasson—but had forgotten about it until now.

"Oh, well you know, it's actually no more than the age-old vanishing hitchhiker story—"

"But it might be the *original* one!" says excited Tiffany. "It's practically a peninsula legend." She nods at Synandra, "I think you told me that story the first summer I was up here."

"Could be, but I don't know if it's *really* true, sometimes people sense that certain places are strange and stories spring-up almost out of nowhere. Plus, there are a lot more centers around the country, and it could be any one of—"

"Oh, let me tell him before you spoil it," says Tiffany. "The version I heard—and Synandra too—is that somebody picks someone up hitchhiking—usually it's a guy picking up a woman, at night—and she gives directions to the MacArthur house. When she's dropped-off the house is standing like new. But the next day the driver of the car finds that the hitchhiker left something in his car, a scarf or something, and when he goes back to return it, the house is empty, abandoned, dilapidated—like it hadn't been lived-in for years. Just like the MacArthur house is today!"

"Okay, okay," says Basil, exasperated, he's heard stories like that plenty of times before—and nothing about the MacArthur place surprises him anymore. "So how'd you bring back Kowalske? Without the machine? Hitchhike?"

"Well, hitching a ride with power, I guess you could say, using the energy of the hill. Captain Jimmy knew essentially what we do, that the house was a window, but he didn't really understand it. He did know, however, that he needed a boost, something to push him into where he wanted to go . . . that was the machine. I used the earth as a conductor, my desire as the guide. What I did was simply go up to the top of the hill and stay on its very center while concentrating on the MacArthur place, and upon Jimmy Kowalske and the place he went to. . . ."

"And ...?"

"Gradually the energy increased, until it became a terrific force, really flowing through me until ... I felt I was dissolving, I guess is how I would describe it, and a fog seemed to come up—kind of like the machine—and then—"

"Oh Basil, I watched her," says Tiffany breathlessly, "and she's right, she just—disappeared! It was too, too freaky...."

"My God ..."

"Anyway, I walked out of that fog and into the little village of MacArthur—it was sort of twilight—right in front of the old house, which was in good shape, so I knew I had made it ... and sitting there on the porch was none other than Jimmy Kowalske." She smiles triumphantly.

"Huh, so you really found him—without the machine. That's incredible."

"See, your machine isn't the only powerful thing around here, Basil."

"Well, pardon me. So how'd you get him to come back?"

"Oh, it was easy. He was bored to death. You know he took a sidestep into an alternate universe, a little backwater of reality is what it was—where the technologies of the twentieth century never occurred for some reason, where life was simple as an Amish farmstead. Apparently everywhere. But for a man of Kowalske's capabilities and interests, it was hell itself. At least that's what he told me. He was really happy to find that I'd come to fetch him. He was actually dying to leave there."

"No kidding ... so how'd you bring him back?"

"Well I was pretty nervous about that ... but it turned out to be just about the reverse of getting there, actually. We walked back into the fogbank that I had come out of—we had to hurry, it was beginning to dissipate—and he just put his arms around my waist, and—"

"What?" interrupts Basil. "Why the hell did he have to do that?"

"Well, Basil, he *had* to hold on to me to get back. Otherwise who knows where he might have ended up? He stood behind me. He was like a passenger on a motorcycle...."

"Hmph. Well I don't have to like it, do I?"

Synandra rolls her eyes. "Anyway, the power brought us back. We ended up on the top of hill, which is where I visualized us returning to. Tiffany says we just—materialized, there."

"They did, Basil," chimes Tiffany, "I watched them. It was really, really freaky." She claps her hands. "Whoo, it gives me shivers just to think about it."

"Me too," says Synandra. "Now, Basil, you can see why I never let myself become totally immersed in those energies. They can literally carry me away. The last time I let it happen was when I was four and look where I ended up."

"Jeeze, well, you sure went to a lot of trouble for me. . . ." He tries to imagine what it would be like to attempt such other-worldly movement without the machine, understands that, as much as he hates to use it anymore, he loves the machine, or the idea of it, anyway . . . loves all machines of steel and oil and brass, all machinery: cogs, gears, cams, idlers . . . operating precisely, dependably, automatically . . . No, it could never be only poor feeble *himself* alone in the vastness, ridiculously fragile flesh and blood and bone, no way, he's in awe of her, has to admit it, her power, her daring, her love for him. . . .

"Well, I couldn't let you take a murder rap," says Synandra, coming over to give him a kiss. "Besides, you're worth it."

There's only one minor detail that still must be attended to this evening, returning Basil to his cell in the Wasson's Bay pokey, via the magic of the timemobile, before he's missed. Basil, of course, doesn't want to do it, as much to avoid another nerve-shaking ride in the crazy car as anything else, but the girls persuade him that it's best to avoid having to explain a jailbreak. Besides, he'll be sprung in the morning when Captain Jimmy shows up, very much alive. Right?

And so, within another great WHOOOOOOOSH! of jail-dust the big black Chrysler appears once again inside the little cell, of course waking the drunk next door, who sees Basil nonchalantly climb out of the car, as if returning from a sort of cosmic late date. They all wave goodbye to him and to the drunk too as the Chrysler POPS! again into nothingness.

"Jesus, kid," says the drunk, "how the hell do you *do* that?"

"Do what?" says Mr. Innocence, climbing onto his cot.

"That-that-that—*car,* that was just there!"

"Car? Maybe you better sleep it off, mister. . . ."

Basil's Journal:

Kowalske is officially back, and I couldn't be happier. Except that he's left the machine with us for a while. We couldn't beg him to take it with him. Says that he's too hot (with the authorities, the press, the church, etc.) to have to deal with it right now. And I believe him. All the hassle was worth it, though, just to see the look on Yate's face when Kowalske walked in. They were transferring me to the Green Bay clink just as Syndy and the gang drove up. Talk about your timing. Yate's mouth dropped a yard. Kowalske stepped up to him and said two words: "You're fired." And Yate's mouth dropped another yard, if you can believe that.

Anyway, Kowalske didn't have much to tell us about the strange place he had run off to other than that it was a world like ours during maybe a more sophisticated version of the middle ages: no electricity, television, telephones, cars, trains, planes. No high technology. Of course, no pollution, either. It's a place where the industrial revolution seemed never to have happened. And also, as Kowalske found, boring as hell. It was obvious he was quite disappointed. When we talked, the first thing he said about it was, "If not there, pal, where?"

This is something I must ask myself.

That night the crazy crew gathers for dinner at the Wasson house to celebrate Basil's release from jail, and to discuss current events and the amazing machine—with the notable exception of Captain Jimmy, already on his way back to the coast to more or less dissolve that once-impressive embodiment of devotional emprise, the Church of the Electronic Trinity. The news of his reappearance would be out immediately, and he wanted to be back at the complex in Barstow, riding triumphantly in on the crest of it, and then to, "set my people free," his exact words. Basil wishes that he had gotten to know him better—the semiconductor savant with a heart—but also understands that perhaps no one ever gets to know him any better, probably a component of his charisma, a whirlwind of dazzle and charm ... and in the end never able to even stay for dinner. But maybe that's the way it has to be, such people must keep on moving; there's no rest on the way to opportunity, adventure, and the American dream. Silicon Valley, watch out.

By now Basil has identified this much-changed Rudy Godwit as the very same tired, frightened Trinnie who appeared at the Jack of Hearts office that rainy L.A. night—providing the break that started him off on this whole adventure. "Why'd you do it?" he feels compelled to ask him, now that they finally have some time to talk.

"I cared about him. I still do. To some extent, I guess. Captain Jimmy was my leader, my teacher, my, ah, messiah . . ." saying this with a certain shrug Basil picks up on, senses that this once-wayward Trinnie has come a long way since their first meeting.

"Well, thanks for that lead . . ." Basil tips his wineglass as Synandra sets a steaming plate of sweet corn on the table. "I owe you one."

"Nothing to it, I was the desperate one . . . Lord, that's the best looking sweet corn I've ever seen—"

"Magic garden."

"Oh yeah . . . well, I certainly believe that . . . pass me over one of those ears and we'll call it even."

"It's a deal."

During dinner it comes out that Rudy is rather heavily into quarks—or at least used to be—and other sub-atomic exotica: photons, leptons, mesons, baryons, neutrinos, quarks, gravitons, and all the rest of the infinitesimally teeny entities that populate the elaborate mythology physicists have created in their attempts to define the nature of the universe.

"It was fascinating work," Rudy explains, "but it started to look like we'd never get to the bottom of things."

"What things?" asks Tiffany.

"The thousand things, I think he means," Synandra smiles cheerfully. "What the Buddhists refer to as the illusory world, isn't that right, Rudy?"

"Er, yes, I suppose. Getting to the bottom of it all is what I, and all particle physicists are attempting to do. To get to the absolute ground zero with a grand unification scheme. The truth. Albert Einstein spent the rest of his life searching for it, but finding himself, regretfully, further and further away from the answer. And the future doesn't look much brighter. It appears that we can divide quarks, which, as I said before, are postulated to be the key components of matter, even farther, through perhaps countless strata. . . . It almost started to look silly to me. It seemed we were going to some pretty elaborate means to understand the workings of the universe, shooting subatomic particles—and they aren't really even particles, just little energetic *concepts,* actually—through a gigantic, so-called, particle accelerator two miles long. You wouldn't believe the equipment we had at Stanford. . . ." Rudy sighs deeply and takes another gulp of wine. "But it seemed that the more we poked and prodded the universe, the less that reality itself seemed to exist!"

"Well," breathes Synandra after a respectful pause, "I can appreciate your confusion. The Hindus say that the world is merely an illusion we conjure up in our minds—something I'm inclined to believe. . . ."

"Me too," sighs Basil. "I can agree to that . . . since the machine came along. Before . . . who would have thought?"

"Yes, the Hindu name for the great illusion is *maya,"* continues Synandra. "Those sages might find it, forgive me, laughable, that scientists could probe around so in a, dream."

"Well, perhaps you're right," Rudy sighs again. "I don't think I know anything anymore. But back then I was certainly confused . . . and also was starting to get pretty depressed about the whole enigma of modern physics."

"Is that when you got involved in the Church, Rudy?"

"Involved? Hah. That's when I did the big one-eighty, when I went from being master of the computers I worked with to becoming a computer, a robot, myself. I wandered into a storefront branch of the Church of Electronic Trinity one afternoon, just out of curiosity—and never wandered out again. I guess I fell in love with the idea of the Three, and the exuberance of Captain Jimmy . . . and their brainwashing techniques are pretty damn effective too, I'll vouch for that.

"At least when Jimmy left the Church I still had a tiny bit of sense left—enough to know that something was wrong. I had become more or less trusted by the higher-ups that really ran the church. That was why I had an opportunity to run out and find you, Basil, to try to help you find Jimmy, which you did an awfully damn good job of doing, by the way."

Basil has to smile. "Aw, it wasn't so much. I just followed your clue. That's what broke the case. But what always seemed so strange—or hypocritical, actually—was how Kowalske strung you guys along. I mean he had the machine all that time and never let you in on it. None of you."

"Yes, yes," Rudy's eyes lower to the tabletop, "I've given that a lot of thought lately. I guess he was an organizer, more than anything else, and the Church just became the end result of his genius. I think he always *wanted* to deliver the machine, the grand embodiment of the Three, to us, but didn't know how. It was, I think even beyond his wildest dreams. How could he control such a thing? It was as much as he could do to give us the promise; the deed itself was beyond him. I tell you, I think that's why he's not here with us—or the machine—tonight. He's happier without it."

"God, I can understand," moans Basil, "the damn thing is a terrible burden. It's the ultimate mechanics, all there is or ever could be, it's—"

"Amen," Synandra kindly cuts him off. "It's the ultimate, that's for sure."

"And we've still got it," says Basil sourly. "Jesus, look at the crazy stuff we've done already. James Dean, my god, how could we have done that?"

"Well, we didn't *mean* to," says Tiffany, she's heard this from him before. "We just couldn't let him *die* there, could we?" something she's said before, too.

Basil can't answer that one. Can't really disagree with her either, but still feels awfully strange inside about that whole episode.

"Yes, yes," ponders Rudy, "Tiffany has told me about your, ah, rescue. It seems funny to me because from my knowledge he never died, or even had the accident you say you prevented—only of the one that followed, in—where was it—Salinas?—the next day. *That* was the accident everybody heard about."

"He survived that one," yawns Tiffany.

"Yes . . . well, the only other thing I remember is that he just dropped out of sight for a while because of alcohol or drugs or something . . . and then he disappeared in India for a few years, as I recall."

"Besides," Synandra chimes in, "what harm has been done? It appears to me we've only changed the world for the better. His Inner Space Institutes are wonderful places I hear, very helpful for spiritual development. He also believes that by teaching people to tune their energies and then gathering them together for deep meditation, the peaceful vibrations they produce will radiate outward and actually penetrate the consciousness of the surrounding community, lowering aggression levels, promoting peaceful relations among everyone. Which, hmm, since they opened the one in Green Bay just might explain the poor performance of the Packers' front line in the last few years ... but anyway, he's turned out to be a very enlightened guy."

"Yeah, yeah, I guess," pouts Basil, "but it still bothers me ... we aren't in the same world that we started out in."

"Well, are we ever?" Synandra smiles.

"I suppose stranger things have happened," offers Rudy, "but I can't think of any offhand ... it reminds me more of something I might have read in a science-fiction story somewhere. Er, do you guys read much science-fiction?"

Synandra and Tiffany shake their heads no.

"I could never really get into that stuff," smirks Basil. "You know, 'Amznx and Darvon marooned on the planet Quaalude a billion light-years from earth ...' It's just too far-out to be interesting—or have any relevance."

"Well, science fiction I think, has a lot of relevance nowadays," sniffs Rudy. "You know, yesterday's science fiction often becomes tomorrow's reality. Look at radio, television, submarines, space-travel ... they were all predicted by science fiction. And time-machines are practically an archetype of the genre. Old H.G. Wells started it with his classic, which still holds up pretty well. Some of the new stuff is terrific. I used to have a wonderful collection but, tsk, I gave it away when I enlisted in the Church...."

"Look Rudy," Basil in a dour mood to begin with, flashes what he takes to be his Jack Nicholson smile, "I admit that we don't share the same literary tastes—actually I happen to prefer Hemingway—but one thing I'm sure we ought to agree on is that the machine is more amazing than anything you could ever read about in a lousy book. This is the real thing—this is reality."

Rudy looks like he's gearing up to respond, but since the conversation has taken a somewhat hostile turn, Synandra intervenes, "Rudy, with your knowledge of physics, I suppose you must have some understanding of the creation of the universe?"

"Er, yes, I'm familiar with several theories."

"Well, my question is, in the big-bang theory, what's in the space surrounding that little piece of junk just before the bang?

Lime Jell-o?"

They all hear the clump-clump-thump before he can answer. It's not very loud, but it's outside by the car, and in a strange way they are all attuned for just such a warning, particularly Basil, he knows it's the Chrysler, dammit, he meant to take that machine out of it, or at least lock the big beast in the garage, but they were involved with other things, up for a party with Rudy here ... loose thoughts jolting through his mind as he leads the dash out to the convertible, top still down, great care here, gang ... but dark and empty-looking underneath the Norway maples alongside the driveway. Maybe it was nothing, a raccoon in the garbage again, though they still approach cautiously, whispering ... and suddenly headlights blare into their eyes, the starter whines and the engine catches, the car lurches toward them and Clyde Mortell's anxious face appears glowing behind the steering wheel, a haunting image as they scatter madly backwards out of the way, but then the car stops hard, and Basil can practically hear a desperate, "Bloody hell!" Mortell can't find reverse to back out of the driveway, Basil realizes as he runs up to the driver's side door and is about to yank it open when suddenly something comes swift and hard for his face, Mortell's goddamn .45, he tries to duck, still catches it soundly on the forehead, sees an explosion of stars and staggers backwards as the gears finally mesh, tires spinning in the gravel as the car pulls away, but someone, Rudy maybe, seems to be hanging onto the car door now, and perhaps Mortell himself ... dark forms struggling behind the headlight glare as the car slows, spins wildly around and then stops midway down the driveway. Basil dashes up to find Rudy, panting, standing helplessly alongside the car while Mortell sits panting himself, but more calmly, holding his gun leveled at Tiffany, who has somehow managed to scramble inside onto the seat next to him, and more or less at Synandra, who is outside behind her, hanging onto the other door.

"So ... we're going to ... have to do it ... the hard way," puffs Mortell. "All right then ... so be it."

"Just-just don't do anything—stupid," begs Synandra.

"Yeah," says Rudy, "just take it easy now...."

"Then you will do ... exactly as I say. Actually, I find that I fancy this arrangement somewhat better than going it alone. I won't have to guess at the precise use of that little instrument," an eyebrow canted toward the dashboard, actually the magical box beneath.

"Uh, we—you, going somewhere?" ventures Basil. His forehead hurts like hell, winces as he wipes away a trickle of blood.

"We all are, it appears. I hope you are all up for a little journey. I certainly am. But let's arrange ourselves, shall we?"

Mortell decides that it will be most prudent to have Basil and Rudy up front where he can watch them, with Tiffany and Synandra in the back with him. He sits back comfortably in the left seat corner, directly behind Basil, cradling the gun in the direction of the girls to his right. "I daresay that this contraption will have no difficulty in shooting through the front seats," he says blithely to them, "if you should decide to cause any, ah, commotion, back here. I hope you understand."

Basil grips the steering wheel, swears under his breath, then sees with a start that the wooden box of the miraculous machine is hanging sideways, a crescent wrench lying next to it. Mortell was in the process of undoing the bolts holding it under the dash, stealing it, that son-of-a-bitch, really makes Basil mad now, wants to slug him or something ... but can't at the moment, can't think of any way out of this, head is throbbing, hurts like hell, the crack with the pistol probably worse than he thought.... "Okay Mortell, where do you want to go, you bastard."

"Tut-tut, my friend, let us not call my lineage into question here, as all of us I'm sure have some—"

"All right, all right, so where, when?"

"All the way."

"What?"

"You heard me. All the way. We're going to test the range of this little, ah, mechanical marvel." He leans forward, jams the barrel of the gun none too kindly into the soft spot below Basil's right ear, and hisses, "Now, move it. All the way. Into the past, yes. We're going to go *way* back." He chuckles gleefully.

Basil's gut twists into a vicious knot, feels sweat pouring out into the humid night, hates this guy, this situation, "Listen, we might not make it, or, or get back okay. This thing's loose now. We don't even know—"

"Just *do* it!" Mortell screams into his aching head. "Do it *now*, do you understand?" cruelly jamming the .45 again below his ear.

"Okay," Basil knows he's trapped, doesn't care now, swiftly pushes the time lever all the way over, pushes the distance coordinate all the way too, what the hell, and flips the switch up. "Hang on everyone. Hang on. We're go-ing . . ."

It's a dead start, but still has its punch as the night performs a giant hiccup, the car shudders terrifically, and they are plunged into the familiar onrushing fog with considerably more force, G-force, it seems, than Basil can remember enduring before, really pressing them back into their seats. Basil thought he might have had a chance to get the gun from Mortell during this onrush, but finds he can't move, can't even turn his head around, is barely able to squint into the whistling mist-stream, never could take roller-coasters either, and this is worse than any of them, all he can do is try to maintain, maintain, this trip is interminable, they never should have done it, it'll never end, he should have let Mortell shoot him, sacrifice himself rather than force them all to endure this, they'll never end up anywhere, there's nothing here, there, anywhere, anyway, it's all nada, nada, nada, y pues nada . . . nada . . . nada . . .

Then it all suddenly—very suddenly—stops. Something, Basil thinks, seems very bright here . . . uh, he's got his eyes closed, didn't even realize, opens them, breathes in the purest air he has ever breathed and sees stretching endlessly before him miles and miles of golden grassland, waving softly in the breeze beneath a brilliant blue sky.

"The veld," whispers an awed voice behind him, Mortell.

"My God . . ." says Rudy, equally awed.

Basil too is captivated by this vast golden land, reminds him of pictures of Africa he might have seen at one time . . . notices that they are perched atop a gradual hill from which the veld stretches out before them, also sees that it is not entirely flat grassland, off to the right the edge of a forest breaks the plain, and to the left the terrain sweeps gradually upwards to form a rise that runs along the horizon, placing them in what appears to be a very broad open valley. The Chrysler has landed.

And then he notices that they are *here*. Not in the ghost-dimension. *Here*. Looks down and notices that the significant lever has been pushed all the way up to place them immediately into reality, can't remember if he did it, head hurting the way it does, but isn't surprised, pissed-off as he was at the time . . . stupid, stupid, and dangerous as all hell . . . but then what about this wasn't?

"Well, where are we?" asks Tiffany. "Looks like someplace in Africa. . . ."

"Wow, maybe we've reached Gondwanaland," says Synandra.

"Oh, no, no," Mortell corrects, "that would be the Paleozoic, at the least—two hundred and eighty million years past. Oh no, not the Permian, Pennsylvanian, Mississippian . . . that would be ferns, cycads, and swamps . . . no, no, we're in the Cenezoic at least, the Miocene or Pliocene, say from, oh, two to fifteen million years ago. Ah yes, marvelous, simply marvelous," Mortell chuckles, obviously quite pleased with himself.

The sight, Basil has to admit, is quite impressive, the huge spread of the earth, as though one-eighth of the entire planet was visible from this perspective, reminds him of the crucial Africa of Ernest Hemingway, one that he, like many others, took great sport from, but understood the sacrifice, the difference between man and thoughtful-man . . . but in the end the result was the same. They were here way before that now, though, the sun-brilliant greens and golds of this pristine land seeming so ripe for, for what? Human development of some sort? What else? It's too depressing. The very thought of humans: coarse, dirty, homicidal maniacs even simply *being here* seems revolting, obscene. And here they are.

"Well, what do we do now?" muses Basil morosely, looks back at the professor.

But before Mortell can answer there is the faint sound of animal-shrieking in front of them to the right, and all heads turn that way to spot a commotion amongst what appear to be large monkeys, or apes, or, uh. . . .

"Oh . . . my . . . God," gasps Mortell incredulously, "they're, they're, expelling them from the forest, the apes, hominids, early man, don't you see? My word, this is it! This is what happened! This is precisely what separated man from the apes. We're seeing it! Right here!"

And sure enough, they are probably almost a mile away, but it is clear that one group of the stooped ape-like creatures is chasing another group from the trees into the open grassland. The chased group appears hesitant, rising up momentarily to look out over the veld, and then crouch down into the grass again.

"Aw, those poor monkeys . . ." says Tiffany.

295

"No, no, don't you see that this is how man *began!*" Mortell sputters. "This, *this* is the turning point, where the apes had to learn to fend for themselves, to continually stand erect so as to watch out for predators, to learn to kill game, and begin eating red meat ..." Mortell turns to look significantly at Synandra.

"And to learn to kill each other," Synandra shoots back.

"In time, yes, perhaps, yes, that happened ... but still, this is the beginning we are seeing now, what a miraculous moment to behold! Those 'poor monkeys' in the trees are the ones you should pity. They are doomed to a life of fruits and nuts, the eternal forest, of, of monkey-dom. It is the ones who are being chased out who are going to become our ancestors, learning to survive on the run, to thrill in the hunt, the glory of the chase, the joy of the kill. Yes, like it or not, Miss Wasson, your ancestors are out there."

"And your's too," adds Rudy. "You know, it makes me kind of edgy that we're here—amazing as it is—because we could screw-up an awful lot of what you're talking about. We're so far back in time that we might—"

"Oh blast," says Mortell, looking fixedly at the apes, rising to stand upon the seat and then fitfully jumping out of the car, "they're in trouble. Lion, or-or," Mortell pants, "a saber-toothed tiger, perhaps."

He's right, they can all see a rounded, darker shape, obviously some sort of big cat, stalking through the grass toward the hapless apes. "Gee, they are in trouble," says Tiffany.

"Right you are!" Mortell suddenly shouts, begins running down the slope, gun drawn, yelling and whooping to scare the beast away.

"Damn," says Basil, "I was afraid something like this would happen."

"Well, why not," says Tiffany. "He's nuts."

"He's also dangerous," says Rudy. "He could off one of our ancestors with his stupid gun."

"Or himself," says Synandra.

No one actually says: "Good riddance," but it is certainly not far from the thoughts of all present. Meanwhile Mortell is plunging clumsily through waist-high grass toward the apes and the cat, who haven't yet seemed to notice his charge.

"Maybe we should just go," says Tiffany firmly.

"And-and just leave him here?" asks Synandra. And for several long seconds no one speaks. "We can't," she answers herself. "You know that. And we've got to stop him."

"She's right," says Rudy, "I'm scared to death he's going to really mess up the past—and thus the future—our, ah, present. We shouldn't really be here at all."

"Maybe," Synandra says softly, "we're suppose to be here. . . ."

"Who knows?" snaps Basil, starting up the Chrysler's engine. "Let's go get him. Hang on."

The car lurches forward, Basil steps on the gas and they begin bouncing terribly across the veld. The apes are a good mile away by now and they catch up with Mortell about a third of the way to them, just as he raises his gun skyward and two fearsome CRACKs fill the air. Immediately all the apes rise upward out of the grass to look in their direction for an instant before turning, crouching, and dashing back into the trees. The cat is nowhere to be seen.

Mortell stands and watches like a man—deflated, is the way it seems to Basil. He turns to sadly face the four of them, like a child whose playmates have deserted him. "They-they all ran away."

"Well, what did you expect," scolds Tiffany, "shooting that gun like that?"

"The cat was about to pounce . . . I had no choice. I certainly didn't aim for the cat, only tried to . . . my God!" His eyes suddenly open wide, looking past them, and the four of them turn around also, and there, beyond where the slope of the ridge to their left has declined into the plain, over in another wide valley is a hill and what looks to be a tall dark something rising above it.

"It's-it's the megalith," gasps Synandra excitedly. "Like the one at the hill we saw . . . unless . . . could it be, that *this* is the hill? My hill?"

"No . . ." says Basil. "It can't be, can it? I figured we were in Africa."

No one can answer that, but all of them want a closer look, including Mortell, the apes presumably to be left to their own evolutionary antics for the time being. So Basil cautiously guides the Chrysler across the veld, following a dry creekbed that leads in the direction of the megalith. It takes them about a half an hour to reach the hill, during which time Synandra has related the time-travel episode in which she and Basil appeared to have discovered the origin of the Mystery Rocks, that being the otherworldly-induced *blitzkrieg* of the black behemoth looming now weirdly before them.

Weirdly—yes. Synandra perceives it more intensely than the rest of them, and perhaps more immediately, but as they get out of the car and begin climbing almost zombie-like up the hill—the great megalith seems to draw them like a magnet—everyone senses a peculiar vibration that seems to emanate from the stone itself. It appears to be haloed by a deep blue luminescence existing just below the limen of perception. Basil, climbing the mound with Synandra, notices that whenever he turns his eyes away, the glow is detectable in his peripheral vision; Synandra says that she can see it quite distinctly. "You know, I didn't notice it at the time, Basil—everything was a trifle hectic—but I realize now that when I saw this megalith before, it glowed in the same way. I had forgotten. . . ."

"Then you're sure this is the same one?"

"Positively."

"Even though its position here . . . the land around it is so different? "

"Yes, you know what I believe is this: that wherever you go, there it is."

"God, my God, it's magnificent!" Mortell exclaims loudly, having reached the summit before them, standing at its base, rubbing his hands together, having stuck the .45 in the waistband of his pants. "It's—I don't know quite how to put it—inspiring! It, it must be nearly fifty feet tall. Yes, quite inspiring."

"It sure is," Rudy agrees, nonchalantly walking over to the professor. "How do you think it got here?"

"That—is a most troubling question," Mortell sighs. "Man, modern man, has clearly not yet evolved. It's as if, as if, there were some *higher* power involved . . . I don't know. Surely no *random* force could have produced such a structure. My homeland abounds with prehistoric earthworks: cairns, dolmens, menhirs, standing stones, and I think everyone speculates that it was early man, in our case the Celts, who might have erected them, but now . . . I don't know bloody what to think."

"What about UFO's?" Synandra calls over. "Maybe our friends in the spaceships put it here," she says jokingly, but still. . . .

"Please Miss Wasson, I am trying my best to forget that, that . . . episode, ever happened. I am forced to relegate that vision to the throes of fatigue and hallucination. I wish I could say the same about this . . . it's so distressing. I'm a man of science and I daresay that all I see here is enough to shake the very foundations of—I say!"

Basil and Synandra have been watching it evolve all along, Rudy sidling-up practically alongside the professor, and then very smoothly snatching the gun from his belt.

He casually points it at the beggared Brit's midsection. "Is there any more to see here?" calling over to them. "Anything else we should do?"

"No," Synandra answers, "everything here is just fine. And there's never been anything for us to *do*. All here will take care of itself, I'm sure."

"Well, then," Rudy spins Mortell around, jabs him in the back with the barrel of the gun, "let's get going, jerkface. Mush!"

And they make a solemn processional back to the car, Mortell inwardly fuming, but cagey enough to put on a shit-eating grin and plea-bargain: "Now, now look, perhaps I've behaved rather badly, yes, I'm sure that in fact I have, but it was all in the name of science, you must understand. What we have here is a superb moment in the history of the planet, of mankind, to observe—"

"And to influence?" Synandra sardonic. "You scared those apes right back into the trees. If a lion or tiger or whatever, was out there you should have let them do battle with it. What about them having to learn the 'thrill of the hunt, the joy of the kill?' Just not if it's the ones that you're studying, huh. Typical scientist, blindsided like all the rest. . . ."

This really angers Mortell, and he tries to lunge at her, but Basil is quickly there to grab him, twist his arm back into a tight hammerlock, feels good, would really like to bang him up against the side of the car, too, yeah, head-first . . . but it is enough to just get him into the back seat with Rudy and the gun, the girls riding up front with Basil, and before anything else can happen, get the hell back home.

299

24

J ust before they take off from the planet of the apes, two
things of note occur: First, Synandra, perhaps fearful of the
great spacetime leap (several millions of years and unknown miles)
that they will have to make to return home, tells everyone to
concentrate on the hill, Mystery Rock Hill in Wasson's Bay. Since
they are embarking in the powerful aura of this megalith, its vibrations extending perhaps throughout the cosmos, it may help to
mentally fix on another landmark existing in a certain time and
space—their own. The other thing is, when Basil reaches down to
flip the lever to take them back, he twists the machine toward him
(fastened now by only one bolt) and his heart skips a beat. He suddenly realizes that the way the machine was positioned when he
threw the switches last night, he must have thrown the time-setting
lever to the *right,* and therefore the future, rather than the past!
So *this,* this aboriginal land-primeval is-is the *future?* God help them.
The time-set lever presently sits at zero, as it always does after a
trip (the time being, of course, *now),* the downward return flip of the
significant other lever their sole means of getting back, so he really
can't be positive, wasn't in any great shape when he set the thing,
anyway, but the uncertainty is enough to scare the hell out of him.

He decides not to mention it to anyone, it would only cause undue alarm, and priority number one is to *get back.*

Get back. Yes. A worried look over at Synandra, who looks back, equally worried, softly murmurs, "Well, I hope your machine works now . . ."

"It got us here, didn't it? Hang on." He flips the lever downward, grabs tightly onto the steering wheel, braces himself, and . . . nothing happens.

"Oh fuck."

"What, what is it?" calls Rudy from the back seat, keeping the gun aimed at Mortell.

"It-it didn't work. Nothing happened."

"Oh no . . ."

"Basil, are you sure you did it right?" asks Synandra.

"Yes, yes, I did it right. God, I was afraid of something like this . . . like maybe its batteries, or something, would wear out someday . . ."

"Good Heavens!" gasps Mortell. "Y-you mean we're stuck here? Marooned? In the ancient past?"

"Or the ultimate future . . ."

"What?"

"Never mind. I-I mean I don't know," and here Basil really slips into a funk, thinking at first that if the *return* function doesn't work, at least maybe he could set the coordinates the reverse of what got them there, and actually *journey* back . . . but, but then, if he is correct that they are really in the *future,* then he would actually want to return to the *past,* but if he is wrong, then . . . it is too much, he's exhausted, battered, too tired to think, maybe the machine has simply run out of juice, like himself. He rests his head on the steering wheel in the silent shadow of the great megalith.

"My Lord," Mortell rambles on, "we would, of course dominate the apes. Why, we would have to in order to survive. We would be the, the embodiment of the Adam and Eve myth. Yes, it's very clear. We, *we,* would be the progenitors of the human race on this planet! Why it's—"

"You," Tiffany turns to eyeball Mortell, "could never get *that* lucky, pal. Not even here."

Everyone chuckles a bit, except oblivious Mortell. "No, no, it's truly astounding. With our superior intelligence, and, and that gun

there, yes, for protection. We shall rule this land. Astounding! Why
. . . oh my, we might actually be our own *precursors* . . . oh my
. . . the implications . . . the reality . . ."

"The horror . . ." mutters Basil.

"Jeeze, and we didn't even bring along any toilet paper," moans
Tiffany. "Why don't you just kick it, Basil?"

"Huh? Kick the machine? You don't just—"

"Sure, like this," and she gives the dangling sacred cask a
righteous kick.

"Hey!!! Don't do that! Who knows what you'll—"

"Well it doesn't work and everyone knows that the first thing
you do then is—"

But the vibration silences her, and all the others, the familiar,
saving, gut-wrenching shuddering has begun. Basil wants to cry for
joy but only gets out, "It worked."

"I told ya—"

And the last thing they hear is Synandra's voice, calmly intoning,
"Think of the hill, everyone, concentrate on Mystery Rock Hill."

And they are into the rushing fog once again, Basil actually
praying to a God he never thought much about before, never really
needed before . . . all through the terrific buffeting, promises he will
never use the machine again, never, ever . . . this time he means it,
is ready to hand the stupid thing over to Mortell, but knows he
can't, or throw it away, but knows he can't do that either . . . doesn't
care right now, doesn't matter, all they've got to do is get back, oh
God, get back to home sweet home, home, home . . . there's no
place like home, no place like home, no place like . . .

Everyone (other than Basil) must have taken Synandra's advice
to heart, for when the telechronic vibrations finally cease, Basil
rouses himself enough to see, in pre-dawn darkness, that the timemobile has landed actually atop Mystery Rock Hill, right alongside
the heart-rocks, like the ark and Ararat . . . rather than the driveway
of the Wasson house from which they had left. . . . His heart leaps
with silent joy, they have returned from never-never-land, returned
home, thank God . . . but he is still absolutely wiped-out along with
everyone else, must rest now, and in an instant drifts off again
. . . only to resurface by the dawn's early light here, felt as though
something brushed against his feet, probably nothing, but there it is
again, along with a clunk or something . . . Basil cautiously opens

his eyes, sees that the car door is wide open, looks down and . . . Mortell! just finished unbolting the machine with the crescent wrench and is rapidly backing out, carefully arched above Basil's sprawled legs. *You bastard!* is all he can think before delivering an upward kick intended for the Brit's head, but only catching the side of the machine, enough though to knock the thing out of the professor's grasp and onto the ground alongside the car. Basil immediately dives for it, initiates a quick clawing scramble punctuated with grunts and puffs, ending with Basil managing to grab the box from Mortell's hands and jump away into the rocky heart, he's got it! But uh-oh, Mortell has his gun again, pulling it grimly from under his shirt, and beleaguered Basil suddenly finds himself facing a .45 caliber point in the schema of the moment, black as eternity. The gun is leveled not ten feet from his pounding chest, as Mortell, sweating, eyes narrowed into dark desperate slits, reaches his other hand out and grunts, "Now please, relinquish the machine."

By this time the others have roused, and Synandra yells, "Give it to him, Basil, he's crazy."

But . . . Basil just can't give the thing up—for just that reason, the guy's crazy, and dangerous, and anyway he figures that he's bluffing, he really wouldn't actually shoot anyone, and says, "No. You're not gonna shoot me, pal. Not over this—"

And KA-WHAMMM! Mortell calls his bluff—but good, just missing Basil but blowing a hole in the windshield of the Chrysler behind as everyone hits the deck. And KA-WHAMMM! fires again, another hole shatters through the windshield as Basil, heart in his throat, twists crazily to dodge the, ah, bullet. He means it! Mortell raises the gun to eye-level now, really drawing a bead on Basil, he's not going to miss this time. . . .

"Basil! Give-give him the machine!" Synandra shrieks. "It's not worth it! Give it to him! Give it to him!"

"Yeah, give him the machine!" chorus Rudy and Tiffany.

"Okay, okay, it's your's, d-don't shoot . . ." stammers Basil as he leans forward, shaking crazily, life in the balance here, can't even think of anything sneaky to try, extends the machine over by its brass handle into the professor's outstretched hand.

Mortell accepts it, takes several steps backwards and holds it at waist-level while with the gun-hand he sets levers, glancing up at Basil every few seconds, puffing, "So we have here . . . what I should call a fair exchange. My career for your machine. Yes, most fair, I should say."

He's finished setting levers, for when and where Basil can't really tell, but it looks like the time coordinate is pushed pretty far over for—past or future? Hmm. Looks like stupid Mortell might actually have the machine upside down, so it's, uh . . .

"Well, now," Mortell says as he straightens up. "I believe this is good-bye. One thing I daresay is that this has to be the ultimate get-away machine, wouldn't you agree?"

Basil feels so helpless here, to think that this jerk is actually going to get away from them, get away completely, actually, without a trace. . . .

"And so farewell, my, ah, friends," Mortell smiling bravely, holding the machine in one hand and reaching to flip the significant brass lever with the barrel of the gun, "Perhaps we shall all meet again some—"

SSSSSSSSSSS-WONNNNKKK! Something, Basil thinks an arrow, suddenly zips out of nowhere, strikes the telechronos, knocking it out of the professor's hands. The machine, its brass handle gleaming in the glow of the rising sun, tumbles backwards in the air, and with a sharp POP! disappears.

And everyone immediately looks down at the bottom of the hill, the direction of the unexpected missile, to see Dr. Bo standing on the forest floor calmly holding his mighty bow.

The arrow has also knocked the gun to the ground. Basil sees it and dives for it, but Mortell quickly bends down and snatches the gun up, fumbles with it briefly before lowering the barrel ala *coup de grâce* at prone Basil's poor wretched head. "You, you, will pay for this—abomination!"

"No-ohh!!" Synandra screams, jumps from the car, but it's too late—KA-WHAMMM! and perhaps a nanosecond later—SSSSSSSSS-WHACK! another of the doctor's extraordinary arrows splits the air, knocks the revolver from Mortell's hand, who can only grab his wrist and utter, after a stunned second or two, "My Lord, what a shot!"

Rudy runs over to restrain the mad professor if necessary, doesn't seem to be at the moment, the man dropping to his knees, beginning to weep . . . meanwhile Synandra immediately by Basil's side, asking, "Basil, Basil, are you all right?"

That depends on what she means. The bullet missed his head by several gigantic inches, blowing a small crater alongside his right ear, which is presently ringing from the explosion, deafening, terrifying . . . but for basic aliveness, for the moment that condition is quite acceptable. . . .

"I-I think it's gone," chokes Rudy, looming above them. "I saw it disappear. Into nothing. . . ." He is blinking back tears.

"All that's left is this," says Tiffany, holding an arrow, its broadhead gone, shaft splintered.

"Agghhhh! Gone. Gone. Gone!" Mortell wails. "All I could have had . . . bloody lost! Lost! Everything gone for me . . . everything . . . nothing . . . nada . . ."

Dr. Bo joins them, gently holding his unstrung bow. "I was afraid this device would not be yours for very long."

"But where is it? Where did it go?" pleads Mortell.

The doctor shrugs. "Another time, another world."

Basil figures it's time to get vertical, with the help of the others rises into a shaky standing position . . . then hears through ringing ears strident voices calling from down below, "Hey there! What's going on up there?"

"Uh-oh," says Tiffany, "I bet it's—"

"Sheriff," answers Synandra grimly. "Mortie McKee and Helmut Thorson."

The first thing they actually want to know is what the car is doing atop the hill, cars out-of-place apparently the most understandable and easiest police matter to deal with . . . and then, who was doing the shooting?

Well . . . as eyes shift back and forth (the Indian doctor's steely blues gazing steadily ahead), it is Mortell who decides, as a full professor and most educated member of the group, to come clean.

"All right, all right, I guess now that it is gone, we might as well tell the truth, right? Yes, I would suppose it is time for the world to learn all about the blasted machine, what? The, ah, bloody Electronic Trinity, yes! The Three, the telechronos, the teleporter, and the anti-grav, all in one! Yes! Yes . . . we had it, we used it, and then . . . we lost it . . ."

Yes . . . brows raise and eyeballs roll all around at this dusty and disheveled fellow who continues ranting on. Dr. Bo speaks to the lawmen, "I'm afraid this man is very disturbed right now. Perhaps if you would let him in my custody. . . ."

But Sheriff McKee and Deputy Thorson will have none of it, for here they have that big-shot British professor who's come to dig up the town's treasured hill, apparently in the throes of profound mental aberration. This is a prize catch.

And then down by the road, as the sun rises higher in the sky, the dissemblers patiently deny each of the sweating, raving professor's ever-wilder pleadings for affirmation of the existence of the impossible machine. Though Basil can see Synandra's cheeks burning as she follows the implacable medicine man's lead in disclaiming all (and for an instant, as her face briefly cuts between Mortell and the sun, thinks he glimpses in the shadow cast upon the professor's face—very odd—a tiny bright red heart glowing like a Brahman caste mark on the desperate man's forehead), she plays her uncomfortable part very well, even to the point of muttering damningly, "how absurd," to Mortell's explanation of how the pyramids of Egypt were constructed by bloody stinking flying saucers.

And after Mortell has sworn innumerable times that he will "get" Synandra *et alii* for this, and is pinioned and handcuffed and shoved into the back of the patrol car, and after the car is on its way to the mental unit of the Sturgeon Bay hospital, Mortie McKee turns to Deputy Thorson, "Well, see, we sure get to see a lot of stuff that no one else does!"

*   *   *

Basil's Journal:

So we lost the most magnificent machine ever. At least we still have the Chrysler T&C, so I can't say that I am all that broken up about it. The damn thing was a real burden, and I have to say that in the end I suppose that we weren't really worthy of it. Of course, there will be no saving the world now, but if things do go all to hell, at least it won't be all our fault. I like to think that in some small way we made our effort—even if it didn't pan out.

I feel bad that we left Mortell holding the bag, but I guess it was his own fault for opening up his stupid mouth. Synandra told Dr. Bo afterwards that she hated lying like that, especially since honesty was one of the virtues he had always instilled in her. The doctor thought for a moment, then answered her, "Complete honesty at all times is nothing more than stupidity. It bears upon the situation. In this instance the game had moved to their playing field"— they being the lawmen—"and we had to play by their rules. Of which such a machine is not a part. The professor did not understand this. To his detriment."

Of course, the doc was right. Mortell must have dealt with theories and hypotheses so much that actually having something miraculous right there in the palm of his hand, and then losing it, was enough to push him over the edge.

Rudy has been taking it, the loss of the machine, especially hard. He's even come up with a pretty way-out explanation about how it might have worked. This after I told him the story that the old Russian told me about what happened in Siberia. Rudy thinks that the machine might have actually contained a teeny-tiny black hole. *That's right. One of those things that float around in outer space like giant vacuum cleaners sucking in anything that comes around (stars, planets, etc.). Pretty wild, but he had heard of that great explosion in Siberia in 1908 (I never had) and said that one of the explanations provided for it was that a very tiny—even microscopic—black hole had passed right through the earth in its travel across open space. Now Rudy figures that maybe the* machine *was the actual destination of the thing, that through the magic of that shaman Nabokoff, it was captured inside. He said that lots of tiny black holes may still be floating around, remnants from when the universe was created, less than a billionth of a second old.*

Anyway, black holes are supposed to terrifically warp space and time, spacetime, they call it. (Rudy has told us all this; I only write it down.) Einstein proved that the force of gravity actually slows time down. The tremendous gravity of a black hole, even a tiny one, would definitely slow time, perhaps reverse it, or fast-forward it into the future. It's impossible to know exactly, because the black hole is a spacetime singularity where all the known laws of physics break down. Rudy said that we might have actually gone through *a black hole when we used the machine. Or maybe we just were bent around its event-horizon in weird ways, whatever, exactly, that means.*

At any rate, it worked for us, for a while anyway. And in that short time it has changed our lives, and in fact our whole world. But the whole thing still gives me the creeps. In the end I know I'm happier without it. Much happier.

Oh, one other thing. We had a big dinner over here last night to kind of mull things over and Tiffany announced that her mother had called from Winnetka, reported that her father had been acting strangely the past month or so—looked as if he had seen a ghost. One day after work he had gone straight to bed and stayed there for three days, though he didn't seem to sleep much. The doctor couldn't find anything wrong, other than overwork and "nerves," and pre- scribed tranquilizers and rest. But when he got back to work he cancelled the entire Dawn—Sex Flakes—project and then decided to introduce a new line of nutritious products at LoFoCo that would complement the present line (and, Tiffany hopes, eventually displace it). He wanted Tiffany to return to Chicago and act as a consultant for the new concept. So we actually have done some good! We made an impact. Tiffany was really excited, and decided to take her father up on the offer. She left yesterday and even took Rudy along to introduce to her parents. Synandra said that this is the first time she can remember Tiffany actually taking someone home with her, so she thinks they're up for bigger things.

As for me, I can sure get over it—the machine, I mean—even if, on a bigger scale, we couldn't do more good things with it than what we did at LoFoCo. At least we tried with poor Ronnie Reagan. A lost cause if I ever saw one. It's too bad, but I think that there is so much to be done to save the world that, even with a miracle ma- chine, for one person, the task is just too huge. Things aren't going to change until a lot more of us get together and try to do the job right.

25

Slowly, inexorably, the little planet whirls onward, the heat and gasp of summer giving way to autumn's cooling breath, August into September, and what is left of the fair season lays heavy upon the Wisconsin countryside like a bloated green and tan beast. Labor Day gusts in and out with leaden skies and a smattering of rain, leaves behind cooler air, a chill in the waters—a mild warning of what is to come. Sunflowers in gardens and fields bow their heavy heads in deference to the great beast's might, purple and white asters glow like stars along the edge of the Wasson woods, goldfinches pick apart spiny thistle heads into floating white fluff, fat grasshoppers fly from brittle lawns at every step. . . .

One night Synandra shakes Basil awake. She is nervous, edgy, says she can't sleep, pulls him over to the window. "There, see, there it is, it's coming . . ."

"Uh, what's coming?"

"Winter."

"Winter? Where?"

"Out there! That's Orion, the hunter, he's back. Winter's on its way . . ."

Basil looks out over the lake, and beneath the glow of the

harvest moon high overhead floats the sparkling diamond constellation on its side, like a sleeping harlequin with star spangled belt and sword.

"Every night now it'll rise a little higher, until—" she breaks off and begins crying.

"Hey, hey, what's wrong?" puts his arms around her, feels her body shaking with each sob. "What's the matter, anyway?"

"I-I don't know," she sniffs, wiping her eyes with the hem of her nightie. "I just don't want it to end."

"What end?"

"I-I . . . the summer. This wonderful amazing summer. I feel that it's going to end." And she begins sobbing again.

"Well, hey, sure it's going to end. Doesn't it always? I mean it's just the natural—"

"Yes, yes, of course, it must, Basil," she says sniffling, straightening up. "It must end. I always knew that, I guess . . ."

Basil takes her hand; it is cold and clammy—unusual for her. In fact, this is very peculiar behavior for normally stable Synandra, but she is a truly sensitive person, and she has been awfully busy lately with the harvest: canning and freezing of fruits and vegetables (Basil grudgingly helping), and the annual ritual of gathering multitudinous herbs and then processing them into various tinctures, ointments, and oils to have ready for next season's customers. Maybe she's just overtired, beat.

"Oh, you know," she whispers huskily, "I wish it would rain."

"Oh. Yeah, me too." He knows what she means. The month of August had been uncommonly dry—Basil had loved it, brilliant hot days, clear blue skies, great swimming weather. . . . But now, with little more than a brief shower on the Labor Day weekend, nearly two weeks into September the drought continues. The leaves of roadside trees hang heavy with dust, lawns are parched, corn leaves clack in the fields. . . . At night they sit atop the hill and watch thunderstorms pass north and south of them, heat lightning flashing pink and amber on the horizon, the soft rolling of distant thunder like artillery battles far away. But the rains always miss Wasson's Bay.

"You know," she says, "I think it might . . ."

"Yeah, maybe it will . . ." Basil yawns, can't wait to crawl back into bed, but then thinks there's something he wanted to tell

her, something that he meant to tell her today but she was too busy
... something that he just can't seem to remember now, he's so
tired, although it strikes him that it was somehow important ... well,
maybe it'll come to him ... maybe, but his head, nodding with
sleep, begins bumping against the windowsill. She is still awake,
gazing at Orion. He says nothing, gives her a kiss and crawls back
into bed. Sometimes he just can't figure her out.

    Basil awakens suspiciously, with a start. Something, he figures,
is up. What? One thing, Synandra is gone, and another, the uncomfortable close atmosphere in the bedroom; if it were a color: dishwa-
ter gray. Outside the window the sky is low solid stratus, unmoving,
ominous, and the lake glassy and dark, vanishing into a pale salmon
haze on the horizon. He checks the clock: a few minutes past one—
he has profoundly overslept. But where is she? He has a strange
feeling that maybe she might be in some kind of danger, but doesn't
know why ... thinks maybe she's at the store, she should be—it's
Saturday isn't it? But then sees her set of store keys on the dresser
top alongside her purse, so she's not there ... and at the same time
an animated pink glow outside the south window catches his eye.
Up on top of Mystery Rock Hill. Oho. *There* she is ... seems to be
... sort of strolling around up there, wearing—Basil knows right
away—a gauzy pink dance tunic, a favorite of hers for skipping
around in on warm twilit evenings, maybe as she enticed him out to
the sultry rosebush circle. But right now her dreamy dalliance is a
disturbing incongruity on this motionless afternoon, not so much as
the fact that it's in broad daylight, but that she's out there at all ...
it's troubling, like something else that he can't quite remember—and
then it comes in a flash.
    Mortell is back in town.
    Yes. Just yesterday as he was on the way to open up the Ars
Aromatica shop, Synandra busy with herb-gathering, Basil had caught
a glimpse of him—he thought it was him, the same assured snoot-in-
the-air—but the man had turned the corner before Basil could be
sure. Then later that afternoon, Rolf, Basil's confidant from the dig,
strode into the shop and confirmed that Mortell was in fact in town,
along with himself and another graduate student to clean up the
remains of their camp. He also told Basil what had happened to

Mortell after his "breakdown." He and Synandra had heard nothing since then. (And perhaps out of guilt had done little to know more.) Turns out that the maniacal prof rather quickly found himself facing a lot of concerned faces, a prolonged regimen of Thorazine and therapy, and a locked ward with most unsavory bunkmates. . . . It did not take him long to change his weird tune. The attending psychiatrist was happy to write the matter off as a brief psychotic break, in exchange for Mortell's agreement that it was, in fact, precisely that. Never to happen again. Yes, yes, of course. . . .

After his discharge Mortell had tried to explain to his University cohorts what, more or less (mostly less) had happened, and after some rather hesitantly accepted apologies, was allowed to come back up here with a couple of students to tear down what still remained of his camp—two large tents still containing some supplies, a huge tarp, and a couple of smaller tents. The sheriff's department had been casually keeping an eye on them, but they really had to be removed.

Before leaving the shop, Rolf told Basil that the professor had been strangely quiet all the time he had been with him—not his usual blowhard self—and it unnerved him. He would be glad to be done with him as soon as he could, when the job was completed, in a couple of days. He had turned to go but Basil stopped him, had to ask him one other thing: which one of their group was the violinist? The one who played the beautiful music every evening at dusk—before the, ah, unfortunate discovery? Rolf scratches his head, says that no one in their crew had played the violin; they all thought it was someone from the Wasson place.

Now back in the clearing on the southeast corner of the Wasson woods, the professor sits silently in his tent on this pallid breathless day, sweating, breathing softly, having asked his two students to be left alone for a while in the shambles of his once-flourishing dig. He sits motionless, gazing out through the doorway at the very dry brown and gold weedy undergrowth leading up to the Wasson woods. He seems to be waiting for something, so still does he sit, idling fingering the brass knob of a kerosene lantern that sits on the camp table next to him. And then he feels it upon the back of his sunbrowned neck, through the mosquito netting, a slight cooling, a hint

312

of a breeze, and then a bit more, the canvas flaps begin to drift ever so slightly with it. . . .

"Hi."

"Oh, hi."

"Uh, what are you doing out here?"

"I'm . . . tuning into my powers. Trying to . . . resonate with them . . . sense them . . . understand them . . . while I still can." She reposes in the rocky heart, propped against one of the boulders, her legs extended toward its potent center as though she lazed beside a deep pool, dangling her toes in its waters. She looks exhausted, her breathing is shallow and rapid, her eyes glazed and dark underneath, as though she hasn't slept at all.

Basil assumes she hasn't. "Er, what do you mean, while you still can?"

She looks up at him, ignores the question, whispers, "Oh, Basil, today, right now, the whole world has stopped."

He can't help thinking she's right. All around them the common transactions of life seem suspended. There is not a breath of wind, and so very still . . . he can hear birds calling from far away, but none seem to be moving nearby. The air feels thick and moist, presses against his skin like it did on a similar day, long ago it seems now, when they were both out here together. . . . How far they had come. Then, he had had no concept of power centers, now understands them all too well . . . notices her arms and legs twitching slightly every few seconds in a sort of rhythmic counterpoint to each of her shallow breaths. Perspiration beads on her upper lip, her stomach rising and falling beneath the cotton-candy chiton with each breath strikes him, hmmm, as fairly erotic here . . . in a perverse debauched-maiden sense he had never noticed an affinity for, something he might actually be able to go with would it occur at another time, under different skies, and did she not seem so appallingly close to a seizure or something. . . .

"Hey, maybe we ought to get down from here. I mean, don't you think maybe you've, uh, had enough?" feeling like he is talking to a drunk at a party.

"No. Not now . . . I have to be here . . . now."

"Aw, c'mon . . ."

"No! This is *my* energy!" suddenly rising to her feet, muscles taut as a cat's, eyes huge, dangerous. She slowly, purposefully, steps to the very center of the heart, momentarily rises on her toes like a dancer, then raises her arms overhead, like an antenna to the sky.

Basil isn't sure what to make of this apparent irrationality. She frightens him; he knows she shouldn't remain very long in that potent center, especially with a storm brewing, but is afraid to disturb her right now ... has to look away ... his thoughts seem muddled anyway ... doesn't understand why she's acting so strangely, but, one thing, the atmosphere certainly can be considered—electric. The clouds are growing darker, more oppressive, lowering as if under their own great weight. A breeze has kicked up from the southeast, and-and, there seems to be a thin scent of smoke in the air, sends a chill through him as he happens to look over at the Wasson house ... to witness the supernatural: gracing each of five glass-bulbed lightning rods protecting the rooftop are the ghostly glowing balls of St. Elmo's fire! Amazing. The house looks like an architect's birthday cake. He's only vaguely heard about this curious phenomena, but Synandra has told him that she's seen them before on the house, usually before a terrific storm. Wow. He turns to tell her ... and gasps as he sees that *she* has a radiant nimbus of similar luminescence crowning *her* head. Good God! Basil can only gape open-mouthed while tears from her closed eyes track down her dusty cheeks and she smiles beatifically, as though concentrating on something extraordinary deep inside.

She opens her eyes, gazes at Basil, "I-I've done it," she whispers. "One with the earth, one with the sky ... their energies are like a great river ... flowing within me, through me ... all of heaven and earth merging ... it's wonderful ..."

"My God ..." Basil gasps. What is happening?

"Oh, oh, Basil, I think it's going to take me. I'm going now ... going ... I don't want to leave you, but I must ..."

And then, Basil can't believe his eyes, it appears that she has begun to *lose solidity,* to *dissolve,* her whole body glowing now, as though she might become pure spirit ... and then he remembers when she had gone after Kowalske, knows that this all is possible, that she might actually *disappear!*

"Goodbye Basil ... I love you—"

"No!" He will not lose her! leaps over heart-rocks and snatches her nearly weightless body out of the heart, feels a shocking jolt of electricity in his arms, face, and chest, and in the same instant an earsplitting CRAAKKK-ROOOOOOOOOMMMMMMMM! of thunder roars angrily overhead, and a flash of lightning that freezes their flight like a strobe. Yikes! Basil's heart is thundering itself, but he's saved her—he thinks. Looks at her lying dazed and trembling—but solid, thank God—safely outside the rocky heart. She seems silently grateful for the rescue from the Invincible Powers ... but the Powers do not. They—or their representatives, the ethereal thunderbirds that Basil had had at least a working relationship with before—seem to be clearly angry. The skies roar again. Yes, well, the priority of the moment is to get off this crazy hill! He pulls Synandra up, she can apparently stand, walk, and he begins to lead her off the lightning-prone summit in the direction of the Wasson house, but she wordlessly stops him, pulls him mightily back in the opposite direction, south, toward the sacred circle of roses. Uh ... Oh. Well ... why not, it *was* low-ground treeless sanctuary, your best bet in an electrical storm and the excitement of fleeing from the angry high-tension skies, thunder rumbling ominously all around them now, and this glowing girl wickedly leading them onward seems to be getting to him here, feels a formidable erection welling up as they make their way to the forbidden spot.

For an instant Basil hesitates before passing through the break in the leafy green wall, really thinks he smells smoke again in the freshening breeze ... but any urgent signals to the alarm center of his brain are shorted by Synandra pushing herself against him, whispering hotly in his ear, "Take me in here, take me in ... nail me to the earth ... keep me here with you ... forever ..."

Oh boy. *You got it,* Basil thinks ... and, two lovers heedless in the path of Armageddon, they begin the fevered rites, fluttering lips and tongues, trembling hands, rippling flesh, caressing the storm away.... But the immortal birds of thunder will not be denied. Terrific concussions rock the earth around them, seeming not to be a component of the fulgurous heavens anymore, but right down there with them, as though *they,* or perhaps just *she,* is an integral part of this heavenly bombardment ... and it is then that Basil understands what she means: that she will cleave to *him,* not the storm gods, the sky, the earth, her benefactors of all these years, surprisingly jealous ... pictures behind eyelids he dare not open now that he is battling

315

a truly awesome force of nature, the goaty god Pan himself, furious with him, poor boy-mortal for stealing away the marvelously sensitive girl from their domain. And all he has for protection *is* this girl, squirming terrifically under him now as he drives her hard against the earth, her salvation . . . and now he *knows* he can smell smoke, dammit, a–a fire caused no doubt by lightning blasting everywhere around them it seems, incredibly exciting, hasn't felt a drop of rain yet, but despite fire and storm, nothing, nothing really matters at this moment than their frenzied flesh in unison, flesh, substance, reality, solid earth, terra firma—what is really important here, flesh and blood and bone, what they are made of, and are able to make . . . and then as she arches magnificently above the energized earth, and he feels an overwhelming contraction somewhere below, all the world is filled by a blinding whitelight and a terrific earth-shattering, mind-blowing VA–RRROOOOOOOOOMMMMMMMMMMMMMMMMMM!

Rolf said later that it was the first sudden boom of thunder that made them look over toward the hill—so long and loud it seemed to shake the earth! He and his companion were on their way back from a local tavern where they had gone for a few beers, honoring Mortell's request to be left alone in the camp for a couple of hours— to reflect—and were shocked to see a thin column of smoke rising above the Wasson woods, drifting in the direction of Mystery Rock Hill. They ran to the nearest house for help, which luckily turned out to be the home of a member of the Wasson's Bay volunteer fire department, who sent out the alarm. The wail of sirens began almost immediately, and a ragged parade of volunteers and vehicles, including the town's two red 1952-vintage fire trucks, began a beeline for the Wasson woods. Rolf and his friend got a short ride with the volunteer fireman to the Wasson yard where veteran smoke-eaters were already organizing the others into a plan of attack—with great concern. Apparently a conflagration in the woods surrounding Mystery Rock Hill had always been a fear among the firemen, nearly ten acres bordered by the homes of the village, with the big Wasson home the first in this particular fire line. . . .

Rolf was shuffled to the side as volunteers continued arriving, were issued hardhats, Indian tanks, Pulaskis, shovels, chain saws . . . and sent scurrying into the now-blazing woods. A trailer carrying two medium-sized bulldozers was unloaded, roaring yellow beasts sent in to help establish a firebreak, these soon followed by two other much larger bulldozers someone remembered being parked down by the lakefront where some grading was being done. Any old dozers in a fire apparently the rule, and since the keys are all interchangeable anyway, it's send 'em in, ask questions later . . . except that in the confusion no one, not even Rolf, noticed that the driver of the second snorting machine, wearing the requisite yellow hardhat, a plastic smoke mask, and a thin smile, was an unlikely volunteer, a college professor who had learned to operate heavy equipment in England, during the second world war. . . .

An acrid tang in Basil's nostrils jolts him back, into a world even more sinister than before, one transmogrified by streamers of smoke blowing by him. Him alone, Synandra is gone. Good God! Where is she? The whole woods must be going up! He leaps up and mechanically pulls his pants and shirt back on, trying to damage-assess as he does: seems to be alive, first of all, not fried by lightning, and then nothing seems to be in serious disrepair . . . but there *was* that debilitating brilliance. And then he recalls a pre-blackout rain of debris pattering his back and guesses what happened: a searing skybolt, nature responding to their impudent coupling, had ripped into the hill and sent a tremendous surge through the fragile energy grid, overloading the underground channels, the power centers, ultimately them. Or at least him. Where the hell was Syndy? Did she get out of the woods? Basil tries to get his bearings here, looks up through treetops now shrouded in billowing smoke, hears what he thinks is thunder roaring overhead—or is it the fire?—wonders when it's ever going to rain. Then he hears an engine growl behind him, and suddenly out of the smoky haze appear four young men wearing yellow helmets, carrying fire axes and shovels. They come running up to him. "Hey! Hey buddy! What are you doing out here? You'd better get out of these woods!"

"Wait! Did you see a–a girl run by here? Dark hair, wearing a pink, uh, dress—"

"You mean there's someone else in these woods?"

"I-I don't know. Maybe she got out."

"We'll keep an eye out. Meantime you better go that-a-way,

pal," pointing in the direction of the Wasson house.

At that moment the diesel roar increases terrifically, and to Basil's amazement a huge bulldozer emerges from the smoky underbrush, mowing down a growth of maple saplings.

"Jesus!"

"We're clearing a firebreak on this side of this hill," shouts one of the men. "That cat's coming through here. Watch out!"

The machine clanks right toward transfixed Basil, the driver waving him out of the way, he only has time to jump before the big steel beast plows into the sacred rosebushes behind him.

"Hey!!! Stop him!" Basil screams furiously. "He can't—" But he can and does. Leaving the leveled bushes behind, the bulldozer rumbles on and the men follow it like infantry supporting a tank. Basil feels like crying at the destruction of the roses, so stupid, terrible, and quick . . . but chokes it down—he's got to find Synandra!—and starts sprinting toward the Wasson house. . . . A deer, a fat red doe, suddenly bounds past him. Another squad of firefighters runs by, two of whom take vicious swings at the animal with their shovels, miss, and laughing, run on. Basil keeps going, crashes around the foot of Mystery Rock Hill, runs past a second big dozer grinding through the haze, and, it's crazy, but the driver kind of looks like— Clyde Mortell! Nah, it can't be . . . tries to get a better look as he runs by, but just at that moment the driver cinches his oxygen mask up against his face, leans forward and charges on in the direction of the hill. Aw, it couldn't be . . . but there's no time to stop anyway, he's got to keep on going. . . .

Reaching the edge of the woods, he finds the Wasson yard transformed into a sort of base camp, with groups of firefighters taking orders before charging into the woods, and fire trucks, sheriff's cars and ambulances idling on the lawn, radios crackling static, a crowd of townspeople milling about in the absurdly festive atmosphere as orange firelight reflects off the tallowy smokeclouds . . . and towering above all, the restive dark sea of the storm.

Basil, panting furiously, sees a familiar face in the crowd, Mrs. Frost, runs up to her. "Is-is Syndy out here anywhere?"

"My lands! I feared that. She's in those woods, isn't she?"

"I-I don't know. I guess you didn't see her . . ."

"No, no. I ran up to the house first thing, but no one was there. I hoped maybe she was off somewhere with you!"

Thunder and lightning crash above the fire and the crowd sighs, "oooh," appreciatively, as though watching fireworks, and the end of everything seems depressingly near. Basil's stomach plunges into the abyss; Synandra is still in there; he is certain of that. But where? He looks futilely up at the murderous clouds, then back at the long edge of smoking woods fronting the Wasson yard—and then suddenly, miraculously, out of them steps the tall saving figure of Dr. Bo! Of course, always there when you need him! solemnly beckoning Basil onward and then turning to point westward—yes! her power center to the west, he remembers it now, the wholly avoidable one of negative energy, *that's* where she is!

"Basil! Son, listen to me!" Mrs. Frost is shaking him. "Is she still in those woods?"

Basil twists away. "Yes, yes, I'll get her!" Turning back again to where Dr. Bo ... but the place where he stood is empty, nothing there now but the smoky forest's edge. Basil couldn't have turned away more than a second, gives him a chill that runs the length of his spine, but there's no time to waste, he's already flying through the crowd, jumping over fat wet hoses, receiving a douse of water as he passes the house some firemen are protectively hosing down, one yelling, "Hey, where's *he* going?" and "Stop him!" but there's no stopping Basil now. He's into the woods again, into the path of the fire-driving winds. Glowing embers rain through the sacrificial forest, igniting small blazes that crews of busy firefighters attack with Indian tanks and Pulaskis, rushing to and fro, Basil dashing wildly around them. On the west side of the hill where a second firebreak is going in, another fearsome vision of hell: ghostly silhouettes of firefighters in a turbulent glowing haze felling trees with ringing chainsaws, two roaring bulldozers scraping clear a wide swath, other wraiths hoeing and shoveling away debris ... the fire apparently having jumped the first firebreak, nearing the hill now, closing rapidly, incinerating trees and bushes in swift sizzling gulps, Basil thinks that this is the end, boy, it's got to be ... and then the trees thin out and he is facing a ragged black curtain of smoke rushing across a field of blackcap brambles. His eyes and lungs burn badly, he rips off his still-damp shirt, ties it over his nose and mouth, realizes he has no idea where, in this treacherous garden, she might be. He's never been to that sinister spot, doesn't even know where to begin, but he can't just stay here, tries to run in, then quickly retreats as smoke-clouds engulf him, waist-high thorns claw at his bluejeans ... tries another route in, but feels that terrible sinking feeling again, he's never going to be able to find her in this ugly expanse, feels the wind begin gusting now, hears the fire leaping ahead, right this way, looks bad, bad ... and then he sees the old woman, yes, the old hag he once glimpsed with Synandra on the hill ... poised now like he'd imagine one of the witches in *MacBeth,* wild hair and sackcloth dress blowing in the hellish gale ... she is off to the left, not even fifty yards away, looking toward Basil, he can't quite make out the expression on her face, assumes it's grim, but his heart leaps at this gruesome sight, he knows she is near Synandra, standing protectively by her—that's where she is! Has to be. He plunges into the clawing canes, ripping clothes and flesh, feeling nothing but icy fear, looks up again, the hag is gone. He's not surprised, but—is Syndy really there? He keeps charging forward as if in a dream, arms bleeding, lungs and eyes burning, until, until, in the surprisingly barren center of the patch he finds her, lying limp, bleeding herself from innumerable scratches, but, but ... breathing! Alive! Thank God! But there's no time to lose, the fire is an angry roar beyond the orange wall of smoke, the heat unbearable, almost upon them as he picks her up weightless in his arms, begins his thorny dash out ... and then ... as though finally bored by the desperate little dramas being played-out on the earth below, the heavens open up and the saving rains begin, sparse sprinkles for a few frantic moments, then blowing in as a great driving sheet against the conflagration, to quench earth, fire, and fevered human psyches alike.

26

Basil awakens late that night in a room at the Sturgeon Bay hospital, sorting through numbing images of smoke, steam, a red-flashing siren-ride with unconscious Synandra ... and is sweating and restless, feeling for cigarettes in imaginary pockets of his hospital gown before remembering he doesn't smoke anymore, wanders on bandaged legs down to the lobby to find a half-asleep Mrs. Frost keeping a lonely vigil on a plastic hospital couch. She tells him that Synandra is all right, recovering from smoke inhalation and exhaustion, primarily, sleeping now in a third floor room, not to be disturbed. Other news is that Clyde Mortell is also in the hospital, several flights below Synandra, in a large cool room—the morgue.

She tells him as much as she knows, what she heard from the firefighters. That the professor had gone berserk with the big bulldozer, had attacked the hill itself, and although he hadn't had that much time at it before the fire raced through, it was long enough to do substantial damage. Basil would have to go out there tomorrow to see for himself ... and anxious query is followed by animated reply until, like an antique toy winding down after a long performance, the dear old lady nods off again. Basil gets a blanket from the attendant at the desk, covers her up, and before returning to bed himself, steps out to look up at the stars. There are millions of them tonight.

The next day comes in bright, cool, and amazingly clear, a truly autumnal day, sweet contrast to the humidity and murk, fire and rain, that marked summer's bitter flight. Basil is driving Mrs. Frost's little Ford Falcon back up to Wasson's Bay, blue skies and sunshine reflecting from the windshield, a bag of caramel corn by his side, small solace against the dismal thoughts that keep leaking through, especially about Synandra's condition. It puzzled the doctors. Though she suffers from shock, mild smoke inhalation, and numerous scratches and small burns, her state of exhaustion, or more precisely—complete lethargy—seems too acute for a healthy girl like her, despite her ordeal. Basil, however, fears he knows what is wrong with her, something that neither the doctors, nor drugs, nor an armada of invisible spirit helpers can heal: her hill of heart-rocks, her power centers, her magnificent lines of communication with the energies of the earth have been destroyed.

This appears tragically clear as Basil pokes among the ruins. The main conflagration had not reached the hill—it was stopped by the rain just short of its base—but left behind a nightmarish expanse studded with charred tree skeletons and a ground cover of black and gray ash. The rest of the magical forest had by no means been spared, defiled by hundreds of burned patches caused by drifting sparks. The larger trees had more or less escaped destruction, apparently due to the short duration of the fire, their bark only charred black by the flames or sliced open by a passing bulldozer, but scores of smaller trees had burned, were uprooted or felled by chainsaws, and wide ugly swaths remained from the big machines which, ultimately, were responsible for doing the magic in.

Synandra had once told Basil about her sporadic dowsing assignments and said that after she had found a good flow and marked it for the well driller, the contractors of the site had to be careful not to drive heavy equipment in the vicinity, particularly if the aquifer was near the surface, because the great weight of the machine might crush the flow and divert it elsewhere. Which is most likely just what had happened here, ruining the elegant symmetry, and thus the magic of the site. Among other things. Mystery Rock Hill had also been ravaged. At the top—or what was left of the top—of the hill, the once gently rounded summit had been gouged, chomped and chewed by the heavy steel blade of Clyde Mortell's bulldozer—which had not yet been removed from where it reposed, dead yellow monster, on its side at the bottom of the hill. Tracing the trampled path of destruction, Basil could see that what Mrs. Frost had told him was true, that instead of following the other dozer around the hill to the firebreak, Mortell had charged the magical mound itself, blade set, apparently trying to level it. Six or seven of the heart rocks had been uprooted and pushed around on the eastern summit—but thank goodness he hadn't time to break through to the very center of the mound, apparently the focus of his attack. In the smoky confusion no one had seen him, or if they had, had not realized the damage he was doing in time to stop him. Indeed, the summit of the hill had been for the most part smoke-hidden, and Mortell's whereabouts unknown. But it was not the smoke that had killed the professor, he was found wearing an oxygen mask; no, it was lightning that did him in. A bolt had ended it quickly, maybe even more than one— Mrs. Frost told Basil that his body had been badly burned, and the fire had not reached that area. She also added, "I can't really say that the professor—or anyone—deserved to be done in like that, but after hearing about the way he tore into Syndy's—our—lovely hill like that, somehow it almost seems fitting. Like it *was* sacred, protected somehow, you know."

It is dusk when Basil gets back to the hospital, bringing from the house an overnight bag of clothes for Synandra. (The proud Wasson house, of course, had been spared from the flames, and when Basil went inside, he could almost swear he heard a very faint musical humming, the tune of "Stormy Weather.") Synandra is awake when he enters her room, but barely, her head sunk deep in the pillow, talking quietly with Mrs. Frost. From the look in her bleary eyes, he knows she has heard everything.

"Oh, Basil ..."

Mrs. Frost pats her tenderly on the arm and excuses herself from the room.

His kiss is light, lest she crumble under its weight. "So, how are you doing?"

Tears run down her cheeks. Her voice rises barely above a whisper. "It's gone ... I knew it ... my hill, my powers ... my strength. . . ."

"I saw it. It's an awful mess, but—"

"I was supposed to go down with the hill," she whispers, a smile fainter than the Mona Lisa's crosses her lips. "You saved me."

"Hey, don't talk like that. It gives me the creeps. But ... it *was* strange that you ended up in those brambles. How did you ever get over there?"

"I-I'm not sure. I remember ... walking ... like in a dream. I didn't know where I was going ... or maybe I did ... I don't know. But you, my wonderful brave hero ... you were so smart to think of that spot ... to rescue me."

"Aw ... well, actually, I didn't think of it. Dr. Bo was there, showed me where you were." He isn't sure why, but immediately regrets telling her that; reluctantly, he gives her the details of his brief saving vision.

"Oh!" Her eyes open wide; she nearly lifts her head from the pillow. "I was afraid of ... I knew it when he wasn't here. He always comes by at times like this ... when I need him." Her face twists into choking tears.

"Hey, hey, it's okay. Maybe he's, uh, busy with something else. I'm sure he's fine," Basil blathers, not knowing why he said that, not believing it either.

"Go to him," she sobs, "go up there and see. Please ... for me. I have to know ... for sure."

"Sure, okay, don't cry," holding her hand firmly in his, then less so as her sniffling ebbs and she drifts again, into sleep. He stares out the window at the deepening horizon, toward the land of the setting sun. Venus, a diamond white in diamond blue, has become the evening star again.

It is not easy driving up to the doctor's digs at night. He would have preferred to wait until morning, but Synandra has to *know,* and so too, he realizes, does he. The nearly full moon helps, illuminating the pines and silent roads with silver light, also bringing out omens in the night Basil cares not to ponder: animals bounding across the beam of his headlights at an astounding rate: deer, rabbits, raccoons, swooping owls ... even a red fox, white tail streaming in his lights, wise old dog of the forest unafraid to sprint in front of silently speeding black death. . . . The moon has risen to overhead when he finally turns down the old logging road, the music he has dialed in on the radio is Mahler's *Eighth,* as full of weird portents as this night. Up ahead he sees lights flickering through the trees, hears voices; it appears that the doc has a great deal of company at this late hour. A lot of cars, mostly older models, but newer ones too, Jeeps and four wheel drive pickups, are parked in the meadow. His headlights flash across several proud bumper stickers: *Red Power, Custer Got His,* and *Geronimo Lives!* He hopes it is a friendly gathering. Farther up a bonfire flashes and sparks, silhouetting shapes of people standing before it, throwing garish shadows on the trees behind. He is about to turn off the engine when—

"You lost, white boy?" growls a deep voice.

"Me? I, uh . . ."

"You, buddy. You *lost?"* And a *heap* big Indian with long black hair bends down to look through his open window.

"Oh. Hi. I, uh, no . . . I was just coming up to see Dr. Bo. Is there a pow—, er, party tonight?"

"Party . . ." the man snorts. "Listen sonny, you just turn your fancy car around and—"

"No! Wait . . . I've got to find out if—"

"Appropriate music," says a familiar voice as someone walks calmly up to them. "Did you listen to that on the way up?"

It is Keno, wearing his feathered fedora. Basil breathes easier, realizes he never turned off the radio. "Yes, I did."

"Mahler, isn't it?"

"Yes."

"Strangely fitting . . ."

"Uh, is he—"

"Yes, his arrow found him. Yesterday."

The bigger Indian steps back from the car. "So he knew Bo?"

"Yes, Running Bear, he's a friend. He's Synandra's friend too. Basil, how is she?"

"She's awfully weak, but she'll be okay, I think."

"She's a strong woman. You probably won't have to worry."

"Good, I—"

"And the hill? Bad scene . . . ?"

"Pretty bad. To fight the fire they brought in bulldozers and made an awful mess of it."

"Aiii!" cries Running Bear. "Mystery Rock Hill. It's a bad time for us all."

"I feared the worst," says Keno, then turns to his cohort. "Let's take him up there ..." points with his chin toward the fire. They lead Basil across the clearing, up to a group of people clustered around a long blanketed cocoon resting on a raised pallet before the doctor's shack. Many of the women, and a few of the men are openly weeping. Basil is surprised to see that the supposedly reclusive doctor had known so many people.

"He was a great one," says Running Bear softly. "He had many, many friends."

"Yes ..." Basil agrees, suddenly finds himself sniffling too for this great Indian doctor, selfless helper of so many, overseer of Mystery Rock Hill and moon-daughter Synandra ... who had attempted through his powerful medicine to guide stubborn stupid Basil in using the greatest power that would ever, *ever,* come his way, and Basil wouldn't even listen ... and now he is gone. Even though, deep inside Basil feared the worst—Synandra had told him about the dangerous ritual the medicine man practiced—it still comes as a shock; it seemed like the man would live forever.

Keno suddenly slips away into the shadows. At the same time, some shouts come from the direction of the bonfire. Basil turns to find a handful of young men whooping it up, shoving one another, popping open cans of beer.

"Look at them," sighs Running Bear. "That's the first time in a long time I've seen them hopped-up like that. It's a shame. With the doctor's passing, they've lost another piece of their heritage, a really big piece, and they know it. At least they've still got Keno. These days the only mysticism left for most of them is the alcoholic vision-quest, and those visions aren't very pretty."

Keno returns, tells Running Bear that he'll walk Basil back to the car. When they get there, Basil notices that Keno is wearing the doctor's medicine pouch. "He gave it to me the day before," Keno explains, sighing. "I knew then. We both knew." Keno reaches inside, pulls from it a packet of heavy paper wrapped with string. "He left this note for Synandra. I hope she recovers soon. Give her my best."

"Thanks. I will."

"We will take care of the body ourselves, according to our

traditions. We don't want the county coroner to hear about this. *Capisce?"*

"You bet."

"You'd better go now."

The next day, back at the hospital, Synandra takes Basil's grim news as might be expected—with tremendous sorrow. She looks as if she's been crying all morning, and then begins again after Basil confirms what she already, obviously, knew. They sit silently for a long while, Basil deciding then and there to hold on to Dr. Bo's packet for a few days until he's sure she's strong enough to bear whatever message it might hold. Somehow it just doesn't *feel* like the right time to give it to her.

She is getting better, but still so weak that it frightens Basil. She understands her condition more precisely than the doctors, however, knows she'll be in the hospital at least another few days to recuperate, tells Basil that although she has an inherent fear and loathing of so much white sterility—and hospital food—this is what she needs right now. A neutral, transitional place to rest and try to find within herself the energies that she had so long relied upon the magical hill to provide. (And as long as Mrs. Frost brings her a basket of fresh food each day, and an herbal tonic from the shop.)

Back home, on the front porch of the Wasson house, there is one other piece of information a misty-eyed Mrs. Frost has for Basil. Apparently another "freak" earthquake occurred the afternoon of the holocaust, just before the fire was discovered, only to be forgotten in the confusion that followed. But Mrs. Frost sensed that something was up, was in fact bothered by an odd sense of dread all day, and when she felt that tremor, she feared the worst, and started over to the Wasson house. The rest is history, duly recorded, Basil finds, in the Peninsula Gazette as a sidebar to the great Wasson woods conflagration, a 3.4, their best, and certainly, unfortunately, their last ever, at least at this particular time and place in the world.

So Basil busies himself with tending the shop during the day, closing early, and cleaning up around the Wasson house in the evening. The lush gardens were trampled, driven over, and otherwise destroyed during the firefighting efforts. Basil does what he can to clean these up, salvaging what he can, dumping the rest in the compost pile. He has nailed a quickly painted board—"CLOSED"—over the entrance sign to the hill, walks through the desecrated forest early in the morning before any vacationers can assemble and gawk, to survey the damage, rake-up debris, and generally contemplate the meaning of the destruction. At night too, he wanders into the woods and sits atop the hill, or walks down by the lake, trying to sort things out. Late one night, the night before Synandra is scheduled to be released from the hospital, he can't sleep, takes a long walk, and ends up down by the lakeshore, feeling thoroughly rotten about the whole thing, dreads tomorrow, when Synandra will see the extent of the damage which he may have been minimizing, just a teensy bit, in his descriptions of it to her.

"Feelin' low, bro?" a deep, somewhat familiar voice resonates in the night, above the murmur of the waves.

"Uh, me? Yeah. You know it."

"Dis heah is what you call a baaad scene."

"Sure is . . ." Basil knows now it is the kindly black fellow he met late one night in Milwaukee.

"Sit down heah, son. Take a load off."

The big man is sitting on a log, facing the expanse of the lake. Basil sits next to him, sees the man is wearing the same Oshkosh B'Gosh overalls he had on the last time he had seen him.

"Yo lady friend be pretty bent outta shape when she see dat mess back dere."

"That's for sure . . ."

"Well, you be understandin' dat dis heah be a good example of da di-chotomy 'tween the genders. Dere be a clash. Dat's all. Happens alla time, ever'where."

"Huh?"

"You hungry, son, heah."

The man passes Basil a warm bratwurst in a bun laden with sauerkraut and mustard, wrapped in a big white napkin. It smells delicious. Basil's mouth waters as he takes a big bite. "Gee, thanks. It really hits the spot."

The man chuckles, chomps down on one he holds, half of it gone in an instant, and continues: "Ya see, son, a woman's life be composed of rhythms, from pu-ber-ty and pregnancy through de change o' life, and dat bein' so, she be fittin' in pre-cisely wif de cosmos. She be followin' de phases of de moon. An' de earth be influenced by de moon, so natch'ly women be in tune wif de earth too. So, all a woman hafs to do is *be*. Her body reg-u-lates itself and her life in dis heah world.

"But a man, he be havin' no real rhythms in dis world—otha than p'haps day n' night. Least-ways none he can be understandin'. He be mo' like the sun, which come up ever' day and goes down ever' night. Nothin' mo'. . . So outta necessity he become a creature of action. Yessuh. He *does*. He be buildin' things—de bigger de bet-ter, makin' wars, biz-nesses, creatin' empires—mostly jes to 'pass de time,' so t' speak."

"That's it, huh?" says Basil, taking another bite of the savory sausage. "To just, ah, kill time?"

"Yessuh. To a man 'dere be birth, and 'dere be death, 'sentially nothin' in be-tween. In be-tween he be confronted wif dat debbil *time*. Dis heah be de reason dat he be makin' clocks and cal-endars and med-icine wheels and stone-henge, ultim'tly dat great machine you be playin' wif dis summer. There you ex-actly be controllin' time. Yessuh. Dat be one hell of a pass-par-toot!"

The man inhales the rest of his bratwurst and chuckles again. "So . . . 'dere be no big mystery. It just be dat man's life is 'sen-tially un-de-mar-cated, and he be doin' the best he can to de-mar-cate it. Dat's all. Just doin' de best he can . . ."

"I guess I never thought of it that way. Thanks. Hey, thanks for the bratwurst, too."

"You be most welcome, son." The man stands up, a towering shadow in the moonlight, brushes crumbs and kraut off his overalls, begins walking slowly down the beach. "You take care, now, heah?"

"Yessir. Uh, you too."

Deep laughter rolls back. "No need t' worry 'bout dat, son. No need t' worry t'all. . . ."

27

It is Synandra's homecoming from the hospital and just as Basil eases the big Chrysler into the driveway, Tiffany's maroon Mercedes zips up behind. "Well, Tiff's as good as her word, hey?" says Basil with forced cheer. He had called her the day after the holocaust with the essential view from the pit, and after understanding that her best friend was for the most part all right, Tiffany apologized that she could not make it up immediately from Chicago—she had scheduled a series of crucial revisionary policy meetings at LoFoCo which she absolutely couldn't afford to miss—but vowed that she would come as soon as she could, certainly for this occasion.

Which turns out to be a dubious one at best, for as Basil feared, Synandra isn't really prepared for the extent of the destruction, doesn't answer him, just keeps staring over at the ravaged woods, the desecrated hill that never before was as visible from the house as this. Basil had driven more quickly than he probably should have past the stretch of woods that fronts the beach road, as though trying to spare her from the atrocity—a foolish futile gesture of course, as she insists on immediately walking over to view the damage. There's no way, really, to put it off. The consolations Basil and Tiffany offer seem minimal, and in the midst of such catastrophe, hollow; they soon give up and follow behind, like the sad faithful servants of a deposed queen.

Synandra bravely tries to hold back tears as she stands on the inert moonscape summit where only a few days earlier she had vibrated with amazing energy. Such a change. The ground here, and below, especially, is damp, even muddy in places from seepage from the crushed aquifers. Basil wants to ask if she feels anything—any, ah, good vibrations—but decides against it, so fragile seems the girl, the moment. The remarkable southern center, once adorned with a lush crown of rosebushes, has become an ugly smear of mud, offensive to the eye as an open wound. Basil sees Synandra avert her eyes from it, wincing as she does. He pretends not to notice, Tiffany too. Neither of them are able to think of anything to say—there's no valid subject other than this awful one they confront. Tiffany can't help herself, the sorrow here is overwhelming, the tragedy so great, sinks to her knees on the damp earth, body shaking with silent sobs. Basil finds it difficult to hold back himself, quietly examines one of many small craters pitting the summit, toes the rubble of rock and sand that has been transformed into odd glassy bead-like lumps by the heat of numerous searing lightning bolts. Mortell's mindless destruction had truly brought the wrath of the thunderbirds upon him.

Synandra starts silently down the hillside, carefully picking her way across the wide gouges the dozer had left behind. She stumbles a couple of times, is propped up by Basil and Tiffany, but manages to lead the way eastward toward the large Bur oak, singular in the forest, that marks the most important of her energy centers, the one that catalyzed her life force. The leaves on its sprawling lower branches have been almost completely burned off, but the magnificent tree has proved itself a survivor, as it had in the peninsula blaze of one hundred years ago, its protection then the aura of the magical hill, and now, the magic fled, through the sheer thickness of bark and trunk, and perhaps something in the huge plant that might resemble *will*. Synandra sits beneath it, leans back against its blackened trunk and sighs, as though once again in the presence of a comforting old friend.

"Basil, is there water running in the house?"

"Yes, yes, there is . . ." realizes the import of her question, adds, "It was pretty dirty-looking at first, though. I had to run it for quite a while before—"

"Good, good." She closes her eyes, her body tenses slightly. "I can feel it, here, the energy . . . it's very weak, but still flowing through this center. I feel better already. . . ."

Both Basil and Tiffany breathe a shared sigh of relief, exchange glances, smile. Basil looks around, notices that other survivors are returning to the forest: swallowtail and sulfur butterflies bouncing around late-blooming dandelions and asters that had survived leeward of the larger trees, warblers and sparrows flitting through the tree-branches, gray squirrels scampering in the ashes, a red-tailed hawk circling above in the blue cirrus-strewn sky. . . .

"So, how are you doing?" ventures Basil. Synandra has sat silently, eyes closed, for several minutes.

"Mmm . . . better, I guess. . . . The main channel, up through the hill, is still flowing—he didn't get to that, thank goodness—but there's no balance here anymore; the flows are obstructed, muddled, the energies diffused back to maximum entropy . . . like any other place on earth."

They are silent for a while and then Synandra speaks again, slowly and clearly, "I've had time to think in the hospital, about what happened here . . . and it really scares me. The great forces have become so unbalanced, the receptive feminine force and the creative masculine force, earth and heaven, passive and aggressive, the ancient Chinese concept of yin and yang . . . the two primary forces that shape this planet. At times one force dominates, at times, the other, but in the end both will balance. I believe that; I believe it to be inevitable.

"The earth, you know, is truly an exceptional planet, at a perfect distance from the sun and also, the moon. Did you know that the sun is exactly four hundred times larger than the moon, but that it is also four hundred times farther than the moon from the earth? That's why, from our humble earthly perspective, they both appear exactly the same size. That's why total eclipses of the sun can occur; that's why the primary forces will always be in perfect balance. At least in the long run.

"The earth previously was dominated by the passive feminine force, the lunar, the priestess, for a very long slow period, with only a small amount of the aggressive force of 'man'kind in the equation. But recently, in the last thousand years, the aggressive solar force, the magician, has dominated beyond belief—which seems in a strange way to make sense: it has a lot of catching up to do. Another reason is that there's an awful lot more of us, population-wise, running around on the planet and the aggressive force is also one of survival. The urge to build upon, develop, and otherwise dominate the earth has become the guiding primal mission of mankind. The whole of western civilization—which more or less means the whole world now—has become a vast arena for the insatiable male force to run amok. The inherent feminine values of caring for and respecting this planet have been nearly forgotten—even by women. The ancient Greeks thought of the earth as a goddess they called *Gaia*. They considered the earth to have its own spiritual awareness, one that can sense what is happening to her graceful body, and perhaps even respond to those abuses in certain ways. . . .

"So I think the destruction of Mystery Rock Hill was more or less inevitable. It's what the old woman tried to tell me. Now I understand. This part of the earth is very energetically linked with the rest of the planet, and it wasn't long before it would have to follow along the same injurious path. We should probably be grateful that it managed to hold out as long as it did. But just look what happened when Mortell did his number on it. The guardians of the hill responded with a vengeance. If the wasteland-machinery keeps running at full-tilt, I worry that something like that storm, on an apocalyptic scale, might happen to the earth as a whole. And who knows what her guardians, her elite special forces, look like? Big and mean as B-52's, I'll bet. . . ."

"Well," says Tiffany, "we tried our best. . . ."

"Yeah," adds Basil, "at least we gave it a shot."

"That's right, we did. But we can keep on trying. I know I will, but I'm not sure just what to do at this point."

"Well, maybe this will give us an idea," Basil takes from his shirt pocket the packet Dr. Bo had left for Synandra—he had been saving it for the right moment, seems to be now—and places it in her hands, says, "It's from him."

"Oh," Synandra understands immediately, carefully unties the string around it, unfolds a thick sheet of paper inked in bold script and reads:

My Dear Daughter of the Earth,

Great changes abound on the earth and in the sky. Fire above and fire below. Death and resurrection. Life beginning anew. It appears that you have lived too long in the shadow of your magnificent hill—and yet not long enough to fully understand the great mysteries to which it held access. Unfortunately I foresee that the end of its powers are at hand. I fear that my time on this earth has expired also. The last years of my long life have been devoted to keeping watch on the hill and you. Now it seems that neither it nor you require my steadfast eye. In a short while my arrow will decide.

I also foresee an awesome struggle between the great forces taking place—with you in the bargain. Our great mother earth is both kind and benevolent, jealous and cruel. She will want you to exist with her forever in the realm of the spirit, of pure energy, with her guardians. She will attempt to capture you with her irresistible subtle charms. Against such powers we humans prove puny indeed—especially one as remarkably sensitive as yourself, Synandra. There is only one power we poor mortals possess that is greater than the forces of nature, a power as omnipotent as it is irrational, as marvelously colored as it is blind, a power that creates bravery in the grip of fear, negates flight in the face of danger, defines beauty in the realm of distaste—the power of love. If the love that binds you and your loved one together is strong—then you will survive.

I cannot yet tell the outcome, but I am optimistic. I believe you are reading this now. If so, you have forsaken your truer nature for a course that at this time I believe is correct for you. At another time, the other force will prevail. Until then, I urge you to joyously welcome a new phase of life. You have been bound to the hill long enough. You have lost, but you have gained.

You are free.

Until we meet again beyond the clouds,
Dr. Bo

Basil's Journal:

Syndy is recovering from the effects of the fire, but slowly. I can sure appreciate now just how close she really was to the hill and its centers. Damaging them was just like hurting a part of her, and a big part, too. Anyway, she's been getting back into the swing of things, has now finished putting up her herbal preparations for the year, and has started working at the shop again, getting it ready to close down for the winter. But she's still not the same old Synandra. She's not as depressed as she had been in the days right after the fire, but she almost never goes out to the hill anymore—or even for a walk through the woods with me. Worst of all, she's not even responding real well to the Caliente y Frio oil—at least not like she used to. Try as I may, I can't seem to snap her out of it.

Well, one thing—I got a call from Tiffany the other day and she said that she had some good news. But she wouldn't tell me yet what it was, other than it was some kind of surprise for Synandra. She said she'd be contacting me again, as soon as some things were worked out. I wonder what she's up to?

Another thing: I happened to pick up an Impossible Destinies *magazine at the newsstand the other day and ran across an article, "Aluminum Flip-Top Rings Found in Egyptian Tomb!" Some archaeologist discovered them during an excavation of a minor tomb around Giza last year. The tomb was about five thousand years old and was still sealed, not even hit by grave robbers when he found it, the article said. I wonder if I should write to him and tell him they came off some Heinenstubers! Ha-ha. Probably not.*

And another thing, the MacArthur house has mysteriously burned to the ground. Apparently the same day as the fire at Mystery Rock Hill. No one saw it happen or I guess even noticed any smoke—the fire in Wasson's Bay I'm sure having everyone's attention—but someone drove by the next day and found only a pile of ashes there. They don't have any idea what started it.

And finally, Synandra is trying to talk me into checking out the Inner Space Institute down in Green Bay. Since she's been feeling so low, she thinks that maybe getting into some meditation might charge her up again. Says I ought to try it too. Well, I'm not sure if I could get into that kind of thing, but maybe, for her, I could give it a shot. Who knows, maybe I'd actually like it.

*   *   *

A couple of weeks later, during a more or less clandestine
meeting with Tiffany and Rudy at a coffeeshop in Green Bay, Basil,
well-fortified with doughnuts and java, says he thinks that what Dr. Bo
meant in his letter to Synandra was that she, probably many years
from now—hopefully many, *many* years from now—will have a similar meeting with the earth-spirit and at that time will follow it into,
uh, whatever's there ... and in the meantime, what they are planning may actually be, essential, geographically speaking, for that
particular rendezvous.

Tiffany agrees and adds that the whole project is experimental
anyway, but exciting, and perhaps may prove more far-reaching in
its effect on the planet than the mere deed they are plotting, a
super-surprise for Synandra: the reconstruction of Mystery Rock Hill
and the sacred centers surrounding it.

Yes, the first thing Tiffany did when she returned to Chicago
was call in LoFoCo's legal counsel to determine what monumental
sum Synandra might extract from the university for the thoroughly
reprehensible actions of its late professor of archaeology, Dr. Clyde
Mortell. But then, barely as the wheels of due process began their
creaky revolutions, she suddenly had a much better idea....

Calls and contacts were hastily made, meetings held, palms
greased, cheeks bussed ... and what emerged was a bold and inno-
vative out-of-court settlement, in the long run cheaper for the defendants in the suit, and more agreeable—and aesthetic—to the prospec-
tive plaintiff than any cash payment. And now it's all set. The preliminary arrangements have been made; all that's needed is the final
go-ahead. The plan is to lure a by now much-recovered, but still
saddened daughter of the earth to a favorite restaurant in Sturgeon
Bay to break the news—a blockbuster if ever there was one....

"We're going to rebuild Mystery Rock Hill? And the centers?"

"Uh-huh," Tiffany beams at her, "at least we're going to try...."

"Gosh, could it actually be done?" Synandra is astonished and
of course pleased by their big surprise, can't seem to stop the joyous
tears that keep leaking down her cheeks into her Chardonnay ... but

tears more, it turns out, for the graciousness of her wonderful friends than the plan itself, as she confesses immediately that she doubts whether such a risky task could be accomplished. (She had never even considered the possibility of legal action against anyone for the misdeed—thinking it exclusively a judgment from the great Goddess herself.) But, any consideration of the earthly placement of the site itself aside—in terms of ley lines, dragon paths, or whatever—the marvelous energies had derived from the perfect flows of subterranean water originating in the hill, one in each of the four cardinal directions. At least two of them have been thoroughly crushed by the bulldozers, the other two reduced to trickles, notwithstanding the damage Mortell had inflicted upon the hill itself. And then it would mean digging again into sacred earth that had already been so cruelly injured. . . .

But in the end even Synandra knows that this course is the only one to be followed; there is so little left to lose, the risk will have to be taken, and, most importantly, it will have to happen soon. The diverted watercourses will quickly establish new paths, especially when the fall rains and then the spring snowmelt comes full upon them. Tiffany has understood this too, which was why she had her lawyers insist on an immediate settlement—pending the plaintiff's acceptance—or else the defendants would not get off so cheaply.

And so it happens. Agreements are made, contracts negotiated, releases signed, and on a bright late September morning two new encampments are erected in Wasson's Bay, a small one in the corner of the woods where Mortell's original site was, and another, much larger one in a rented local YMCA campsite, housing more than one hundred able-bodied workers whose implements of reconstruction are old-fashioned picks and shovels, rakes and wheelbarrows—absolutely no heavy equipment. Tiffany has to return to Chicago to attend to business at LoFoCo (her work, combatting decades of junk-food fascism at the corporate level, simply can't be neglected at this tender stage (she'll be up on weekends)), leaving the three of them to manage the project, to coordinate the provision of food, water, shelter, tools, portable toilets . . . and to organize the workers into five different crews (North, South, East, West, and Hill Center), to explain to them exactly what has to be done in terms of earthwork repair and flowage realignment, and in general what care is necessary in carrying out this extraordinary reconstructive task.

Synandra decides upon where, precisely, the actual digging will be done through her dowsing. She and Basil go out each night after the crews have left, and, armed with a forked branch, she determines in which direction the flows have been diverted, Basil pounding in painted wooden stakes to mark the line of the next day's attack.

And for the next several weeks the Wasson woods buzz with activity, the clink of picks and the clank of shovels resounding through the autumnal forest as gangs of ditch diggers sing beloved chain gang ditties, rhythmically heft their tools in unison into the rocky northern soil until foot by foot, scoop by scoop, trenches are dug down through wet earth to flowage-level, each section then carefully cleared of rocky obstruction, relined if necessary with coarse quartzite gravel (specially selected by Synandra for its piezoelectric qualities), and refilled.

The abundance of help makes the work progress faster than they ever expected, Synandra, Basil, and Rudy flowing constantly from crew to crew monitoring practically each shovelful, until—at the end of nearly three long weeks the last trench has been filled and the earth raked over, the valentine rocks returned to their original positions (possibly the most meticulous part of the project as Synandra tried to recall exactly their previous placement), and the hill reshaped as nearly as possible to what it once was—the work is done. It comes at the end of a long day and three weary "eco-re-constructionists" (plus one delighted health food consultant up from Chicago) breathe a shared sigh of relief, crack open the first of many bottles of champagne to celebrate with one and all a job well done.

Come next spring there is still much to do in the way of re-planting the burned forest (the roses, especially), but for now it appears that a minor miracle has been performed. Synandra is able to detect moderate flows in each of the centers—not anywhere as strong as before, but the earth needs time to heal. Maybe next year, or even the year after, as the water courses reestablish themselves, the sacred centers might return to semblances of their former selves.

But more exciting still is the fact that they may have proved Mother Goose wrong, that all the king's horses and men *could* put the humpty-dumpty hill back together again. Or as Rudy is quick to point out, that—as they seemed to do with the miraculous machine—they again were able to cheat the troubling second law of thermodynamics, which states that all roads lead to eventual disorder.

Rudy makes this statement a couple of days later, leaning pensively back from the head table of the huge feast they hold on the Wasson lawn for all the workers and the townspeople of Wasson's Bay—and anyone else who comes along—to celebrate the resurrection of Mystery Rock Hill. Synandra is especially excited by what their accomplishment might mean for the troubled goddess, Gaia. A reversal of forces, an effort of loving repair of an injured area of the earth, performed as elegantly as surgery here, that might send its own positive currents back out into whatever plexus of earth energies it figures into. Who knows where the good vibrations will end up? Hopefully, *everywhere!*

To this Tiffany raises a mug of Heinenstuber to her friends, proposes a toast, "May the good vibrations created here proceed onward and outward through our small planet earth, healing wherever it goes!"

"And being wherever it is," adds Synandra.

"Amen," Basil and Rudy agree, all of them raising their mugs together in a salute to the earth, the heavens, and a man of medicine, who, if he is able in any way to see them now, is very, very proud.

28

During the weeks of the hill's reconstruction, unnoticed by perhaps everyone busy with the project but a fey girl who knows every tree in the forest, every star in the sky, and once in a time out of time danced so lightly, so gracefully, upon the magical mound—fall fell gently, floatingly, like a blue-gray feather dropped from heaven upon the place beneath. October, the orange month of cider and beer, cornstalks and pumpkins and silent yearnings for Packer victories, has arrived in a swirl of warming days, crisp nights, and a dazzle of color. The leaves of elm and birch have turned to gold, oak to russet, sumac to scarlet, and maple to all the hues of fire itself. Great V-lines of Canadian geese honk their way southward, fat red apples fall of their own weight from the trees, and the last wave of tourists crash the Jack Frost xanthorama and then ebb quickly away.

Basil is on the road once again, hitchhiking, not sure where he's come from, no idea where he's going, but the direction is definitely westward, a long straight highway ahead and flat empty land, a big chunk of blue sky in front of him opening up into that sunny southern land from whence he had come. . . . But he can't seem to get a ride here, having no luck at all, nothing, *nada* . . . but over there beyond the ocotillo cacti is a roadside diner gleaming of chrome and bright red trim. He's thirsty in this heat, has no real deadline that he knows of, so he shuffles over, looks inside for somewhere to sit, the place is air-conditioned, very cool, but noisy, full of people, should've known from the cars in front . . . and suddenly sees sitting off to the right, facing him across the big L-curve formed by the counter, his parents! beaming at him, gesturing to folks around them that there he is, *their* son, the Peeper! Just like they used to do, embarrassed the hell out of him, so many years ago. . . . But what are they doing here, out in the middle of nowhere? Figures he ought to go over and see them . . . but suddenly hears a raspy voice calling his name from the other direction, way in the back, it's . . . Pop Dawson! grinning ear to ear, cigarette-hand waving him over, wearing a–a cowboy hat and that same old gaudy red-green-yellow Hawaiian shirt he'd wear around the set, just to piss-off the director. God, it's Pop! He's got to get over to see him, right away, feels tears welling up really big now, he's got to see that crazy guy again, seems like there's no time to lose . . .

"Basil, Basil . . ."

Now someone *else* is calling him, what the—

"Basil, wake up."

"Huh?"

"Telephone. It's, it's your friend, Stinky Harrison. Your Pop . . . er, Jack Doughtery, just passed away. Stinky wants to talk to you. . . ."

"You haven't said anything all night," says Synandra. They are sitting atop the newly reconstructed hill, watching over the lake. The night is clear and crisp, the moon brilliant in the bright fall sky. The Great Square of Pegasus hangs above them like a window to the rest of the universe. "I'm sorry to have had to wake you like that, but—"

"S'okay. Serves me right for trying to catch a nap."

"I guess you were quite close to him—back then," she says through a warm breath-cloud.

"Sort of. I really liked the guy."

"I'm sure you did. From what you told me. . . ."

"I'm going to miss him. Even though I never really saw him.

341

Funny, isn't it. Just to know he was still around. . . ."

"I do know what you mean. . . . You know, I'm awfully nervous about flying out there. For the funeral. I've never flown before. In an airplane, that is."

"Say, Syndy, listen. What do you say we really take-off. Split. Leave Wasson's Bay for a while. Like Dr. Bo said, you're free. And you've never been anywhere else." Which is quite true. Early in their relationship Basil had been surprised to learn that she had never left Wasson's Bay for any length of time. She'd never really been *anywhere*. Her ties to the hill were too strong to permit an extended separation.

"You mean just, go?"

"Sure, why not. Everything's taken care of around here. The shop's closed down. Mrs. Frost can keep an eye on the house. We'll drive. We'll take the car. We've got three days before the funeral, that's plenty of time to get there."

"But where will we go? I mean, after Los Angeles."

"Anywhere. North, south, east, west. There's a heck of a lot to see out there. Out anywhere."

"Well . . . why not?"

"That's right. Why not."

*   *   *

There is an automobile gliding smoothly westward, a big black 1948 Chrysler, lavish with wood trim, heavy on the chrome. It is a warm October Sunday afternoon and the top is down. Basil is behind the wheel, contentedly driving the elegant machine, which, as it cruises steadily down this long stretch of Interstate 90 through southernmost Minnesota, hardly seems like driving at all. That's good, for he can afford to take his eyes off the road and snatch long glances at Synandra sitting comfortably across from him on the leather seat. Her eyes are closed. She is smiling. She is wearing a Green Bay Packer T-shirt and a short green jersey skirt. Right now she allows the skirt to blow rather rakishly upwards so the Indian summer can rush against her knees and thighs, against her bright green and gold panties, a tender patriotic gesture because the Pack is playing today and Synandra is a big fan. Basil too, now. He had the game on the radio until it started fading hopelessly in and out. At the half they were ahead, in the third quarter they were behind; the fourth quarter dissolved in the ozone.

Sioux Falls, straight ahead. The sun is only a few hours away from setting. Already a marvelous sunset is shaping up. A good sign. Basil is keeping an eye out for a motel to spend the night in, preferably one with waterbeds.

But why is Synandra smiling? Is it because the Packers have won? There is really no way she could know, although Basil understands that long-time Packer backers sometimes develop a sixth sense about such things. Or is she smiling because of the postcard they received just before they left? From Tiffany, that kooky kid. Seems that she and Rudy have contacted Jimmy Kowalske about working for LoFoCo, helping them start a west coast operation for their new line of healthy foodstuffs. Why not, the guy is awfully sharp and is probably looking for something else to get into about now.... But no, her smile today is the smile that passes by a woman's lips only once on its way to the infinite grin-bin. Once in a lifetime, when she first thinks that for the first time, she may be pregnant. Yes indeedy. Though the sublime and mysterious powers of the hill may be dormant for quite a while, it seems that a tiny lightning bolt remnant might have survived, beyond the silent flow of earth energies, beyond the hill itself, captured within her. Will it be a boy or a girl? Synandra isn't positive, but the hearts sneaking out behind her sun-glowing eyelids have all been bright pink. Electric pink.

Basil hates to disturb whatever reveries she's up to, she looks so content. Anyway, he's happy too, has to smile himself when he remembers that dream he had, even though seeing Pop always tears him up, he realizes now that that dream was actually in *color*. For the first time ever. He dreamed in color! Feels like he's escaped from someplace he'd been locked up inside of for a long time. He has to chuckle, thinks that maybe, from wherever he is now, Pop wanted to help out—was why, in the dream, he wore that crazy shirt! Sure, that's just like him, what a guy! What a guy he was. Perhaps, like the sunset, a good sign, that a new life is beginning for him too. For both of them. Is that true? Is that terrific? He can't wait to find out.